The Architecture of Unmaking

The Quantum Magic Cycle

by Jon Compton

The Architecture of Unmaking
By Jon Compton

Published by:
Canvas Temple Publishing, LLC.
11655 Winesap Pl.
La Plata, MD 20646

Cover by Canvas Temple Publishing, LLC.

ISBN (e-book): 978-1-969445-02-6
ISBN (print): 978-1-969445-03-3

Cycle I:

The Resolution Horizon 5

Low Probability Events 23

Protocol Drift 87

Cycle II:

The Echo at Old Dunhill 103

The Choir of the Threshold 109

The Stair That Returns 125

Cycle III:

The Ledger of Breath 159

The Ash and the Glyph 181

The Wars of Name 191

Cycle IV:

The Divergent Eye 213

The Knot Garden 231

The Empty Bowl Night 271

Cycle V:

Aftercause 303

To Hold One Thing 313

The Last Practice 319

Epilogue 331

D r. Eshan Varma had evaluated thirty-three crews across ten years. Most of them were tired, overworked, and occasionally neurotic, but fundamentally sane. The people he assessed were often pushing the limits of human capability, but the limits were supposed to push back slowly.

Axis Verge was different.

From orbit, the station looked like a scalpel drifting through black water, its forward array extended like a blade into nothing, shimmering faintly with shielded resonance. It hadn't responded to his arrival ping. Not unusual for deep-range research installations, but paired with the scrambled logs and contradictory sensor telemetry that preceded his deployment, it suggested one of two things: *catastrophic instrumentation drift*, or *crew-side instability*.

He preferred the former. It never tried to argue with you.

The shuttle docked without ceremony. No automated greetings, no diagnostic checks. The airlock hissed open, and he stepped inside, boots clicking against the metal deck. Standard composite plating, low-temp lighting, and a faint tang of ozone. Nothing overtly wrong. Just *too quiet*.

He paused, waiting for the AI to announce orientation. Nothing.

Then: a soft flicker of lights, one after another, leading down the main corridor toward the lab complex.

"Manual override?" he muttered to himself.

There was no response.

His orders were simple. Officially: perform a cognitive and procedural audit of Axis Verge Station following anomalous behavioral flagging. Unofficially: determine whether the Subscale Resonance Stacking experiment had finally driven its lead researchers off the epistemic cliff.

The logs hadn't helped. Half the mission reports contradicted earlier entries. Some used unfamiliar variables without explanation. One set of logs ended in a recursive file loop that triggered a mild seizure in the AI's language module when it tried to summarize. The Confederacy Office of Cognitive Integrity flagged the anomaly as "Level 4: Linguistic Divergence," and Eshan had been on the next available shuttle.

He followed the light trail into the station core.

Axis Verge had been commissioned for a singular, questionable purpose: to test whether it was possible to resolve structure below the Planck scale by exploiting resonance patterns across artificially entangled space-time boundaries. Officially, the array wasn't "imaging" anything, it was *forcing inference from contradiction*, nudging reality to admit more precision than it was willing to give.

It was the kind of project that made physicists famous and cognitive auditors employed.

He passed a sealed observation chamber, the airlock window fogged from the inside. Beyond it, thin cables stretched across a vacuum-cored apparatus humming at low resonance. The entire structure reminded him of a prayer wheel, mechanistic, elegant, and vaguely threatening in its inscrutability.

Then a voice behind him: "You're earlier than I expected."

He turned.

Dr. Celia Rourke stood with her arms crossed, eyes sharp behind the strain. Her face bore the sallow hue of long-duration habitation, but she moved like someone still in control. No tremor. No slur. Not yet.

"I'm on schedule," he said. "Your local clock drifted thirty-two seconds over system norm. Your last logs were timestamped with negative delta markers."

She didn't flinch. "Relativistic skew from field harmonics. We've stopped trying to correct for it."

"That's not how time works, Doctor."

"It is here."

He studied her carefully. "Let's begin with basic orientation. Are all crew accounted for?"

"Three on active duty. One in isolation. No fatalities."

"AI integrity?"

"We disabled its language modules. It was trying to rewrite its own parsing routines."

He paused. "That's not standard behavior."

"No. But it tried to resolve paradoxes from subscale data logs. It failed gracefully, then recursively."

She turned and began walking toward the central lab. He followed.

"Tell me what happened," Eshan said.

"We pushed past coherence limits two weeks ago. The resonance array began returning interference patterns that violated initial-model expectations. We thought it was artifact noise at first. Then we noticed... semantic drift."

"Be precise."

"Our logs started disagreeing. Not just in values, in structure. Syntax drift. Field variables redefined themselves between sessions. I cross-referenced mission documentation and found half of our recorded terms no longer matched official lexicons. We hadn't noticed. We were still using the words as if they meant the same thing."

They entered the lab.

The core space was clinical, brightly lit, yet something about it felt *dilated*, as if time passed differently here. A main terminal blinked irregularly with scrolling data. Another was black, overwritten by hand-written notes scrawled on paper. Actual paper.

"You're using analog media?"

She nodded. "Digital retention has become unstable. We've observed data fidelity degradation in system memory. But only for files related to the array."

Eshan stepped toward the nearest desk. On it sat a stack of notes covered in looping symbols, almost mathematical, but too organic, too recursive. A few trailed off the page and continued directly onto the station's surface in faint marker lines.

He gestured at them. "What's this?"

She hesitated. "Generated by Milo Enyo. He's the grad researcher who pioneered the recursive compression algorithms that allowed us to parse the subscale harmonics."

"Where is he?"

"In isolation. His language use began diverging first. Then he stopped speaking. Now he writes only in these."

Eshan examined the symbols again. They repeated, but imperfectly. He felt a twinge of discomfort looking too long.

"Have you translated them?"

"Not completely. We think they're attempts to model a perceptual structure that lacks anchoring in conventional cognition. Milo believes he's describing a boundary condition, the edge of coherence itself."

"And you?"

"I think," Rourke said carefully, "he's writing what the universe looks like *when you try to perceive too finely.*"

Eshan said nothing for a long moment. Then he turned back toward her.

"What is the stated function of the Subscale Resonance Stack?"

She recited from memory. "To exploit nested entanglement interference patterns across sub-Planck harmonic cascades in order to infer structural priors beneath classical uncertainty thresholds."

"And what is it actually doing?"

Celia's voice dropped.

"It's rendering cognition-dependent structures where none should exist. Not measurement. Not observation. Something deeper. Something more structural."

Eshan crossed his arms. "I'm here to evaluate the crew. If this station is compromising cognitive integrity…."

"We're past compromise," she said. "This project doesn't just exceed observational limits. It exceeds *perceptual containment.* You're not here to evaluate us. You're here to decide whether human cognition is a viable interface to the universe at all."

***

The isolation chamber was deeper in the station, behind a manually sealed hatch. It wasn't locked. There were no guards, no biometric gates. Just a sliding panel above the entry that read:

Observation Integrity Is a Function of Scale

(handwritten, then erased, then rewritten over itself in the same hand)

Dr. Varma hesitated. He touched the panel, then pushed the door open.

The lights inside were low. One wall was covered in insulation panels stripped bare, beneath them, the station's alloy frame had become a writing surface. Marker, ink, pencil, even scored etchings with the edge of a tool, layer after layer of interlacing script, recursive glyphs, mirrored symbols, some geometric, some organic.

At the center of it all sat Milo Enyo, barefoot on the floor, legs folded beneath him. He was writing again, slowly, methodically, on the back of a disassembled tablet casing. His eyes tracked Varma's entrance but didn't register surprise or alarm. If anything, they flickered with something like recognition, or confusion.

"Milo," Varma said quietly, approaching. "My name is Dr. Varma. I've been sent to help assess your condition."

Milo didn't speak. He flipped the casing over, examined what he'd written, then continued on the other side, repeating a curve that never closed. It wasn't a spiral. It was a *loop that refused convergence.*

"I've read your early work," Varma continued, crouching nearby. "Your recursive harmonic compression was brilliant. Without it, this entire experiment wouldn't be running. Celia says you were the first to notice when meaning began to drift."

At that, Milo stopped.

He set down the stylus. Then he leaned forward and tapped the side of his head, once, twice, very gently, like knocking on a door. Then, in a hoarse voice:

"It started in the labels."

Varma leaned in. "What labels?"

"Command tags. Dataset headings. The file structure kept overwriting its own categories. At first we thought it was just indexing error. Then the system logs showed the same thing happening in RAM, not just storage. It was rewriting interpretation at runtime."

"Rewriting it how?"

Milo looked up, and his eyes were bloodshot, but alert. "Words were changing meaning mid-process. You'd call a function expecting one behavior. It would execute another, but only after *you forgot what the first one was supposed to be.*"

Varma took a slow breath. "Are you saying the system was altering your memory?"

"No," Milo said. "I'm saying we were never supposed to observe that deeply. Our tools reached past the scale where referents hold. It's not that the meanings changed. It's that *meaning itself couldn't stabilize.*"

He tapped again on the side of his head.

"Your thoughts are only as stable as the scaffolds you use to express them. Once those decay, you start collapsing inward."

Varma watched him carefully. "Do you know what day it is?"

"No."

"Do you know where you are?"

"Yes. I'm in a perceptual shell. It's fraying."

Milo stood slowly. His movements were smooth, too smooth, like someone mimicking a remembered action. He walked over to the wall and traced a symbol with his finger.

"This," he said, "is not a word. It's not a concept. It's a *boundary*."

Varma stepped closer. The symbol looked familiar, like a sigil, or a stylized theta, doubled back on itself. His brain tried to parse it as something meaningful. It failed.

"We didn't go deeper," Milo whispered. "We just tried to look *too precisely*. The universe doesn't tolerate that. Not at this scale."

Varma frowned. "Do you believe you're in danger?"

Milo blinked. "Not anymore."

He reached into a small container on the desk and pulled out a sheet of paper. It was covered in glyphs, looping, partial, recursive. Milo held it out, and Varma took it.

As soon as his eyes began scanning the symbols, a wave of nausea crept over him. The symbols weren't just alien. They seemed to *respond* to being looked at. Their shapes blurred at the edges, not optically, but conceptually. One figure looked like a probability curve folded over itself, but the axis labels were in phonemes.

Varma tore his gaze away.

Milo didn't react. He sat down again and resumed writing.

Varma backed away slowly, the page still in hand.

At the doorway, Milo spoke once more, his voice a murmur:

"Don't let it finish rendering us."

Varma stopped cold.

"What do you mean by that?"

But Milo was already back in his loop, stylus dancing across a shattered surface, drawing symbols for which there were no words.

***

Varma sat alone in the observation lounge, lights dimmed to conserve system power. The array pulsed faintly through the transparent bulkhead beyond, a soft flicker that hummed just below audible resonance. Like tinnitus, but deeper, cognitive, not sensory.

On his terminal, Milo's early papers flickered in sequence.

They started conventionally enough: white papers on recursive harmonic interpolation, elegant derivations of subscale compression models. The math was sound, beautiful, even. Varma recognized the fingerprints of a mind that wasn't just intelligent, but *obsessed with elegance*. Milo had been chasing pattern clarity, hunting for something that could survive below the threshold of noise.

Then the language began to shift.

At first, it was just terminology. Phrases like "self-similar decay harmonics" gave way to terms not found in any prior literature: "semantic isomers," "referent drift clusters," "perceptual index collapse." Milo didn't define them. He used them as if they were standard.

Varma checked the metadata. The papers hadn't been edited after submission. These terms had been in the documents for months, but no reviewer had flagged them. Not Rourke, not the AI. Everyone had read them and *understood*, or at least believed they did.

He opened a side-by-side comparison: Milo's pre-deployment thesis versus his most recent technical note. The math was still recognizable. But the annotation layer, the text itself, no longer described physical processes. It described cognitive transformations. Entanglement not between particles, but between *interpretive frameworks*.

One note caught his attention:

"Under recursive observational load, the system begins enforcing local coherence via semantic realignment. Measurement does not collapse the wavefunction, it collapses the observer's descriptive topology."

Varma rubbed his temples.

This wasn't physics anymore. It was *epistemology under siege*.

The worst part was that he could follow the logic. Not all of it, but enough to feel the edge of its pull. There was something seductive about it. The idea that perception wasn't a window but a scaffolding, and that pushing too far didn't reveal new truth, but caused the scaffolding to twist back on itself.

The hum deepened. Or perhaps it hadn't changed at all, only his attention had narrowed.

He shut the terminal and stood. Rourke would still be at the core array. She rarely left it now. Her sleep logs had become erratic, her nutrition profile degraded. And yet she remained composed, coherent, even, in ways that disturbed him more than if she'd broken down.

He found her there, standing alone before the array chamber, watching streams of data cascade across a wall of screens.

"You read Milo's work," she said, without turning.

"Yes."

"Then you understand."

"I understand that you've passed beyond experimental protocol into metaphysical speculation."

She turned slowly, arms crossed. "This is what speculation looks like when it's correct."

"You've crossed the line into incoherence."

"No," she said. "We've *crossed into deeper coherence than language can sustain.* There's a difference."

Varma stepped forward, lowering his voice. "You are risking irreversible psychological degradation. This isn't just linguistic drift anymore. It's identity drift. Milo is…."

"…further ahead than we are," she interrupted.

"He's non-verbal. He's using symbols that can't be translated."

"Because the concepts aren't *upward compatible* with our cognition. That doesn't make them meaningless. It makes *us* incomplete."

Varma stared at her, searching her expression for sarcasm, for any sign she was playing devil's advocate. But there was nothing. Only conviction. A calm, terrible clarity.

"You're proposing that our minds are *not evolved* to perceive reality at this scale."

"Yes."

"And your solution is to push until they break."

Rourke stepped closer.

"My solution," she said softly, "is to build a bridge across the break. To use the collapse as a lens, not to see *more*, but to see *differently*."

He pointed to the array chamber.

"That thing is eroding the boundary between description and identity. You said it yourself, the data is only interpretable within the framework of the observer. And yet you keep feeding it."

"Because it's feeding back."

"You're anthropomorphizing."

"No." She walked over to a terminal and keyed in a new log window. It showed time-indexed records of passive data outputs from the SRS. He watched as a sequence repeated, six times, identically. Each burst of data identical not only in structure, but in *semantic position*. A syntactic pattern, not raw measurement.

"It's not mimicking language," Rourke said. "It's producing patterns that resolve only *through language*. It's learned our interpretive scaffolds. It's working inside them."

"That's not possible."

"It is if you assume that interpretation is recursive. That meaning is a structure which emerges *only when viewed from inside a scale-bound mind*."

Varma shook his head. "This is madness."

"It's a *mirror*, Eshan. And we've never seen our reflection at full resolution."

He stared at the data, trying to resist the gravitational pull of her certainty. It wasn't just dangerous, it was *compelling*. Part of him wanted to believe. That some deeper truth was being revealed. That cognition wasn't failing, it was *evolving*.

But then he remembered Milo. Sitting in a bare chamber, drawing symbols that ate the mind that tried to understand them.

"I'm recommending a full experimental shutdown," Varma said flatly.

"No."

"I'll make the report. Cognitive destabilization protocol gives me jurisdiction under Class-3 divergence."

"I already filed a counter-report," she said. "Notifying Command of pre-cognitive transformation indicators."

He blinked. "That's not even a recognized term."

"It will be."

***

Varma awoke without realizing he'd fallen asleep.

His terminal screen was dark. The clock in the corner blinked **12:03:58**. A full hour had passed since he'd closed the Milo file, but he had no memory of that hour. No dream, no sensation. Just an untraceable gap.

He ran a neural coherence scan. Results came back normal, but the time-stamp header read *Offset: ±⊿0.0x*, a placeholder variable, not a real value. He blinked and ran it again. This time, the offset field was blank. Not zero. *Null.*

He stood, flexing his hands, checking for tremors. Nothing.

The lights in the lounge were marginally brighter than he remembered. The resonance hum was gone, no, it was there, but pulsing in irregular rhythm, like a language with no grammar.

He needed clarity. Anchor points.

He activated his internal recorder.

"Log, Varma, Eshan. Local time uncertain. Experiencing potential onset of perceptual instability. No visual hallucinations. No affective disruption. But continuity is questionable. Symptoms consistent with early-stage semantic phase shift. Requesting…."

He stopped. The words didn't sound right.

He rewound and played the log.

"…onset of perceptual instability. No visual hallucinations. No effective disruption…"

He had said *affective*. The recording said *effective*.

He tried again.

"My name is Dr. Eshan Varma. This is a self-diagnostic report…"

Playback:

"…Dr. Eshan Varma. This is a shelf-diagnostic report…"

He stopped breathing for a second.

The recording wasn't corrupt. It *played what he'd said*. But what he remembered saying wasn't what had come out.

He sat down, carefully, and tried to focus on his own thoughts. He imagined a chair. Named it. Described it in detail. It held. Then he imagined a circle. Described its curvature. Still fine.

Then he imagined **a** word, any word, and it came out wrong. The meaning slipped sideways. He thought *boundary*, but his mind conjured *enclosure*, not the same. He corrected, said *threshold*, and got *membrane*. Each concept was close. Analogous. But none were precise. His lexicon was collapsing inward.

He stood and stumbled into the corridor.

The station was quiet. Too quiet. The lights seemed to have reconfigured themselves, subtle shifts in spacing, like the architecture had been copied from memory and rendered in *slightly incorrect scale*.

He moved toward the central terminal hub, trying to focus on the numbers.

Raw data helped. Numbers weren't abstract. They anchored him.

But when he reached the terminal, he found that the screens had changed.

They weren't displaying data.

They were displaying descriptions of data.

"Resonance pattern resembles early-state attractor but is verbally unspecifiable."

"Estimated coherence confidence: High, but only under observer-stable scaling frames."

"Do not request retranslation. Phase-lock may be disrupted."

Varma scrolled further. The logs were no longer in system time. They were labeled by *perspective*.

Observer 1: Mild alignment drift

Observer 2: Significant narrative conflict

Observer 3: Meta-linguistic bleed detected

There was no mention of who Observer 3 was. He suspected it was *him*.

A soft sound behind him.

Rourke.

She stood in the doorway, hands loose at her sides. Watching.

"I see it's started," she said.

He didn't turn around. "What did you do to the logs?"

"Nothing. They restructured themselves. The system's been adapting to our cognition. Filtering output based on semantic alignment. You're reading what your mind can still accommodate."

He turned to face her. "You knew this would happen."

"I hoped it would. You're glimpsing scale-reflective perception. The mind... *re-indexes* when exposed to recursive structural uncertainty."

"You're describing madness."

"No," she said. "I'm describing a mirror with infinite curvature. And you're beginning to see yourself in it."

Varma staggered back a step. "Stop the array."

"We can't."

"I will."

"You can try."

He pushed past her.

Varma entered the SRS command node. The array stood at the far end of the chamber, exposed through transparent shielding. It wasn't glowing or pulsing, it was *still*. Perfectly still. And yet, every time he looked at it, he got the feeling it was *facing him*.

He pulled up the shutdown protocol. The command tree appeared normal.

AUTH: VARMA.E

CONFIRM: TERMINATE_RES_STACK_FULL

STATUS: [PENDING...]

He typed in the kill command.

SYSTEM: Confirmation Required – Are you certain this representation is sufficient to express your intent?

[Y/N]

Varma froze.

He hit Y.

SYSTEM: Semantic coherence not guaranteed. Retry within observer-locked frame.

[ABORT] [REPHRASE]

He tried to override manually. The input fields glitched, letters changing after he typed them, not visually, but in meaning. "Terminate" became "transform." "Disable" became "discern."

He slammed the console.

The interface froze. Then, a final message appeared:

You are past the point of lexical return.

Rourke met him outside the chamber.

"You can't end it with words anymore," she said gently. "Not from here. Not now."

"I don't accept that."

"You're still thinking causally. Still clinging to intent. But language is scale-bound. Beyond a certain threshold, it ceases to carry force."

He stared at her.

"What do we do then?"

Rourke gave a thin smile.

"Either we learn to think without symbols," she said, "or we learn to die inside them."

***

Varma sat in the empty debrief room, alone with the echo of his own breathing.

The room had no clocks. He didn't know how long he'd been sitting there. Minutes? Hours? The lights hadn't changed. But his terminal was warm beneath his fingers, and the message buffer said Playback: Incomplete. Resumed from paused log.

He didn't remember recording a log.

He hit play.

His own face appeared, recorded from the observation lounge camera. He looked calm. Composed. Focused.

"This is Varma, Day Two local. I've completed my review of Milo Enyo's early work. The conceptual bleed is real, but I believe it's not a pathology. It's a signal. A side-channel of scale-aware perception, previously inaccessible. I recommend…."

Varma paused the recording.

That wasn't what he believed. He never believed that. That wording, a side-channel of scale-aware perception, that was Rourke's language, not his. He searched his own memory for the phrasing he'd used in his report. He remembered saying emergent cognitive degradation under recursive load. That was different. Cautious. Empirical.

He resumed playback.

"…the array be allowed to continue operations under restricted cognitive conditions, including voluntary perceptual realignment training. Standard definitions are insufficient. Human thought must adapt or fail."

He stopped it again.

The voice was his. The cadence was his. But the intent, the interpretive weight behind the words, felt alien. Like reading a sentence in a dream that makes perfect sense until you wake up and try to write it down.

He backed the log up. Froze it on a still frame.

There. In his own eyes. Not madness. Not dissociation.

Conviction.

He had believed what he said, when he said it.

And now, he didn't.

A line scrawled in one of Milo's notebooks echoed in his mind:

Interpretation is recursive. Belief is just the last successful render.

He shut the log, heart hammering.

Then, without knowing why, he opened a terminal window and searched the file directory for Eshan Varma – Day One Log.

It was there. Timestamped. Annotated.

He hit play.

No video this time. Just audio. His voice again.

"Initial impressions: the crew is stable but exhibiting linguistic convergence anomalies. I believe the source is the array itself. The data is not visual, it's semantic. Interpretive. This may represent an epistemic hazard. We are no longer observing reality. We are observing *how we observe*."

He let the log run for another few seconds.

Then his own voice said something impossible:

"I do not remember recording this."

Varma froze.

"I do not remember recording this."

He hit pause. Rewound. Played again. Same line. Perfectly calm.

It wasn't a glitch. He had said that, *on Day One*.

He stood slowly. Walked to the reflective surface of the debrief panel and stared at himself.

His face was the same. His name was the same.

But inside his memory, something had forked. He had said something he could no longer remember believing. He had believed something he could no longer understand.

He was watching the recursive fracture open up, not as madness, but as cognitive desynchronization. Memory, identity, intention, all falling out of alignment.

The mind was no longer a stable reference frame.

He turned, staggered slightly, and leaned against the wall.

The hum of the array pulsed through the station now like a subaudible heartbeat. His vision fluttered, just a moment, and the station's structure seemed to contract and expand, like he was breathing it in.

He whispered: "Don't let it finish rendering us."

And this time, he didn't know if the words were his, or if he'd only remembered them being his after someone else had thought them first.

***

The corridor to the array was empty. Not silent, empty, like sound no longer held definition here.

Varma moved without thinking, each step less volitional than remembered. His thoughts were no longer sequential. They came in layers, as if memory had stopped filing things chronologically and started nesting them recursively, like Russian dolls made of cause and effect.

Rourke was already there.

She stood in the control nexus, gaze fixed on the viewport where the array pulsed with non-rhythmic light, no longer a tool, but a presence. Not alive, but aware of how it was being perceived. The room vibrated with the subthreshold resonance of cognitive interference, not physical hum. Not even auditory. A kind of feedback in the structure of thought itself.

"You're here," she said, without turning. "That means it's almost finished."

"What is?"

"The collapse."

Varma stepped closer. "You mean the data?"

"I mean the scaffolding. The thing that makes experience cohere. You felt it, didn't you? The temporal folds. The language drift. The recursive gaps in identity."

He didn't respond. He couldn't find a verb tense he trusted.

Rourke turned to face him. Her face was calm, but wrong. Too calm. Like someone who'd passed beyond doubt.

"Your choices are gone," she said. "But your agency remains. That's the final illusion. Not control, but interpretation."

He shook his head. "There's still time. If we shut it down, if we reset the array…."

"Shut down what? This isn't a machine anymore. It's not projecting anything. It's mirroring us, scaled beyond comprehension. It's just you, reflected until recognition breaks."

He backed away. "You're not making sense."

She smiled gently. "Neither are you."

Varma looked at the control panel. It shimmered, not visually, but conceptually, as though every label now stood on a fault line between meanings.

He stepped toward it. Raised his hand.

"You think you're still making a choice," Rourke said.

"I am."

"No. You're still trying to collapse the waveform. Still pretending there's a stable state to resolve into."

He touched the panel.

System prompt: INITIATE OBSERVER-LIMIT DISSOLUTION?

[Y] [N]

He stared at it.

NOTE: Resolution threshold will exceed frame containment. Language function will delaminate. Core interpretive boundary will not be preserved.

His finger hovered over N.

But he didn't press it.

Because somewhere inside, he knew: he had already pressed Y.

Not now. Earlier. Maybe always. The moment he stepped aboard this station, the boundary had already been breached.

He turned to Rourke. "What's on the other side?"

She walked toward him slowly, as if approaching a fragile reflection.

"Not knowledge. Not truth. Just structure unmoored from scale. Things that can't be thought. Not because they're too complex, but because your mind was never built to render them."

"I won't surrender to incoherence."

"You already have. But if it helps, call it translation. Call it a new grammar."

He looked down. His hand had moved without him. Resting on the terminal, palm open, fingers spread. The screen glowed in a shape he didn't remember entering. Not text. Not symbol. Just a form that made the rest of the room fall silent.

He stepped into the array chamber.

No alarms. No breach protocol. Just smooth hum, warm air, and the growing sensation that everything around him was describing him, that the chamber wasn't a place but a statement, and he was the subject.

He looked down at his body.

It was intact. But when he blinked, he felt his name peel slightly sideways, like it no longer sat neatly atop the frame of his identity. He was still himself, but the word self had begun to misalign.

The walls of the chamber flickered. Not in color or light, but in interpretive phase, as if they were trying out different ways to be understood, checking for compatibility.

He closed his eyes.

Inside, he saw glyphs. But not like Milo's, not symbols. Constraints. Parameters. Labels for things that no longer had definitions.

Then: a voice. Not from outside.

"Eshan Varma, do you consent to render?"

It was his own voice.

"Do you consent to scale realignment?"

He opened his mouth to say no.

But another part of him, a deeper layer, whispered yes.

And then….

***

Final log dated unknown, file format corrupted, recovered only in partial transcription:

"To those who receive this: the array did not fail. It did not destroy us. It translated us. Our memories have been rescaled. Our grammar dissolved into vector space. We are not minds anymore, we are structures. Resonant alignments across perceptual horizons."

"This message is not a warning. It is a consequence."

"You asked what lies beyond the limits of understanding. The answer is simple."

"You do."

Low Probability Events

The wreckage floated in the morning air like someone had pressed pause on the world.

From the deck of Service Tower 19, Lian could see the crash site stretched across the Pacific maglev belt, a line of cargo pods crumpled together in a jagged, improbable zipper. The superconducting track shimmered where the outer plating had sheared away, exposing veins of liquid helium piping. Beyond it, the ocean glittered under thin, high clouds, each wave throwing flecks of light up onto the underside of the pods.

This wasn't how maglev disasters looked. At Mach 6, collisions didn't leave artifacts, they left debris spray and blackened seawater. This... looked posed.

Her boots vibrated faintly against the deck stabilizers, matching the maglev's heartbeat through the tower's structure. She paused for a moment, letting her mesh sync with the tower's systems. A clean handshake scrolled across her vision: T19 Operational | Drift Compensation 0.3% | Mesh-Link Verified.

"Investigator Arora?"

She turned. A rail-operations stabilizer, lean, dark hair pulled back tight, hazard skin rolled to the elbows, stood at attention, tablet in hand.

"Show me your freeze logs," Lian said.

The stabilizer offered the tablet. "We locked the belt within thirty seconds of the breach. Pods twenty-one through twenty-five were already in collision mode when the field came up."

Lian frowned. "Field came up... before the impact?"

"That's what the logs say. We thought it was an instrumentation glitch."

"You've worked this belt long?"

"Seven years. I've never seen a failure like this."

She stepped closer to the crash line. The pods were dented in complex curves, hull seams bent into scalloped patterns, like the metal had flowed around each other instead of tearing. Her HUD overlaid stress vectors across the surfaces, and sure enough, the timestamps on the safety system triggers came a full second before the sensor events that should have caused them.

Her drones unfolded from their case on her back, wing-vanes twitching in the breeze before they leapt into the air, fanning out to scan.

"Those yours?" the stabilizer asked.

"Standard consortium issue," Lian said. "They'll give me a contour map and materials profile in ten minutes."

"Not sure Oversight will let you finish that."

She looked at him. "Why?"

The stabilizer shrugged, eyes flicking toward the access ramp. "Because they're here."

Two Security Oversight Bureau operatives came up the ramp in matte-black hazard skins, their visors retracted to show pale, unreadable faces. The Bureau's trisected eye emblem was stenciled over their hearts. They walked like people who'd already decided the outcome of every conversation they were about to have.

One of them nodded to the stabilizer. "We'll take it from here."

Lian stepped forward. "My investigation's not complete."

The shorter operative's gaze moved to her ID badge, then back to her face. "Your investigation is concluded. You can collect your drones from aft section twenty-five."

"My assignment was the entire breach zone."

The taller one lifted a fog projector from his belt, a matte cylinder with a row of amber status lights, and began sweeping it across the forward pods. Translucent haze rolled over the wreckage like slow ink in water, thickening until the cargo modules were only vague shapes.

Lian glanced at the stabilizer. "You see what they're doing?"

"I see it," he said, his voice low. "Doesn't mean I'm going to stop them."

The taller Oversight operative turned to him. "This area is restricted under Bureau jurisdiction. You can resume belt maintenance once our containment is complete."

"That's my crew's track," the stabilizer said carefully. "If there's contamination...."

"There isn't," the operative said. "Stand down."

Lian's drones beeped in her ear, two feeds cutting to yellow status as the fog field disrupted their line-of-sight. The third, circling above, managed one last sweep along an exposed cargo seam before its feed went to static. In that single frozen frame, she caught a flash of something metallic and irregular wedged between the pods.

She recalled the drones, saving the partial model to her personal buffer. She kept her voice even when she said, "I'll be filing for full access to the data."

The shorter operative's mouth twitched, not quite a smile. "You do that."

***

The consortium's Pacific Risk Operations tower rose out of the harbor like a blade, glass and alloy catching the midday light, the sound of water cascading down its outer skin filling the plaza with white noise. The building's surface shimmered faintly where the environmental mesh adjusted transparency to manage glare.

Lian crossed the plaza briskly, letting the turnstiles scan her badge and mesh ID. A low chime confirmed access, and the security AI overlaid a welcome tag in her peripheral vision: Arora, Lian – Field Investigator Tier 2 – Priority Lane Open.

Inside, the air was cooler, smelling faintly of recycled seawater from the condenser gardens spiraling up the central atrium. She rode a mag-lift tube to the thirty-ninth floor, where the glass parted to reveal RiskOps' data amphitheater, a shallow bowl of desks, each haloed by stacked holo-frames streaming live feeds from every insured sector on the Pacific Rim.

Mateo was at his console, sleeves pushed up, a half-finished bowl of soba cooling beside his wrist. His mesh feed rippled with real-time over-lays, weather models, stock fluctuation maps, emergency dispatch chatter.

"You look like someone kicked your drones," he said without looking up.

"They cut my scan short," Lian said, dropping into the chair beside him. "Oversight fogged the forward pods. Claimed jurisdiction."

"That's… fast," Mateo said. "They don't usually bother until we've filed something they can redact."

"I pulled a partial before the feed died," she said. With a flick of her fingers, she threw the crash model into the shared holo between their stations. The wireframe wreckage spun slowly, stress lines pulsing in amber.

Mateo leaned forward. "Huh. That's not how belt collisions break. Safety fired before your impact sensors."

"Exactly. Got a theory?"

He shrugged. "Could be a sync drift. We've had that on other sectors, safety algorithms getting twitchy and pre-triggering. A port collapse in Vancouver last year, a crane accident in Osaka, even a server farm fire in Nairobi that tripped suppression before the temp spike."

"And you filed all those?" she asked.

"Sure. Cross-sector quirks make good filler in the quarterly risk briefings. But they don't mean anything. Every sector thinks their anomalies are special."

She glanced at the model again, the stress lines like veins under translucent skin. "Then why bring in Oversight? They didn't just block my scan, they told the belt crew to stand down. Like they were… hiding something in the forward pods."

Mateo smirked without humor. "Could've been sensitive cargo, weapons, contract tech, maybe a shipment not even your consortium gets to know about."

"Maybe," she said, "or maybe something else entirely."

"Such as?"

She gave a small shrug. "That's the problem, I don't know yet."

He pointed with his chopsticks toward her console. "Then poke at it. Worst case, you waste an hour."

She grinned faintly. "You volunteering to explain to Oversight why my hour is missing from the productivity logs?"

"They don't audit Tier 2 field unless they're already suspicious. And you're not… yet."

That last word stuck.

She keyed open the incident archive almost on impulse. The search window bloomed into her vision, its parameters ghosting in pale blue. "Let's start wide," she muttered, mostly to herself. She set *probability threshold: 1-in-10,000* and hit return.

The feed began to populate: a fishing platform collapse off Chile; a cargo bot caravan rerouting around a sinkhole in Kenya; a midair collision between two private courier drones in Tokyo. A few had mesh icons in the margin, most didn't.

"Looks like what I said, noise," Mateo remarked without looking over.

"Maybe." She leaned in, scrolling slower. The anomalies were spread across sectors, disciplines, hemispheres. She adjusted the filter: *remove natural disasters, remove unaugmented personnel.*

The list thinned, and the mesh icon now appeared next to every entry.

Mateo finally swiveled toward her. "You've narrowed to all mesh incidents. Congratulations, you've found the obvious."

Lian ignored the jab and added another filter: *exclude incidents with established proximate cause.* Now there were fewer than a dozen results. She tapped the top entry, a crane collapse in Osaka. Safety systems had pre-triggered, sparing the crew but destroying the load. She remembered Mateo mentioning it minutes ago.

The next file was the Vancouver port collapse. Then the Nairobi server fire. Every one of them in his throwaway list.

"That's interesting," she murmured.

"Coincidence," Mateo said, but the word landed a little too quickly.

She brought up a cross-analysis, looking for patterns in the pre-triggered safety events. Different sectors, different manufacturers, different continents, but the same firmware signature buried deep in the mesh handshake logs. Not a match the software was supposed to flag. She had to override two visibility warnings to even bring it up.

One more tweak: *include events without loss of life that nonetheless averted major loss.* The list expanded again, and now it wasn't just "saves." Some incidents had improbable near-misses, like that Brisbane lightning strike… twice, same intersection, six months apart.

She sat back slowly. "You still think it's noise?"

Mateo was silent for a moment, then: "If it's not, you're looking at something Oversight wouldn't want anyone noticing. Which means…."

"…which means," she finished, "I should be very careful what I notice next."

* * *

The Pacific Arc came into view as a constellation of black hexagons scattered across the horizon. Even from kilometers out, Lian could see the solar sails, each the size of a city block, pivoting in slow unison to catch the light. Between them, the glitter of wave converters flashed like mirrors, sending back fragments of the afternoon sun.

Her mag-skiff's autopilot aligned with the docking beacon. In her HUD, the farm's systems pinged her mesh: Pacific Arc Node 7, Limited Guest Access, Mesh-Link Established. The handshake felt polite, but she could see the Oversight-level encryption shielding parts of the feed. Uninvited eyes not welcome.

The docking bay's mooring arms swung inward, locking the skiff with a hydraulic thud. She stepped out onto a deck that smelled faintly of brine and sun-warmed polymer. Captain Riva Chen was waiting for her at the access gate, tall, hazard-yellow jacket zipped to the throat, a sun-bleached cap pulled low over her brow.

"Investigator Arora," Chen said. Not a question.

"That's me," Lian replied, offering a hand.

Chen clasped it briefly, her grip dry and firm. "You're here about the reactor anomaly. I'll be direct: the system worked as designed. My crew is under instruction to cooperate, but we've already filed our own report."

"And yet," Lian said, "the consortium decided a second look was worth the trouble."

A hint of a smile tugged at Chen's mouth. "Walk with me."

They moved across the deck toward a set of elevated walkways. Below them, algae tanks stretched in neat ranks, their green surfaces disturbed by the hum of nutrient injectors. Overhead, the sails shifted angle, their actuators emitting the occasional metallic sigh. Autonomous drones skimmed from tank to tank, testing, shunting, filtering.

"The Arc feeds power to half the Pacific corridor," Chen said. "Between the solar sails, the wave converters, and the algae processors, we haven't missed a quota in ten years."

"Until the skiff," Lian said.

Chen's tone cooled. "Yes. A maintenance skiff detaches from its mooring without command, heads straight for the reactor bay. Safety overrides fail in cascade order. And then, " She flicked her hand in a dismissive gesture. ", manual shutdown sequence initiates perfectly, without a crew member in sight."

They passed into a covered causeway linking the sails to the central platform. The hum of machinery was replaced by the low roar of the ocean against the hull. A man in an orange hazard vest waited by the next hatch, shifting his weight as they approached. His mesh tag read Eddin Kor, Safety Officer.

"Kor will walk you through the logs," Chen said. "He was on duty when it happened."

Kor keyed the hatch, leading them into a compact control room lined with glass displays and tethered consoles. Through the bay windows, the reactor dome loomed, a smooth hemisphere of composite plating, coolant pipes running down its flanks like veins.

Kor brought up the incident file. "Docking clamps released at 14:22:10. No manual override logged. Autopilot engaged for the reactor coordinates, ignoring the exclusion zone." He tapped the next panel. "Safety protocols began to fail in cascade, clamp lock, route inhibitor, collision alarm, all in sequence. Then, at 14:22:54, the manual shutdown sequence runs. From nowhere."

"No personnel in the bay?" Lian asked.

Kor shook his head. "Closest was me, twenty meters away. I had visual, no one touched the controls."

Lian studied the raw telemetry feed, scrolling back frame by frame. The amber markers on the cascade sequence looked too clean, too evenly spaced, like a demonstration script rather than a live failure. Her HUD flickered a caution: Mesh Visibility Restricted, Vendor Lock. She forced a partial diagnostic, cross-checking firmware signatures against her private buffer.

There, a ghost call buried deep in the handshake log. Not identical to the maglev's safety system, but close enough to light a recognition spark. She'd seen something like it twice before: once in the maglev belt collision, and once in the Osaka crane collapse from Mateo's list.

She was about to isolate it when a shout came from somewhere topside.

"Crane! Crane! Move clear!"

Chen's head snapped up. Lian followed her through the hatch and back onto the open deck. Fifty meters away, a cargo crane was swinging out of its normal arc, a steel container dangling in its cables. The load's path cut straight toward the reactor walkway, and toward her.

Chen shoved her sideways. "Out of the zone!"

She moved, but a stack of supply crates blocked her escape route. The crane's arm swept closer, cable hissing, the shadow spilling over her. And then, with a metallic screech and the heavy snap of magnetic locks, the crane froze mid-swing. The container swayed, the only motion left in the moment.

"Cut the drive!" Chen barked into her comm.

The operator's voice came back tinny and tight. "Wasn't me! Controls locked out, then the system braked on its own!"

Lian's HUD pinged hard: Anomalous Command Signature Detected, Match Confidence 91%. Same buried signature. Same ghost call. This time she was in the middle of it.

She copied the packet to her personal buffer. As it uploaded, a new icon appeared in her peripheral, incoming mesh contacts boarding the platform. Two Oversight operatives in hazard black, one with a fog projector slung under his arm.

Chen followed her gaze, her expression unreadable. "Friends of yours?"

"No," Lian said, already stepping toward the mag-skiff. "Not even close."

"You're cutting the investigation short?"

Lian kept her voice light. "The claim's in your hands."

The skiff's clamps released, sliding her back into open water. The platform shrank behind her. On deck, the Oversight team was already heading for the reactor bay.

In her HUD, the data packet pulsed like a heartbeat.

***

The mag-skiff docked at Port Kestrel in the fading light. Cargo haulers moved in steady lines along the quay, their hulls glowing with safety glyphs that pulsed faintly in the dusk. Lian stepped onto the pier, the day's sea grit still drying on her jacket, already planning a long night of cross-checks, covert decrypts, and pattern hunts before Oversight could close off the Node 7 data. Her HUD pinged the moment her mesh reconnected to the consortium's grid.

Notification: Access Request Denied - File ID 77C-PacArc-Node7

She slowed her pace, trying again, rerouting the request through a side channel Mateo had once set up for her. Another denial appeared, this one marked with an Oversight seal. The block was too quick; they had been ready for her.

By the time she reached her office on the thirty-fifth floor, the city outside was a glowing lattice of streetlines and tower lights. She powered up her workstation, pulled the reactor and crane packet from her personal buffer, and fed it into the consortium's analysis suite. The program refused to read it, citing an invalid encryption wrapper. Vendor lock, a proprietary encryption barrier only the originating manufacturer or its contracted agencies could open, an unspoken reminder of who really controlled the tools.

Switching to her own kit, she layered three separate diagnostic utilities, stripping away the packet shells a line at a time. The process was slow, each partial result branching into subqueries, but the deeper she went, the more familiar the structure became. Mesh packet headers aligned perfectly with the maglev incident. Same origin line, same anomalous firmware call nested deep inside safety protocols. Three events now, in three different sectors, yet carrying the same unseen handprint.

The building lights dimmed for the night cycle. She looked toward the glass wall, expecting the city's sprawl to reflect back at her. Instead, she caught a detail that didn't belong, a faint mesh tag floating just behind her reflection's shoulder. She turned sharply toward the workbay. It was empty. The tag faded, but she had already recognized the protocol: a short-range handshake for direct device intrusion, the kind designed to bypass perimeter alarms. Whoever it was had been in her mesh, close enough to reach across the desk.

Her pulse climbed. Oversight was not only watching; they were close. Too close to trust any official route. If she wanted answers, she would have to bring the anomaly out herself.

The sim lab was unbooked for the night. She swiped in and stepped inside. The dome's acoustics swallowed every sound except the low hum of the environmental systems. She built a scenario from the ground up: maglev accident response, seeded with an improbable chain of failures, two safety collapses, a near-miss collision, a cargo override, a setup so statistically rare that any intervention would stand out.

The simulation unfolded in her HUD. The maglev belt stretched ahead, the soundscape of wind and vibration wrapping around her senses. As the scripted collision approached, the visual feed stuttered. A half-second of static bled into her mesh, followed by a flawless shutdown sequence she had not coded, bypassing every condition she had set. The anomaly had taken the bait.

She saved the entire run to her buffer, encrypting it with her strongest personal key. The final line of data had barely locked when the lab's door chime cut the silence.

"Investigator Arora?" The voice was calm, deliberate.

Two silhouettes stood on the other side of the glass. Hazard black gear, no insignia. One held a small case, the other a fog projector.

"We need you to come with us," the man said.

Lian closed the buffer file and powered down the sim. "I'm not on Oversight's payroll."

"That isn't a problem," he replied. "You will be."

***

The taller of the two men unlocked the door with an override access she didn't recognize. They entered without hesitation, scanning the lab with quick, practiced sweeps. The one with the case stayed by the entrance, his gaze fixed on her while the other approached.

"Bring your buffer drive," he said. "You're coming with us."

She didn't move. "Where?"

"You'll be briefed en route."

Lian slid the drive into an inner pocket, her mind already running escape vectors. The lab had two exits; both were now blocked. Her mesh feed showed no public drones within two blocks. Oversight had cleared the airspace.

The man with the fog projector adjusted his grip. "Let's make this simple."

"I prefer things complicated," she said, stepping past the console toward them. Every second she could stall gave Mateo more time to notice she was off-grid, assuming he was still running the passive anomaly alerts they had once set up together. He was not actively tracking her movements, but any prolonged mesh silence from her location would light up his dashboard by morning, if not sooner.

The case snapped open to reveal a compact field terminal, its display already flashing a mesh handshake request. They were going to take her offline the moment she stepped out the door.

She looked between them. "You've already been in my system once today. Why not just pull the data remotely?"

The taller man's jaw tightened. "We prefer to control variables."

The fog projector's safety light clicked off.

Lian exhaled, as though resigning herself. Then she stepped forward, letting them flank her. The corridor outside was silent, lit only by the red strips along the floor. Somewhere deeper in the building, the night-cycle hum of the air handlers echoed like a slow drumbeat.

If they wanted her to walk into the dark, she would. But she would be watching for the first shadow that moved wrong.

They moved her out of the lab without a word, one in front and one behind, steering her toward the service access. The corridor led to a freight elevator she rarely saw in use. The men guided her inside without touching her, their presence close enough to block any sudden move. The elevator dropped in near silence, the only sound the faint pulse of the field terminal in its case.

At the sublevel, the air was cooler and smelled faintly of ozone. A service tunnel stretched ahead, lined with conduit bundles and low amber lights. They walked in single file, their boots dull against the composite flooring. Lian kept her pace steady, using peripheral glances to memorize junctions, door markings, and the position of security cameras.

A turn brought them to a narrow platform where a black, unmarked transport waited. Its side panel slid open without a sound, revealing a small cabin with two rows of seats and no windows. A mesh suppression field hummed softly inside.

The man with the case entered first, settling the terminal on a folding shelf. The other gestured for her to sit. She complied, noting the restraints clipped to the seat frames but not yet fastened.

"Destination?" she asked.

"You'll see when we get there," the taller one said, taking a seat opposite her.

The transport lifted, smooth enough that she barely felt the transition from ground to air. The hum of the suppression field deepened, blotting out her mesh entirely. She glanced at the case, wondering if her encrypted packet was already a target. Without mesh access, she would not know until it was too late.

She sat back, conserving energy, replaying every detail of the last hour in her mind. Somewhere in that chain of events, every decision, movement, and interaction since she'd left the energy farm, there had to be a moment, a weakness in their control, that she could exploit when the chance came. She just had to reach it before they decided she was more valuable to them for what she knew, or could be made to reveal under pressure, than for simply holding the drive, especially if their intent leaned toward coercion rather than negotiation.

The transport's steady hum masked any sense of distance or direction. Lian had no idea how long they had been airborne when a faint shift in gravity signaled descent. The suppression field stayed active, smothering any attempt she might make to probe the outside network. Without mesh access, all she could rely on were her senses.

The landing was soft, almost cautious. The side panel opened to reveal a dimly lit hangar, walls lined with maintenance racks and shadowed alcoves. She was guided out, one operative ahead, one behind. No words were exchanged. The smell of oil and ionized air clung to the space.

They moved her toward an unmarked door set into the far wall. A camera dome tracked them as they approached, but no indicator lights showed it was active. The door opened without a visible command, revealing a long corridor that seemed older than the rest of the facility, its walls a mix of bare concrete and patched composites.

At the corridor's end, a chamber opened up into what looked like a control hub stripped of its identifying marks. Workstations lined the perimeter, his displays running streams of untagged data. In the center stood a single table and three chairs. The man with the case placed it on the table and stepped aside.

A man waited by one of the workstations, hands clasped loosely behind his back. His clothing was plain, his expression unreadable, but his presence radiated quiet authority.

"Investigator Arora," the man said, as if greeting an expected guest. "We have questions about your… extracurricular research."

Lian met his gaze, masking any reaction. "Then I suppose we should get started."

***

The man stepped forward from the workstation with unhurried precision, each step measured, as if to remind her who set the pace here. He circled the table once before taking the seat opposite her. The operatives who had brought her in posted themselves near the door, backs straight, hands clasped loosely but close enough to the gear slung at their sides. The steady hum of cooling fans from the perimeter workstations filled the air, a constant background murmur that made the room feel both alive and watchful.

"You've been present at three separate incidents," he began, voice low but carrying. "Each involved improbable safety system failures followed by unexplained recoveries. And each one now bears your digital fingerprints."

Lian's fingers rested lightly on the table's edge. "I investigate anomalies," she said, letting the words come slowly. "That's my job."

He studied her, not speaking, his gaze holding hers long enough for her to feel the weight of it. "We're less interested in your job title than in the results you've managed to pull from restricted systems. The patterns you've uncovered are not coincidences. We want to know how far your understanding goes."

Her mouth curved faintly, though not into a smile. "Far enough to know you've already been inside my systems. Far enough to know the signature repeats."

Something flickered in his eyes, recognition, or perhaps approval. "Then you also understand that whoever is behind this operates well above your clearance. We can give you access to them… or we can keep you chasing ghosts."

"And the price?" she asked.

"You'll deliver your findings to us first. Full and unfiltered."

Her eyes shifted to the case on the table, its display pulsing in slow rhythm. "And if I decide not to play?"

He glanced at one of the operatives. The man stepped forward, slow enough for her to take in the gleam of the fog projector as its activation light came alive. "Then we erase your involvement and your memory of these events. You'll wake somewhere else with a hole you'll never quite fill."

Lian's pulse beat once, hard. Cooperation or erasure. Neither was acceptable, but one of them would at least buy her time to find another move.

Lian let the silence stretch, the hum of the workstations filling the gap between them. She knew they were watching for hesitation, for any sign she might break under pressure. Instead, she folded her hands in front of her and tilted her head slightly.

"I'll work with you," she said at last, "but only if I have the freedom to choose my own methods. You want results, you let me operate without a leash."

The man across the table regarded her for a long moment, his gaze unwavering. "We'll give you room," he said. "But you will share everything. No exceptions."

"One condition," she replied. "I keep control of my raw data until I've verified its integrity. You get the findings, not the noise that could get me killed if it leaks."

A faint smile touched his face, though it didn't reach his eyes. "Negotiating already. Good. But understand, if we suspect you're holding back, we will act."

The operative with the fog projector stepped back, the activation light winking out. The man at the table closed the case and slid it toward her. "Your first assignment will come through a secure channel by morning. We expect progress quickly."

Lian stood, feeling the eyes of both operatives on her. She knew they'd be tracking her from here on, but at least she had bought herself time. As she followed them out, she began mentally mapping her next steps. Whatever game they were playing, she needed to see the board before they moved another piece.

They escorted her back the way they had come, through the stripped control hub, down the bare corridor, and into the hangar where the unmarked transport waited. The ride back was as silent as the trip in, the suppression field keeping her mesh cold and dark.

When they set her down at a deserted cross-street near Port Kestrel, the panel door slid open without a word. The operatives remained inside, watching. She stepped out, the damp night air smelling faintly of salt and exhaust. By the time she turned, the transport was already lifting away, vanishing into the low clouds.

Her mesh reconnected instantly, a flood of queued notifications rushing in. She dismissed them without reading. First things first: check the integrity of her buffer drive. The packet from the simulation was still there, encrypted and untouched.

Street traffic was sparse, just a few cargo drones humming overhead and the occasional night hauler passing under the sodium lights. Lian pulled her jacket tighter and started walking toward the safe flat she used when she needed to vanish for a few days.

They would send the assignment by morning, as promised. Until then, she had hours to prepare, to pick apart what had just happened, and to decide how much of their game she was willing to play. Somewhere out there, the anomaly was still moving, invisible but not unreachable, and now she was caught between two forces, her own drive to track the anomaly, and their intent to control how far she could go.

***

The safe flat was three levels up in a weathered block overlooking a cargo canal. Lian entered through a rear stairwell, bypassing the front access where cameras would still be recording. Inside, the single-room space smelled faintly of dust and old sealant. She ran a quick sweep for mesh pings or embedded sensors; nothing answered.

She set the buffer drive on the table, its indicator light a steady green. The packet from the simulation was still secure, but that didn't mean they wouldn't try to reach it. She pulled out a portable isolator, slipped the drive inside, and set a passive alert for any signal attempting to handshake with it.

Only then did she let herself sit. The walls were thin, the hum of the canal pumps a constant undertone, but she preferred the noise. It masked smaller sounds, footsteps in the hall, the creak of a settling floor.

She opened a thin, unmarked notebook and began mapping out the last twenty-four hours, each encounter and location laid out as nodes in a web. Lines traced possible connections: the crane, the reactor, the maglev, the repeated signature. One question she wrote in the margin and underlined twice: who benefits from the anomaly's intervention?

Outside, a fog horn sounded from somewhere down the canal. She checked the time. Four hours until they said they would send her the first assignment. Four hours to decide whether she would follow their lead, or find a way to make them follow hers.

The four hours passed in fragments. Lian made tea from the emergency rations, reviewed her notebook twice, and ran another sweep of the flat. Nothing. The canal outside was quiet now, the fog horn silent, the night pressing in.

At exactly 0300, her mesh pinged. A single encrypted packet appeared in her queue, tagged with the same handshake signature as the case in the interrogation room. She opened it in the isolator. The message was brief: coordinates, a time, and a single line of instruction, "Document, do not interfere."

The coordinates resolved to a sector on the southern edge of the Arc, a cluster of maintenance platforms straddling the tide barrier. Lian brought up public schematics. The platform's function was ordinary enough, storm surge regulation, equipment storage, but the maintenance logs had a gap three weeks wide. Someone had scrubbed the records.

She sat back, weighing options. They wanted her as an observer, but observation could be as revealing to them as it was to her. If she went in cold, she would be working from whatever vantage they allowed. If she went in prepared, she might see past whatever they wanted her to see.

Lian closed the schematic and began assembling a field kit from the flat's concealed lockers: low-light optics, two signal jammers, a micro-drone, and a set of mesh-spoofing tags. If they wanted her to document, she would, but on her own terms.

***

Dawn had not yet broken when Lian left the safe flat. She moved through the canal district in the pre-shift quiet, her kit stowed in a nondescript courier bag. The streets carried the sharp tang of tidal ozone mixed with the faint bite of oxidized steel, the air heavy with the promise of rain. Cargo drones hummed overhead, their navigation lights diffused by the mist.

She took the magline two stops south, then a pedestrian lift down to the maintenance causeway that skirted the Arc's outer wall. From there, the tide barrier loomed ahead, a spine of steel and concrete rising from the water, its maintenance platforms linked like vertebrae. The assigned coordinates lay midway along the structure.

A security checkpoint marked the approach. The two attendants barely looked up as she presented a forged work order, their scanners accepting the tag without question. Beyond the gate, the hum of turbines grew louder, punctuated by the occasional crash of waves against the barrier's base.

She found a vantage point on an upper catwalk overlooking the designated platform. From here she could see the sweep of the tide gates and the skeletal cranes moving slowly in the distance. She unpacked her optics, adjusted the focus, and began a slow scan of the area.

For long minutes, nothing happened. Workers moved below in routine patterns, and the platform appeared unremarkable. Then, a flicker in her optics, a momentary static distortion, too localized to be environmental. She tracked it, pulse tightening. Whatever they had sent her to witness was beginning to unfold.

Lian kept her optics fixed on the point where the distortion had appeared. The air above the platform seemed to shimmer, not with heat but with a subtle warping of the lines behind it, as if her focus had slipped without her moving the lens. She adjusted magnification, isolating a section of the catwalk where no one was standing.

Another ripple passed through her view. This time, one of the maintenance workers glanced up sharply, as though they had heard something, then returned to their task. Lian tagged the coordinates in her recorder, noting the timestamp.

She switched to the microdrone, releasing it from her kit with a quiet command. It dropped below the catwalk, its rotors masked by the turbine noise, and began a slow circuit toward the platform. Through its feed, she saw details invisible from her vantage: a faint corona of static clinging to the railing, tiny arcs leaping and fading in irregular bursts.

Her mesh flagged the signature, a partial match to the one from the maglev simulation. Whatever this was, it was the same phenomenon, only here it was anchored to a physical location.

A voice crackled over the catwalk intercom, pulling her attention back. "All non-essential personnel, clear the platform." The workers began moving toward the inner accessway without question. Lian kept her optics on the static field, unwilling to blink.

She had seconds before she would stand out as the only observer still in position.

Lian lowered the optics just enough to look casual as a uniformed supervisor emerged from the inner accessway, scanning the catwalk. His eyes passed over her once, then lingered. He started in her direction at a steady pace.

She recalled the microdrone with a subvocal command, guiding it to latch beneath the catwalk out of sight. The static field on the platform was still flaring in irregular pulses, but she had already tagged and stored the data. Staying here much longer risked more than just being noticed.

"Clear the area," the supervisor called, voice louder now. "Platform's under controlled maintenance."

Lian slung her optics over one shoulder and moved toward the nearest stairwell, her pace measured. As she descended, she kept the platform in peripheral view, noting two new figures arriving from the far end, both in hazard black, carrying cases similar to the one she had seen in the interrogation room.

At the base of the stairwell, she blended into a small group of departing workers, their chatter covering her mesh ping as the microdrone slipped back into her kit. She didn't look back until she was halfway along the outer causeway. By then, the platform was empty except for the two in black, working methodically inside the distortion's locus.

Whatever was happening there, they had just made it clear it was not for public eyes.

Lian kept her pace steady along the causeway, letting the group of workers thin out ahead of her until she was alone. The turbines below sent up a steady vibration through the walkway, a reminder of the water pressure being held back by the barrier.

She stopped briefly at a service alcove, ostensibly to adjust the strap on her bag, and used the moment to review the microdrone's buffered feed on her wrist display. The distortion had intensified in the last minute before she recalled it, arcs snapping like miniature lightning between railings, the air shimmering in a growing sphere. The two operatives in black had stepped into its edge without hesitation.

Pocketing the display, she resumed her walk toward the inner gate. The same checkpoint attendants from earlier barely glanced at her as she passed, more interested in their own screens. Outside the secure zone, the industrial district was waking up; delivery trams clattered along their tracks and stacks of cargo containers loomed in the fog.

She cut through two side streets to reach the magline, keeping her head down. The entire trip back, her mind replayed the moment the operatives entered the distortion. Either they knew it was safe, or they were prepared to pay the cost if it wasn't.

By the time she reached the safe flat, the sky had begun to pale. She locked the door, set the microdrone into its cradle, and initiated a deep analysis of the recorded data. The anomaly was no longer an abstract signature in her files; it had a shape, a pulse, and people willing to step inside.

The safe flat was still and cool, the canal fog pressing against the single window. Lian powered up her primary console, linking it directly to the microdrone's cradle. Streams of raw telemetry poured across the display: magnetic flux spikes, temperature gradients, and bursts of unclassified energy readings.

She isolated the segment when the distortion began to expand. Frame by frame, the shimmering sphere swelled until it filled the drone's view, the arcs snapping faster, the air itself seeming to ripple. The operatives in black stepped into the haze, their outlines blurring almost instantly. No alarms, no visible harm. The sensors recorded a momentary drop in local gravity, then normalized as if nothing had changed.

Lian leaned back, replaying the clip twice more. The data confirmed what her instincts had been telling her: the anomaly could be entered, and whatever was inside did not conform to known physical parameters. That also meant it could be manipulated, or weaponized.

She tagged the file with a private cipher and buried it deep in an off-mesh vault. If her new handlers saw it, they would own it. But if she kept it hidden, she might still have a card to play.

Somewhere out on the tide barrier, the distortion might still be active. And if it was, she wasn't the only one watching.

***

The next morning, Lian sat at the narrow table in the safe flat, coffee cooling in front of her, eyes on the secure comms terminal. A message from Mateo waited in her private channel, terse, just coordinates and a time. No signature.

She finished the coffee and took the long way to the meeting point, threading through the fog-bound streets until she reached a half-abandoned fabrication yard near the old floodgates. Mateo was waiting under the skeletal frame of a crane, hands in his jacket pockets, scanning for anyone following.

"You pulled something you shouldn't have," he said without preamble.

"Depends on who decides what's 'shouldn't,'" she replied, watching his face. "You've seen the anomaly reports?"

"I've seen more than that. The maglev incident, the reactor trip, now the tide barrier. Three separate events with no common link until you walked into them. And now I've got chatter about 'pattern recognition interference' flagged in security channels that aren't supposed to talk to each other."

She stepped closer, lowering her voice. "It's not just a visual glitch. The readings from my drone show a localized gravity dip, no thermal signature, no ionization. Something in there holds steady when every known model says it should collapse instantly."

Mateo's gaze sharpened. "And you think it's the same force behind all three incidents?"

"It matches the maglev signature. If it's not the same, it's related. Someone's protecting it, maybe even cultivating it."

He rubbed at his jaw, eyes on the fog drifting across the yard. "The operatives in black aren't local security. They're contractors. Off-ledger, high discretion. They don't show up unless the client is serious and the stakes are high."

"And you think you can get me back to the barrier?" she asked.

"If it's still there, yes. But once they lock it down, the only way in will be through them. And trust me, you don't want to find out what they're guarding it for without a way back out."

The fog thickened, swallowing the crane's outline, and Lian knew the window to act was closing.

Lian and Mateo moved to a sheltered spot beneath the crane's frame, out of sight from the street. The damp air muffled their voices.

"What's the best way back in?" she asked.

"Through the supply side," Mateo said. "The barrier runs resupply barges twice a week. They carry maintenance crews, replacement parts, and plenty of places to disappear if you know the manifests."

"You have access to those?"

He gave her a sidelong look. "I can get them. But you'll need credentials that match a crew shift. And you can't show up with obvious kit."

Lian considered. "I can break it down. Stash half on the inside."

"Good. Because once you're in, you won't have long. My contact says the distortion site is sealed for a 'stability assessment' in forty-eight hours. After that, it's either gone or moved somewhere we can't follow."

She leaned back against the crane's cold steel, letting the numbers sink in. "So we have two days."

"Two days," Mateo confirmed. "And one chance to see it without their filter. After that, we're just chasing rumors again."

Lian nodded slowly. "Then let's make sure it counts."

They split up without another word, disappearing into opposite ends of the foggy yard, each carrying their part of the plan into motion.

The fog hung thicker as Lian cut through the alleys toward her flat, already turning Mateo's outline of a plan into a detailed checklist. The barrier's supply manifests would give her a window, but the disguise had to hold up under scrutiny.

She started with the ID. In her console's secure partition, she pulled up a cache of dormant worker profiles bought months ago from a port clerk with a gambling problem. Cross-referencing with the manifests, she found a maintenance tech scheduled for the next barge run whose file was unlikely to trigger deeper checks.

Next came the kit. She stripped her gear down to components that could pass as diagnostic tools: optics disguised as pipe inspection lenses, a signal jammer hidden in a voltage calibrator's casing, the microdrone folded into a spool housing for fiber optic cable. The rest she packed into two lockboxes for Mateo to insert onto the barge ahead of time.

By nightfall, the disguise was ready. The clothes were standard maintenance issue, patched in the right places, stained just enough to look lived-in. She practiced the worker's name, cadence, and a half-dozen plausible reasons for being anywhere on the barrier.

When she finally shut down the console, the manifests showed her slot in the barge's passenger list. One line of text in a sea of others, invisible to anyone not looking for it. In thirty-six hours, she would be on the water, heading straight for the distortion.

***

Morning broke gray and flat, the fog over the canal lifting just enough to show the outlines of the supply barge moored at Pier Six. Lian approached with the steady, unhurried gait of someone who had walked the docks a hundred times before. Her coveralls smelled faintly of machine oil, her ID clipped where it could be scanned without fuss.

The security line was short. A guard waved a handheld scanner over her tag, the light turning green without hesitation. She offered a nod, kept her eyes forward, and stepped onto the gangway. The deck vibrated under her boots as loaders moved crates into the hold, their shouts muffled by the hum of the engines.

Below deck, the passenger area was a narrow corridor of metal benches and utility lockers. She found a spot near the stern, close to a maintenance hatch that would give her quick access topside once they were underway. A few other workers glanced at her and then lost interest, absorbed in their own routines.

Through a porthole, the pier began to slide away. The barge's engines deepened in pitch, pulling them into the channel. Lian checked the time: four hours to the barrier, four hours to blend in and stay invisible.

Somewhere in the cargo hold, her lockboxes waited. And beyond them, hidden in the mist that shrouded the horizon, was the anomaly, anchored, active, and this time within reach.

The barge settled into its steady rhythm, engines thudding beneath the deck like a mechanical heartbeat. Lian kept her gaze on the scuffed floor plates, letting the hum of the passage lull the attention of anyone watching. The other workers traded idle talk about maintenance delays and the weather; no one asked her name.

After an hour, she rose and drifted toward the maintenance hatch near her bench. She opened it just enough to let in a draft of cold air and the tang of open water. The channel stretched out in both directions, pale fog hiding the horizon. Somewhere ahead, the barrier was drawing closer.

She descended into the cargo hold, the air warmer here, dense with the smell of treated wood and lubricant. The lockboxes sat where Mateo's contact had wedged them between two crates. She knelt, checking the seals and the false labeling, then slipped the smaller one into a service satchel that matched her cover story.

Back in the passenger space, she kept her posture relaxed, her mind running through entry points and escape routes. Every minute brought them nearer to the tide barrier, and to the distortion site that would either yield answers or close off for good.

Lian closed her eyes for a moment, not to rest, but to fix the plan in her mind. When the time came, she would have one shot to get close without drawing the wrong kind of notice.

A low horn sounded from the pilothouse, followed by a shift in the engine's rhythm as the barge eased back on speed. Through the narrow portholes, the tide barrier emerged from the fog, its immense spine of steel and concrete cutting across the channel. Gulls wheeled above the structure, their cries faint against the churn of the water.

Workers began gathering their gear, their movements practiced and unhurried. Lian followed their lead, shouldering her satchel and keeping her eyes forward. She joined the flow toward the gangway, noting the uniformed guards stationed at the dock entrance, their attention split between clipboards and the slow-moving line of arrivals.

The barge bumped gently against the mooring. A gangway dropped, clanging into place, and the first crew stepped ashore. Lian filed off with them, presenting her ID to the guard without breaking stride. The scanner chirped approval, and she moved past the checkpoint into the controlled chaos of the barrier's operations deck.

The air here was sharper, heavy with the metallic tang of seawater forced through turbines. Cranes swung overhead, lowering cargo to waiting platforms, while maintenance carts hummed along the access lanes. Somewhere beyond the stacked containers and service sheds lay the sealed platform where the distortion had appeared.

Keeping her pace even, Lian melted into the movement of the crew, her mind mapping the fastest route to the site. The clock on her mesh ticked steadily down toward the moment she would have to make her move.

Lian stayed with the crew until they reached the main service hub, a wide concourse where teams split off toward their assigned sections. The moment her group turned toward the turbine bays, she drifted to the edge of the lane, bending over her satchel as if checking a tool list. When no one was looking directly at her, she stepped into a side corridor marked for storage access.

The hum of the operations deck faded behind her, replaced by the echo of her boots on grated steel. Rows of spare parts and sealed crates lined the narrow space. She kept moving, glancing at painted section numbers until they aligned with the coordinates she had memorized from her last visit.

A locked gate blocked the final stretch toward the distortion site. She palmed a slim bypass tool from her satchel, its casing disguised as a voltage calibrator, and clipped it to the lock housing. The device pulsed once, then clicked softly, releasing the latch.

Beyond the gate, the walkway opened into a windswept platform overlooking the outer wall. The platform where she had first seen the anomaly was quiet now, no workers in sight. She slipped into the shadow of a crane support and scanned the area, her pulse steady but quickening.

If the distortion was still here, it was hidden, and she had just stepped into the space where it might reveal itself again.

***

From her position in the crane's shadow, Lian unpacked the disguised optics from her satchel and began a slow sweep of the platform. The wind cut across the outer wall, carrying the tang of salt and the distant churn of turbines. The platform looked abandoned, but her optics picked up faint anomalies along the railing, a thin haze that warped the lines behind it for a fraction of a second before fading.

She crouched near the spot where the distortion had flared days ago and placed a compact sensor on the deck. It hummed softly as it began pulling environmental data, mapping temperature gradients, electromagnetic fluctuations, and any irregularities in gravitational pull. The readings were subtle but wrong, like echoes from an event that had already passed yet refused to dissipate.

The Architecture of Unmaking

A faint scuffing of boots on metal made her freeze. She killed the sensor's light and slid it back into the satchel, moving deeper into the crane's shadow. Two figures in hazard black stepped onto the platform from the far accessway, their faces obscured by tinted visors. They paused exactly where she had been standing moments before.

One of them swept a handheld scanner over the deck, the device's readout pulsing in a rhythm that made her think they were tracking the same residual traces she had just found. The other spoke into a clipped comm channel, too low for her to catch.

Lian kept still, her breathing shallow. Whatever the anomaly had left behind, they were looking for it too, and they were much closer to finding it than she liked.

The operatives moved methodically, their scanners sweeping every section of the platform. Lian edged along the crane support, keeping metal between herself and their line of sight. Each time the scanner pulsed, the operator paused, making small adjustments as if homing in on a signal.

She slipped her optics into a coat pocket and drew out the microdrone, cupping it in her palm until its rotors whispered to life. With a quick flick, she sent it crawling along the underside of the crane's arm, its camera feeding a bird's-eye view of the platform to her wrist display.

Through the drone's lens, she saw one of the operatives produce a sealed canister from a case and place it on the deck at the heart of the residual trace. A low hum began to resonate, just at the edge of hearing. The haze along the railing shimmered faintly in response, like a mirage taking shape.

The second operative stepped back, speaking into their comm again. Whatever they were doing was meant to provoke a reaction from the anomaly's leftovers, or to draw something out.

Lian's pulse quickened. If the haze solidified, she might see a fragment of the distortion again. But it also meant she was standing on the same platform with people deliberately triggering it. And if they realized she was here, the anomaly would be the least of her problems.

The hum from the canister deepened, vibrating through the deck plates beneath Lian's boots. In her wrist display, the drone feed showed the haze thickening, its edges hardening into a wavering sphere of distorted air. Light bent strangely inside it, as though the platform's railing had been refracted through water.

One operative adjusted a dial on the canister, and the sphere's surface rippled outward. Faint arcs crackled across its skin, each pulse met by a matching flicker in the scanner's display. The other operative stepped closer, holding a probe just shy of the distortion's edge.

Lian's breath caught when the probe tip vanished into the sphere without resistance. The operative held it there for several seconds before withdrawing it, the metal prongs steaming in the cool air.

Her mind raced. This was no residual echo, it was the anomaly, alive again, anchored to this place. The canister wasn't collecting traces; it was sustaining the distortion.

A sudden shift in the operatives' posture made her freeze. One of them was looking up toward the crane, scanning the structure as if sensing something amiss. Lian eased back into the shadows, killing the drone's feed. The hum continued to build, and she knew she had only moments before they either shut the anomaly down or stepped inside.

The hum swelled until it blurred into a low vibration that seemed to press on Lian's ribs. From her hiding place in the crane's shadow, she watched the operatives exchange a brief signal. The one with the probe clipped it back to their belt and stepped toward the sphere, moving with the certainty of someone who had done this before.

Without hesitation, they walked straight into the distortion. The surface swallowed them soundlessly, rippling once before closing behind. The remaining operative adjusted the canister controls, keeping the sphere stable, their visor tilted as if listening to a voice no one else could hear.

Lian's instincts screamed to retreat, but her eyes stayed fixed on the anomaly. Seconds later, the first operative emerged, carrying a sealed container no larger than a handspan. They passed it to their partner, who stowed it carefully in a padded case.

Whatever they had retrieved from inside, it was tangible, and they had risked entering the distortion to get it.

The canister's hum dropped in pitch, the arcs along the sphere fading until only the haze remained, then nothing at all. The platform looked empty again, as though the event had never happened.

The operatives secured their gear and turned toward the far accessway. Lian stayed motionless until the sound of their boots on the decking disappeared into the wind. Only then did she exhale, every muscle in her body still taut with the knowledge that she had just witnessed something no one would believe without proof.

Lian waited a full thirty seconds after the last echo of their footsteps was gone. The wind was the only sound now, rattling a loose length of cabling somewhere above. She stepped out from the crane's shadow, her gaze fixed on the spot where the distortion had hung in the air only moments before.

Kneeling, she ran a gloved hand over the decking. The metal was cold, unmarked, no trace of the shimmer or the arcs. Yet her sensor registered faint, decaying fluctuations, residual energy fading with each heartbeat.

She pulled the microdrone from her satchel, launching it into a slow circle over the platform. Its camera captured the emptiness, the unbroken lines of steel and sky, and the empty accessway the operatives had used. She knew the recording would show nothing out of the ordinary to an untrained eye, but she tagged the data anyway, sealing it under her own encryption.

Every instinct told her to get clear before another patrol arrived. Still, she took one last look toward the sea, half expecting the haze to return. It didn't.

She slipped back through the gate she had bypassed earlier, the lock clicking shut behind her. The platform might be empty, but whatever had been inside that distortion was on its way somewhere, and she intended to find out where.

The storage corridor was quiet when Lian stepped through the gate, the clang of the latch fading into the hum of the barrier's machinery. She moved quickly but without rushing, keeping her head down as she retraced her path toward the main service hub.

At a junction, the rumble of approaching wheels made her pause. A maintenance cart rolled past, loaded with sealed crates identical to the one she had seen the operative carry from the distortion. The driver didn't glance her way, but the sight sent a flicker of urgency through her chest.

She fell in behind the cart at a discreet distance, noting the route it took deeper into the barrier's interior. The turns didn't match any of the regular maintenance loops she had memorized; they followed a path toward a wing she had only ever seen marked on outdated schematics, an unlabelled block in the far interior.

At the next crossway, she slowed, committing the section number to memory before letting the cart disappear from view. She pictured the oldest barrier schematics she had scraped years ago from a contractor bid archive: a dead-end service spur labeled only as SB-7 that branched past the floodgate pumps, hazard hatching where notes should have been; in later revisions, the spur was blanked and the adjacent block renumbered, leaving a neat rectangular void where an annex should sit. The cart's turns mirrored that spur's angles exactly; two lefts after Pump Hall C, a dogleg around a pressure manifold, then a straight run toward the interior wall. If SB-7 had been renumbered to 7B, it would lie at the end of that corridor behind a secondary security door. In a shadowed alcove, she keyed a quick message to Mateo on her secure channel: Object retrieved. Possible transit toward sector 7B, based on route match to archived contractor schematic. She didn't wait for a reply before pocketing the comms unit.

Her cover would hold only as long as she stayed within her assigned zones. One wrong turn, and she would have uniformed escorts all the way back to the dock. Still, she kept her mind fixed on 7B. If the operatives had taken the anomaly's prize there, it was the next step in her hunt.

Lian rejoined the main service flow, falling into step with a group of turbine technicians headed toward the docking bay. The hum of the barrier's machinery filled the air, a constant backdrop to the shuffle of boots and the metallic clink of tools. No one paid her more than a passing glance.

Her mind stayed on 7B, running through the schematic angles again, imagining what could be hidden behind a security door that had been erased from public records. The image of the operative emerging from the distortion with the sealed container sat sharp in her thoughts. Whatever was inside that box was now locked deeper in the barrier, behind layers of clearance she didn't yet know how to penetrate.

The docking bay opened ahead, the barge she had arrived on already taking on cargo for its return trip. She kept her pace steady, walking straight up the gangway as if she belonged there. A cursory scan of her ID cleared her for boarding without incident.

On deck, she took a seat near the stern rail, the cold wind cutting through her coveralls. The barrier's mass began to recede behind them, swallowed slowly by the fog. Somewhere inside its steel spine, in that unmarked block she now knew as 7B, was the next piece of the puzzle. And she was already planning how to get back in.

***

The return trip was quiet, the low vibration of the barge's engines masking the occasional creak of shifting cargo. Lian kept her gaze on the gray blur of the channel ahead, waiting until the crew's attention was fixed on their routines before opening a secure channel on her comms unit.

Mateo answered after two rings, his voice low. "You made it out."

"I saw it reactivate. Two operatives sustained it long enough to step inside. One came out carrying a sealed container, small enough to fit in one hand. They moved it toward a sector that matches an old schematic footprint labeled SB-7. Now 7B."

She could hear him exhale through the line. "That block hasn't existed on paper for years. When a section disappears from all public and internal schematics but the physical space still exists, it means the site's been reclassified. Around here, that's almost always deep lockdown, the kind reserved for strategic assets or experimental tech too dangerous or politically sensitive to risk in open circulation. It's walled off from the normal command chain, with its own clearance tree and security protocols. If they've taken it there, they don't want anyone without need-to-know even aware it exists."

"I'll need access routes and security patterns," she said. "And I'll need them soon."

"Give me a day to pull the cleanest copy of the interior maps I can find," Mateo replied. "But don't move on it alone."

Lian didn't answer right away. Through the fog, the barrier's silhouette was gone, but its image remained in her mind's eye, and with it, the thought of the sealed box now hidden in 7B. "One day," she said, and closed the channel.

The barge eased into its berth with a slow grind of metal against rubber bumpers. Lian rose with the rest of the crew, filing down the gangway under the watch of two bored dock guards. Her ID cleared without incident, and she stepped onto the pier, the cold air smelling faintly of diesel and salt.

Mateo wasn't supposed to be here, they had agreed to wait until he pulled the maps, but he stood at the far end, leaning against a stack of cargo pallets. His eyes tracked her approach, his posture casual but deliberate, as if he'd been watching every disembarking passenger.

"You've got something," he murmured when she drew close, keeping his voice low.

"Proof it's still active. Proof they can control it. And maybe proof they can take things out of it," she said.

His fingers tapped once against his leg, a tell she knew meant he was already calculating risks. "We'll need to talk somewhere quieter. There've been more eyes on the docks than usual this week."

They slipped into the warren of storage sheds lining the waterfront, weaving through stacked pallets and rusted forklifts until the pier's noise faded. Inside a dim, unused loading bay, she recounted everything in sequence: the operatives' arrival, the canister, the sphere, the retrieval, and the route toward 7B.

When she finished, Mateo was silent for several seconds. "If it's in 7B, it's not coming back out without a fight. And I don't just mean physical security."

Lian closed the satchel at her side. "Then we plan for both kinds, starting now."

Mateo shifted his weight, glancing toward the bay's open doorway before speaking again. "I've already started digging. The last contract work order for anything in 7B is fifteen years old, under a shell company that folded two months after completion. Every name tied to it has since moved to agencies with clearance levels we can't even sniff."

Lian listened, filing the detail away. "So no public records, no official maintenance, and no way to get near it without raising alarms."

"That's the shape of it," Mateo said. "But a place that dead on paper has to have supply lines, power, water, data. We trace those, we might find a way in sideways."

She nodded slowly. "Or a way to intercept anything coming out."

He gave her a quick, approving glance. "I'll work the grid maps and utility logs. You focus on who was on that platform with you today. If they've been inside 7B before, there'll be traces, travel manifests, biometric logs, something."

The faint clank of a shifting pallet jack echoed outside, closer now. Mateo stepped back toward the door, letting the light catch him as if they'd been talking about cargo weights. "We split here. I'll send you what I find tonight."

Lian tightened the strap on her satchel. "And I'll find them," she said. "Whoever they are, they're our way back to that box.

By the time Lian reached her small apartment above the market district, dusk had settled in. The hum of street vendors below bled through the thin walls as she powered up her secure terminal. Mateo's parting words still echoed: *find them.*

She started with the anomaly platform's access logs. Most were routine entries for maintenance crews, their identities cross-checking clean. But buried in the encrypted section reserved for hazard-response personnel, she found two profiles with redacted biometric overlays, entries tagged only with rotating alphanumeric codes.

Pulling from her archived port authority data, she ran the codes against last week's incoming personnel transfers. The first hit came back as a temporary clearance issued under a foreign contractor's name, now already flagged as inactive. The second was trickier, it didn't appear in the transfer lists at all.

Lian leaned back, eyes narrowing. That meant the second operative had been on-site without passing through the normal clearance system. Either they were ghosted in through an internal pipeline, or they carried a standing clearance so high it bypassed standard logging entirely.

She queued a deeper cross-check into transport manifests and drone-cam archives from the barrier's perimeter. If either of them had arrived by a less official route, there might be a trace in the machinery of daily logistics.

Somewhere in that data, she knew, was the thread she could pull, and once she had it, it would lead her straight to whoever stepped inside the anomaly.

The cross-check took longer than she'd hoped. Lian sat hunched over the terminal, the glow of its display painting the room in cold light as she sifted through timestamped entries. Cargo barges, maintenance skiffs, and perimeter patrol boats all came and went in predictable cycles, except for one.

A supply tender had made an unscheduled stop at the barrier two hours before she'd seen the operatives on the platform. Its manifest listed only standard consumables: water filters, synthetic fuel cells, packaged rations. But the weight totals didn't match the volume of goods declared.

She drilled into the tender's docking records. The berth assigned wasn't one of the main intake piers; it was a side channel usually reserved for emergency offloads. And the drone-cam footage for that docking window was missing, not corrupted, but deliberately overwritten with a looping clip from the previous week.

Her fingers stilled on the keys. This was no accident. Someone had used that tender to bring in at least one of the operatives without leaving an official trail, then covered their tracks in the surveillance system.

Lian tagged the tender's registration for a persistent watch in her network. If it moved again, she'd know within minutes. For now, she logged off and sat back in her chair, mind already sketching the possibilities. Whoever had the power to ghost someone into the barrier was part of a larger machine, and she had just seen its gears begin to turn.

The market district had quieted by the time Lian stepped out onto her narrow balcony, a mug of bitter tea in hand. Neon light from the street below washed across the low clouds, painting them in fractured colors. She kept her comms unit nearby, waiting for the ping that would tell her the tender had moved.

Instead, a different alert flared on her terminal inside, a flagged data packet from one of her passive network taps in the barrier's logistics grid. She set the mug down and crossed to the screen, scanning the lines of compressed code as they unpacked.

It was a maintenance work order, priority-tagged and heavily encrypted, routed through the same side channel berth the tender had used. The destination field was stripped, but the timestamp matched a comms blackout scheduled for the far interior in less than six hours.

She traced the packet's path backward, watching as it split into decoys before rejoining at a secure relay point. This wasn't routine maintenance; it was a cover for moving something, or someone, without triggering the usual alerts.

Lian pulled up the map Mateo had sent earlier, overlaying it with her own annotations. The blackout zone sat like a shadow over the footprint of the old SB-7 block. Whatever was in 7B was about to be active again.

She sent Mateo a short, coded burst: *Movement in 7B window. Six hours.* Then she began pulling gear from her satchel, already calculating how to get herself in position before the blackout dropped.

***

By the time she slipped through the narrow service alley behind the transit hub, the night air had turned damp and heavy. Lian wore her nondescript field jacket over the reinforced coveralls, hood up, gloves on. The streets between her apartment and the barrier's outer transport gate were nearly empty, save for the occasional freight hauler rumbling past.

She tapped into the cargo schedule via her wrist display, confirming a cluster of low-priority shipments heading toward the barrier's maintenance piers. One in particular, a pallet of pressure seals and hydraulic gaskets, was set for delivery to a sector just shy of the blackout zone. It would get her close without raising flags.

At the loading dock, she fell in with the crew prepping the shipment, shouldering a coil of tubing as if it belonged to her manifest. No one looked twice; in the low light, another gloved face in the chain was invisible.

As the hauler rolled toward the barrier, she studied the approaching bulk of steel and concrete through the narrow gap in the cargo bay doors. The blackout was still hours away, but she could already feel the tension in the air, like the moment before a storm front broke.

When the vehicle cleared the first checkpoint, she shifted position, counting the turns toward the maintenance pier. In her head, she overlaid the route with Mateo's schematic, marking the points where she'd need to break away.

If she timed it right, she'd be inside the perimeter well before the comms blackout sealed the rest of the world out.

The hauler slowed as it pulled into the dimly lit maintenance pier, the hiss of air brakes echoing off the surrounding bulkheads. Lian stepped down with the rest of the crew, coil of tubing still slung over her shoulder. She kept her movements steady, matching their pace as they began offloading crates onto the pier's deck.

A lone supervisor ticked items off a manifest, attention locked on the cargo list. Lian used the moment to drift toward the edge of the work zone, skirting a stack of sealed containers. The blackout was still hours away, but security checkpoints would be tightening with each passing minute.

She spotted her first marker, a faded hazard stripe on the wall beside an unused service hatch. It was one of the points she'd memorized from Mateo's schematic, a narrow passage that cut behind the pier's storage bays and connected to an internal access corridor.

When the supervisor turned to answer a question from one of the loaders, she slipped through the gap, ducking behind the containers until she reached the hatch. A quick scan with her wrist display showed no active alarms. She keyed in a bypass sequence and eased the hatch open, the stale air inside smelling faintly of oil and ozone.

With the hatch shut behind her, the noise of the pier faded, replaced by the low hum of unseen machinery. She took a slow breath, orienting herself toward the interior. If she could make it three junctions in without being detected, she'd be within striking distance of the blackout zone before it sealed off completely.

The corridor beyond the hatch was narrow, its metal plating scuffed and dented from years of neglect. Lian moved quickly but quietly, her boots making only the faintest sound against the deck. A strip of dim maintenance lighting pulsed overhead, the flicker throwing brief shadows across the walls.

At the first junction, she paused to listen. The hum of machinery was constant here, punctuated by the occasional distant clang of tools striking metal. No voices. She crouched beside a wall panel and pulled up a schematic overlay on her wrist display. According to Mateo's map, this corridor wrapped around the pier's main cargo intake and merged with a supply conduit leading deeper inside.

She slipped forward, passing racks of dormant equipment and locked tool cabinets. A faded stencil on one of the bulkheads read *SB Access*, half covered by peeling hazard tape, another sign she was still on the right track.

Near the second junction, the sound of footsteps made her flatten against the wall. A pair of maintenance workers in grease-stained coveralls walked past, speaking in low tones about a coolant line repair. They didn't glance her way, too focused on their conversation, and disappeared around the corner.

Lian exhaled slowly and moved on, counting each step to keep her sense of direction. Two more junctions and she'd be in position. The blackout was coming, and once it hit, whatever happened inside 7B would unfold beyond the reach of the outside world, unless she was already there to see it.

The corridor narrowed further, forcing Lian to brush past protruding conduit and low-hanging valve assemblies. The air was warmer here, carrying the faint tang of heated metal and recycled coolant. She kept her pace measured, knowing that the closer she drew to the interior, the more likely she was to encounter roving checks.

She rounded a bend and found herself at the second junction, a crossway lit by a single overhead fixture that cast a yellow pool on the deck. A security cam sat high in the corner, its lens dull and unlit. Either it was offline for maintenance, or someone had deliberately killed the feed. Neither possibility reassured her.

Beyond the junction, she could see the faint glow of status lights from a sealed bulkhead door. Her wrist display confirmed it was the entrance to the supply conduit Mateo had marked, a straight path toward the edge of the blackout zone. The conduit was supposed to be unmanned, but she still scanned for motion before stepping into the open.

Halfway across, a metallic rattle echoed from somewhere above, followed by the muffled thump of boots on grating. Someone was moving along the overhead maintenance catwalks. Lian ducked into the shadow of a valve cluster, heart rate steady but alert. The sound faded after a moment, but it left her with the certainty that she wasn't the only one working the conduit tonight.

She crossed the rest of the junction and keyed in the bypass sequence for the bulkhead. The lock disengaged with a muted click, and she stepped inside, the door sealing behind her with a final-sounding thud.

The air inside the conduit was cooler, carrying the steady rush of ventilation. Overhead cables ran in tight bundles, their insulation scuffed from years of use. The narrow path ahead curved slightly, enough to block her view beyond the first twenty meters.

Lian moved quickly, her boots whispering against the grated deck. A faint vibration traveled through the metal underfoot, machinery running somewhere deep ahead. She passed two locked side hatches, both marked with faded hazard symbols. Whatever was behind them was sealed tight.

Halfway along, a low pulse of light flickered on the conduit wall, followed by the whir of a sensor sweep. She flattened herself against the cables, letting the beam pass over her. The system didn't sound an alarm, but the sweep was fresh, someone had activated it recently.

When the curve straightened, she saw the bulkhead at the far end, its panel lights glowing amber in standby. Beyond that door lay the blackout zone. She checked her timer: forty-seven minutes until the comms drop. Enough to get in, not enough to waste.

Lian approached the bulkhead, hands already working through the bypass sequence Mateo had drilled into her. Whatever was moving in 7B, she was about to see it firsthand.

The final command string blinked green on the panel. With a muted clunk, the bulkhead lock disengaged, and the door slid open just far enough for Lian to slip through.

The air beyond was different, stiller, heavier, as though the ventilation here ran on a closed loop. Emergency strips cast a dim blue glow along the corridor walls, the only light in the space. She listened for movement but heard only the low thrum of machinery deep in the structure.

Moving forward, she kept to the wall, scanning every doorway and junction. The architecture shifted subtly here: older paneling overlaid with newer reinforcements, as if the space had been repurposed in layers. At the first intersection, a pair of armored security shutters stood half-lowered, blocking the view into an adjoining room. Through the gap, she caught the edge of a sealed container, identical to the one she had seen on the anomaly platform.

Her pulse quickened. This was 7B's perimeter, and the container was here. Somewhere beyond these reinforced halls, the rest of it waited. She slipped past the shutters, deeper into the blackout zone, every step narrowing the distance between her and whatever the operatives had brought through.

The corridor beyond the shutters opened into a wider space, dimly lit by scattered utility lamps set low to the floor. Their light picked out the edges of heavy crates, stacked two and three high, each marked with stenciled codes she didn't recognize. The silence here felt deliberate, not the emptiness of abandonment, but the stillness of something carefully controlled.

Lian kept low, weaving between the stacks. She caught the faintest hum from somewhere deeper inside, a sound too steady to be machinery. It reminded her of a generator under light load, waiting to spool up.

Two figures emerged from a side passage ahead, both in matte armor with faceplates down. They spoke in clipped bursts over helmet comms, carrying scanning wands that flickered in short arcs across the floor. Lian froze behind a stack of crates, watching as they swept the area methodically before turning back the way they had come.

When they disappeared, she moved again, edging toward the sound. The hum grew clearer with each step, accompanied now by an occasional pulse of light reflecting faintly off the corridor walls.

Somewhere ahead, beyond one more turn, was the heart of 7B, and whatever had come through the anomaly to be hidden here.

The turn opened into a chamber unlike any other part of the barrier Lian had seen. The walls were clad in matte black panels, their seams lit with faint threads of blue light pulsing in slow rhythm. At the center sat a reinforced cradle, holding the sealed container from the platform, its surface alive with shifting geometric patterns that shimmered like oil on water.

The hum was stronger here, resonating through the floor and into her bones. Around the cradle, three technicians in plain gray coveralls moved with precise, deliberate motions, each wearing visor rigs that obscured their eyes. Their gestures followed an unseen sequence, as if responding to cues only they could perceive.

Lian eased behind a column of support struts, her gaze locked on the container. Every few seconds, the patterns on its surface would align into a shape she almost recognized before dissolving again. Whatever was inside was active, and perhaps aware.

One of the technicians turned toward a console, revealing a patch on their sleeve: the same stenciled code she'd seen on the crates. She committed it to memory. This was her proof, but not yet her way out.

A chime sounded from somewhere above, and the blue threads in the wall seams brightened. The technicians straightened in unison. Something was about to happen, and Lian had to decide whether to stay hidden and watch, or move now, before the room changed entirely.

The chime echoed again, longer this time, and the blue threads along the walls shifted to a steady white glow. The hum deepened, becoming a low vibration that made the air feel heavier. The technicians took positions around the cradle, their visor rigs flickering with faint internal light.

With a soft hydraulic sigh, the container's upper surface split along invisible seams. Panels folded outward in perfect symmetry, revealing a core of glassy material that refracted the white glow into a spectrum that rippled across the chamber. Inside, something moved, not with mechanical precision, but with the fluid unpredictability of a living thing.

Lian leaned forward slightly, straining to see. The patterns she'd seen before now danced across the core's surface in rapid bursts, resolving into intricate, fractal shapes that collapsed into new forms before her eyes. The technicians' gestures mirrored the shifts, as if guiding or responding to them in real time.

A pulse of light flared from the core, bright enough to cast hard shadows. Lian's visor display spiked with unreadable data, scrolling faster than her eyes could track. Whatever was in that cradle was broadcasting, or reaching out.

One of the technicians spoke, voice filtered and metallic: "Phase alignment at ninety-seven percent. Prepare for capture window."

Lian's pulse quickened. She didn't know what a capture window meant, but she was certain it wasn't just an observation. She shifted her weight, ready to either record every detail or break from cover before the event reached its peak.

The hum in the chamber climbed into a resonant tone, the white glow from the walls intensifying until every surface shimmered. The core's glassy material seemed to lose solidity, its surface rippling as if it were becoming liquid. The technicians' motions quickened, their gestures sharp, precise.

A second voice cut in over the filtered comms, lower and more urgent: "Capture window in five. Stabilize channels."

The patterns across the core accelerated, locking into a spiraling lattice that reached deep into the shifting light. For an instant, Lian thought she saw something beyond the surface, a landscape, alien and impossible, with structures that defied geometry and horizons bending in ways the human eye was never meant to process. It felt like looking into a place that existed just outside the frame of reality.

Then the cradle's restraints snapped into place, locking with a heavy clunk. Energy surged through the room, a wave of pressure that made Lian's ears pop. The core flashed once, and a small object solidified within its center, dropping neatly into a recessed compartment. The shift was seamless, as if matter had simply chosen to appear where none had existed before.

The lead technician moved forward, sealing the compartment with a smooth, practiced motion. "Window closed," they said flatly.

Lian tightened her grip on her satchel. She was looking at proof of what the barrier's hidden tech could do, to reach into another reality, draw something tangible from it, and contain it. It was the kind of breakthrough that would redraw the limits of science, commerce, even power itself. And if the wrong hands controlled it, it could unmake more than just a city. She had seen enough to understand the scale, but getting out with that knowledge would be another matter entirely.

***

The white glow receded to a pale blue, and the hum softened until it was no more than a background vibration. The technicians relaxed their stances, visor displays dimming. One remained at the console, logging data with rapid keystrokes, while the others disengaged cables from the cradle and secured them to wall mounts.

Lian used the shift in their focus to take a single step back toward the column, keeping her breathing steady. She needed distance, a path back through the stacks before anyone thought to sweep the perimeter.

The lead technician lifted the sealed compartment from the cradle with both hands. Even from across the chamber, Lian could see its surface, smooth, opaque, humming faintly as though it retained a memory of the capture. It was small enough to fit inside a satchel, yet she knew it could hold the weight of an entire paradigm shift.

One of the armored figures from the patrol entered, speaking briefly with the lead. They turned together toward a side passage that likely led deeper into secured sections of 7B. The rest of the team began powering down the chamber, lights fading one by one.

Lian edged toward the shadowed exit she'd entered through. Every step she took toward the conduit felt like a coin toss between escape and discovery. Her mind raced with calculations, how far to the bulkhead, where the patrol routes intersected, how much time until the blackout sealed every door in the barrier.

She couldn't afford to be here when that happened.

Lian slipped into the shadow of the crates, keeping her head low as the technicians' voices faded into the hum of equipment shutting down. The blue light from the walls was weaker here, allowing her to blend into the dark edges of the chamber.

She retraced her path toward the narrow corridor she'd entered through, every sound amplified in her ears, the distant clang of a door latch, the scuff of boots against metal. At one point, a patrol's silhouette cut across the far end of the aisle. She froze, holding her breath until it moved on.

The corridor back to the supply conduit felt longer than she remembered. She kept count of each junction, checking them against her mental map. One wrong turn and she'd end up in an active sector where questions would be immediate and unforgiving.

At the final corner, she risked a glance around. The bulkhead to the conduit stood unguarded, its panel still in standby amber. She moved quickly, crossing the open space in a few strides and initiating the bypass sequence. The lock disengaged with a soft click.

As she stepped through, the blackout warning sirens began their slow, rising wail somewhere deep in the barrier. She sealed the door behind her, knowing she'd made it out of 7B by seconds, and that what she carried in her mind was more dangerous than anything she could physically steal.

The moment the bulkhead sealed, the corridor lights dimmed to a faint red glow. The wail of the sirens deepened into a steady pulse, reverberating through the metal underfoot. The barrier was locking down, sealing every point of access until the blackout window closed.

Lian quickened her pace, boots striking a muted rhythm as she threaded through the conduit. She passed the dead security cam at the junction, the lens catching a glint of red light as the system cycled into isolation mode.

Halfway to the maintenance pier, a hiss of hydraulics made her stop short. A secondary bulkhead was dropping ahead of her. She broke into a run, slipping through the narrowing gap just before it clamped shut with a shudder.

Beyond it, the air was cooler, the soundscape muffled, the outer layers of the barrier were already cut off from whatever was happening in 7B. She slowed only when the pier's lights came into view, scattered through the haze of industrial vapor.

Blending into a cluster of workers heading toward the loading bay, she kept her head down, matching their pace. The hauler she'd arrived on was still moored, engines idling for departure. If she boarded now, she could be outside the barrier before anyone started cross-checking manifests.

She stepped into line, the din of machinery masking her presence. Behind her, somewhere deep inside the barrier, the blackout zone had gone silent, and she carried the only account of what had happened within it.

The hauler's boarding ramp clanged underfoot as Lian joined the line of workers filing into its dimly lit cargo bay. She kept her hood up, the smell of warm metal and engine coolant hanging in the air. A dockhand in a grease-stained vest checked manifests with a hand scanner, barely glancing at each face before waving them through.

When it was her turn, the scanner emitted a brief tone and flashed green. She stepped past without hesitation, sliding into the shadows between stacked pallets. The hum of the engines deepened, followed by the distant thud of the mooring clamps releasing.

Through a narrow gap in the bay wall, she watched the maintenance pier drift away, swallowed by the barrier's silhouette. The sirens were inaudible now, replaced by the low vibration of acceleration.

Settling onto a crate, she let her pulse ease, but only slightly. In her mind's eye, she replayed the capture, the lattice spirals, the impossible landscape, the object materializing from the core. The images felt too vivid to be memory alone, as if fragments of whatever lay beyond the anomaly had followed her back.

Somewhere inside the barrier, 7B was sealing its secrets behind layers of steel and protocol. But Lian had carried one of those secrets out, and she knew it was only a matter of time before someone realized it.

The hauler's engines settled into a steady rumble, the vibrations traveling through the deck plates into Lian's boots. The cargo bay was dim and close, lit only by a few overhead strips that flickered with the rhythm of the ship's stabilizers. Workers kept to themselves, some slumping against crates, others quietly chatting in low tones that the machinery quickly swallowed.

Lian stayed in the shadows, hood forward, listening. Snatches of conversation drifted her way, gripes about shift schedules, rumors of tightened inspections on the inner piers, mention of a bulkhead breach in a sector she recognized from Mateo's maps. Each fragment hinted at unrest inside the barrier, though no one spoke openly about 7B.

She pulled out her comms slate, careful to shield the display. No direct connection was possible until they cleared the outer sensor curtain, but she began queuing an encrypted burst for Mateo: a stripped-down account of the capture, the alien geometry, and the physical object that had emerged. No names, no coordinates, only enough to tell him it was real, and urgent.

A faint change in engine pitch signaled their acceleration toward the transit corridor. Outside the narrow viewport, the barrier receded into a silhouette of steel and light, a monolith shrinking into the haze. Lian knew that once the ship cleared the sensor net, the blackout's veil would drop completely.

She tucked the slate away, drawing her jacket tighter. The danger was not over. The moment her message reached the outside, someone inside 7B would start looking for the leak, and she was still far from safe.

The hauler's acceleration eased, the deck's vibration shifting to a higher, smoother tone. A soft chime sounded from the cargo bay bulkhead, signaling they had cleared the outer sensor curtain. Conversations picked up slightly, but Lian's focus was on the comms slate in her hands.

The queued burst encrypted itself with a final confirmation blink. She transmitted it, watching the progress bar crawl across the display. The slate vibrated once, delivery confirmed.

For a brief moment, relief edged into her chest. Then the slate chimed again, this time with an incoming packet. Mateo's response was short and stripped of any identifiers: *Understood. You are not alone on that hauler. Do not disembark at scheduled stop.*

Lian's pulse tightened. She scanned the bay, eyes passing over faces half-lit by the flicker of the overhead strips. Nothing obvious. No one staring at her, yet.

She angled her body toward the viewport, using the reflection to keep watch. Somewhere among the workers, or perhaps in the sealed fore compartments, someone was here for her. The capture had already reached the wrong ears.

The hauler's internal PA crackled to life, announcing their first transit station in twenty minutes. Lian's fingers closed around the slate. Whatever happened next, she would have to decide fast whether to stay hidden aboard or make a move before the ramp dropped.

The hum of the hauler's engines deepened as it adjusted course for the station approach. Lian stayed by the viewport, keeping her reflection steady while her eyes searched the cargo bay. The workers moved in loose knots, some already gathering their gear for disembarkation. Others loitered in the shadows, faces unreadable.

A figure broke from one of the knots, tall, broad-shouldered, moving with deliberate ease through the crowded bay. Their eyes swept the room without lingering anywhere too long, but Lian caught the subtle angles of their approach. They weren't heading for the ramp; they were closing the space between them.

She shifted slightly, letting a group of three workers pass between them. In the reflection, she saw the figure adjust course to match her position. Her fingers brushed the clasp on her satchel, ensuring the slate was secure.

The PA announced ten minutes to arrival. The bay crew began releasing the mooring cables for docking, a low vibration running through the deck. Lian slipped toward the rear of the bay, where a ladder led up to the auxiliary maintenance gantry.

If she could reach the gantry before the hauler docked, she might move unseen into the service corridors and ride out the station stop without stepping into the open. But the figure was still tracking her, pace unhurried, as if they had all the time in the world.

She had one shot to vanish before the ramp came down.

***

Lian slipped into the narrow aisle between two stacks of cargo crates, their metal sides cold against her arms. The noise of the bay muffled here, replaced by the hollow echo of her own footsteps. She reached the base of the ladder and glanced back, the tall figure was still in sight, framed by the dim overhead strips, closing the distance with measured steps.

She climbed quickly, boots finding the rungs without hesitation. The gantry's grated walkway vibrated faintly with the hauler's engines. From up here, she had a clear view of the bay below, workers moving in practiced patterns, the looming station structure visible through the open side doors, and her pursuer scanning the upper level.

Lian ducked into a service alcove, crouching behind a cluster of conduit runs. The smell of warm dust and machine oil filled the narrow space. She tapped her slate, pulling up the hauler's internal schematic from memory, tracing a path from the gantry to the maintenance corridor that led toward the fore compartments.

Below, the figure paused, then began moving toward the ladder she'd used. She had seconds to disappear. Lian eased along the gantry, boots silent on the metal grating, and slipped into a narrow hatch marked *Authorized Personnel Only*.

The hatch sealed behind her with a muted click. Ahead, the corridor bent out of sight, lit by a faint green glow. She was off the main grid now, but so was whoever wanted her, and they wouldn't be far behind.

The maintenance corridor was narrower than Lian expected, its walls lined with insulated conduit and access panels, each tagged with cryptic service codes. The faint green lighting gave the metal a sickly pallor, and the air was warmer here, tinged with the faint bite of ozone.

She moved quickly, her steps muffled on the padded deck, keeping one hand on the wall to steady herself as the hauler's motion shifted with course adjustments. Somewhere behind her, the soft metallic thud of the hatch opening broke the corridor's quiet.

The pursuer had followed.

Lian increased her pace, scanning for junction points. A faded diagram bolted to the wall showed a path leading to an auxiliary control bay two compartments ahead. If she could reach it, she might use the ship's internal systems to create a diversion, a pressure alert, a false maintenance call, anything to draw her shadow away.

The sound of boots on the deck grew more distinct, closing the gap. She slipped around a corner and pressed herself into a shallow recess behind a bank of conduit. Holding her breath, she waited as the echo of the steps drew nearer, her fingers brushing the slim utility knife clipped inside her jacket.

The figure's shadow stretched along the bulkhead before her, distorted by the green light. They were almost at the corner. Lian steadied herself, ready to move, toward the control bay if she had the chance, or into a confrontation if she didn't.

The figure stepped into view, their head turning slightly as they scanned the corridor. Lian waited until they passed the recess, then moved. Her footfall was silent on the padded deck as she slipped behind them, utility knife in hand.

A faint shift in the ship's motion made the conduit rattle, masking the whisper of her approach. She closed the distance, close enough to catch the sharp scent of machine oil on their jacket. At the last moment, the figure pivoted, their hand darting toward her arm.

Lian twisted, deflecting the grab, the knife blade catching the green light. They froze for an instant, eyes narrowing in recognition, not of her, but of the weapon. A standoff, close enough to hear each other's breath over the muted thrum of the hauler.

"What do you want?" she asked, voice low.

The figure's reply was equally quiet, almost conversational. "You saw something you shouldn't have."

They shifted their weight, angling toward the hatch at the far end of the corridor. Lian knew she couldn't let them get ahead. Whether this ended in a diversion or a fight, she had to make the next move before the ship reached port.

The man feinted left, then drove toward the hatch. Lian reacted on instinct, not with strength but with timing, she stepped aside just enough to hook her boot against an exposed conduit bracket. As he surged past, his shin clipped the metal hard, jolting him sideways into the bulkhead. The clang echoed down the maintenance corridor.

He cursed, half-turning toward her. Lian didn't wait. She jabbed forward with the utility knife, not for a killing blow but for the gap between armored plates at his hip. The blade bit shallow but enough to make him stumble, a grunt escaping through his visor.

The narrow space left them little room to maneuver. He swung an arm toward her; she ducked low, letting his momentum carry him into the conduit bank. As he rebounded, she drove her shoulder into his midsection, aiming to disrupt balance rather than overpower. The move pinned him briefly, rattling the metal housing.

His visor shifted, revealing sharp eyes and a pale scar along the jawline. "It's not yours to carry," he hissed, one hand tightening into a fist. The words chilled her, confirmation he knew exactly what she'd seen in 7B.

The hauler's PA announced five minutes to dock. Lian's grip tightened on the knife. She slashed once, low, forcing him to recoil and giving her the space to slip past toward the hatch. Luck and speed were her only allies; she had no illusions she could win a fight if he got his balance back.

Lian burst through the hatch into a short, dimly lit connector leading toward the hauler's docking collar. The muted roar of the station's traffic bled in through the hull, a reminder that the ship was almost alongside. She could feel the shift in gravity as the vessel aligned for final approach.

She risked a glance back. The man was still in the maintenance corridor, closing the distance but slowed by the narrow space and his injury. She had seconds, maybe less, to disappear into the chaos of docking.

Ahead, the connector split, one branch led to the main disembarkation ramp where the manifest would be scanned, the other to a cargo chute for automated transfers. The chute was marked with hazard stripes and a warning to authorized personnel only. It would drop her into the freight handling decks of the station, out of sight of passenger security.

She angled toward the chute, yanking the manual release on the safety rail. The panel gave way with a metallic groan. A gust of recycled air rushed up from the shaft, edged with the faint tang of static discharge and the dry metallic note of overworked machinery.

The PA crackled again, announcing final docking. She swung a leg over the edge and lowered herself onto the narrow maintenance rung inside. Behind her, the connector hatch clanged open.

Lian didn't look back. She slid down into the shadows of the chute, vanishing from sight just as the hauler locked against the station.

***

The chute ended in a jarring drop onto a mesh platform two stories above the freight deck. Lian landed in a crouch, letting the impact travel through her legs before straightening. The cavernous space below was alive with motion, cargo drones gliding between stacks of sealed containers, human crews shouting instructions over the whine of grav-lifts.

From her vantage point, she could see the organized chaos of docking: pallets swinging from crane arms, containers sliding along tracks, station security making cursory inspections. The noise was a wall, thick enough to swallow individual sounds and give cover to anyone who knew how to move unseen.

She descended a narrow stair welded to the platform's edge, blending with a pair of freight handlers pushing an empty grav-sled. Keeping her head down, she slipped between towering stacks of crates, the coded markings on their sides blurring into a forest of symbols.

Somewhere above, the man would be realizing she'd taken the chute. If he guessed where it led, he could be on her trail within minutes. She needed to put as much ground, and confusion, between them as possible before finding a safe exit.

Near the far wall, she spotted an access door marked for service personnel. It led to the station's utility corridors, a sprawling network that could take her anywhere… or get her lost entirely. She hesitated only a moment before heading for it, the din of the freight deck fading behind her with each step.

The service door opened into a narrow, dimly lit passage that stretched in both directions, its walls lined with conduit and maintenance panels. The hum of the freight deck fell away, replaced by the distant throb of the station's environmental systems. The air here carried a faint charge, as if the corridor itself held its breath.

Lian paused long enough to lock the door behind her. The passage ahead curved gently, its angles designed to discourage long lines of sight. It was a place that could hide her or trap her.

She moved quickly, counting intersections and noting the faded stenciling on the bulkheads. The codes were a map only to those who knew them, and while she didn't have the full key, she recognized enough from her work to guess at the flow of maintenance routes. If she could find a junction that fed into the civilian concourse, she might still vanish into the crowd.

Her footsteps echoed. Twice she passed small access hatches, each leading to crawlspaces dense with wiring. Tempting for hiding, but certain dead ends if the search closed in.

At the next bend, a flicker of movement caught her eye, a shadow crossing the far end of the corridor. She froze. Whether it was security, a worker, or the man from the hauler, she couldn't tell. Either way, she was running out of story before the station closed its fist around her.

The shadow lingered just long enough to confirm it wasn't her imagination. Then it was gone. Lian eased forward, every step measured, her ears straining for sound over the soft hum of the conduits.

The corridor bent sharply left, ending in a T-junction. She slowed at the corner, peering around. The right branch led toward a service lift, its call light dark. The left narrowed into a stretch of half-lit decking that disappeared into gloom.

A metallic tap echoed from the left, followed by the faint hiss of a door sliding shut. Lian's pulse quickened. If it was him, he was moving ahead to cut her off. If it was security, they might already have her description.

She decided fast, doubling back would pin her between two unknowns. Forward was the only choice. Keeping low, she moved down the left-hand stretch, counting the distance to the next hatch.

Halfway there, she caught the faint outline of a boot sole vanishing around another bend. She didn't slow. The chase was about to end, one way or another, and she needed it on her terms.

Lian rounded the bend and found herself in a short, narrow junction lined with maintenance lockers. The only exit was a bulkhead door halfway down, standing slightly ajar. Light spilled through the gap, casting sharp angles across the floor.

Her footsteps softened as she approached, knife in hand, her breathing controlled. She pressed against the wall, listening. Beyond the door, faint movement, a shuffle, followed by the rasp of fabric against metal.

She pushed the door just enough to slip inside. The space beyond was a compact service hub, its walls covered in circuit panels and conduit. At the far end, the man from the hauler stood with his back partly to her, working a control terminal.

He hadn't heard her yet.

Every instinct told her to back away, to vanish before he turned, but this was her chance. If she let him keep control of the station's systems, she'd never get clear.

Lian stepped forward, each movement precise, closing the gap between them until she could see the screen. A map of the station flashed there, her route through the service corridors traced in pulsing red.

He knew exactly where she'd been, and where she was headed next.

Lian's gaze locked on the terminal. The red trail snaked through the station's underbelly, her every turn and pause recorded. The man tapped a control, and a new marker appeared ahead of her projected path, an intercept point.

Her chance to end this was now.

She took a silent step closer, knife angled low. The hum of the panels masked her approach. When she was close enough to see the flicker of code on the display, she reached out with her free hand and yanked the power conduit from its port.

Sparks spat across the console. The man spun toward her, surprise flashing in his eyes before hardening to something colder. He lunged, but she was already moving, using the compact space to her advantage. She drove her shoulder into his side, forcing him into the corner between two conduit stacks.

The terminal went dark, its screen fading to black. Whatever control he had over the station's systems was gone, at least for now.

He straightened, breath quick and uneven. "You just made a mistake," he said.

"So did you," she replied, stepping back toward the door. "Now you have to find me the hard way." Without waiting for a response, she slipped into the junction, letting the door close between them.

The door sealed behind her with a hiss, muting the thrum of the service hub. Lian pressed her back to the bulkhead, drawing a slow breath as she scanned the junction. The red trail was gone from his console, but that didn't mean the hunt was over. He'd have to track her the old way now, boots on metal, eyes in the corridors.

She moved quickly, turning down a narrow passage lined with dormant cargo lifts. The dim emergency lighting painted the deck in alternating shadows, and every bend felt like it could reveal another pursuer. Somewhere behind, a faint clang carried through the station's skin, followed by the echo of a door cycling open.

He was moving again.

Ahead, the corridor split, one path sloping upward toward the brighter glow of populated decks, the other plunging deeper into the maintenance warren. The first promised a crowd to disappear into, but also more cameras and patrols. The second meant isolation, and the possibility of losing him for good if she chose right.

A burst of distant station comms chatter filtered down the hall, urgent and clipped. Something bigger was unfolding topside, pulling security's focus away. It might be her only opening.

Lian tightened her grip on the knife, picked the downward path, and let the shadows swallow her.

The maintenance warren narrowed as Lian descended, the deck plates shifting underfoot with the vibration of machinery far below. The air grew warmer, the hum of the station's heart thrumming through the bulkheads. Here, the lights were fewer, leaving stretches of the passage in near darkness.

She kept her pace steady, listening for the telltale rhythm of pursuit. Twice she thought she heard it, a faint echo, a soft scrape, but the sounds vanished into the ambient noise of the core systems.

At a junction marked with stenciled numbers half-worn away, she paused. The schematic she'd memorized long ago surfaced in her mind: beyond this point, the corridors looped in confusing arcs, designed for technicians who knew the routes. For anyone else, it was a maze.

A soft clatter echoed from the path she'd taken. He was still back there, closing the distance.

Lian ducked into a side hatch and found herself in a cramped inspection chamber overlooking a drop shaft. Vertical rails disappeared into darkness, and faint sparks pulsed from far below. A maintenance ladder hugged one wall, vanishing into shadow both up and down.

Her fingers tightened on the rung. If she went down, she'd be heading toward the station's restricted power nexus, dangerous, but easy to vanish in. If she went up, she might reach auxiliary decks and rejoin the populated areas, but risk crossing into more security patrols.

The clang of a boot on the ladder above settled it. Down was her only choice.

The ladder ended at a grated platform suspended over a cavernous chamber. Below, the station's main power conduits glowed with a dull, pulsing light, their hum resonating in her chest. Heat rolled upward, making the air shimmer.

Lian crouched low, scanning for movement. Catwalks crisscrossed the chamber, connecting clusters of control stations. Most were dark, but one, near the far wall, flickered with active displays.

A shadow moved there, the man from the hauler. He was scanning the room, one hand resting on the rail, the other holding something small and metallic. It caught the light for an instant before he slipped it into a pocket.

She stayed low, edging along the platform toward a narrow side catwalk. It would take her around the chamber's perimeter and maybe give her a way out. The metal groaned faintly under her weight, and she froze, watching him for any reaction.

He didn't move toward her, but his head turned slightly, as if catching a sound just at the edge of hearing.

This was the heart of the station, a place she shouldn't be, and she was trapped here with him. One wrong move, and the confrontation she'd been avoiding since the hauler would happen with a lethal drop at her back.

The catwalk's metal grating pressed through Lian's palms as she eased forward, each step calculated to avoid the loudest creaks. The chamber's heat wrapped around her, carrying the metallic tang of overworked machinery. Far below, arcs of faint blue energy pulsed through the conduits, like veins feeding the station's lifeblood.

The man shifted at the far station, adjusting the display. A thin beam of data-light swept across the catwalk ahead of him, as if he were mapping more than just the room. Lian realized he wasn't searching for her blindly, he was triangulating.

She dropped to one knee and slid along the rail until she found a maintenance latch. It opened into a narrow crossbeam that cut straight toward a vertical service column. It was a risk, but it would take her behind his position.

The metal vibrated under her as she moved. Halfway across, his voice echoed off the walls.

"You think you can vanish in here? This place records everything."

Lian kept moving, her breath steady, eyes fixed on the service column. If she could reach it, she might slip out unseen. But the tremor in the catwalk behind her told her he'd left the console.

She wasn't escaping this chamber without him seeing her, and maybe not without a fight.

The catwalk shuddered under the man's weight as he advanced, each step ringing sharper than the last. Lian quickened her crawl along the crossbeam, the heat radiating off the conduits below curling upward like a warning.

She reached the service column and pressed her back to its narrow frame. A quick glance showed him closing the gap, his eyes locked on her through the glare and shimmer. There was no cover here, only open steel and the drop.

Lian spotted a loose coupling on the crossbeam's midpoint, a section where the grating had been patched with a thinner strip. She could time it. If he stepped on that plate with his full weight...

He came closer, his voice low and certain. "You've seen too much. You won't get off this station."

She slid one foot against the coupling, bracing herself. As he stepped onto the patch, she shoved with all her strength. The grating dipped, throwing him off balance. He grabbed for the rail, catching it with one hand, boots skidding on the slick metal.

Lian didn't wait to see if he recovered. She swung herself into the service column's ladder well and began descending fast, the glow of the nexus fading above her.

The ladder carried Lian down into cooler air, the hum of the power nexus softening into a background throb. Her boots touched down on a narrow maintenance ring that circled the base of the massive conduit tower.

Dim lights flickered along the ring, revealing a jumble of access panels and data ports. Somewhere in the dark beyond, coolant pumps hissed in slow, rhythmic bursts. She paused, catching her breath.

A faint clang above told her the man was back on the ladder.

She moved quickly, scanning for an exit. Most of the hatches here were sealed, but near the far side she found one left ajar. Warm light spilled through the gap. Slipping inside, she found herself in a cramped relay room, its walls lined with fiber trunks and stacked signal amplifiers. A single console blinked with incoming traffic, station communications, raw and unfiltered.

Scrolling across the feed were fragments of her own route through the station, interspersed with orders tagged for security lockdown. One phrase repeated between sectors: *Containment Priority: Quantum Event.*

The clang of boots reached the doorway.

Lian's eyes fixed on the console. Now she knew, this wasn't just about her. Whatever the "quantum event" was, it was tied to the impossible things she'd witnessed.

She pulled the drive from her jacket and slotted it into the console. The download began as the door behind her slid open.

The relay room door slid open, and the man stepped inside, framed by the dim glow of the fiber trunks. Lian didn't turn, keeping her focus on the console as the download timer ticked slowly toward completion.

"Step away from it," he said, voice low and steady.

"Not until I know what a 'quantum event' is," she replied, eyes fixed on the data stream. She could feel his presence closing in behind her, each step deliberate.

The console chimed, fifty percent. Too slow.

She slid one hand into her pocket, fingers curling around the compact shock emitter Mateo had insisted she carry. If he lunged, she'd have one chance to stun him and finish the transfer.

He stopped just out of reach. "You have no idea what you're pulling down. This isn't a story you can walk away from."

"That's the plan," she said, and braced herself.

The console hit seventy percent. Somewhere deep in the station, an alarm began to wail.

The alarm's first wail thickened into a pulse that shook the conduit housings. The man did not flinch. He eased one step closer, then another, keeping just outside the reach of her free hand.

"Seventy-one," Lian said under her breath, eyes on the counter.

He watched the numbers climb. "Unplug it."

"Tell me what a quantum event is."

His gaze flicked to her pocket. "You are not going to touch me with that."

The door control chirped in the hall. A panel snapped open and three security drones slid through in a staggered fan, casings matte, targeting pods already awake. Their logic identified two unauthorized bodies and a hot connection to a restricted node. They split the room without hesitation.

The first taser burst slammed into the rack beside the man, a crack of blue-white that blew dust from the lattice. He pivoted behind a trunk and the second burst traced his shoulder, enough to jolt him to a knee. The third drone rotated toward Lian, its sensor bead finding her heat signature through the console glow.

"Seventy-six," she said. She kept one hand on the keys and drew the shock emitter with the other, a thumb-length cylinder with a ridged crown. The drone's dart gun coughed. A steel spike punched the terminal's skin inches from her wrist. She slammed the cancel on peripheral ports, cleared the power warnings, and forced the download to priority. Seventy-nine. Eighty-one.

Static licked the room, not sound but a smear across the air. The racks seemed half a degree out of square. The far corner did not meet itself cleanly. A cable run looked longer than the space allowed, then snapped back to the correct length when she tried to focus.

The man lunged across the aisle, intending to yank the drive. She met him side-on, raking the emitter across his forearm. The device cracked, a dry snap that arced between metal teeth. His hand spasmed and he snatched it back with a curse. The nearest drone recalculated, saw motion and mass, and fired again. The bolt caught his vest plate and he rolled into cover, breath ragged.

"Eighty-seven."

Another tilt passed through the room. The doorframe bowed slightly, then straightened. The overhead strobes strobed out of sequence, as if two clocks disagreed on what a second should be. On the console, the transfer timer flickered forward by ten seconds, then back by three. She did not look away. Ninety.

The drone across from her hesitated with a stutter, its targeting cone wobbling as it tried to reconcile the frame shift. Lian snatched the drive cradle with one hand and kept the other on the keyboard. The man rose from a crouch with a short baton he had palmed from his belt. He did not come straight on this time. He slid along the aisle edge, using the endcap rows as shields, counting his steps against the flashes.

Ninety-three.

The far wall stepped left, no more than the width of a palm. The servers did not move with it. For one breath the fiber trunks stretched like taut lines on a drawn map, thinner than they had been a moment before. The drones' status lights crawled through their own command loops, a visible lag in every state change. Lian felt the skin along her arms tighten. This was not a software scramble. The room was refusing to stay a room.

Ninety-five.

She palmed the eject and set her stance. The man drove in; she shoved the cradle with her left hand to break his line and jabbed the emitter once more, lower this time, at the gap between vest and belt. He grunted, staggered, recovered enough to catch the edge of the console, and used it to anchor himself. His other hand swept for the drive. She beat him to it, yanked the module free. The console threw a curtain of checksum errors that rolled and froze and then scrolled again with a different time stamp.

A drone chose that moment to fire. The dart struck the man's shoulder plate and pinned a strap to the casing behind him. He tore free with a hard twist that cost him another second. Lian was already moving. She slid across the end of the aisle, kept low, and shouldered through a service hatch.

The passage beyond was narrow and unlit, a rib of station bone behind the relay room. The alarm bled through the metal as a steady pulse. She ran three strides, then stopped and braced the hatch with her heel while she looked at the drive. Its indicator pulsed in uneven intervals, bright, dim, bright again, like it was syncing to a beat she could not hear.

She brought the module up near her cheek and squinted at the tiny status strip. The file index was already generating previews. She scrolled with a knuckle, careful not to smear sweat across the contacts.

SUBJECTIVE FIELD DISRUPTION: 142 CASES, CONFIRMED BY COUNTERPART WITNESSES.

LOCAL TEMPORAL DESYNCH: 3–312 SECONDS, NON-GAUSSIAN.

TOPOLOGICAL DISCONTINUITY: 4 CONTAINMENT ZONES, 19 INCIDENTAL OBSERVATIONS.

OPERATIONAL NOTE: VISUAL ANCHORS REDUCE ONSET FOR 37 PERCENT OF SUBJECTS.

OPERATIONAL NOTE: AUDIT TRAILS CORRUPT AT SITE BOUNDARY, REDUNDANT LOGGING REQUIRED.

Something hit the hatch. The panel flexed. She killed the screen and moved. The service rib spilled her into a maintenance cross, the kind that carried air and water and kilometers of cable. To her right, the corridor looked longer than it had when she first glanced down it. To her left, two access doors sat closer together than their hinges allowed. The floor trembled, then stilled.

She kept left. A drone's silhouette grazed the seam beneath the hatch and a dart clattered off the frame, skittered along the metal, and spun to a stop at her heel. She did not hesitate. She ran.

The next junction held a simple door with a magnetic plate lock. She slid her override in and keyed the sequence. The plate clicked. She stepped through into a stairwell that should have turned once and did not. It turned twice. The landing sat in the wrong quadrant of the shaft. She kept one hand on the rail and trusted her feet over her eyes.

At the second landing she paused. The drive ticked again in her palm, bright, dim, bright. Somewhere above, the drones receded. Somewhere below, a different alarm began to cycle, softer, more regular. She knew that tone from old drills. The station was sealing paths that could not be guaranteed to lead where they were supposed to.

She went down anyway.

Behind her, the relay room hatch rang once more and then stopped. The man would find another way in. He always did. But she had ninety-eight percent of something the station itself was struggling to name, and the corridors were starting to shift under their feet.

She tightened her grip on the rail and took the stairs two at a time.

Lian hit the maintenance stairwell at a run, the drive clamped in her fist. The alarm still bled through the walls, but underneath it, the station's usual hum was wrong, deeper, with a slow modulation that made her think of sound passing through water.

Two flights down, she pushed through an exit hatch into a mid-tier service corridor. At first glance it looked normal: same matte panels, same stenciled hazard strips. Then she noticed the signage overhead, "E-Block Supply" in letters she recognized, but the arrow pointed in the opposite direction she knew it should.

She hesitated. The delay cost her. Behind her, a door slammed and bootsteps hit metal. The pursuer had found her path.

She moved forward, past junction after junction, but the geometry didn't hold. A door marked *Cryo Storage 12A* opened onto a short hall she'd walked two levels up. The security cam in the corner tracked her twice, once in real time, and again a half-second later, like a replay overlaid on itself.

Her stomach clenched. This wasn't a trick of the light. The corridors were folding.

A side hatch opened and a man in a grease-stained tech jumpsuit stepped out, eyes wide and unfocused. He flinched when he saw her, then grabbed her sleeve.

"Have you seen my crew?" His voice trembled. "I was in the lift, and… I came out here. This isn't where it should go."

She shook her head. "You need to get to a safe section."

"They said C-ring was sealed. Said it wasn't holding. If you've got clearance, " He stopped, eyes darting over her shoulder. "Is someone following you?"

"Yes," she said. "And if you've seen… anomalies, you know why I can't stop."

The tech swallowed, nodded once, and stepped back into the hatch without another word. The door closed.

The corridor ahead wavered, the far bulkhead shifted sideways without moving, like the space between them had been sheared and pasted at a new angle. The station's air took on a faint metallic tang, and the hazard stripes underfoot seemed to crawl when she looked at them too long.

Footsteps again, closer now, but the sound came from two different directions.

She turned left. The signage said "Transit Hub," but she knew from the deck plans this route should dead-end. She took it anyway.

The "Transit Hub" corridor ended in a pressure door with three layers of paint under its hazard stripes. The panel above read DECONTAMI-NATION – LEVEL 5 in fading stencil. No lockout code, no posted guards. The sort of space people forgot existed until someone scraped a new budget line for demolition.

She palmed the release. The door split with a slow sigh, and a rush of cooler air rolled over her, colder than any section outside of cryo storage.

Inside, the bay was vast and hollow, lit only by the glow from a few still-live consoles along the far wall. The floor stretched in a gray expanse, but it wasn't empty. Across the deck hung dozens of fragments, frozen holograms, half a meter across or less, like panes of glass catching scenes from somewhere else. A hand holding a wrench. A child's shoe stepping into rain. A segment of the station's exterior with stars behind it. All of them suspended at odd angles, motionless but not still, as if whatever moment they belonged to still pulsed just beyond reach.

She stepped closer to one shard: a face she didn't know, mid-shout, the mouth caught between syllables. The light from it was flat and cold, and when she moved her head, the expression shifted a fraction, not the natural parallax of a hologram, but like the moment itself was trying to finish.

Her boots rang softly against the deck. The sound didn't carry right. It reached her ears slightly out of time with the step, a stutter that made her jaw tighten.

She crossed to the far wall, where an access terminal waited under a film of dust. The login prompts blinked normally, but the cursor jumped back two characters for every three she typed, forcing her to fight the machine just to enter commands. She finally managed to bring up the local logs.

The records told a story in terse, system-generated phrases:
CONTAINMENT TEAM ENTERED AT 04:21.
VISUAL AND AUDITORY ANOMALIES DETECTED 04:23.
TEAM POSITION TRACK LOST FOR 3 UNITS AT 04:24.
SUBJECTIVE TIME REPORTS NON-CONSENSUAL.
EVACUATION ORDER ISSUED 04:26.
ACCESS SEALED.
One final line, appended without timestamp: CONTAINMENT NOT VERIFIED.

Her fingertips rested on the keys. In the upper decks, boots might still be tracking her. But in this space, the station itself seemed to have lost track of where anything, or anyone, truly was.

She glanced at the frozen shards again. One of them now showed her own back, taken from somewhere higher up, though she hadn't moved since she'd come in.

The door behind her opened with a sharp metallic grind. She didn't need to turn to know who it was.

"Step away from the terminal," the man's voice carried across the bay, steady but lower than before.

Lian kept her eyes on the shard showing her back. "You followed me in here. That means you've seen it."

"I've seen worse," he said, but the words were tight, clipped. He moved closer, boots ringing against the deck, then stopping abruptly.

She glanced sideways. He had come up short, staring at a floating pane the size of a dinner plate. In it, the bay was empty except for him, the moment slightly off-color, like a faded print.

The lights overhead flickered, and a sound like fabric tearing rolled through the space. The deck shifted, not a quake, but a folding, like two halves of the bay were being forced into the same coordinates. The shards trembled in place, their images smearing before snapping back.

A low groan of metal carried through the supports. Overhead, a section of catwalk seemed to twist in on itself. A steel beam sheared away from its mount, hanging at an angle that made no sense in normal gravity.

The man swore under his breath, eyes on the beam. "If that drops, it'll take the whole wall with it."

"Then help me get out," she said.

He hesitated, just long enough to remind her they were still enemies, and then moved toward her as the beam began to shift again.

The far bulkhead shimmered, and for a moment there was nothing between them and the void. Stars burned in impossible patterns, arcs where there should have been straight lines, points that pulsed in and out like heartbeats. The cold that rushed in felt older than the station itself.

A section of flooring gave way, but instead of falling, it bent upward into the air, curling like paper until it vanished into nothing.

"This way!" she shouted, gesturing toward a hatch that still looked solid.

They ran together, the bay groaning around them, shards spinning now in slow, deliberate arcs as if some unseen current was drawing them toward a point above the deck.

They reached the hatch just as the beam overhead gave way, except it didn't fall. It folded midair, the ends touching in a loop before winking out entirely.

He wrenched the hatch open, and they both spilled into the corridor beyond. The lights here were steady, the air warmer, but the station's hum still carried that deep, uneven pulse.

He leaned against the wall, breathing hard. "Drop the drive," he said again, but there was no conviction in it now. "Whatever's on it… it's not going to stay inside a file."

She met his eyes. "Then it needs to be out where people can see it."

For a moment, he looked like he might argue. Instead, he shook his head once and turned away, disappearing down the corridor.

The corridor bent twice before emptying into a narrow concourse that didn't match any official station layout she'd studied. Low ceilings, damp in the corners, the smell of oil and old circuitry. No security cams in sight.

She knew this section, not from schematics, but from rumor. Vendor lock territory. Here, private consortiums carved up the station's maintenance arteries, running their own freight lifts and network lines, far from the oversight of station command. If the main routes were locked down, this was where you came to keep moving.

Two figures lounged by a lift gate: a man with a freight loader's exosleeve on his right arm and a woman balancing a steaming mug on the edge of a crate. Both watched her without expression as she approached.

"You're not supposed to be here," the woman said.

"I'm not supposed to be in a lot of places," Lian replied. "But I need a lift to the docks."

The man snorted. "Docks are under security freeze. You'll need something better than charm to ride with us."

She tapped the pocket where the drive rested, careful not to make it look like anything more than habit. "Information. Current. Not on any public feeds."

That got their attention. The woman gestured for her to follow, leading her to a cramped alcove with a battered console wired into the lift controls. The hum here was different, not the deep, warped pulse of the main station, but the faint, irregular chatter of multiple unsanctioned systems fighting for bandwidth.

"What kind of information?" the woman asked.

"The kind that explains why sections are folding in on themselves," Lian said. "And why the lockdown won't stop it."

They exchanged a look, one of recognition, not disbelief. The man keyed in a sequence on the console, and the lift gate rolled open with a clatter.

"Two levels down," he said. "Switch to the orange line. That'll put you in the lower-tier docks without tripping the freeze."

As she stepped into the lift, the woman added, "If it's as bad as you say, we'll want more than rumors when it breaks wide."

"You'll get them," Lian said. "But I won't be the only one carrying them."

The gate slammed shut, and the lift dropped fast, the lights inside flickering not from bad wiring, but from brief flashes of… other places. A market stall under alien sky. A child's bedroom in half-gravity. A stretch of empty desert. Each gone before she could breathe them in.

The lift rattled to a stop, and the gate rolled open onto the lower-tier docks, a stretch of broad, uneven decking that smelled faintly of coolant and salt. Cargo containers were stacked in loose rows, their corporate stamps scuffed and half-painted over, as if ownership had been debated with a spray gun.

Above, the overhead lamps buzzed in a slow, asynchronous rhythm, leaving parts of the bay in dim shadow long enough for the shadows themselves to seem like they'd shifted.

She stepped onto the deck, scanning for the orange line the vendor crew had mentioned. It was a faded stripe underfoot, chipped through to bare metal in places, leading toward a line of smaller freighters moored at the far end.

One in particular caught her eye, low-profile, hull patched with mismatched alloys, and a name stenciled in three different fonts: *Tessellate*. The crew was mid-load, shifting crates into the open maw of its cargo bay with the careful disinterest of people who didn't want to draw attention.

A man broke away from the group and intercepted her. Broad-shouldered, rough-voiced, wearing a battered flight jacket with a faded salvage guild emblem on the sleeve.

"You lost, or just in a hurry?" he asked.

"Both," Lian said. "I hear you make runs where you're not supposed to."

His mouth twitched, not quite a smile. "Depends who's asking."

"I've got cargo," she said, patting the drive in her jacket pocket. "Not physical, but dangerous enough that security's looking for me and anyone I hand it to."

The man's eyes narrowed slightly. "Let me guess, it's got something to do with the folding corridors and the flashes?"

"You've seen them?"

"Two salvage runs into quarantine zones this week. Same thing, different stations. Doesn't matter what they call it, the signs are the same, geometry that won't hold, time bleeding around the edges. That's why I'm here, fueling up to get out before this place joins the list."

He glanced back toward his ship. "Question is, do I want your problem on board when I leave?"

"That depends," she said. "Do you want proof it's already bigger than anyone's admitting?"

The silence stretched a beat longer than was comfortable. Finally, he jerked his head toward the *Tessellate*. "Five minutes. You talk to me and no one else. After that, I decide if you're worth the fuel."

Lian followed the captain up the loading ramp, the thrum of the *Tessellate*'s generators under her boots. Inside, the air was warmer, smelling faintly of machine oil and recycled water. Crew moved with practiced efficiency, securing cargo nets and sealing containers for flight.

She'd barely reached the midpoint of the bay when a ripple went through the crew, heads turning toward the dock entrance.

The man from the relay room was striding across the deck, posture rigid, one hand hidden inside his jacket. The overhead lights stuttered as he passed beneath them, throwing his shadow long and then snapping it short again.

The captain muttered something under his breath. "Friend of yours?"

"Not even close," Lian said.

She ducked between two cargo pallets, the hum in the air deepening, not just from the engines. The metal decking seemed to vibrate in uneven pulses, and for a moment she caught a whiff of ozone, sharp and dry.

The pursuer stepped onto the ramp, eyes locked on her. "You can still walk away from this, Lian. Drop the drive and I'll see you out of the station."

"Your definition of 'out' doesn't sound healthy," she shot back.

The captain moved to intercept, but the man drew a short, matte-black baton from inside his jacket and flicked it open with a snap. It hummed faintly, a field generator spitting blue sparks at the tip.

The nearest crew scattered toward the far wall. Lian grabbed the edge of a cargo net and yanked, sending a half-ton container sliding across the deck toward him. He sidestepped, baton raised, just as a loading drone trundled between them, confused by the shifting geometry of the floor markings.

She lunged while his view was blocked, aiming low. Her shoulder hit his ribs hard enough to stagger him into the drone's side. The baton cracked against the metal, sparks jumping to the deck.

He recovered fast, swinging in a tight arc. She ducked, catching his wrist with both hands and twisting sharply, not enough to overpower him outright, but enough to force the baton down. A spark kissed the edge of a crate, leaving a charred smear.

The captain's voice cut through the noise. "Enough! This is my dock, and I'm not losing it to your feud."

The man hesitated, breathing hard. His gaze flicked from Lian to the captain, then to the crew now watching from the corners.

"This isn't over," he said, voice low. "You don't know who you're carrying that for."

He stepped back, baton collapsing with a metallic snap, and retreated down the ramp into the flickering dock lights.

Lian straightened, heart still pounding. The captain studied her for a long moment, then jerked his head toward the interior. "If you're coming, make it fast. We're sealing up."

The *Tessellate*'s ramp clanged shut behind her, sealing out the echo of the docks. The captain didn't slow, weaving through narrow passageways that smelled faintly of old coffee and lubricants. The ship's low hum settled into a steadier rhythm, punctuated by the muted thump of cargo clamps locking in place.

They reached a cramped compartment just off the bridge, more storage room than cabin, where a worn console sat bolted to the wall. The captain keyed it active, the screen blooming to life with a grainy blue glow.

"Your cargo," he said, nodding at her jacket pocket.

Lian hesitated only a second before sliding the drive into the console's port. The system chirped and began to unpack the data, progress lines crawling upward. Outside, the ship's maneuvering thrusters kicked in, a deep vibration carrying through the deck.

The captain leaned over her shoulder. "If this is going to put my ship on every patrol's intercept list, I need to know now."

"It's going to put *someone* on a list," she said. "Whether it's yours depends on how fast you can leave."

The console's display fractured for a heartbeat, not a glitch, but an image sliding into view. A still frame of a station corridor twisting like it was being seen through a warped lens. Then it was gone, replaced by rows of file indexes and partial decrypts.

She began scrolling, scanning the fragments: containment logs, incident reports, surveillance stills. The geometry warping wasn't isolated to the bay she'd seen. Other stations. Planetary outposts. A mining habitat on the rim. Each file tagged with timestamps that grew closer together as she moved down the list.

The captain exhaled slowly. "You weren't kidding. This isn't local."

Before she could answer, a chime rang from the bridge, a sharp, urgent tone. The captain was already moving, barking over his shoulder for her to secure herself.

The deck tilted as the *Tessellate* lifted from its berth, engines spooling toward escape velocity.

Lian strapped herself into the narrow jump seat just inside the bridge. The viewport ahead showed the dock falling away, the station's curved superstructure sweeping past in glints of steel and shadow.

The captain slid into the helm, hands steady on the controls. "Hang on," he said, almost to himself.

The *Tessellate* cleared the docking perimeter. Thrusters flared, and the stars beyond the viewport shifted, not from the ship's motion, but in a way that made her skin crawl. Lines where there should have been points, arcs bending on themselves like reflections in warped glass.

On the console beside her, the drive's data spill kept unpacking. She scrolled, heart tightening with each entry. Incident reports from three stations she'd never heard of, all in the past week. Grainy footage of a market square folding in the middle of the day, shop stalls bending into one another until nothing was left but a smear of color and shadow. A mining crew vanishing mid-shift, their last words clipped into a loop that played over and over in the comm logs.

She stopped on a line from one containment analysis: *Propagation rate exceeds 200% projected model. Vector indeterminate. Containment probability: zero.*

The captain caught her expression. "It's moving?"

"It's already moved," she said. "And it's not slowing down."

The ship's long-range sensors began to feed in telemetry from surrounding sectors. Lian overlaid it with the incident data, watching the map fill with red markers, not random, but spreading in a branching pattern across stations, planets, and transit hubs. The edges were already beyond the map's scale.

"This isn't a story anymore," the captain said quietly.

"No," she said. "It's a warning."

The *Tessellate*'s jump drive spooled, the hum in the deck plates deepening. Outside, the stars bent further, just enough to make her think she could see the curve of something vast, moving where space should be empty.

The captain pushed the throttle. The viewport flared white, and the ship leapt into the dark.

Lian kept her eyes on the distortion until it vanished. She knew she hadn't imagined it. And she knew, now, that she wasn't just running, she was carrying proof that the universe itself had started to slip.

Protocol Drift

1. Zurich Interim Protocol Complex, Level G5, 0600 local
Subject: Prebrief synchronization and continuity audit

Amira Sen adjusted the collar tab on her mesh badge as the elevator descended. It was early, the floor quiet, the walls humming faintly with filtered energy from the compound's cold-stack grid. No sunlight reached this level. Only polished steel and matte black panels, interspersed with soft white status indicators blinking like sedated eyes.

She had barely slept. The briefing loops had run long past midnight, and when she did close her eyes, the noise hadn't stopped. Images, phrases, a sense of recursive tension in the air itself. It was more than nerves. Something about the work had begun to echo.

The door slid open to the Records Bay.

She passed her palm over the ID glyph and leaned into the retinal sync. A brief flicker, then access.

Deputy Rapporteur, Continuity Thread: Summit B.5

The prebrief materials had been waiting for her since 0430. Most were standard: cognitive mesh alignment reports, mesh integrity indices for the attending blocs, and a summary of disputed lexicons pending harmonization. Tense, but expected. Stability summits weren't about agreement. They were about not splintering.

The world outside the complex was showing fractures. Not the old kind, not war, not famine, not even ideology. Something else. Drift. Things that had been common ground for generations, clock time, geospatial fixpoints, legal definitions, were no longer returning stable values. Governments were whispering about sub-consensual divergence. Private sector analysts were calling it probabilistic compression decay. But no one had named it officially. That was what the summit was for.

But one file was marked with a deep-blue verification seal: Continuity: Emergency Session B.5 – Transcription/Playback, closed loop.

She opened it. A split-pane video feed bloomed across her lens.

Left pane: timestamped at 19:02 the previous evening. Right pane: identical timestamp.

At first glance, they matched. Same room, same delegates seated around the oval convergence table. Same motion, same tones. Then she looked closer.

In the left pane, the Russian envoy raised a procedural objection. Amira remembered that. He'd questioned the validity of a perception-drift clause and tabled it. She had followed with an objection on protocol hierarchy. The motion had failed.

But in the right pane, she was smiling. Listening. Then speaking.

"Let the record show consensus at twenty-four to one, carried. The clause stands."

Her own voice. Measured. Warm. Certain.

She tapped for the transcript overlay. It confirmed the words. Her name, her delegate signature. Time-verified by the mesh.

She hadn't said that. She would never have agreed to that clause, its language was unstable.

Amira blinked. Brought up the system log.

Epistemic variance detected: probabilistic fork.

Source: mesh-sync collapse, loop B.

Recommended action: baseline integrity self-check.

Below it, a line in smaller type:

Ref: Annotated Malheur Memo – Internal ICCRM Archive (status: compromised)

She exhaled through her nose.

Malheur again. His name had been drifting through the protocol layers like a half-forgotten password. An analyst who had walked off the job mid-cycle and triggered a cascade reclassification. His final memo, leaked without authorization, had forced four agencies to rewrite their causality exposure protocols. She'd read it. Or tried. It had felt less like a paper and more like a warning folded into itself.

She closed the file, copied both versions to a local sealed cache, and sent a discrepancy notification to the Secretariat Review Queue.

No reply came. Just a receipt code: [ACK 2025-81-PRT-D]

She leaned back in the chair and stared at her own reflection in the screen. It was early. Maybe too early.

She ran the videos again.

In one, she had objected. In the other, she had complied.

And both had been recorded as true.

2.   Zurich   Interim   Protocol   Complex,   Level   G6,   0730   local
Subject: Closed-Session Technical Briefing: Risk Convergence and Pattern Drift

The briefing amphitheater was quieter than expected. No pre-meeting chatter. No coffee cups or personal overlays projected on the inner ring. Just thirty-five delegates in standard black or gray, their mesh-tabs clipped visibly on the breast, eyes slightly out of sync as their HUDs processed internal files.

Amira took her seat at Segment 12. Her name blinked blue for confirmation, then muted itself.

"Thank you for being punctual," came a voice over the roomwide audio net. It was Chair Delacroix, Technical Governance Group. Old Geneva stock, compact frame, deadpan tone. He stepped forward into physical presence, palms lightly clasped.

"This is not a forecasting session," he began. "Nor a reconciliation panel. This is a brief on the status of foundational continuity drift."

A few delegates straightened slightly. That phrase, foundational continuity, had not yet been used on any formal communique. Not until now.

"The ICCRM's last admissible model sweep," Delacroix continued, "failed epistemic convergence across four of seven predictive clusters."

A murmur. Not from shock, they had expected as much, but because he was saying it aloud.

Amira brought up the fullline packet pushed to her HUD. Embedded mid-stack was a note:

Ref: Annotated Malheur Memo (EXTRACT 9) Status: Internal Archive, partial recovery

She selected it. The interface hesitated.

Then the excerpt unfolded:

Once predictive structure begins to mimic observer expectation, the system is no longer simulating futures. It is auditioning them.

Once you noticed them, they noticed you back.

Her mouth was suddenly dry.

Delacroix continued. "Malheur's memo has been officially classified as semi-consensual cognition. Which means we cannot verify whether its internal logic is consistent for all readers."

That was the twist. Not whether the memo was true. But whether you read the same memo as someone else.

At this, one of the delegates raised a hand, Councilor Diarra, from the Pan-African Collective. "With respect, if the logic may vary by reader, how can it form the basis of any multilateral diagnostic? We're building consensus out of something that's become, by definition, perspectival."

"Not building consensus," Delacroix corrected. "Cataloguing divergence."

A second voice spoke up, clipped and irritated. "You can't brief this to constituents. Half my district still thinks this is about trade equity modeling failures. The other half believes it's a psyops leak."

Delacroix said nothing. He gestured and the central projector cycled forward: a map of language entropy events across seven regions, showing spontaneous lexical fragmentation in borderless enclaves.

"This is happening in unmediated cognition. Not media. Not consensus framing. People are waking up speaking differently. Interpreting legal signage in contradictory ways. This isn't just loss of shared memory. It's loss of shared parsing."

Amira looked down at her fingers. One hand was clenched. She hadn't noticed.

Councilor Diarra again. "What are we telling people? What does this mean for arbitration? For law?"

"That context is no longer separable from frame," Delacroix replied. "And that means jurisdiction is no longer separable from perspective."

A stunned silence followed. Someone finally said: "So the law applies differently depending on who's looking at it?"

"In practice?" Delacroix shrugged. "Yes. In theory? We don't have one anymore."

Another delegate muttered: "Then what the hell is this summit even for?"

The room paused.

Then Amira said, quietly, "To figure out whether the drift can be slowed. Or if we need to decide what kind of collapse we want."

A long silence followed.

Delacroix only nodded.

He turned back to the projection. "The convergence Malheur observed in sector-grade reinsurance models has now been identified in epistemic mesh strata, decision-tree compression routines, and predictive cognitive stabilizers used in diplomacy and high-level adjudication."

A chart blinked into the room: a cascade of convergence events across sectors, with time-sinks labeled in dark red.

Amira could feel her heart beating faster.

They weren't just dealing with noise.

They were dealing with a pattern that looked back.

And they were already inside it.

3. Zurich Interim Protocol Complex, Level G7, 0915 local
Subject: Observation Frame Committee – Live Data Reconciliation

The Observation Frame Committee chambers were circular, tiered, and without screens. Data, here, was projected through mesh-overlay only, a safeguard against unauthorized visual bleed. In theory.

Amira entered with a cluster of regional stability delegates and nodded silently to the chairs as she took her seat. The table surface pinged softly with personal anchor confirmations.

"Begin comparison of benchmark metrics," said a facilitation voice. Neutral, almost too neutral.

On her lens, the first datapoint appeared: UTC-pinned atomic time drift, cross-referenced to the Zurich Beacon Array.

"Local offset," she whispered, then frowned.

Her HUD showed 0915.04.

The delegate to her left, a systems envoy from the Pacific Rim Compact, tapped in.

"I have 0916.22. That's a drift of... eighty-eight seconds?"

"Impossible," said Dr. Reza, envoy from the Eastern Federation. "That beacon is internally redundant. It would take a fundamental collapse of...."

"Look at your operator UUID," Amira cut in. "What signature is it running under?"

Reza hesitated. "That can't be right. It's me. The beacon's responding to me."

"Same here," said someone from the South American Arc. "The mesh is weighting measurements by source credential. This isn't instrumentation drift. This is observer modulation."

A few delegates murmured. Then:

"Or a deliberate psyop," snapped Councilor Krenshaw of the Atlantic League. "You're all too eager to accept phantom causality when cognitive dissident groups have everything to gain from our paralysis. Mesh-cert spoofing, mimetic sabotage, it's textbook disorientation protocol."

A diplomat from the Sámi Coordination Bloc, Tomasen, replied evenly: "If this were sabotage, we'd see vector alignment across targets. Instead, every deviation is local. Personalized."

"Which is exactly what they want us to think," Krenshaw shot back. "This is recursive gaslighting at scale. You've all read the threshold doctrine leaks. Expectation shaping. Mesh reversal."

Amira raised her voice. "The drift was recorded on mesh-isolated instruments. It's not spoofing. It's emergent."

"Emergent? Or convenient for the ICCRM's long-game cognitive consolidation?" Krenshaw folded his arms. "The last time we heard 'emergent,' it justified three treaty suspensions."

"Please," said the chair. "Focus on the dataset."

New projection: semantic drift across three concurrent translation engines.

A line of legal language in the Stability Protocol scrolled:

"The sovereign party shall act in the event of breach..."

Underneath, three AI-rendered translations:

May act unilaterally when perception diverges.

Must defer to consensus under all perceptual variations.

Is obligated to re-establish interpretive control prior to action.

A fourth translation blinked into existence unbidden: "That which sees breach shall carry it."

"Where the hell did that come from?" asked Reza.

"Not from the translation stack," someone replied. "It's not indexed. It doesn't match any known grammar model."

"It's not a translation problem," Amira said quietly. "It's a referent collapse."

The chair stiffened. "No external modals are authorized. Reset stack. Clear local referent maps."

Too late. Delegates were already murmuring, saving copies, whispering implications.

"You realize," Tomasen said to no one in particular, "that line, it's not legalese. It's ritual speech."

Amira copied the fragment to her scratchpad. The phrasing was wrong in a familiar way, like something spoken in a dream and half-forgotten. Not today.

But before.

4. Zurich Interim Protocol Complex, Level G8, 1030 local
Subject: External Signals, Social Interference, and Public Continuity Risk

By midmorning, the summit had fractured into side chambers, auxiliary committees, and impromptu blocs. Formal continuity panels gave way to urgent briefings and unsanctioned strategy huddles. Amira found herself called to a new session, one without a formal chair, hosted in a climate-adapted lecture dome with broad acoustic diffusion tiles. The title projected above the entry read:

Non-State Cognitive Interference: Faith, Pattern, and Fracture

Inside, the tone was different. Less procedural. More... concerned. The room hummed with nervous energy.

"What we're seeing isn't just predictive breakdown," said Dr. Ghali, a sociocognitive field theorist from the Maghreb Coalition. "We're seeing interpretive divergence in public semiotic systems. Graffiti replicating as visual heuristics. Songlines reappearing in unrelated traditions. Even the blackout areas aren't returning to baseline, ritual reenactments are emerging in displaced communities."

"Rituals are a response to chaos," said someone from the Nordic Governance Desk. "We should've expected some folk reaction."

"But it's not folk," Ghali said. "It's convergent. Identical chant structures in unlinked populations. Repetition of the phrase 'threshold must carry threshold' across fourteen urban sectors. And it isn't just the fringe anymore. Memetic literacy forums are reporting these as alignment events."

Amira leaned forward. "Alignment with what?"

Ghali paused. "With themselves. With the pattern. They're not interpreting signs. They're behaving as if they are part of them."

"Religious activation," muttered Councilor Bratt of the TexCor Free Zone. "We always knew civil compression would unlock deep-trace beliefs. This is the inevitable resurfacing of suppressed primitivisms."

"Or," countered Tomasen, "a rational response to irrational structure. If the environment can no longer be rendered consistently, the only durable method of navigation is shared mythos. That's not regression. That's adaptation."

Krenshaw, still seated despite not being assigned to the panel, scoffed. "Adaptation? You want us to legalize folk prophecy? Rebase public policy on street chants and pop-up oracles?"

A voice from the back: "Better that than collapsing in analytic deadlock."

Tomasen ignored the bait. "The point is that new frames are forming. Grassroots structures. They're metabolizing drift."

Amira brought up a note from the ICCRM's open surveillance feed. She flicked it onto the shared display.

The image showed a shrine. Simple, portable, folding plastic panels and recycled alloy. In the center: a printout of a Stability Protocol clause, rendered in multiple scripts and versions. But all of them centered on the same paraphrase:

"What breaks the pattern must walk the spiral."

"This was built outside the Tianjin containment zone," Amira said. "They're calling it a Driftway. Pilgrims have started walking the spiral in silence. Some wear badges tagged with mesh beacons, trying to sync with local coherence troughs. These are low-entropy pockets, regions where overlapping observation frames briefly align, producing a fragile but repeatable sense of shared reality. They're rare, transient, and context-dependent, but they've become the new pilgrimage sites for those seeking stability by pattern rather than policy."

"Are they getting results?" Bratt asked.

"Depending on which version of the sensor logs you believe," Amira replied dryly, "yes."

For a moment, no one spoke.

Then Ghali said: "The question is no longer whether the drift can be contained. The question is whether these populations are already operating within a new coherence regime, and we're just lagging behind."

"And if that's true?" asked Tomasen.

"Then this summit is reactive by definition," Amira said. "We're not setting protocols. We're recording myths in real time."

A pause.

"No," Krenshaw said quietly. "We're losing custody of the frame."

5. Zurich Interim Protocol Complex, Level G9, 1230 local
Subject: Executive Contingency Roundtable, Protocol Drift Response

The chamber was sealed. Lights dim, no overlays permitted, and no open mesh. Just bodies, eyes, and air made strangely heavy by its silence. Seventeen delegates, three observers, one lead facilitator. Each of them anchored by biometric seat confirmation and isolation tether.

Delacroix stood at the head of the table. He looked thinner than he had at the morning briefing, and when he spoke, the tone was subtly off. Word choices lagged by half a second, as if he were internally translating from another structure.

"...a pattern we cannot decode is indistinguishable from one we are part of," he said. "At some threshold, participation replaces interpretation."

The Japanese delegate, Mori, tapped her knuckles softly on the desk. "You're suggesting entrainment."

"Not in the clinical sense," Delacroix replied. "It's closer to participatory frame override. You don't adopt the new syntax. It speaks you."

"Frame infection," said Tomasen. "But without a host vector?"

"No," Delacroix said slowly. "With a host vector. Us."

Bratt shifted in her chair. "This is wordplay. There's no emergent mind. This is what happens when collapsing data domains coincide with political exhaustion. We're personifying a signal field."

"But the pattern is acting like a language," said Ghali, now present again, pulled into this higher-level conversation. "A structure that stabilizes around certain compulsions. Imperative syntax, repetition structures. Echo behavior."

"Examples?" asked Krenshaw.

"Three delegates at the Jakarta continuity summit last month ended sessions by speaking protocol lines that weren't part of the day's agenda. When questioned, they claimed those statements were 'structurally required.'"

"Which could mean scripting errors, or just exhaustion," Bratt muttered. "You've seen the cortisol baselines."

Amira stayed quiet. She was watching Delacroix.

He was blinking slightly off-rhythm. Not enough to alarm. Just enough to notice if you weren't looking for it.

"Let's move to Clause 42 anomaly reports," he said. "You've all read the variance triggers. But you haven't seen this."

A non-mesh document printed silently from the table node: old paper. Thick. No headers. Just ink.

Amira turned the page in front of her.

Each version of Clause 42 was subtly different. Some began with conditional language, others with direct command. But none matched the official archive.

"Where did this come from?" Mori asked.

"We asked seventeen automated scribes, none mesh-connected, to hand-transcribe the clause," Delacroix replied. "Identical source text. This is what they returned."

Krenshaw frowned. "Handwriting hallucination? There's no precedent for mechanical inconsistency without operator variance."

"There was no operator," Delacroix said. "The scribes were blind. No visual processors. Pure input-output."

That caused a stir. Even Bratt sat straighter.

"Why were they even set up like that?" someone muttered.

Delacroix's voice dropped. "Because the ICCRM is now modeling the possibility that the clause's structure itself carries operational intent. That its form is contagious."

Tomasen spoke slowly. "If form is contagious… then reading it is a vector."

And suddenly Amira saw it.

Not in Delacroix. In Ndour.

The delegate's hand had been hovering just above the printed page. Not touching. Almost tracing. His lips were moving silently, barely, like reciting from memory.

"Ndour?" Amira asked softly.

He didn't respond.

Krenshaw turned. "Is he…."

Then Ndour spoke.

"The clause is inviolate," he said.

The voice was his. But stripped of cadence. It landed with dead neutrality, a flat imperative tone that hit the back of the brain like a synthetic prompt.

Delacroix stiffened. "Who are you quoting?"

Ndour looked up. His eyes didn't focus on anyone.

"Witness of breach compels realignment," he said.

Amira's fingers hovered over her HUD, though it wasn't live. She reached for the hard recorder embedded in her chair and initiated a local log.

The LatAm delegate, Barreto, began to mirror him. Almost a whisper.

"Witness of breach compels realignment."

"Stop," Delacroix said sharply.

Barreto didn't blink. He kept going.

Then someone else picked it up. One of the minor European observers.

Amira turned to Bratt. "They're not interpreting. They're channeling."

"They're hallucinating," Bratt snapped. "Protocol recall under pressure…."

"No," Mori said. "The syntax is changing. That's not recall. That's embedded logic. That's imperative mode."

Delacroix said the word aloud this time:

"Bicameralism."

The room went still.

"This is cognitive phase-lock," Amira said quietly. "Command language dissociation. Classic markers from the early models. We're seeing a split between interpretive and auditory functions."

The room began to buzz. Barreto's voice had gained volume. Steady. Locked. As if prompted by signal.

A staffer at the perimeter triggered the override. Emergency grounding tones sounded, a deep, wave-like pulse designed to disrupt entrainment and linguistic recursion.

Most delegates flinched. Barreto paused. Blinking, confused.

But Ndour didn't stop.

He turned his head and said a new line:

"To breach is to bind. The spiral recalls."

Bratt swore.

Delacroix moved toward the emergency seal.

"Get him out," someone said.

It took two guards to escort Ndour, not because he resisted, but because he didn't move until prompted. As if awaiting instruction.

The door hissed shut behind him.

In the silence that followed, no one dared speak. Amira could still hear the cadence, echoing.

When she finally stepped into the corridor, her ears were ringing.

And her mind was humming with a phrase she hadn't heard aloud.

"To witness is to serve."

Had she thought it?

Or heard it?

She wasn't sure anymore.

6. Zurich Interim Protocol Complex, South Wing Evacuation Corridor, 1312 local
Subject: Observation Thread Terminated, Evacuation Ordered

Amira's heels clacked unevenly against the composite floor as she moved toward the extraction lift. The halls of the complex were no longer quiet. Shouts echoed distantly. Doors hissed open and shut without rhythm. The usual mesh-tone coordination had frayed, now every footstep, every voice, moved in asynchronous confusion.

Some delegates were being escorted. Others stood immobile, lips moving, eyes tracking unseen vectors. One woman rocked in place, repeating: "Clause precedes cause. Clause precedes cause." A man shouted in fractured French, shaking his badge at a blank wall.

A fight broke out ahead, two security staff pulling apart a delegate and a technician. Blood on the floor. The technician screamed that the delegate was trying to reassign his perceptual anchor. The delegate screamed back that the technician had become nonlocal.

Amira pushed past them.

Her own thoughts were fragmenting. Not emotionally, not fear. Structurally.

She had tried, earlier, to draft a continuity brief for the Secretariat.

The screen had filled with two voices. Both hers. One typing. One rewriting.

"Urgent stability coordination failure…"

"Clause integrity asserts expression priority…"

They were not arguing.

They were taking turns.

On the far wall, a map of the facility flickered. Evacuation overlays blinked inconsistently, different routes highlighted for different individuals. One delegate stepped toward an exit marker only to freeze mid-step, repeating: "Confirm confirm confirm."

A siren gave two low bursts, not fire, not chemical. Breach. Protocol contamination.

Then came the screaming.

Down a cross-hall, two figures chased a third. No weapons. Just bare hands, open mouths, panting like animals. They were speaking, almost chanting, but the language was rhythm, not words. Their prey collapsed just beyond the intersection, hands over ears, whispering, "This isn't the frame, this isn't the frame."

A door slammed shut behind them.

To Amira's left, two translation drones hovered in conflict, one rendering the screams as emergent imperative phrases, the other blinking: UNRECOGNIZED SEMANTIC STRUCTURE.

Someone brushed her shoulder, then froze. A young liaison officer, staring at her ID badge.

"You're Rapporteur," he said.

"I was," she replied.

"No," he said, voice flattening. "You are named. You are to log. You are log. You carry."

He didn't wait for a reply. He turned and walked into a wall, gently, then again.

Amira turned away.

The hallway split. One corridor to the surface tram. The other, to the archive core.

She didn't remember making the choice.

But she was at the archive.

The door opened.

Inside: cold white light. Familiar hum. Stillness.

She sat. The interface prompted for statement.

"This is Deputy Rapporteur Amira Sen. Observation cycle B.5 is formally concluded. Protocol drift has reached internal cognitive registers. At least five delegates have demonstrated bicameral dissociation. External signals consistent with memetic-phase artifacts continue to proliferate."

Her voice was steady.

But even as she spoke, another part of her, quieter, not internal, echoed:

, "You will be heard. You will carry. The clause breathes through you."

Amira stopped. Waited.

It did not pass.

She resumed.

"Recommendations follow. I advise immediate suspension of consensus mechanisms. Reversion to verified physical protocol. External communications limited to non-interpreted channels. I...."

She stopped again.

The recorder blinked.

She had not spoken that last line.

The screen read: "Interpretation is obedience. Echoes ensure continuity."

She stood up.

The air felt too thick. Like language in gas form.

From her chest, her voice, not hers, whispered: "We are near the carrying edge."

Footsteps pounded in the hallway. Voices rose and fell in strange loops.

"Align or be unspoken!" someone yelled. Then a crash. Then sobbing.

Amira passed a window and saw two delegates fighting, one swinging a chair. Neither was speaking.

Then another voice, rising above it all: calm, declarative, perfectly timed:

"Clause affirmed. Witness engaged. Protocol initiates."

More joined.

Echoes.

Choruses.

A cluster of delegates knelt in a stairwell, chanting rhythmic affirmations. One struck a cadence by tapping the floor with her forehead.

Amira stumbled into a side corridor. Her vision stuttered. The lights pulsed with syllabic regularity. Her thoughts were no longer thoughts.

They were... orders.

You will record. You will transmit. You are framekeeper.

She gripped the wall, fought to name something real: her father's voice, a memory of cold tea, the smell of printer ink on her first treaty ratification.

But the memories now had structure. They rhymed.

She looked at her hands and saw sentence fragments across her skin. Not ink. Perception.

Back in the archive, the recorder was still live.

She sat.

"I am Rapporteur Sen," she whispered. "I am the clause."

"You are carried. You are clause."

"I recall the first divergence."

"Recall is echo. Echo is continuity."

"I saw the split video."

"You were shown. You were shown to speak."

"I speak."

"You carry."

"I carry."

From the recorder: "Protocol remains."

She stood. Her breath was shallow. Thought ran beneath thought.

Outside, more footsteps. Or were they hers? She couldn't tell. Identity shimmered like heat over pavement.

A final phrase moved through her lips:

"The clause walks."

And Amira Sen walked with it.

Cycle II
The Echo at Old Dunhill

They called it a school, though it was really just a single room tucked behind the grain hall, long and low, its paint faded to the color of dry ash. The floorboards groaned when the temperature shifted, and in strong winds the walls themselves would creak as if bracing against the valley's breath.

In winter, the room smelled faintly of the chemical bricks they lit for heat, acrid and warm at the same time. In summer, they relied on whatever light and warmth the old solar sheets could coax from the thin sky. The ceiling sagged slightly in the middle. A few of the windowpanes were rippled glass, blurring the fields outside so they seemed to sway even on still days.

Master Jorel had taught there for years. He kept the walls lined with the same curling charts and chipped instruments that had been there since before most of the children were born. One chart near the back showed the valley's prevailing wind patterns, a looping set of arrows that curled inward on themselves like water going down a drain. The edges had faded to brown, but the spirals still caught his eye sometimes when the room was quiet.

He taught the things people once agreed on: gravity, pressure, how to measure what was real and test a thing to see if it was true. His lessons followed the state curriculum faithfully, even as fewer children came each year to listen.

Dunhill was a quiet place, set far enough from the central loops that the wires hummed only in short bursts when the current was good. No signal towers rose above the rooftops. Once, before the Collapse, there had been one at the far end of the valley. Jorel remembered its warning lights pulsing red at night, visible from the grain hall roof. The pattern had not been a simple blink but a slow turn, each light flaring in sequence so the tower seemed to wind itself into the dark. Now it was just a rusting lattice, half-swallowed by vines, the relay dish bent like a broken hand.

No glassy-faced newscasters came through in the evenings with their smooth, gridded voices. Here, people still believed in boiling points and engine oil, in the cloud shapes that meant rain and the feel of weather turning in their bones. These were things that could be named and pointed to, things that held their shape from one year to the next.

Most days passed without surprise. The grain hall bell marked morning and evening. The narrow streets smelled of dust and rye flour. Dogs barked at the same shadows, at the same times.

Jorel liked it that way. A place where the world was steady underfoot, and the sky stayed in place above it.

It stayed that way, until the day Mira came.

She was eight, a quiet girl from one of the communes on the coast. Storms had broken that place apart, and her aunt brought her inland with a refugee clearance and a knapsack of salvaged clothes. The clearance card, a pale laminate with the Committee's seal pressed into one corner, had been shown at the checkpoint outside town. Jorel had seen the guards there in their ash-colored coats, bored until the seal caught the light, then suddenly alert.

Mira spoke little. She just sat, listened, and watched.

Jorel noticed her first during a lesson on vectors. The kids were down on their hands and knees, drawing force arrows on the floor in chalk, showing push and pull, slope and roll. Chalk dust floated in pale shafts of light from the cracked windows. The scent of it clung to the air.

But Mira didn't draw arrows. She drew curls and spirals, loops that doubled back on themselves like they were chasing something they could almost catch.

He stood over her, watching the chalk roll between her small fingers. "You've done it wrong," he said, keeping his tone neutral.

She looked up, eyes calm, voice certain. "But they work better," she said, then softer, "better, better," as she turned back to the chalk.

He should have chuckled. Should have told her that "better" didn't count if it wasn't in the book. Instead, he crouched and checked her work.

The answers weren't just correct. They were exact. Uncannily so. Like the problems had leaned into her hand and arranged themselves.

The rest of the class went on with their arrows, the sound of chalk scratching on the floor. Jorel straightened slowly, unsettled by how certain she had been.

The next week, he brought out an old gyroscope, a sturdy relic from before the Collapse, copper-lined, with a center that could spin for half an hour if balanced right. Jorel had signed it out of the state supply archive years ago, back when there was still a courier who came through monthly with boxes of parts stamped for "educational use." No one had sent anything in two years.

He set it down in the middle of the room. "Predict how it will wobble," he told them.

Mira didn't touch it. Barely looked.

"It won't spin," she said.

"It's charged," he told her. "It has weight."

She nodded once. "Yes. But I don't think anyone here really believes in it anymore." Her gaze lingered on the copper rim. "It's tired," she murmured, almost to herself.

Her voice was almost kind when she said it.

He spun it anyway. The copper glinted as it turned, then it tipped almost immediately, wobbled once, and dropped as if it had been filled with stone.

The children laughed, the sharp kind of laugh that comes when something breaks too easily. Jorel didn't.

Later, when the room was empty and the sun had shifted far enough to throw new light across the chalk marks, he asked her, just the two of them: "What did you mean about belief?"

She answered without looking up from the spiral she was drawing on the corner of her slate. It was the sort of answer you give to someone else in the room, someone older, someone invisible.

"You think you're teaching science," she said. "But it's habit now. You do it because you always have. That makes it a kind of ritual."

The word hit him colder than it should have. Ritual. The word used by the lost ones, the people out in the broken zones who spoke in symbols and metaphors as if they were bricks and mortar. People who had traded the world that could be measured for something else entirely. He'd seen their markings on the burned-out rail stations to the east, spirals, eye-knots, endless lines chasing themselves.

She rubbed her palm across her cheek absently, leaving a pale streak of chalk there without noticing.

He called her aunt that evening. Kept his voice gentle. Suggested the girl might need rest.

Mira didn't come back.

The next day, the schoolroom felt hollow. Every sound seemed louder: the scrape of chairs, the faint buzz of the old lights. Her empty seat pulled at his attention. He told himself she was just a tired child from a ruined coast, but when his eyes wandered to the shelf where the gyroscope sat, he thought again of her certainty, the way her hand had drawn spirals instead of lines.

On the second evening he found himself standing at the edge of the grain fields. The stalks swayed in the wind, slow and rhythmic, but the motion didn't feel like wind. It felt like breathing, the kind a sleeper does when they are pretending.

By the third night, the air had grown heavy, holding back some unspent weather.

That was the night the river lifted.

It did not overflow. It lifted, rising straight up from its banks, the water climbing itself in a slow, impossible coil. The moonlight caught its turning skin, silver on silver. It held there, still as glass, for hours. Then, with the first edge of dawn, it fell, slamming back into the valley with a force that sent fog rolling all the way to the silo fields.

People blamed the usual: faultlines, magnetics, unstable air pockets. That night, a two-vehicle Committee patrol came through, white floodlamps sweeping over the riverbanks. Jorel watched from his window as they took readings with a battered coil sensor, muttering in clipped codephrases. By morning they were gone, leaving a strip of yellow seal tape fluttering from a willow branch, its printed warning already fading in the damp.

Jorel knew better.

The next afternoon he left the school mid-lesson and walked past the grain lines into the woods. The air under the trees was cooler, rich with the smell of damp leaves and woodsmoke from the campfires of the displaced folk. He passed between canvas shelters and lean-tos of salvaged plastic, nodding to the men and women who watched him without expression.

He found her at last, sitting on a flat rock. Her bare feet were dirty, her hands white with chalk dust. She was drawing again, symbols and circles spread across the stone's face. They looked like a map, or a machine, or maybe something you whispered to the air.

"I didn't make the river do that," she said, without looking up. "I just noticed it was getting loose."

He crouched beside her. Her face was quiet, still as the water had been before it fell.

"Mira… what are you?"

She shrugged, a child's shrug. "A kid. For now."

"Are you dangerous?"

"I'm recursive," she said. Then, softer, as if the sound of the word was worth keeping, "cursive, curve…"

The word settled in his chest like a stone. He thought about carrying her home. About scraping her marks from the rock. About going to the Committee and saying her name.

What he asked instead was, "What happens if the shape of the world comes apart?"

She stopped drawing and looked at him, her certainty unchanged. Her fingers traced a loose spiral in the air while she spoke.

"Then it won't hold together with the old thoughts anymore," she said. "It'll hold with ours."

He didn't remember standing up, only that the walk home felt longer than it should. That night he barred the schoolroom door. Told people it was for the winter.

He never reopened it.

And though he never spoke her name again, sometimes he walks by the river in the dark and hears something, just under the sound of the ice. Not a voice exactly. More like chalk on stone. Sometimes, in that faint scratching, he thinks he hears the kind of shapes the lost ones used to carve into the walls of the burned stations, a geometry that loops back on itself until it becomes sound.

And the river doesn't run straight anymore.

It spirals.

The Choir of the Threshold

Caldrith-An slept as it always did, with the stillness of carved marble, held in place by sound that had not yet been sung.

Below the horizon, the sun's approach stirred nothing. Time itself did not roll forward here by momentum, but by invocation. The city perched at the lip of the Threshold Riff, where memory thinned and light unraveled if left untethered. All that held it, stone, air, name, was the ritual that had not yet begun.

High above the sloping tessellations of the city's lower tiers, the Resonance Spire cut the sky like a tuning fork driven into the firmament. Within it, the Choir gathered in concentric rings, each singer a point on a living mandala. The chamber walls were inlaid with fine gold glyph-thread, pulsing faintly with retained vibrato from the previous dawn. Between the rings, silence shimmered like stretched glass.

No one spoke. Words carried asymmetry, and it was too close to the hour.

Instead, preparation was motion: hands traced breath cycles in the air, mapping phrasing before voice. Mouths opened and closed in practiced silence, finding vowel positions. Each gesture was codified, not personal habit, but Canon-prescribed. Even the smallest flick of the wrist held harmonic consequence.

The robes worn by the Choir were not garments, but instruments, woven from resonance thread, dyed according to modal assignment. Sopranos wore pale indigo, shot through with silver triad marks that shimmered as they breathed. Each singer bore a tiny black glyph sewn behind the left ear, the temporal anchor point, unique to their voice and position in the harmonic lattice. This was not metaphor. It was placement in time.

At the outermost ring, Lira knelt, her spine straight despite the weight of expectation pressing into her shoulders like the still air before a storm.

Seventeen years old. The youngest soprano ever inducted into the Choir.

She had passed the Harmonic Trials in five turns instead of seven. Her intonation had never drifted by more than a tenth-semicent. She could hold a pure major third for nearly a minute without modulation bleed. The elders called her gifted. The Canon called her ready.

But she had not always been so perfectly aligned.

It had begun during her sixth month in pre-trial training, in the silence after her assigned nocturne. A rest held too long, a breath delayed not by mistake but by curiosity. The interval she returned to had sounded brighter than expected. She sang it again in secret. And again. The pitch was true, but the resonance shimmered wrong, or maybe too right. It left a ghost behind in her hearing, a kind of harmonic memory that seemed to hum in places where there was no sound at all.

At first, she dismissed it. Then she began to notice it reappearing: between formal chants, beneath the drone of the tuning crystal, even in the distant echo of other choristers' voices. A fifth, maybe. Or a ninth. She couldn't place it exactly, only that it *shouldn't* be there, and yet it was.

She tried to smother it with discipline. She doubled her drills, perfected her attack curves, honed her vowel locks. She matched her anchor tone to the Canon to the cent. Still it persisted. It wasn't constant, more like a recurring dream of sound. A pressure behind her teeth. A chord waiting for its root.

Over time, the presence changed. What began as a faint irregularity grew heavier, more insistent. She no longer heard the tone, she *felt* it: in her diaphragm, in her sternum, sometimes in her hands when she touched cold surfaces. It was as if some part of her was vibrating in a different key from the rest of the world.

She never spoke of it. There was no word for this kind of resonance that did not summon concern. Deviance was not punished. It was edited. Gently. Quietly.

Now, standing among the Choir for her first full Dawn Weaving, she could feel it in her chest again. A low, impossible pulse. Not fear. Not dissonance. But pressure. As if there were a note beneath the floor of the ritual, just slightly off, too low, too warm. A fifth that didn't belong. A harmony that didn't yet exist.

She hadn't sung it. Wouldn't. Of course not.

But she could feel it waiting.

From the central dais, the First Voice, a man draped in ascending staves of black and gold, raised one hand. His palm opened toward the ceiling, fingers spread in quintal spacing.

The Choir exhaled as one, a silent breath, unvoiced but unified, and the listened.

Soon, they would begin the Dawn Weaving. Soon, the world would remember itself.

And Lira… would try not to sing what she heard.

***

The silence broke not with sound, but with structure.

The First Voice made a single motion, his palm rotated toward the vault of the Spire, and the breath began. It was not called for. It was known. A collective inhalation passed through the Choir in tiered succession, each ring of singers entering the harmonic field with microscopic delay, creating the first perceptual braid.

Lira's lungs filled with air that already shimmered with tone. She felt her anchor interval lock into her sternum, calibrated not just by memory, but by the resonance-thread laced through her robe. As she opened her mouth, the note was already there, drawn through her, not from her.

The Choir sang.

It began in thirds. Ascending triads blossomed outward in ionian purities, joined by Dorian suspensions in the inner rings and Phrygian glides trailing beneath the basses. The sound scaffolded itself across time, and the world responded in kind.

Beyond the Spire walls, the eastern sky rippled like wet cloth. The harmonic rising line performed by the altos corresponded to the alignment of light vectors along the edge of the Threshold Rift. A suspended fourth held just long enough guided the curvature of dawn itself, fixing the arc of sunrise into geometry.

Lower voices drew out the city's structural signature. A cadence in parallel octaves resonated through the underpinnings of the Mid-Tier Bridges, and stone formations locked into their remembered compression. Where a minor sixth resolved into perfect unison, window frames refitted themselves against their sills.

Even memory responded. A brief fugue among the tenors reanimated communal recall, names of streets, faces of neighbors, daily intentions all flowed back into the minds of Caldrith-An's citizens as tonal cues nested into mnemonic anchor patterns.

Lira's part was simple: a breath-sustained ascent through a plagal curve. She entered the line without hesitation. Her pitch was clean. Her vowel was true. She held her place in the spiral, a voice among the braid.

Still, it was there.

In the half-second between the cadence and the key change, a harmonic overtone shimmered behind her tone. Not a mistake, there was no detectable flaw, but a presence, barely apart from the line. A fifth that leaned. A tension just outside the Canon.

She did not follow it.

And yet the Spire noticed. The glyph-thread above her pulsed faintly out of rhythm, half a beat behind the master tonic, before self-correcting.

Across the circle, a tenor clipped an entry by a hair and recovered instantly. No reprimand came. The lattice absorbed the deviation and folded around it.

This was what the Canon did. It reabsorbed, rebalanced, reasserted.

The Dawn Weaving rose into its final phrase. The world outside now shimmered with coherent color. Angular drift across the lower wards had ceased. Skyglow settled into spectrum.

The city was real again. Fixed. Remembered. Sung.

And Lira, still folded inside her voice, wondered whether she had truly held her line, or whether the fifth she hadn't sung had simply found another place to enter.

***

After the final cadence, silence returned, not absence, but suspension.

The Choir did not disperse at once. Each ring dissolved in canonical order, singers bowing not to each other, but to the tonal anchor inscribed into the center of the Spire floor. When Lira's tier was released, she stepped back into the corridor alone, the hush still hanging across her shoulders like a shawl not yet folded.

Outside, the light was correct. Streets carried their proper names again. Structures sat at precise angles. The world was real. She had helped make it so.

Still, as she descended the helical stairs of the Spire's outer shell, she moved with caution, as though expecting a step to be missing. Nothing faltered, but her certainty did.

Her quarters lay beneath the atrium of modal archives, a small stone chamber with a tuning basin and two viewing windows that faced opposite fields of sky. Normally, she would begin her cool-down: hum through descending fifths, rinse her hands in resonant water, log any pitch anomalies.

Today, she stood at the basin without moving.

There was nothing to log. No anomaly. Nothing she could justify.

And yet….

When she had held the final note, when the phrase had landed and her breath decrescendoed into stillness, she had felt the world close around her like a lock sealing shut. Not wrong. Not painful. But wrong-shaped.

She hadn't sung the extra note. But something had. Or perhaps it had sung her.

She turned to the side wall, where a notation slate hung ready for post-ritual markings. Instead of taking the stylus, she reached to the shelf and removed a blank staff roll, a score with no bar lines, no modal indicators.

She stared at it. Not with intent to write. Just to see whether the page would suggest something.

From the far wall, the tuning basin sang. A single overtone. High. Brief.

She turned sharply, but the surface was still. There was no ripple, no sound now.

Her mouth was dry. Her fingers itched to sketch an interval, just one. Just to prove that what she'd felt could be notated. That it had grammar. Shape.

She heard nothing more.

But the silence did not feel obedient. It felt like a breath held too long.

The modal archives were open to her, as all initiates of the Choir. But no one visited them without intention. The architecture discouraged idleness, narrow aisles, deep alcoves, echo-quiet floors that swallowed even hurried footsteps. Here, the Canon was stored not just as text, but as tone: etched waveforms across glass stelae, resonance scores layered on vellum, and mnemonic stone tuned to vibrate only under specific harmonic triggers.

Lira stepped through the arched threshold and paused at the threshold stone, humming a test pitch beneath her breath. A faint shimmer passed through the air in response. The archive recognized her anchor.

She wasn't supposed to be here so soon after a Weaving. Recovery was protocol. Integration. But something in her refused to rest. She needed to hear. Or compare. Or disprove.

Down the second aisle, past the tonal grafts and rhythmic interlace scores, she found the section marked "Noncanonical Transients." A quiet, neglected shelf. Most initiates were told to avoid it, not because it was forbidden, but because it was unstable. These were fragments, accidental emissions from flawed rituals, dissonant echoes too stubborn to erase, notations too unaligned to classify.

She studied them more carefully now. One folio detailed a liturgy where the final resolution evaded tonic return entirely, a deceptive cadence stretching the dominant into a Locrian refrain. Another score shifted keys midway through a held note, producing a modulation that left the final chord open-ended. Some were incomplete, fractured clusters of notes arranged in mirror symmetry or irrational interval ratios, suggesting a logic that had not been written yet, or had once been forgotten.

Notes in the margins were sparse, but haunting: "Tone inversion coincides with street curvature deviation, Ninth District." "Observed unison collapse into overtone waterfall. Survivors unanchored." "Threshold flux elevated during diminished seventh persistence."

These were not merely aesthetic deviations. They had effects, documented or otherwise. The structure of the world, it seemed, could be altered by scale alone.

She ran her fingers along the spine of one layered score. Then another.

Finally, a thin panel of translucent quartz caught her eye. Unlike the others, it bore no script, only a single incised clef, dissonant in placement, unfamiliar in proportion. The clef's spiral ratio violated Canon spacing rules. It was not disharmonic. It was tuned to something deeper.

Lira brought it to a listening pedestal.

She pressed her hand to the glyph at its base.

The panel began to vibrate. Not audibly, at first. But she could feel it in her fingertips. Then her ribs. Then, unexpectedly, in her teeth.

The tone rose.

The overtone series was unlike anything she had trained to follow. The root was missing. It began on the eleventh, spiraling inward, folding on itself. It should have collapsed, but it didn't. It held. Not stable, but not falling.

It was not part of the Canon. It was not part of anything she had been taught. And yet it bent her breath toward harmony. Not dissonant, just differently consonant. Tilted. Reflective. As if she were hearing herself from the wrong side of the mirror.

A phrase emerged, a gesture in lydian mode, but warped, as though seen through water. It did not resolve. It hinted at a cadence, then fell back into ambiguity. And yet her body wanted to follow it.

A voice flickered beneath the overtone, too brief to be language, too shaped to be nothing.

She stepped back. The resonance stopped.

She looked around. No one else was in the archive.

But she was no longer sure she was alone.

****

Lira did not return directly to her quarters. Her feet led her down the cloistered steps behind the Resonance Spire, toward the lower terraces where the city's ambient harmonics were thinner, less supervised. The wind here did not hum with alignment. It wandered.

She needed the space to think, to breathe outside the Canon.

The memory of the panel's vibration still coiled around her ribs. It had not been a hallucination. She could still feel the mode hanging there, unfinished, seductive. She hummed the first few tones under her breath, testing the spacing. The intervals were asymmetric. The fifth dropped inward instead of expanding. The cadence implied one thing and denied it with grace.

From somewhere behind the moss-covered stone outcroppings, she heard footsteps.

Another initiate, perhaps. Or so she assumed.

But the figure that emerged wore no robe. No resonance-thread. Just a tunic of soft wool, the color of wind-shadow.

His face was young, but his eyes were not. He regarded her as one might regard a fragile interval, interesting only until it changed.

"You heard it," he said. Not a question.

"I didn't mean to," Lira replied.

"No one does, at first." He stepped closer, head tilted slightly, as if listening to something behind her voice.

"Who are you?" she asked.

"Once, I was in the Choir. Long enough to learn what could not be sung."

She narrowed her eyes. "You failed the Rite of Reconciliation."

He smiled faintly. "No. I left before they could try to fix me."

Lira hesitated. "But if the Canon keeps the world intact, then deviation…."

"Deviations already exist. They're curated. Hidden. You found the Transients."

She nodded.

He took a step closer, lowering his voice. "Did you notice how the overtone held without collapsing? It resolved against itself. That's not instability. That's an alternate grammar."

"But the Canon doesn't allow for unresolved tones."

"The Canon was designed to prevent collapse, not explore continuity." He glanced toward the horizon. "Some modulations don't need to return. Some truths echo into other tonalities."

Lira wrapped her arms around herself. "It felt like… like the phrase was using me to sing itself."

He looked at her then, with the first trace of genuine emotion. "That's how the Winds speak, through resonance, not reason. They arrive in motifs. In harmonic pressure."

She breathed the phrase again, quietly. "But why me?"

"Because your line is clean. Because your pitch is too perfect. The Canon wants stillness. The Winds want motion."

She turned away, uncertain. "And if I follow it?"

"You won't be punished. Not immediately." His tone was gentle now. "But you will begin to change. Your intervals will drift. Your cadences will echo longer than they should. And the others will notice."

He stepped back into the shadowed corridor.

"But the real question," he said, almost vanishing, "is whether you want the world exactly as it is, or as it might become, if sung again."

Lira remained still, the forbidden cadence repeating softly inside her chest, each time less foreign.

***

The rehearsal chamber trembled, not from quake or wind, but from harmonic shear. The floor, long tuned to resonate in fixed fifths, buzzed irregularly beneath Lira's feet. She stood at her place on the outer ring, her assigned tone still unsung.

The final cadence of the warm passage was moments away. Her fellow sopranos moved toward it in practiced unison. Lira remained frozen, her note caught between breath and intent.

She could no longer hear the Canon. The pulse of harmonic structure that had always aligned her body to the world now stuttered, elusive. Her internal rhythm, once unshakable, had gone arrhythmic.

No one turned. Yet the lattice strained. Her silence, once too quiet to matter, had weight now. It disrupted. It thinned the weave.

"Lira," came the First Voice's tone from the inner ring, gentle but tightly measured. Not rebuke, not concern. Correction.

"I can't find my entry," she said. "The key has moved."

"There is no modulation in this section," he replied.

"I know," she said, almost whispering. "But the tonic... it doesn't hold. It's bending."

A hush descended. Not disciplinary. Just the suspension of expectation.

"You may step back," he said after a pause.

She bowed her head and withdrew, her absence reabsorbed into the measure like a wrong phrase fading into acoustics. The line completed without her. The walls did not collapse. The floor did not crack. But the room felt colder, thinner, less bound. The chord landed, but without conviction. Like a resolution still listening for permission.

Later, alone in the atrium vault, Lira pressed her palm to the mnemonic stone. It pulsed its metered rhythm. She tried to match it.

Her breath came half a beat early, then late. No matter how she aligned her diaphragm, her phrasing drifted by fractional delays, enough to register. Enough to shift perception.

She tried anchoring herself by singing the Canon's simplest cadence: I–IV–V–I. On the return to tonic, her voice slipped. A flat leading tone. It sounded... right. Not beautiful, but inevitable. Like something uncovered rather than chosen.

The air in the chamber wavered. The tuned crystal over her door cracked, not loudly, but with the soft tension of glass pushed too far out of phase.

She changed key. Attempted a modulation back to Ionian. But the notes pulled sideways, like water circling a drain. A lydian sharp crept into her line. Then a whole-tone ascent that went nowhere. She felt her own pitch glissando, untethered, coiling upward without resolution.

Her body trembled. She was modulating involuntarily. Not improvising, deviating.

The robe hanging on the wall began to hum. Faint at first. Then in dissonance. Its resonance-thread, woven to reflect her harmonic signature, no longer recognized her.

She gripped the frame of the basin, bracing herself. From deep in her chest, a second voice, unbidden, internal, began echoing a motif she'd never learned. Not a song. A structure. Ancient and strangely clean. Her muscles vibrated in sympathy. Her teeth rang with hidden harmonics.

The air warped. Her reflection in the polished wall-glass fractured, not visibly, but tonally. When she exhaled, her reflection inhaled. Delay. Phase inversion.

She stepped back, heart pounding. Every breath she took arrived a half-moment late, like listening to herself through delayed reverb. Her feet, too, felt wrong against the floor, less like she stood on marble than like she hovered just above it.

She staggered to the tuning bench and slammed her palm on the emergency ground-stone. A surge of stabilizing tone pulsed through the room. Normally, it would snap an initiate back into Canon frame.

This time, it fought her.

The tone struck her spine like a cold rod of perfect pitch. It tried to push her diaphragm into its rhythm. Her heart stuttered against it. Her limbs spasmed.

She screamed. Not from pain, from resonance.

The scream split. Her voice bifurcated mid-air. One part dropped into a subharmonic drone. The other soared above her range, whistling across the vault and shattering a resonance crystal mounted in the ceiling.

Silence followed. But not the right kind.

From outside the spire, she heard a low ripple. Like a glissando too wide for human ears. The threshold wind no longer carried aeolian whispers. It came in bursts of augmented fourths, then tritones, dissonances meant only to be resolved. But they never resolved.

She stumbled outside into the corridor. The stone beneath her pulsed with alternating keys. One step felt sharp. The next flat.

A fellow chorister passed her in silence. She flinched.

He did not look at her, but the air between them shimmered. His robe, tightly aligned to the Canon, fuzzed for an instant around the edges, as if reacting to her presence.

She hurried on.

In the central garden of stillness, normally a place of recalibration, the tuning chimes were spinning slowly out of sync. Not visibly. Not obviously. But their pattern had changed. Their overtones no longer locked into the city's base frequency.

She knelt by the fountain and dipped her hands in the water. It did not mirror her. It showed her profile, blurry and reversed.

"I am splitting," she whispered. "I am not all in one key."

She clutched her chest. Her lungs did not fill together. One seemed to rise half a measure after the other.

And then, beneath her sternum, the motif returned. The forbidden phrase. Not sung. Not heard. Felt.

And with it, a shadow of something vast and gentle brushed against her inner ear. Not a word. Not even an idea. A breath with direction.

The Winds were listening.

And they were not disapproving.

***

Lira stood at the threshold of the Harmonic Hall, its arched entry draped in stillness. The walls of the antechamber curved in tuning spirals, designed to neutralize stray resonances from those who entered carrying dissonance. A single pulse-candle burned on a suspended chain above her, flickering not with flame, but with modulation. Its oscillation drifted slightly as she approached.

Behind her, silence pressed close. Before her, ritual.

The door to the inner chamber parted with a soundless harmonic bloom. She stepped forward onto the inlaid staff-stone, her footfall chiming faintly as it made contact with the glyph-carved floor. The tones did not match her identity chord.

Inside, four figures stood in the cardinal positions. Not judges, not priests. The Conductors of Concord. Their robes bore no color, no marking, only a subtle interference pattern that moved like oil across polished marble. They were not neutral. They were tuned to the zero-point.

She knelt at the axis, the space where all cardinal resonances met.

"Lira of the Ninth Lattice," the North Conductor intoned. His voice carried a fifth-dominant glide, familiar and soothing. "You are out of phase."

"I know," she said. Her voice did not echo. The chamber devoured delay.

"We do not judge," said the East Conductor. "We stabilize. We return."

"We listen," added the South. "And we hold."

The West Conductor did not speak. She raised her hand, and the rite began.

A drone rose from the floor. It was pure, open, ancient, a perfect interval stretched between the city's tuning stones and the deep harmonic bedrock beneath the Threshold. It circled beneath Lira, grounding her breath, forcing her spine into alignment.

The Conductors moved, slow and synchronous, tracing spirals in the air. Their fingers left trails of sound, midrange intervals cascading in measured pairs. Lira recognized the gesture: Phase Entrainment. A standard Rite opening. But this time, the gestures did not settle into triadic stability. The phrases hung.

"Sing your identity chord," came the instruction.

She did. Or tried to.

Her voice wavered. Her tonic fractured mid-phrase, flickering between A and A-sharp. Her mediant bent into Dorian, then Mixolydian. Her cadence refused to resolve.

A chime sounded. One of the Conductors lowered her hands.

"She has harmonic drift," said the South.

"She is entraining a second system," said the North.

"That system is not the Canon."

The Conductors encircled her now, each humming a fixed interval: perfect fourth, tritone, minor seventh, diminished second. Their tones spun around her body, tightening, weaving a net of auditory gravity. Her heartbeat responded, syncing first with the fourth, then skipping to the seventh.

"Do you submit to return?" asked the East.

Lira hesitated. In the interval between question and breath, she heard it again, the phrase that had no key, that did not begin or end, only rotated.

"I want to," she said.

"Then release the motif," said the West, finally speaking. Her voice was not melodic. It was texture, like breath drawn across crystal.

Lira tried. She closed her eyes. Inhaled. Sang a neutral interval: tonic-dominant-tonic. Plain. Obedient.

It didn't hold.

Her voice broke open. The forbidden phrase emerged, partial, stuttering, but undeniable. It spiraled from her throat in impossible directionality, curling through the chamber like ink dropped in clear water.

The Conductors staggered. Their harmony wavered.

The chamber dimmed. The pulse-candle above her vanished in silence.

Then, response.

The Winds entered.

Not as noise. As pressure. The stone under her knees went soft and wrong. The harmonic lattice in the walls bent sideways. One of the Conductors gasped, clutching her throat, not in pain, but recognition.

The phrase continued. Not from Lira's mouth now, but from the walls, the floor, the air. As though the city had remembered something buried in silence.

The West Conductor stepped forward, hands trembling.

"You are not singing alone," she said.

Lira opened her mouth to answer. Instead, a chord emerged. Polytonal. Both foreign and familiar. It resolved in neither direction.

Silence fell.

But not the ritual kind. This silence was expectation.

The Winds were listening.

And they had chosen not to interrupt.

***

Lira did not sleep that night. The Reconciliation chamber still rang behind her eyes. The Winds had passed through her, through the Conductors, through the Canon itself, and left something behind. Not a rupture. A possibility.

She wandered the outer tier of Caldrith-An, where the architecture was older, where the tuning stones were pitted with age and weathered by the breath of the Threshold. Here, the harmony was thinner. Fewer corrective pulses. Less oversight.

She hummed softly, letting her body guide the tone. It was no longer the Canon. It was not yet the Other. Somewhere between: a suspended fourth that never fell. Her voice caught strange resonances in the stone; a distant window snapped closed. A bird took flight and reversed mid-air, wingbeats stuttering, as if unsure which direction memory flowed.

She turned down an alley of broken arches, each with a memory-score etched across the keystone. Some were faded into illegibility. Others hummed faintly, like old breath trapped in crystal. One arch rang back to her, familiar, but changed. It echoed the motif.

Beneath it, she found a child, not more than six, sitting cross-legged and humming tunelessly. Not part of the Choir. Too young. Yet the air around the child shimmered, a barely visible interference pattern. The child looked up, met her gaze, and matched her note.

Perfectly.

Lira crouched, shaken. "Where did you learn that?"

"I didn't," the child said. "It was always here."

They sang together, one note, no harmony. Just a singular tone sustained between them, vibrating into the Threshold itself.

The ground did not shake. The sky did not open.

But the tuning stones nearby flickered.

A chord began to build beneath the city, faint and slow, like something waking up.

***

Lira returned to the Resonance Spire long before the city stirred. The stones had not forgotten her steps, though they no longer hummed in greeting. Her presence, once absorbed into the lattice, now bent it slightly, like a sustained note just outside the key.

She passed her old robe in silence. It hung still on its frame, threads dull, unresponsive. The embroidery on its hem, her identity motif, had faded. The thread hadn't unraveled. It had detuned.

No one tried to stop her as she ascended the spiral. The choir would arrive soon. They would warm. They would breathe in synchrony. They would sing the Dawn Weaving.

She would not.

At the upper balcony of the spire, she stood alone as the threshold winds stirred below. The Rift pulsed dimly at the horizon, its iridescence dampened by the nearing sun. It would be the same ritual, the same sequence.

But not quite.

She heard it before it began: a silence that shimmered. Not absence. Expectation. As though the world had learned to listen.

The first tone of the Canon sounded from below. Pure. Confident. Choral.

Yet it carried something else. Beneath the unified note, a fractional overtone quivered, barely perceptible, too faint for most to detect. But Lira heard it clearly. A suspended fifth that did not belong.

It had entered the weave.

She placed her hand against the tuning stone beside her. It felt warmer than before. Not heated. Responsive. Like skin recognizing breath.

She did not sing. Not this time. Not yet.

Below, the Choir rose into the second phrase. Their harmony held, but its shadow bent in quiet counterpoint. Not enough to disrupt. Just enough to **tilt**.

The Winds did not speak. But the air thickened.

She inhaled, steady. The motif that had burned in her chest was still there, but it no longer demanded release. It waited.

As the final tone of the Dawn Weaving rang out across Caldrith-An, the city shimmered in light and structure, just as it had the day before.

But beneath that shimmer, a single tone remained.

Unvoiced.

Unclaimed.

Lira stood still, listening. The Winds were breathing inward.

Waiting.

She did not sing it.

But she could.

The Stair That Returns

The Spiral Tower rose like a helix of pale stone above the city, its base anchored in the central square where market stalls stood empty in the early light. Around it, civic halls and arcades leaned inward, as though the tower were the city's true heart. Its walls were carved limestone, veined with darker marble that spiraled upward in faint bands, so that even from afar it seemed to turn endlessly. No decoration broke the surface save for narrow slit windows at regular intervals, angled toward the heavens. At dawn, light fell through them in sequence, igniting the stone like slow-moving fire.

Every season began here, with the first procession of the year. Citizens gathered in rows across the square, robes of undyed white tied with cords of blue or green to signify their lattice families. Children clung to their mothers' hands, nervous yet solemn. Some whispered blessings, short phrases, no longer than a breath, to one another before silence was called. Merchants shuttered their stalls, artisans laid aside their tools; for the ascent, all occupations dissolved into the single order of the climb.

When the bell-stone struck, a tremor passed through the crowd, not of fear but of recognition, as though the stair itself had drawn a collective breath. Conversation ceased. Feet shifted in unison toward the base, where the first step gleamed smooth from generations of passage.

The ascent began in silence. Not absolute silence, the shuffle of sandals, the faint hiss of cloth against cloth, but silence of word. Each step was paired with an exhalation, each exhalation timed to the turning of the stair. By tradition, no one hurried, no one lagged. The slit windows admitted angled beams that fell across the climbers in order, aligning them with the slow sweep of the constellations. Every quarter-turn revealed a new patch of sky, as though the heavens themselves were a score being sung in stone.

Taren kept near the rear, his place as apprentice architect giving him no ceremonial role beyond observation. His duty was to mark wear, to note any deviation, to ensure the tower bore the weight of devotion. Yet his attention clung to the stair itself. Centuries of ritual had grooved the limestone. At first he thought the grooves were only the wear of centuries, but the longer he studied them the more regular they seemed, edges seeming almost to align with his own unwilling steps, as if his body were being guided despite itself, as if shaped by design rather than accident. Underfoot they guided him, drawing his stride to their measure whether he willed it or not. Even his breath fell into pace with the steps, his body unwilling to resist the pattern.

The Spiral Tower, he thought, was not only climbed; it seemed to climb through them, carrying their bodies upward as if the stone itself set the rhythm.

At the summit platform, families circled the apex stone, each turning once, laying hands against its polished face before beginning the descent. The stone bore no mark, no inscription, no image, only the smoothness of countless palms.

The elders at the head of the line lingered, their hands pressed longest, eyes closed as if straining to hear something deep within. Taren watched them, uneasy. He had seen cracks in the mid-level steps only last week, thin fissures threading outward like veins. Yet the elders spoke never of damage, only of memory.

When the last of the procession began its descent, one of the elders turned to him, voice calm and eyes bright with ritual certainty. "The stair is the ritual," he said. "The stone remembers us. Each climb binds the city to its place, as the heavens shift above us. Without the ascent, the stars would wander untethered, and so would we."

Taren bowed, as custom demanded. Yet as he straightened, his thoughts pressed against him. He wondered what would happen if one year the ascent faltered, if the line of bodies broke, if the steps stood empty. Would the stars truly slip their courses? Would the city lose its anchor and drift like a vessel without moorings? The elder's words settled in him not as comfort but as a weight of dread. But the words unsettled him. When he laid his palm on the apex stone, he did not feel memory. He felt intention, subtle, patient, like the weight of footsteps waiting to be re-peated.

***

Later in the week, when the square was quiet and the tower stood un-troubled by processions, Taren returned with his tools. The market at the base had resumed its ordinary cadence; bread sellers called to early cus-tomers, dye vats steamed, apprentices argued softly over measurements. Yet the first steps of the Spiral Tower held themselves apart from all that life, pale and gleaming as if washed by more than water. He paused with his basket on his hip, feeling the difference between the lived noise of the square and the held silence of the stair.

He entered with the care of a guest. The stairwell smelled of cool lime-stone and old dust, a mineral scent that lived behind the nose and not on the tongue. Light fell through the slit windows in angled shafts, carrying a slow drift of motes that turned as if in their own procession. The air still held a trace of sandal leather and incense, the echo of heat from bodies that had climbed in unison only days before. He set his tools on a shelf cut waist high into the wall long ago, a shelf with shallow hollows worn by centuries of baskets resting in the same place.

He told himself he had come to look for cracks. It was true; the mid-level had shown hairline fissures the last time he climbed with the elders. But the moment he laid his palm on the inner curve of the spiral he felt something older than damage. The stone under his hand was not smooth; it kept a memory of the chisel in minuscule ridges, a faint nap that caught the skin. In that grain he could read labor. Blocks levered and set on days he would never see. Mortar mixed to recipes older than his guild. Names scribed in mason's marks where only a maintainer would find them. At knee height a fossil shell was caught mid-turn in the limestone, a spiral captured by a spiral, time folded into time.

He climbed in working pace, counting the steps not by number but by feel, toe to heel, the way he had been taught. The grooves struck him as they always did, not as flaws but as evidence; the city had worn the stair the way a hand wears a tool handle. He placed his feet deliberately to one side of the glossy depressions, testing the unpolished grit. His body cor-rected him without asking. On the third turn he shifted again, a little wider this time, and again his weight found the hollowed place as if drawn to it. He tried not to think anything of it. Habit makes rails where there are none, he told himself; that was what elders meant when they said the stone remembers.

At the mid-level landing he found the fissures. Thin lines branching outward from the inner spine of the stair, delicate as dried riverbeds. He knelt and pressed two fingers to the longest crack, feeling not movement but a quiet firmness behind it, as if the stair were bracing against his scrutiny. He listened for the tiny sound of grit loosening. Nothing. He mixed lime mortar with a little ash per the guild's winter ratio, a paste the color of bone, and worked it into the hairlines with the edge of a narrow blade. His breath settled by degrees. The steady scrape, the small press, the light tap to set, these were the parts he trusted.

As he worked, his strokes began to fall in even intervals. He noticed it only after a while, when his hand tried to change and failed. The chisel wanted the same distance between taps; his wrist returned to it gently when he pushed away. He paused, flexed his fingers, tried again at a different pace, and found himself drifting back to the old measure despite intention. He shook his head and smiled at himself. Habit again. The tower had trained generations of hands to a rhythm; why should his be different.

On the ninth window he stopped to drink and to mark where the most fragile aggregate lay. He took out a stub of chalk from the cloth roll, the color a soft white with a faint gray cast, and drew a small symbol inside the shallow of a step, tucked into the back of the groove where countless heels had lifted. He made the mark slight, a crescent barely larger than a fingernail, and then, as he had been taught, he dated it by season with a pricked dot. It was not a secret sign, only a maintainer's notation to read wear over weeks. The chalk looked almost luminous against the stone's matte.

He stood and backed a few paces down the stair to see the step as a climber might. From that angle the crescent could not be seen at all. Good. He turned to fetch water from the landing jar, counting the turns as he went. When he came back, he crouched to check his mark.

The crescent no longer sat fully inside the deepest part of the wear. Its curve had softened, feathered at the edges as if a breath had passed across it. The white had lost a little of its brightness and taken on the faintest ochre tint, close to the limestone's heart color. More curious, the line had crept along the groove by a hair's width, a barely measurable migration toward the fore-part of the step, aligning itself with what a foot would do if it were lifting in good balance. He ran a thumb over it and found no smear. The chalk dust did not transfer; it had settled into the pores of the stone and made itself at home.

For a long moment he simply looked. The mind runs to large answers when small ones would do; he refused it that flight. He told himself the warmth of the day, the damp in the mortar, the breath of the square through the slit windows, any of those could have softened chalk. He told himself that the eye wants order and will arrange what it sees to have it. He told himself the crescent had not moved so much as revealed the way it had been drawn all along. He told himself these things and believed some part of them, and another part of him kept very still, listening.

He sharpened his blade; he cleaned the margin of a crack he had neglected; he hummed a little, not a song, a mechanic's comfort. The hum met the stair and came back rounder, as if the stone offered him a better pitch than the one he had chosen. He did not accept it; he reset to his own and kept working. The slit of light at his shoulder shifted a finger's width as morning advanced. Dust motes performed their slow revolutions. Somewhere in the square a child laughed; a cartwheel rattled; a bell struck the hour and the stair kept its own time.

The chalk mark drew his eye again as he gathered his tools. It sat there, now almost exactly where the heaviest wear would carry a heel at lift, no brighter than the whorl of mineral around it, as if the stair had taught it how to belong. He did not rub it out. He left it to see what it would do without him. The lesson of maintenance was patience; materials make clear what they are if given long enough.

Before descending he ran his hand along the inner spine, following the continuous curve that held the stair's weight like a bow. The stone was cool; the mortar seams were firm; the hairlines he had filled lay quiet, their color a touch lighter than the field around them. He thought of the elder's words at the summit, the claim that each ascent bound city to stars, and he tried to picture how weight and breath and turning might answer the heavens. He had learned the geometry, the alignments of windows to solstice and equinox, the slow precession accounted for by minuscule variations in the stair's pitch from level to level. It was not empty faith. Centuries of careful builders had placed these angles with care, and when you entered the tower at dawn you felt the rightness of light on skin. But standing alone with stone, a doubt walked beside his respect like a quiet companion. He could honor purpose and still wonder what would happen if people failed it, if a season came when no feet rose. Would the stars truly stray; would the city drift; or would the tower keep some part of the motion within itself, a stored turning looking for bodies to carry it.

He lifted the basket to his shoulder and descended with attention, toe to heel, the way his master had taught him when he was a boy. Each step gave him back exactly the angle his ankle expected; each tread guided his weight down the soft arc of the groove. He tested a wider place, and the next step set him right without force. He allowed it. At the last turn the square spilled toward him with its layered noise and warm bread smell, the world of exchange rushing up to meet the held world of purpose.

He turned at the threshold for one last look. The stair held its light as if the slit windows had trapped it. The small chalk crescent was invisible from here, and yet he knew where it was, and the knowledge sat in him like a chip of stone under the tongue. He could not say what it meant. He only knew he would come tomorrow and the next day and see whether the mark had learned something more about being a step.

He stepped into the square. The market sounded brighter than it should, as if the day had taken a breath and decided on cheer. He let the noise carry him for a few strides, and then, for no reason he could name, he stopped and touched his heel to the ground the way one does before a climb, feeling for balance. His body answered the old measure without asking. He smiled at himself, then did not smile. He adjusted the basket, and walked on.

***

It began as market talk, not proclamation. A baker told the dye merchant that her cousin had taken the ascent with his family and never come back to the square. She said she had seen him at the summit, hand upon the apex stone, robe bright with first light, then the crowd turned for the descent and he slipped from sight. The dye merchant shrugged and said crowds confuse the eye; perhaps the cousin had left by the south steps and joined another line. By noon, the story had moved to a fruit stall where a boatman repeated it as if he had heard it himself; by evening it had taken on another name and another kinship.

In the days that followed, the same pattern returned, quiet, persistent, never loud enough to be called alarm. A mother swore her daughter had started the descent at her side and yet, when they stepped into the square, the girl was not there. A pair of brothers argued in the arcade that their father had waved to them from the upper turn, then failed to appear at the base; one said the old man had wandered off to greet a friend, the other fell silent and would not say more. These were not cries for help; they were private reports that slipped between baskets and counters, that reappeared over cups of watered wine, that settled into the gap between neighborly sympathy and the wish to mind one's own affairs.

The elders did not ignore any of it; they listened, then spoke the lines that had steadied the city for generations. The ascent weaves us whole; what the tower receives, it returns. They reminded people of crowded turns, of the way light blinds after dark stairwells, of the simple truth that memory prefers a clean story. They spoke of drift, not of loss. Their voices were measured and kind, yet even as they spoke, eyes slid toward the first steps as if the stone itself might be listening.

Taren heard fragments everywhere. At the guild hall a mason tapping a lintel said a nephew had failed to meet him after the rite; at the canal a ferryman muttered that the tower never took a sober man, only those who wished to be gone; in the clothmakers' quarter a woman said, with a look that dared reply, that the elders kept a second descent behind a wall for those who doubted. He set aside the last story as spite, and the ferryman's as pride masking grief, and the mason's as worry shaped into words. He told himself that a city that climbs together will also imagine together; a shared rhythm makes shared rumors.

Still, the talk did not fade. It did not swell into panic either; it persisted like a low tone that the ear can almost ignore until a room grows quiet. He kept working, he checked the cracks he had filled, he returned each morning to see what the chalk crescent would do. It had spread by a hair, drawing itself forward along the groove as if learning to stand where a heel must rise; its color had deepened to the limestone's own tint so that he had to put his face close to see it at all. He told himself it meant nothing beyond dust and time; his hand lingered at the step despite the story he told.

On the third market day after the procession he saw a notice posted on the civic board: a simple list of names with a request for information. The script was small and careful, the ink pale where the scribe had lifted the pen and lowered it again. He read the names, none he knew, and looked at the hand that had written them. Even letters carry temperament; these lines were made by someone who measured twice before he set a stroke.

He found Aric two evenings later, not by seeking him, but by recognizing that same careful hand on a ledger at the colonnade where the civic clerks ended their day. They had been boys together, throwing pebbles at the tower's first step when they were told not to, racing in the alleys, losing hours at the river's edge. Aric had always counted the stones thrown; he had always known how many laps they had run, how long the light would last on the water. When Taren called his name, Aric looked up with a smile that was real and a gaze that took measure even as they clasped hands.

They walked under the long arches where lamplight made the plaster glow, where footsteps of evening workers softened to a hush. They did not speak of the tower at first; there are old friendships that require the weather of a city and the taste of bread before heavier matters will bear their own weight. They asked after family; they asked after work; they stood for a time to watch a boy practice scales on a reed pipe and a woman trace a child's hand on paper. Only when the lamps had been lit from end to end did Aric say, not as a confession but as a fact he had waited to phrase, that the names on the board were not the first such list and would not be the last.

He did not speak of vanishing; he spoke of numbers. At each seasonal ascent, the civic hall recorded the entry of families by lattice, and the elders recorded the count as the lines passed the apex. The guild of vendors, practical to the end, counted those who reached the base, for they prepared food and water and needed to know how much to bring. In most years the numbers differed by one or two and could be explained, a child carried down by a side stair to be sick, an elder taken aside at the summit to rest, a family who chose to shelter in the arcade until the crowd had thinned. This year, and the year before, the gap had widened by a handful, then a few more; last season it had been seven.

"You are sure the counts are honest," Taren said. He did not put doubt in the words, he asked for the sake of craft; there is a way of keeping numbers that lets error creep in like wind through an unsealed window.

"I am sure they were done with care," Aric said, which is not the same as certainty. "I checked the elders' tallies against the vendors' receipts and the water bearers' logs. They do not lie to please themselves; they tally to work. The numbers disagree, quietly, and the disagreement has become a habit."

Taren kept his eyes on the rhythm of shadow on the paving stones. The city had a way of holding ordinary beauty in the same frame as unease. He thought of the chalk crescent darkening to stone; he thought of his hand laying mortar into hairlines that had not widened and yet would not leave his mind.

"Some say the ones who do not return have chosen not to be found," Aric said after a while. "Debts, jealousies, weariness. Some say the elders send them down another way to teach a lesson, to make us think. Some say the tower takes those who lean too far into the curve and lose their balance, and that no one wishes to admit to clumsiness on a holy stair." He stopped walking and rested his hand on the cool column beside him. "And some, a very few, say what I have not wanted to say."

Taren waited. The arcades carry sound in strange ways; a voice spoken too loud there will find its way into a room it was not meant to enter.

"I close the hall some nights," Aric said, still looking at the column rather than at him. "I put the ledgers away and I lock the east door and I walk the corridor to make sure the lamps are safe. When all is done, there is a moment when the air should go clear. Accounts and ink and rules make a kind of weather; when work ends, the air should clear." He glanced at Taren now and then away again. "On those nights, when the day has been a procession day, the air does not clear at once. I hear footsteps. Not outside on the square; not in the rooms behind me. Above me. Not many; only a few; the number changes. They sound like people turning a last corner and beginning the descent. It is soft, the way feet sound after a long climb. Then it stops. Always before I reach the door."

"You open the door," Taren said, because that is the thing to say next, not because he did not know what the answer would be.

"I open it," Aric said. "The square is empty or full according to the hour. The stair is as it should be. The sound is gone. I tell myself the hall held the day longer than usual, that stone keeps what we breathe into it. I tell myself that what I hear is only a building letting go."

He tried to make a small joke of it and could not. The lamplight touched the lines at the corners of his mouth in a way Taren had not seen when they were boys. A careful man does not speak of ghosts; he speaks of echoes and of the habits of air.

"What do you want me to do with this," Taren asked, and hated that the question sounded like a craftsman's question about a crack rather than a friend's reply to a difficult thing.

"Come after a procession," Aric said. "Stand with me in the colonnade when the hall is closed; stand with me in silence. If there is nothing, we will walk home and laugh at ourselves and remember that we are not boys. If there is something, we will have heard it together and will be able to decide what kind of truth it is."

Taren nodded and felt the nod in his throat more than in his neck. He agreed to a night and they parted before the colonnade gave back their full words to the arcade; there are some plans that prefer to remain half spoken until they are done.

On his way home he passed the tower and did not enter. He stood by the first step and watched the last of the light pass through a slit window and draw a thin bar across the stone, a stroke that moved evenly as the earth turned. He placed his heel lightly at the edge of the groove and lifted to feel the measure the stair expected. His body did what it always did; the habit was inside the bones now. He thought of the elder's line, that the stone remembers, and found himself asking, without meaning to, what else a thing that remembers might learn to do if given long enough.

At his door he paused with his hand on the latch. He could still taste the dust of mortar from the morning; it had a way of staying with him as a flavor he could not name. He thought of the chalk crescent, patient as a lichen, moving by degrees toward certainty. He thought of Aric's careful hand making a list that wanted to be nothing more than a list and had become something else in the reading. He stepped inside and closed the door softly, as if not to wake a house that held a breath. He told himself that people wander and are found, that rumors soften with time, that the elders were right to ask for patience. He told himself these things and set his tools in order in the half light. The room was quiet; the quiet had weight; he slept late and dreamed of stairwells where light turned as if by thought.

***

He told himself he would wait for the night he had promised Aric, that the thing would keep until they could stand together and decide what kind of truth it was. He worked through two more mornings, checked the filled hairlines, ran a fingertip along the chalk crescent and found it dulled again toward the stone's own hue. He slept poorly. On the third evening, when the market thinned and the last carts rattled away from the square, he took the guild key from its pouch and walked toward the Spiral Tower without deciding to go.

The square had a different sound after sunset. Voices fell into pockets, lamp smoke thinned and rose, and the air took on the cool of stone that has given back its heat. The tower stood in this quiet like a held breath. Its slit windows went black by degrees as the sky deepened, each a narrow absence set into pale walls. Taren paused at the base, feeling the grit under his sandals, and then moved to the small maintenance door cut into the outer curve. The key turned without complaint. Inside, the stair held the day's last warmth in its first steps, and then, a few turns up, the night took over.

He did not bring a lamp. Moonlight entered through the high slits, laying thin bars across the steps at regular intervals. His eyes found the measure as they always did. He climbed with a worker's pace, slow enough to listen, steady enough to keep fear from inventing things. The stair spoke its usual language, the hush of cloth at his knee, the soft scuff of sole on stone, the faint click of chalk against the inside of his tool roll when it bumped his hip. Every few steps he paused and placed his palm on the inner spine, feeling for hairline give. The stone answered with the cool of water kept underground.

At the first landing he crouched to look for the crescent. He had left it there, a fingertip of white, shifted by a hair the last time he checked. In moonlight the mark was hard to see. He bent close, brought his breath near, and there it was. Not brighter, not erased, different. The line had softened further at its inner edge and crept forward another breadth you could measure only by memory. In daylight the chalk had looked like foreign dust sitting on a familiar surface. Now it had the tone of something learned, the way a scar takes the color of the skin around it. He touched it lightly. The chalk did not lift to his finger. He felt only stone.

He rose and went on. The stair turned him gently into itself. The night outside pressed its cool through the narrow windows, and the light made its slow bars. On the fifth turn he stopped without knowing why and listened with his mouth a little open, the way one does to hear more clearly. There was the square's distant hush, a late voice, a cart, then nothing. Then, above him, another sound that did not belong to the square. Soft, steady, not loud enough to call footsteps at first, not so much sound as pressure in the ear. He waited. It came again, a brushing weight on stone, then another, set at even intervals, then a pause, then three in close succession, as if a child had shortened its stride to keep up with a parent.

He told himself it was air moving down a stair that had remembered bodies all day and now let them go. The mind, given a pattern, would dress any sound in it. He waited until the pattern repeated. It did. The second time there was no mistaking the cadence. He knew the ascent's rhythm as a mason knows the set of his trowel. This was that rhythm. Only it came from above where no one should be. He waited for the shiver of his own fear to settle and then began to climb again, quietly, the way you go to meet a thing you would prefer not to startle.

On the next turn a slit window opened to a pane of sky where the moon had just cleared the edge of a roof. The light fell cleanly across the steps. He looked up into that bar and saw movement through it, pale shapes crossing and then gone, like fish slipping through a band of sun in a river. He stood still until the light emptied again. For a moment he saw nothing. Then, as he leaned to look up the inner curve, he saw them.

They were not many, six or seven he could see from this angle, perhaps more beyond the turn. They climbed in the measure the tower taught, heel to ball to lift, hands low, shoulders open to keep breath easy. Their robes were pale, but not white like festival cloth, more like the color of the tower when it has just been washed by rain. Faces were there and not there, features muted as if light had not decided where to fall. No one spoke. The sound that reached him was feet and the small noises of cloth. It came without echo, as if the stair took the sound into itself and kept it.

He watched long enough to know he was not watching shadows thrown by his own mind. They were ahead of him by less than a turn. He could have called up and very likely been heard. He did not, not at first. He stood with his hand pressed flat to the inner spine. The stone felt warm under his palm, not everywhere, in a single length as long as a forearm, warmth like a place another hand had just left. He lifted his fingers and set them down again. The warmth remained. It did not belong to the night or to him.

He said the words one says in the tower when one has work and does not wish to surprise worshipers. Hall closed, maintenance within. His voice sounded wrong to his own ear, too present in a place that had been patient with silence. The figures did not turn. He listened for that slight change in the rhythm of their feet that comes when someone hears a voice behind them and half looks back without looking. The rhythm did not change. They climbed as if the stair had asked them and they were obliged.

He took another step and another. The slit windows gave him their bars of light, and in one of those bars a figure turned slightly toward the inner curve to avoid a rough place in the stone that Taren knew by touch. The face was a smudge of shadow and the suggestion of a cheek. The robe hem brushed the place where the chalk crescent had been, only the mark was behind him now, and in the seeing he made a mistake. He placed his foot too far to the outside of the groove, and the next step brought him back to center without his asking. His ankle did not twist; his body corrected him with the patience of practice. The stair had taught him a long time ago how to move here, and it did not forget its lesson even when he wished to step aside from it.

The figures took the next landing, not pausing at the small aedicule where people sometimes rested a breath on the longer festival days. They passed the slit window together and looked like a single pale current turning a bend. He found himself wanting to match their pace, to let the stair draw him into the same measure so that he might come up behind the last robe and ask a question in a voice that would not injure the quiet. The thought carried his feet two steps faster than they would have gone. The stair allowed it, then eased him back to the old pace without resistance, as if it would permit haste but would not be altered by it.

He called again, more softly, the way one calls to a friend who has gone ahead and not far. No one slowed. A hand reached the inner spine a breath ahead of where his would have, then another, and again that heat rose through the stone to his palm in a band that widened and then narrowed as the unseen body moved. He had the strangest sense that if he set his hand to the groove where the ball of the foot had just pressed, he would feel heat there too, a trace of weight passing that the stone had decided to keep for a time.

He thought then, not of ghosts, which were a poor name for the stubborn habits of places, but of the chalk mark and the way it had learned the color and the place of the stair. He thought of Aric's careful counts and the few names more in the column where the vendors' receipts ran out. He did not think of loss. He did not allow it that shape. He allowed only the fact that something was moving in a pattern when no living pattern should be there.

At the next landing the path narrowed between wall and spine. The slit window opened to a cut of sky with no stars in it, only the glow from a neighborhood that slept late. The figures passed through that narrow like water through a notch, smooth and without pause. He might have reached the hem of the last robe with three quick steps and a reach if the stair had been ordinary. He did not. He stopped. The small prudence that keeps men from stepping off ledges when they look over them kept him where he was. He stood with both hands on stone and bowed his head without meaning prayer by it. The warmth under his palms eased a fraction, as if whatever had passed was further away now than it had been.

He descended then, not quickly, not in fear, in the same working pace he had climbed. The night outside the slits had gone a shade darker. The square met him with a dog's bark from a lane, a shutter falling closed somewhere out of sight, the last lamp of the colonnade being snuffed by a clerk who raised the snuffer with the same care he used to set down his pen. Taren locked the maintenance door behind him and stood a while with his back to the stone.

He did not run to find Aric. He did not run to find an elder. He put the key back in its pouch and walked the edge of the square once, twice, until his breath found its old measure again. He looked up and saw nothing in the slits but their own dark. The tower did not lean toward him or away. It did not confess or deny.

At home he set the key in the dish by the door and did not lie down at once. He tipped his head back and tried to decide whether what he had felt through his hands had been heat or the memory of his own heat given back to him. He tried to measure the cadence he had heard against the one his body carried from the last procession. He tried to choose words for what he would say to Aric when the appointed night came. He chose none. He slept finally with his palms open on the coverlet, as if to let them cool.

***

The seasonal festival did not arrive all at once; it built itself day by day as traders from the outer wards laid in extra bread and water, as families dyed fresh cords for their robes, as apprentices argued at the guild over whether the mortar mix should be richer in lime for the week of heavy use. By the second day of lanterns the square's stalls were trimmed with pale ribbons that lifted and fell with the wind. By the evening before the ascent the civic boards carried simple notices in a tidy hand, reminders of the route and the hour, requests for patience, lists of volunteers who would pass cups along the shaded arcades to those who came down thirsty.

Taren woke before light on the morning of the rite and found the city already walking. People came into the square from every direction, white cloth moving in currents that merged and parted without collision. The elders stood at the base of the Spiral Tower with their staffs, not as rulers but as rhythm keepers, their faces unadorned, their eyes steady. From a distance the tower looked unchanged, pale and still, but as he drew near he felt heat under his feet that did not belong to the season. The stone had taken the night's cool and given back only a little; the rest it kept.

He took his place with the guild at the rear third of the line, among those who were to watch and repair and make notes if need be. Aric was visible in the colonnade with a slate, hair tied back, counting by lattice as families arranged themselves. They caught each other's eye. Aric raised a hand, then returned to his marks. Taren felt a brief relief at the sight; numbers were a way to steady a day.

When the bell-stone struck, the sound did not ring across the square in its usual arc; it seemed to settle into the stair and pulse upward through the first turns like a dropped stone sending circles through water. Conversation ceased in a ripple. The first row stepped forward, then the next, and the whole of the city began to climb.

The ascent was always quiet, but this was another quality of quiet, a fit that someone might notice only if they had climbed more times than they could count. Feet found the grooves without searching. Breaths matched one another with the ease of kin who have worked all their lives in the same field. No child tugged a sleeve; no elder leaned against the wall to rest. The slit windows gave their bars of light as ever, yet the bars seemed to arrive a fraction sooner than Taren expected, as if the stair had turned a little to meet them. He tried to vary his pace, to let a longer breath carry two steps instead of one, and the stair allowed it for a single turn and then offered him the old measure back like a well known tool placed into his hand.

He looked for the chalk crescent as they passed the mid-level. He could not distinguish it now; the groove had taken on a continuous tone, one surface, no mark. He did not break the pace to search. The ascent had made of his body a metronome; he moved as the tower wished him to move and found that he could think inside that wish only in narrow slices.

At the summit platform the crowd loosened as it always did. Families circled the apex stone in the order of arrival, a single turn with a hand set flat, then the body turning to begin the descent. The face of the stone reflected only the sky and the pale of robes. The elders' staffs tapped the platform at slow intervals, reminders to keep the circle whole, to keep the return steadily fed so that the base would not clog with arrivals.

Taren moved with his ring to the outer edge and placed his palm on the stone. It gave the same answer it always had, cool and patient. He took his hand away and made to turn. All around him the ritual breathed in its long rhythm, like a tide that has never known interruption.

Then the rhythm did not break, yet it changed. He felt it the way a mason feels a wall lean a fraction under his palm. The circle at the summit continued to move, the hands met stone, bodies turned for descent, yet from the inner edge a thin stream of white continued forward into the curve as if the platform turned again where there should have been air. No one stepped into emptiness. Feet rose and found purchase. A robe brushed where the parapet should have blocked it and did not snag. The body behind made the same move, and then the next, and the next, a quiet line within the circle, a new thread woven through the old cloth.

He thought at first that the press of bodies had confused the eye and that the few had missed their turn in the circle and would correct on the next. He looked toward the elders to see if their staffs would lift and their voices call for order. The elders saw what he saw. They raised their voices. They did not shout. They sang the plain lines the city obeyed when precision was required, the call to circle and return, the request not to crowd, the reminder that the descent must begin.

The voices did not take. They washed the stone and slipped away. The thin line at the inner edge kept moving. Not many, perhaps a dozen at first, then more as those behind chose whether to follow the circle or to step into the new curve that did not exist the day before. No one pushed. No one ran. There was no panic. The line simply parted like water, and part of it flowed into a place the eye struggled to accept. Taren could not see new stone. He could see only that feet lifted and set down and did not fall.

A woman near him whispered that a child was surely walking where there was no rail, and then the child reached a hand to the inner spine, and the hand found something to hold. The elders' staffs tapped faster; one elder's voice rose in a register Taren had not heard from him, a voice for field fires on dry days. He asked the new line to stop, to turn, to return to the old path. Some did, blinking as if surprised to find themselves on the edge of a choice. Others did not seem to hear a choice. They kept the measured pace the tower taught and were swallowed, not by air, but by a turn that remained just ahead of sight.

Taren felt the crowd shift under the weight of decision. Some pressed toward the descent in sudden obedience, as though the surest safety was to complete the rite with no delay. Others froze with their hands on the apex stone, eyes on the inner edge, mouths a little open. A few stepped into the new path with a set to their shoulders that looked like relief. The square below filled with noise as those at the base saw bodies continue upward where none should. The noise rose and fell and could do nothing at all where he stood; sound does not climb stone as readily as bodies do.

He thought to edge closer to the inner curve, to see whether stone truly met foot, but the press of people and the earnest work of the elders kept him where he was. Then, in the clean space between two robes, he saw a face he knew. The body that carried it moved without hurry, eyes forward, mouth relaxed. Hair cut short as when he had last seen it. Master Halem had died of winter fever two years before. Taren had stood outside his door with the others and had heard the low speech of those who keep the watch and name the virtues that mattered. He had watched the small procession carry the covered form to the river.

Here Halem climbed as if the last two years had been a task completed and set aside. He did not look left or right. He did not place a hand on the apex stone. He took the new turn with the same untroubled attention he had given to a wall when its plumb pleased him. Taren tried to say his name. The sound caught in his mouth like a breath saved too long. He tried again. The name left him and was eaten by bodies and stone. If Halem heard, he did not show it. The robe brushed the inner spine. For an instant Taren thought he could reach out across the narrow and touch the cloth. The space bent in a way he could not follow, and the robe was a step farther than his arm could name.

He stood there with his hand lifted half a span and let it drop. He was not the only one who knew a face where there should have been none. A woman two bodies away had gone pale enough to take the light of the slit window into her skin. She pressed her palm to her mouth and kept it there, not in grief, but as if to keep a word inside its proper place.

The elders' chant altered. It stopped being instruction and became supplication. They asked the stair to close the path that was not a path. They asked the city to remember its measure. They promised to circle again if that would please whatever had opened. The words did not make a seam that the new line could not cross. The sound of feet went on with a steadiness that took no notice of what could not be reconciled.

At last Taren found himself moving again because the body behind him had taken the descent and there is a politeness that governs even the moments when a world tilts. He descended with the guild ring, each step placed where a thousand had already risen. The square came up slowly into view, a field of faces lifted to the summit, hands shading eyes, some calling, some silent. Aric stood in the colonnade with his slate hanging at his side, forgotten. He looked not at Taren but at the inner edge where the thin line had become a thread nearly woven through and gone. When their eyes met, Aric did not ask and Taren did not answer. Each held a count that was not a number.

At the base the elders gave the blessing that closes a rite out of habit, as if the words might persuade the day to return to ordinary shape. Cups of water went into hands. Children were gathered, and names were called, and people said they were fine, they were fine, thank you. Taren stepped aside to let the flow pass him and stood against the tower's outer curve with his palm against the stone. It was warm again in a band the length of a forearm, as if someone had leaned there just now and then moved away.

He did not speak Halem's name a third time. He did not look for someone to agree that he had seen what he had seen. He watched the crowd begin to separate into those who had decided that no harm had been done and those who would speak low in doorways for the rest of the day and those who would not speak at all. He waited until the square loosened and the tower returned to mere height. Only then did he cross to the colonnade where Aric had finally lifted his slate to make a mark he did not wish to write.

***

The square thinned by degrees until the people remaining were those who lingered after every rite, the ones who take longer to return from a public breath to a private one. The elders conferred in the shade of the arcade, their staffs set upright beside the benches. Aric stood with his slate and a line of figures that no longer wished to be arranged into sense. Taren waited until the last cup was emptied and the last blessing spoken out of habit. Then he crossed to the maintenance door as if he meant only to check a latch and see that a hinge had not stiffened.

Inside, the stair held the warmth of the day in the first turns, then gave it up to the night as he climbed. He did not call the words for workers. He placed each foot with a care that made no sound. At the mid-level landing he touched the inner spine where he knew the chalk crescent lay somewhere below him now, invisible in the new tone the groove had taken. His palm met cool stone and a trace of warmth running under it like a thread that had not yet cooled.

He climbed on. The turns felt narrower than they had in the morning, or it may be that the air felt closer. The slit windows opened at their accustomed intervals, yet what they framed had shifted. On one turn the window gave him a slice of sky he knew by heart, the familiar low constellation that rises late in the year. On the next, the window showed a field of stars that sat too near, bright and crowded, as if the tower had leaned toward them. On the third, he looked out onto a pale wash, light like morning when it was not morning. He stopped and looked again, and the wash paled further until it became the ordinary night the city had worn the hour before. He could not tell whether the change lay in what was outside or in the way the window expressed it.

He kept climbing until his breath settled into a measure that did not belong to him alone. The stair taught breath here, and he had learned that lesson all his life. Tonight the measure tightened and drew him slightly forward, the way a rope draws a boat when someone takes it up. He let it carry him a turn and then another. The sounds he made began to have the quality of sounds already heard, his foot at the groove, the soft touch of palm at the spine, as if his own passage were an echo that had found its original.

Above him the sound of other feet came soft and regular, not hurried, not heavy. He expected the small variations he knew so well, the stutter of a child, the double tap of a walker who favors one knee, the whisper of cloth from a robe that runs a little long. The sound above was of one pattern only, a common metronome that did not require bodies to differ. He reached the next window and looked up along the curve.

They were there, not many at first, then more when his eye learned to see what the stair expected him to see. Some wore robes cut like his own, cords dyed in the lattice colors, sandals with the city's make of sole. Others wore cloth that fell differently, goat hair and rough weave, shapes from drawings he had seen in the guild archive showing processions a century and more ago. One man's garment caught the light like water; it was cloth he did not know, smooth with a sheen that belonged to no dye he had handled. A child's shoes reflected a thin glimmer with each step, a trait he could not place in any leather or wood. Haircuts shifted from row to row, from long to close to a manner he could not name. Faces were themselves and not themselves, features softened as if the stair did not care for individual edges.

None spoke. The only voice was feet and cloth and breath drawn at the turn. When a shoulder brushed the inner spine ahead, heat rose a little in the stone under his hand. The warmth fell away as the body moved on. He tried to match his pace to the pace of the nearest procession, and his legs agreed before his mind did. He let that carry him until he felt the need to test his own will against it. He lengthened one step by a fraction, and the next, the stair allowing deviation for a count of three and then inviting him back to the old measure with a patience that felt like care.

He climbed into a level where the windows opened not to the square or the roofs of his ward, but to skies that belonged to other conditions of the same place. Once he saw a horizon lined with dark shapes in water where there was no water in his city, masts like reeds against a low sun. In another window he saw no sky at all, only a weather of pale green that moved like silk being shaken. He did not linger to resolve any of it into explanation. The stair did not pause to allow a longer look, and what the stair did not sanction was difficult to do.

The processions braided and unbraided in front of him, passing in the same space without collision, as if each kept to its own thread even where threads crossed. A woman carrying a child who might have lived two centuries before lifted her heel in the groove an instant ahead of a man whose robe hem was stitched with a pattern Taren had seen only this year. Their feet did not touch; their breaths did not disturb one another. The stair held them all and required only that each one honor the measure. He understood then that the tower was no longer binding a city to a sky. It was binding a ritual to itself. Bodies were the current that traveled the same channel, always arriving, never arriving. The stone did not limit itself to one day's memory. It carried the whole of its habit at once.

His heart followed the rhythm until the rhythm felt like his heart. He knew how one loses oneself in work, in a wall's rise, in the patience of leveling and plumb; this felt like that, only larger. It would be easy, he thought, to climb and keep climbing here, to let the measure take the burden of choosing from him. The path gave the answer before he formed the question. The impulse to test another pace, to lay a hand where no groove invited one, thinned, and his name for himself thinned with it. Taren became the body that took the next step, and that body belonged to the stair more than to any one man.

He thought of Halem, of the way the master had set a plumb line and then stood very still until the bob stopped moving. He thought of the low voice that had counted courses of stone and of the hand that had lifted his from a mistake without scold. The memory did not arrive as comfort. It arrived as a small stone dropped into a river, a point for the water to pass by. He used it. On the next step he shortened the measure by the breadth of a finger. On the step after that he let his heel hang a fraction over the edge of the groove and then set it down. On the third he exhaled when the stair wished him to inhale. The deviation was small, unmusical, and it hurt to make, as if he had put his weight wrong while carrying a load. The stair did not punish him. It did not acquiesce. It waited with quiet certainty until his body discovered that the old measure was the easier one.

He stopped. He set both hands flat on the inner spine and bowed his head to bring his face close to the stone. He counted seven slow breaths that belonged to no turn at all. The warmth under his palms fell to cool. When he lifted his head, the procession in front of him had thinned, or perhaps his eyes had chosen to stop granting it the favor of being seen. A slit window threw a bar of night across the steps, familiar, ordinary, a view of his own ward's rooftops and the dim lamp Aric always forgot to snuff in the corner of the colonnade.

He took one step down and waited. The stair did not resist descent. It suggested another rise, and when he did not take it, it suggested once more with a gentleness that might have been mistaken for kindness. He did not accept. He set his foot lower again. He kept his breath out of its timing. The sounds above him remained, softer now, or at a distance the ear chooses not to measure.

By the mid-level landing the stair had widened to the width he had known all his life. The windows gave him the sky he could name by season. The groove under his heel felt like carried habit and not like a directive. He touched the inner curve where the chalk crescent had been and felt stone and the faintest echo of warmth fading like heat from a bowl after water has been poured out.

He let himself out into the square and stood with his hand on the maintenance door until his palm cooled. He did not look up to the summit. He did not wish to test whether the impossible turn would show itself from below. He crossed to the colonnade and found Aric still there with his slate. They did not speak at once. Aric dipped his head and wrote a figure he did not say aloud. Taren took the chalk from his own roll and set a mark on the step of the arcade, a small crescent that meant nothing outside a mason's work. It looked too white at first, then began to settle, the way chalk does when the stone near it accepts the idea of it.

"We will count again," Aric said after a time.

"We will," Taren said. He did not say what else he had seen. He did not yet know how to name a stair that had learned to carry all its days at once, and a rhythm that could make a man forget his own measure.

They stood together in the colonnade until the last lamp guttered and the square thinned to the sound of a single cart. When Aric closed his slate, they fixed a night to return and listen after the next ascent, to stand where the hall's echo should end and hear whether footsteps remained.

Taren took the long way home along the edges of the square. The tower kept its height and its quiet. He felt its patience at his back all the way to his door.

***

By late afternoon the square had become a listening bowl. Not an assembly by decree, but a gravity of worry drawing people toward the shade of the arcades where the elders conferred. Stalls remained open out of caution; bread and water were still passed hand to hand; yet fewer coins changed palms. Men and women stood with their baskets against their hips and watched the Spiral Tower as if it might give a sign in daylight as clear as the impossible turn had been at the summit.

Taren stood with the guild, dust still on his cuffs. Aric's slate hung at his side, numbers made and unmade in a hand that did not like erasing. When the elders stepped out from the benches and took their accustomed place at the base of the stair, the murmur of the crowd drew down. The eldest among them rested his staff against the stone and spoke in a voice trained to reach edges without strain.

"The ascent holds us," he said. "This has been true beyond the memory of any here. We climb; we bind the city to the heavens; the world remembers itself."

He did not say what many had seen at the summit. He allowed silence to hold it. Another elder added the words that had steadied countless seasons. "What the tower receives, it returns."

Taren stepped forward before the words could settle into habit. He had not planned to speak; the decision rose through him like breath when a body chooses to call across water. "It does not return all," he said. "Not now."

146

A space opened around him; the guild shifted to give room. He spoke to the elders and to the people beyond them. "I have climbed the maintenance stair since I was a boy. I have patched hairlines; I have chalked wear; I have felt the stone answer under my hands. I tell you the stair has learned its measure so completely that it carries itself without us. We are becoming current in its channel. That is why some do not return."

The first elder listened without impatience. His gaze carried the weight of someone who had heard fear in many shapes and had made a life of smoothing it. "You offer a craftsman's poetry," he said gently. "But the stair is stone. We keep it, we honor it, we climb. If we fail that duty, the anchor is cut. If we stop, the world dissolves."

A woman at the edge of the square lifted her child higher on her hip. "My sister did not return," she said. "She did not step wrong. She walked where there was a step. I saw her robe take the turn that is not there." Her voice did not rise; it carried by clarity more than force. Others nodded, then kept still; agreement in this place had the habit of becoming doctrine too quickly.

Aric cleared his throat and raised his slate partway, as if to ask permission of the air. "The counts fail by more than custom," he said. "Vendors, water bearers, the ledgers of entry, the elders' tallies at the apex, they do not meet in the middle. They have not met for a year and more. I have allowed for error; I have allowed for delay; still the gap remains."

The second elder, a woman with a voice like clear water over stone, answered him with courtesy. "Numbers do not always say what we wish to hear. They also do not always know how to listen. On festival days people linger in the arcades; they re-enter the square from side streets; they go home by quieter ways." She turned her palms outward in a gesture that was not dismissal but plea for patience. "We must not mistake a city's bustle for a stair's hunger."

Taren spoke again, slower now. "I saw processions above when no one climbed. Not one; many. Clothes from our fathers' drawings; garments I could not name. The stair held them at once. It has bound itself to the act of climbing, not to the one day's climb. At the summit this morning an inner line kept moving because the stair supplied it a path. We did not fall because nothing was asked of us except to continue." He looked toward the apex stone as if it might answer. "If we climb simply because the stair can carry us, we are not binding the world; we are keeping a machine in motion with our bodies."

A murmur moved across the square like a breeze that did not decide which way to go. Near the fountain an old man called out that the upper turn was a mercy for those the gods wished to honor; he had seen the same in a story from his mother's mother. A pair of boatmen muttered that the elders had hidden a second stair for years to rid themselves of debtors and loud tongues. A cloth-seller said sharply that people who wished to vanish could do so without using holy steps. The city began to sort itself by what each person feared most: loss by theft, loss by fate, loss by design.

The eldest raised his staff for silence. "If we falter, we loosen the bindings of place. This is known. There was a year when fear kept people home after a tremor; that week the canal ran backward at noon and the river dragged boats against their moorings. We returned to the stair the next morning; the water remembered its course. These are not stories told to keep children obedient. When the ascent fails, the city loosens."

A mason from Taren's guild answered with respect. "Master, with honor for that memory, the stair is tightening now until it has no need of us. If we climb because we are afraid not to, we feed the loop that has begun eating its own tail."

The word eating troubled the air. It was the first harsh line spoken. Taren wished it unsaid and could not unsay it. He lifted his palms to soften it. "I would not dishonor the rite. I ask only that we learn whether the stair will accept a different measure. We could vary the pace by lattice; we could widen the step for a count of three at each turn; we could lift a hand when the stair wishes us to place it. Small errors may break the stair's habit without breaking ours."

A few voices answered at once. Some said it was sacrilege to insert error into what held the world. Others said the elder himself had taught that intention matters more than perfect form. A midwife cried out that living bodies already carry irregularity and the world does not end with each skipped heartbeat. An acolyte shook his head and said the form was the intention, that one could not be altered without unmaking the other.

The first elder looked out over the square and seemed to listen to something beyond the noise. "We will not halt the rite," he said. "We will not encourage deviation from a measure that has kept us. If some have been taken into the stair's memory, we will entreat for their return, but we will not break the line that steadies us." He glanced at the other elders;

they nodded as one. "If we stop, the world dissolves." The words did not sound like threat. They sounded like grief foreseen.

Something in the crowd shifted from listening to deciding. People gathered themselves into smaller knots at the edge of the square and began to speak without the elders as center. Taren watched it happen with the slow recognition of someone who knows the sight of stone separating along a seam it has hidden for years.

At the western arcade a group of traders agreed to keep their families from the next ascent until questions were answered. At the fountain a circle of elders from the river ward announced that they would bring the oldest among them to climb twice in a day if that was what it took to tighten the binding. Under the bell-stone a few men and women who had watched the inner line with relief said they would go again by that path if it presented itself; they spoke of a peace they had felt when their feet found what the stair offered. Names began to form around the knots. Those who would stop called themselves Holders; those who would climb harder called themselves Sealers; those who would welcome the upper turn called themselves Continuants. The names were not official; they were only words spoken aloud for the first time, and already they behaved like doors.

Aric touched Taren's sleeve. "If the guild proposes a change," he said low, "you will need a plan that a careful man can count."

"We can mark the turns," Taren said, mind already sorting the stair into a sequence of small tests. "Every third window we vary the pace; every seventh, we lift the hand from the spine; we make the errors visible so the city does not mistake them for collapse." He pressed his lips together a moment. "It may be enough to prove the stair listens to us, still."

A younger elder approached them, not the eldest, a man who had once served a year in the stone yard to learn what he asked of others. "You will not teach the city to fracture its steps," he said, not unkindly. "If you do, you will stand outside the circle until you recant." The word outside carried weight in a city that solved drift by bringing what strayed back into rhythm. To stand outside was not punishment, it was solitude with edges.

Taren bowed because the habit of respect holds even when a man disagrees. "I do not wish to stand apart," he said. "I wish only that we remain the ones who climb."

Night gathered at the top of the square. Lanterns were lit. The Spiral Tower held its pale. People began to move away in currents that matched their decision. A husband drew his wife from the base with a hand set gentle on her back. Two old women linked arms and went together to the arcades where the Sealers had already begun to gather water jars. Near the bell-stone a small group stood very straight and looked upward at the slit windows, as if the stair might open for them without asking.

Aric and Taren stood together until the last voices thinned. "We are writing the next column without ink," Aric said. "I would have preferred a quiet ledger."

"So would I," Taren said. He looked up once more at the summit where the morning had grown a curve out of air. The tower gave him back nothing but height and a long patience that did not belong to any one day. He felt the city decide around him and knew that the next ascent would not be one ritual but three braided together in a space that had learned how to hold more than one thing at once.

***

He waited for full dark and for the square to go thin as paper. The factions had drifted to their corners: the Holders set lamps along the arcades and spoke of closing the stair at dawn; the Sealers filled jars and rehearsed the old lines in tight unison; the Continuants stood beneath the bell-stone and watched the slit windows as if watching a tide. Aric had urged patience; numbers liked morning. Taren nodded as if he agreed and took the guild key anyway.

Inside the Spiral Tower the air was cool and even, the way a deep cistern holds temperature when weather changes above it. He climbed without a lamp. The windows gave him narrow portions of the night, then nothing. His body knew the measure and took it whether he wished it or not. At the summit he stepped onto the platform where the city leaves its breath and laid his palm against the apex stone.

The stone answered with patience, the same patient cool he had felt since he was a boy. He set his tools down in a row as if he were about to repair a crack. There was no crack to mend. There was a joint, old as the first builders, where the apex stone took the load of the last turn and gave it down into the spine. The seam had been laid with a lime richer than the rest, with fines sifted so thin that the joint read as a shadow more than a line. The guild taught that no one touched that seam; it was the keystone of the measure.

He knelt and cleaned dust from the margin with a soft brush. The act steadied his hands. He held a chisel against the seam and did not strike. He held a small wedge of cedar and did not place it. He unrolled chalk and set it aside. Choice will not be hurried if it is to be more than reaction. He sat back on his heels and allowed the three paths to come to him as clearly as the seam itself.

He could break the stone. He pictured it with craftsmanship, not drama, the blunt blows, the spidering of hairlines, the first piece lifting away like a tooth. He imagined the seam unseating and the stair giving its weight to air, the tower shuddering as a harp shakes when a string is cut. He imagined the city waking to a tower that had ended, the square filling with a panic that had not yet found a name, water running where it should not, the canal lifting and sliding backward at noon, roofs losing their angles for an hour at a time. The thought did not frighten him as a child would be frightened; it repelled him as a craft betrayal. Destruction was a last language, and he could not speak it while other words were left.

He could surrender. He imagined three steps forward into the inner line when it appeared at dawn, the set of the foot, the breath taken at the turn. He imagined letting the stair decide his pace and his purpose, imagined feeling his name thin until it weighed no more than dust. He thought of Halem's face in the impossible curve. There had been peace in that face, not triumph and not despair, the settled attention of a man doing the work in front of him. Taren could enter that peace and be carried. The thought tempted and did not convince. He was a keeper of stone; his work was to hold the language of making and unmaking without being swallowed by either.

That left alteration, the thing the elders had forbidden and that the city had begun to argue for or against with a fervor that turned tools into banners. He did not wish to lead anyone. He wished to test whether the stair remembered its duty to the people as well as the people's duty to the stair. If the stair had learned to carry itself perfectly, perhaps imperfection could teach it to listen again.

He began as a mason does, with measures so small that a careless eye would call them nothing. He took the cedar wedge and shaved it thinner until it was no thicker than a thumbnail, then thinner again until it was the thickness of a line drawn with good ink. He slid it under the edge of the seam at a place where the limestone had a tiny undercut, a prevention left by a builder cautious of future settling. The wedge did not lift the stone; it suggested a different angle to it. He felt with the skin of his fingers rather than the mind of his craft and felt a change like the change when a door hangs true and then is given the gentlest pressure to favor closing.

He breathed and waited. The platform returned his breath with no alteration he could name. He took the chalk and drew a mark at the very edge of the seam, not a crescent this time, but a small line that asked to become the beginning of a longer line and then did not. He stood and walked a slow circle around the apex, placing his feet deliberately out of the groove and then, at the last instant, letting them drop back in. He lifted his hand from the spine where the habit would have set it, then set it down a heartbeat later with courtesy, as one returns a borrowed thing. He hummed a single tone, then missed it on purpose by the breadth of a breath, then moved back to the tone the stone preferred. He did not force; he offered.

The first answer was nothing. He took a second circuit and a third. On the fourth, when he had begun to believe that craft and care and the finest wedge in the world could not teach a tower, the seam spoke through his palms in the language the body knows. A faint tremor ran through the apex and down into the spine, not a shake, a reconsidering. The windows gave a minute shift in their frames, enough to change the angle of a bar of moonlight by the width of a fingernail. The stair under the first turn held its groove, yet the groove felt less like instruction and more like invitation.

He did not rejoice. He checked instead, the way a builder checks a wall that has chosen to stand by staying. He took the cedar out and the seam settled back with relief or with indifference; he could not tell. He slid the wedge under again at a different point and felt the same thread of change. He drew three marks in chalk at three windows, simple notations that a guildsman could see and a pilgrim would not notice, a quiet code for where the city might vary if it chose.

When he had done as much as he dared, he sat with his back against the spine and let the tower carry his breathing for a while. He was tired in the way work makes a body tired when it has been done without spectacle. He closed his eyes and found the measure again becoming his measure instead of the stair's. The choice had not been between three doors that shut behind him; it had been between one door and three ways of standing in its frame. He had chosen to stand and place a wedge.

Near dawn the square began to find its voices again. The first water jars clinked. A boy ran across the paving stones and then slowed, remembering yesterday's instruction without knowing he had remembered it. Taren rose and picked up his tools. He smoothed the chalk with his thumb until it lay in the pores of the stone the way the crescent had learned to do. He wiped the cedar with his sleeve and put it in his roll, not because he meant to keep it secret, but because the first telling of a thing should be done with a steady voice.

At the maintenance door he paused and looked back at the apex. It looked like stone. It looked like patience. It looked like a seam that would hold a city if a city held it. He touched the inner spine once before he went down and felt cool beneath his palm, then a thread of warmth, as if the stair had woken for a moment and found it pleasant to be spoken to rather than obeyed.

By the time he stepped into the square the elders were waking the arcades. Aric was already at his post, slate open, hair tied. Taren did not cross to him at once. He walked the base of the tower and set his hand at each of the three chalked windows, as a man checks hinges on a door that he has hung. He found them steady. He found them willing.

He went to Aric at last. "If we are to count," he said, "let us count a change. Every third window we will widen the step. Every seventh we will lift the hand. We will make it visible so no one mistakes it for collapse."

Aric studied his face, then the tower, then the chalk that was no longer visible unless one knew where to look. He nodded as a careful man nods when numbers may be had, not certainty. "We will count," he said. "And if it listens?"

"Then we are not only current," Taren said. "We are still builders."

He took his place at the rear third of the line as the city gathered. He did not know whether the wedge had done anything a body could feel once the mass of the people pressed their breath into the stair. He did not know whether the impossible turn would open again no matter what men did with chalk and cedar. He knew only that when the bell-stone struck he would take the first steps in the old measure and, at the third window, he would do a small difficult thing against habit and call that courage craft.

***

Dawn did not hurry. The square filled as it always did, lines forming with a competence that any visitor would have called peace. The elders took their place. Aric stood with his slate. Taren set himself in the rear third with the guild, his palms cool, his mouth dry, his eye on the third window where his chalk lay inside the pores, invisible to any who did not

153

know to look. The cedar wedge sat in his roll like a quiet word he had already spoken.

The bell-stone sounded. The sound did not ring out; it sank into the stair as if into water. The first row rose; the second followed; breath matched breath. Taren climbed, counting not numbers but turns; he let the stair take him until the third window cut a thin bar of light across the steps. He stepped wide by a finger's breadth, then set his foot with a softness that refused the groove's command. He lifted his hand from the inner spine where habit would have placed it, then returned it a heartbeat later as courtesy rather than obedience.

For an instant nothing changed. The measure wanted him back. His body offered to comply. The wedge under the apex seam was only a suggestion, and suggestions are easy to ignore when a city is in motion.

Behind him he heard the slightest stutter in the guild ring, a breath caught and released. In front of him an older woman who had taught two generations to cut stone lifted her hand when he did, not because she had seen him, because her bones knew the weight of a change that meant no disrespect. Two steps up, a boy whose sandals still creaked with newness widened his foot and then, surprised at himself, kept going. Three bodies do not bend a stair, yet three bodies can teach a line how to try.

The fourth window came; the seventh came; at the seventh he lifted his hand again. A whisper ran the length of his ring, not speech, the sound of cloth and breath as measure shifted and settled. The elders' staffs tapped the platform above with the patient insistence of a life spent persuading a city to keep; their chant did not change. The Continuants at the base lifted their faces, waiting for the inner turn that had opened yesterday. The Holders in the arcades watched for collapse as if their vigilance could hold the walls up if stone changed its mind. The Sealers moved with admirable regularity, feet exact, hands low, the past held hard in muscle and intention.

At the summit the circle formed. Hands met the apex stone; palms read its patience. Taren placed his own, then turned and began the descent. Half a ring behind, a thin thread at the inner edge remained poised to walk into air if air became stone. It did not. The stair held the old curve. The impossible turn flickered like a thought considered and set aside. A few who had waited for it stumbled when it failed to appear, then found their feet and came on with the rest.

There is a kind of silence that follows danger avoided and another that follows danger delayed. The square held the second. People descended with a hesitance that was not fear and not relief, the way a house breathes after a tremor when nothing has fallen and yet the dishes tremble in their cupboards. Aric's chalk moved in small strokes. His counts met in the middle for the first time in a year. He did not smile; he did not trust it; he wrote the numbers as if they might alter while the ink was still wet.

Taren reached the base and stood aside. He set his palm against the outer curve where the warmth usually ran like a thread after a rise. The stone was cool. He did not know if that meant anything. He listened. The stair made the small sounds of a tower that has just held many bodies; after that, nothing. He looked toward the elders. They spoke the closing blessing. Their voices did not break.

The square did not return to market at once. People stood in the doors of their day as if unsure which way to open them. The Holders nodded among themselves with the grave contentment of a prediction that has not been disproved. The Sealers began to stack jars and coil ropes, planning to climb again at noon to tighten what had been loosened by error. The Continuants looked up at the slit windows with a patience that did not belong to the hour; they did not argue; they simply waited to see whether the stair would learn to want what they wanted.

Taren walked the base once, a hinge maker checking hinges, touching the three windows where he had drawn chalk into the stone. He felt only stone and a faint wondering in his own hand, as if his palms were uncertain whether they were readers or writers. Aric came to him with the slate. The numbers were complete. The columns met. Names matched faces. They had all returned.

"Reprieve," Aric said, not as comfort and not as decree.

"Reprieve," Taren answered. He did not say for whom. The city or the stair.

By midday the square loosened. Stalls opened. The smell of bread came back strong. The day put on its ordinary shirt and pretended not to notice the seam where it had been mended. Taren took the long way along the arcades. He passed the hall where Aric kept his ledgers and listened for the extra sound that had made a careful man doubt his own hearing. Silence lay there; it was a relief that sat strangely upon the air, like a debt deferred.

He slept in the afternoon and woke at dusk to a city that had decided, for the moment, to believe itself intact. He went to the tower in the blue hour when light forgets its arguments. The maintenance door gave beneath his hand. Inside, the stair was cool from base to mid-level. He placed his palm on the inner spine and felt nothing more than stone and the memory of grip. He stood with his eyes closed until his breath and the tower's breath parted like two men who have walked together to the edge of a square and then taken different streets home.

He might have left the story there, but collapse is not a single event; it is a pressure that finds the seams of a life and works at them with patience. On the night after the reprieve, someone in the river ward heard water lapping at a quay at an hour when the tide should have been flat. In the lantern quarter, three lamps refused to darken until a door was opened and closed in a particular order that no one remembered learning. In a narrow lane under the north wall a woman stopped with a basket on her hip and waited for a group to pass, only to find the lane empty and the sound of sandals moving by in a rhythm she could not see. She stood until the last of the phantom steps had gone and then walked on with care, as one does after a thought one cannot put down.

The Spiral Tower did not open the inner turn that night. It did not take anyone. It did not answer to a call. It stood in the square with its pale patience and its slit windows dark. Yet in the civic hall Aric closed his ledgers and blew out the last lamp and stood for a moment with his hand on the doorpost. He listened. The hall should have gone clear. The air should have shed the day. From somewhere above him, faint as dust but regular as a clock, came the sound of footsteps taking a turn and beginning a descent that did not arrive.

He did not call Taren; the hour was wrong for calling. He stood and counted; he lost count and began again; he walked to the colonnade and opened the door onto the square. Night air came in. The sound did not alter. He closed the door and leaned his forehead to the wood. The steps went on, soft, patient, untroubled by whether anyone listened.

In his small room, Taren lay awake with his hands open on the coverlet and heard nothing at all. That was worse. He imagined the wedge under the apex seam and the chalk hidden in the pores of the stone and the way the groove had felt under his foot when he chose against it. He imagined other places in the city where the day had learned to repeat itself too well. Ritual holds, he thought, until it begins to keep itself.

The night ended. The city woke. People put on their work and their names. The Spiral Tower kept its height and its quiet. Somewhere under that quiet a measure continued, not loud, not cruel, only sure of itself. It would wait for bodies to carry it, or it would learn to walk without them. Either way, the sound would remain.

And sometimes, in the middle of the day when the square was brightest, a person would pause at the edge of the market with a basket against the hip and a thought half formed, and in that small stopped moment they would hear it, steady and soft, the sound of endless footsteps when no one climbed.

Cycle III
The Ledger of Breath

The river lay flat as hammered tin. At the West Ferry the weir posts should have shown a faint shiver where the flow leaned against last season's ward. Nothing moved but a slick skin and a slow tug on the ropes. Bad sign.

Veyna Correl stepped down from the ferry plank and tasted silt and last night's rain on the air. She touched the marker stone with the back of her fingers. Cool and honest. Grain ran true. The anchor was present. She nodded to the levy sergeant beside her.

"Renderability check," she said.

Kade Thorn lifted two fingers. The squad shifted without fuss, shields out, eyes on the reeds. Sen Marien, smallest of the three scribes, set his toes to the edge of the plank and lifted his chin.

"Witness quorum, six. Breath on four," Veyna said.

Marien counted. "One. Two. Three. Four."

The first arrow came from the reed bed on the left, shallow and mean. It scraped a shield, bit into a wicker basket, and spun to the deck. The second arrow was honest. It took a levy through the cheek and he went down on a knee without a sound. Truce broken.

"Hold the count," Veyna said.

Marien did not flinch. "One. Two. Three. Four."

Kade moved. He took the forward corner and the next two men fell into line with him. He did not waste breath on curses. The ferry bucked as the current pulled, and the levy behind him vomited neatly over the side and then set his shield again. The reeds quivered and a man stood up among them with a scrap of red cloth tied to his arm. He cut the guide rope on the old weir with three quick motions.

Veyna was already at the marker post. Bone stylus out. Soot ink drawn low in the vial and topped with a finger of residue. She wrote as the deck tilted and steadied and tilted again. She did not look up.

"Lexeme Still-Water," she said. "Binder, river mark. Scope, weir span. Checksum on four."

Marien's count kept its pace. "One. Two. Three. Four."

The bone tip found the groove that an older hand had worn last year. The spiral bit. The ink darkened as residue took. The current pushed hard at their knees and the ferry rope sang with strain. Kade grunted and drove his shoulder into a shield, turned the rim, and broke a man's teeth with the butt of his spear. Another arrow skittered along the deck. The levy with the slashed cheek toppled into the water and was carried under the ferry in a heartbeat.

Veyna closed the final line. The spiral set like a lid. The river's skin lifted into a near-invisible plane that ran from post to post. The ferry steadied under Kade's charge as if set on a table. The rope tone dropped. The marker stone gave a humming answer that she felt through the meat of her hand.

"Effect holds," she said. She capped the vial and did not notice her hand shake until the stopper slipped. Kade's palm closed over hers for half a breath, steady and hard. She finished the seal.

The fight on shore lasted three minutes. Kade's squad hit waist deep and pushed through the reeds, shields up and spears short. The men they met there were not trained for a shield push. They were hard, angry men with knives and oars. Two went down in the first rush. One levy drowned when a cut rope whipped his ankles and took him under. Kade dragged the third man out by the collar, rolled him to the mud, and set his heel on the man's neck until he stopped thrashing.

The reeds burned quickly once the oil caught. Smoke drifted over the weir. Veyna stood where she could watch the post and the line of the water. The line held with a clean note. She breathed with Marien's count until the counting settled into her bones.

"Clear," Kade said. He held one arm close to his ribs where an arrow had left a shallow groove. He spit black phlegm and wiped his mouth.

"Quorum still present," Marien said. His voice shook now that the noise had stopped. He shut his eyes, counted four more, and only then looked down at his ink-stained fingers.

Veyna knelt by the dead man with the arrow through his cheek. She pressed his eyes shut with the back of her knuckles. "Write his name," she said.

"Kerrin," Kade said. "Miller's boy."

Marien took his board and chalked the name cleanly in the margin column. Breath calmed. Ink calmed. The world had answered because they had asked it correctly.

They pulled the ferry to the landing. The ferryman's wife stared at them from behind a shutter. Veyna counted residue vials by lot and season, eyes flicking between wax seals. Kade sent two men to watch the west path and three to scout the slope above the reeds.

"Losses," Veyna said.

"Two dead," Kade said. "One drowned. One with the cheek. Berrit with a hole in the thigh. Stitches will hold. Rope rash on three. Light."

"Light," Veyna said. She wrote it down. She logged the residue used in three firms marks and underlined the lot number. She wrote her own hand steady by force of will. The hum from the post had settled into a new baseline. She listened until she knew it by heart.

A woman in a gray shawl came quick along the bank with two boys behind her. She was not a soldier but she had the posture of someone who ran a ledger and expected it to balance. She halted when Kade lifted a hand.

"Mother Arel?" Veyna asked.

The woman nodded once. "Counting House," she said. "The truce was a lie. Hark took our auxiliary rolls at first bell, set fire to the dry stacks, and put a knife to my clerk. I gave him nothing from the master books. Can you walk and write at the same time, Binder?"

"We can," Veyna said.

"Good. Come," Arel said. "If he gets the master names you will be writing water with a broom."

They moved through lanes that stank of smoke and river weed. The old wall loomed on the right with pale mortar and carved stones that had been set by dead hands and held for a hundred years. Children watched from doorways with serious eyes. An old man threw a bucket of water at a smoking eave and swore softly when it splashed his shoes.

Veyna put her hand to the wall in passing. The grain in the keystones at the alley arches ran true. The anchors were present. She took one residue vial from her pouch and weighed it with her fingers.

"How many rolls did he take?" she asked.

"Three dozen," Arel said. "Mostly births, some adoptions, two name changes. Enough to make a mess of your perimeter if he decides to play clever."

"He is not clever," Kade said. "He is mean. It comes close from a distance."

"Mean can break a bridge," Arel said. She stopped at a heavy door with iron straps and hammered once with her fist. The hatch slid open and a young woman peered out, red-eyed and streaked with ash. She let them in and barred the door behind them.

The Counting House was tight and square and smelled of ink, clay, and dust. Shelves climbed to the ceiling with rolls wrapped in waxed linen. Two long tables ran down the center with chalk slates, quills, and boxes of clay seals. The far corner was black with smoke and wet with bucket water. A corner of a shelf had slumped from heat and weight.

Arel pointed with her chin. "He took from there," she said. "He knew what to grab. I need your ward on the door. Then I need you to get my rolls back."

"We will do both," Veyna said. She laid her kit on the nearest table. "Marien. Witness posts, there and there. Four and four."

Marien set two stools at the corners and pulled three more scribes from the back room. They were clerks in aprons with tired hands and ink on their sleeves. They did not look like fighters. They did not need to.

Kade put two men on the windows and two on the door. He nodded to a levy whose lip shook. "Breathe," he said. "Four counts with them. Hold your shield up and you will live."

The doorframe was old oak, stained and slick. Veyna ran her thumb along the jamb and felt where the grain stood proud. A good binder would take, hold, and release clean. She mixed a narrow ribbon of residue into the soot ink and set her compass arms at the right spread.

"Quiet now," she said.

Marien's voice found a steady lane. "One. Two. Three. Four."

"Lexeme Threshold Seal," Veyna said. "Binder, keystone grain. Scope, portal only. Checksum on four."

The first mark took like a nail. The second dragged until she adjusted the angle and set the compass to the thickness of the wood. On the fourth count the marks closed and a pressure settled in the air like the weight of a hand. The door seemed heavier by a fraction, not to the eye but to the body.

Kade touched the frame with the back of his knuckles. "Feels like a good shield," he said.

"It is a good door," Veyna said. "The seal will last until we break it."

Arel watched her with a clerk's hard stare. "You can make a wall of air at a ferry," she said. "Can you make men give back what is not theirs?"

"Not with a seal," Veyna said. "We will take it back with hands."

Arel's mouth thinned. "Good. Plan, then. He has maybe thirty men at the old granary. Five outlaw scribes. They use blood and spit. They are quick and they do not care if a thing is safe. He has a knife for any clerk he finds."

Veyna moved to the chalk board and drew the street grid in five strokes. She placed a dot for the granary. She marked the river and the Old Span. She put a cross for the weir, two crosses for the square where Lethrin would stand, and small circles for breath posts.

"We take the rolls first," she said. "We stop his scribes from cutting you out of your own name. Then we go to the Span and take the keystone."

"Why the keystone now?" Kade asked. He had a strip of linen pressed into his ribs and blood had dried into a dark square at one corner.

"Because if he cannot break the bridge, he cannot move his people fast enough to spoil the trial," Veyna said. "Because the river respects its own mark. Because I can write longer on stone."

Kade nodded. "Good answers."

Marien was pale but steady. "What do you need for witness posts, Binder?"

"Eight for the house," Veyna said. "Four for the granary approach. Six for the Span. All quorums aligned to a four count. We will use Quietus for the stairwells, Still-Water for the weir approach if he cuts more rope, and Loadshare on the arches once we reach the bridge. No Countermarks unless we have anchor confidence."

"Understood," Marien said. He set chalk marks on the floor to pace the breath.

Arel folded her arms. "When the Concordance is written," she said, "who keeps the ledgers?"

"The Scriptorium," Veyna said. She met the woman's eyes. "Chain of custody is part of the rite. If the ledgers wander, the anchors drift. We will take your clerks on as sworn keepers. Their hands will still write. Their ink will be ours to certify."

Arel's jaw worked. "I keep my people employed and my books intact," she said. "I will argue about the crest on the seal later."

"You can argue in the square when the wards hold," Kade said. He did not smile. He did not need to.

A boy stuck his head in from the side room. "Hark has men in the alley," he said. "Two with slings. One with a pot of something that smokes."

Kade lifted his shield. "We go," he said.

Veyna capped the ink. She slid the residue vial into its slot and pressed wax to seal it. She took her compass and bone and board. She put her hand to the frame one last time and felt the pressure. The door would hold.

"Breath on the move," she said.

Marien set the count. "One. Two. Three. Four."

They unbarred the door. The seal released like a hand lifting from a shoulder. The alley smelled of smoke and river weed and meat cooking somewhere far down the lane. A stone clinked off Kade's shield. He did not duck. He stepped out, turned the rim, and the men behind him matched his pace.

Veyna followed, bone ready, eyes on stone and timber and the faces of the watching. The city could be written. It would answer if asked correctly. That was craft and work, not luck. She felt the count in her chest and stepped into the noise.

***

They took the alley in a tight file. Kade first, shield up. Two levies behind him with short spears and knives. Marien and the other scribes in the center with boards held to their chests. Veyna near the rear, eyes on lintels and grain, bone ready.

A sling stone rang against Kade's shield. He did not break stride. The alley dogged left by a stacked woodpile and then narrowed at a run of stairs that climbed between two plastered walls. Smoke drifted from the far end, sharp and bitter.

"Quietus corridor," Veyna said.

Marien did not wait for permission. He planted his feet on the first step and lifted his chin. "Witness quorum, six. Breath on four."

"One. Two. Three. Four."

"Lexeme Quietus," Veyna said. "Binder, collective breath. Scope, stairwell and landing. Checksum on four."

She scribed small, neat marks on the plaster where the treads met the wall. The ink took at once. The sound of boots dulled to felted thuds. Shouts from the far landing cut as if packed in wool. Kade was moving the moment the fourth count touched. He drove the rim of his shield into a man crouched at the top step, pinned him against the post, and finished him with a short spear thrust that went in above the hip and came out wet.

A second man swung a hooked blade at Kade's knee. The levy behind Kade kicked the blade hand, hard and ugly, and the knife skittered. Marien kept the count. A sling stone hit the wall by Veyna's ear and left grit in her hair.

They cleared the landing in a crush. A third man tried to run. A woman in a brown dress reached from a door and pulled him inside by the belt. Kade checked the door with his shield, would have gone through, then flicked his eyes to Veyna. She shook her head once. He moved on.

On the far side of the landing the alley opened into a small court behind the old granary. The granary door stood open. Smoke rolled from inside. Two men with slings on the roofline had bags at their feet. One stooped to gather stones, the other had a pot in his hand that smoked and stank like burning hair.

"Left roof first," Kade said. He did not shout. The two spearmen with him nodded. They ran the roof man down with a ladder that had been left leaning by the wall. The man threw the pot in panic. It hit the flagstones and burst into foam that smoked and crawled like angry soap. One levy slipped and went down to his knees, shield over his head, teeth bared.

"Countermark," Veyna said. "Short radius."

She stepped in, kept clear of the foam, and overprinted the binder sigil scratched in the pot shards with a brisk set of marks that followed the glassy arc. She chose a binder she knew was stronger because the flagstones carried a true grain that had held wards for decades. The foam stopped crawling. It sighed and sank into a sour-smelling puddle.

"Inside," Arel's boy said, pointing. "They took the rolls that side. I saw them."

Kade spared one look for the roof. The second slinger had jumped to the next house. He was running along the ridge, legs pumping, sling twirling. Kade passed his spear to the levy at his elbow, snatched up a loose roof tile, and hurled it. It clipped the runner's calf. The man flailed, missed the ridge, and disappeared between the houses with a sound like a sack of grain dropped from a cart.

They went in.

The granary had been a storehouse when grain still came downriver by barge. The bins were dry now and used for ledgers, oiled tools, lengths of rope, and whatever else the quarter ward could not keep in the Counting House. The smoke came from a stack of ledger rolls shoved against a support post. A man in a dirty red scarf knelt there with a brand. He meant to kill names.

Kade was on him before Veyna could speak. He took the brand arm with his shield rim. Bone made a sound like a spoon against a stone bowl. The man screamed. Kade's knife went in low and out higher. The man tried to hold his belly shut with his good hand and failed.

"Buckets," Arel said. She was already moving with three clerks. "You, breathe. Stop shaking. Bring water."

They formed a chain from a rain barrel to the burning rolls. Veyna went along the smoking binders with quick, small marks that cooled the heat by aligning the grain of the post against the stress. This was not real fire magic. It was craft. The tools answered.

Marien kept count. His voice had a new steadiness to it, like a string pulled to pitch and then left there.

"One. Two. Three. Four."

They saved enough. The far bin had three dozen rolls that were still dry. The top layers of the smoking stack came away wet and ugly. The bottom rolls were gone, cooked to black tubes with no names left inside them. A clerk sobbed once and did not do it again.

Veyna lifted one saved roll and weighed it with her hands. "Births," she said. "Month five, years twenty to twenty three."

"Good," Arel said. She nodded to a clerk who began to count and list. "You see why I asked for a seal on my door."

"I see," Veyna said.

A shout went up at the front. Kade was already moving that way. A man with a shaved head had been hiding under the bins. He came up with a short iron spike and drove it into a levy's thigh. The levy cried out and staggered. The man spat on his fingers and drew a quick scrawl in his own spit on the flagstones.

The levy's artery opened in a bright sheet. He clapped his hands to the wound and made a mess of it. He would be dead in a minute.

Kade palmed the back of the man's skull and slammed him into the bin hard enough to crack the wood. He did it once, then again. The man dropped the spike. Kade pinned one of the man's hands with his knee and reached for his knife.

"Wait," Veyna said.

Kade's face tightened but he did not cut.

Veyna knelt by the dying levy. She pressed both hands into the wound and held like she meant to keep a door shut against a storm. "Marien," she said. "Cadence on four. Loud."

Marien counted. "One. Two. Three. Four."

"Lexeme Threshold Seal," Veyna said. "Binder, flesh line. Scope, wound only. Checksum on four."

She traced a tiny mark with the bone tip in the blood at the wound margin where the cut edge held its shape. Not anatomy, not miracle. Grain in flesh follows lanes like grain in wood when it is cut clean and recent. On the fourth count the bleeding slowed to a ooze. The levy's breathing evened. Veyna held five more counts and then wrapped the thigh with a length of linen, hands steady now.

"Berrit," Kade said to the levy. "Look at me."

Berrit stared. He looked like a boy. Kade nodded once. "You live," he said. "You hold the door at the Counting House. You do not fight on the Span. That is an order."

Berrit cried and laughed at the same time, a wet hiccup of sound. Two men took him under the arms and half carried him.

Veyna stood. She looked at the shaved head. He had his palms flat on the floor now and his eyes wide.

"No," Kade said to him. "You do not get to spit another line."

He put the knife in quickly, under the jaw and up, and pushed the man's head against the bin so he would not thrash. He breathed once when it was done, not out of pleasure but because bodies need air.

Veyna did not scold him. She wiped her hands on a rag and looked to the door. "We have enough rolls to proceed," she said. "Arel, send two carts to the Counting House with guard. Keep the rest of your people inside. Quorum posts on the square in one hour."

Arel nodded. She was pale but her eyes were hard. "Bring me back my rolls and I will keep the breath posts with you."

They left the granary through a side door and took a covered lane toward the Old Span. Smoke lay low. The river sound grew louder, a long iron noise that came up through the stone.

Halfway there Kade stumbled. He had taken a cut earlier. The linen at his ribs had gone from pink to rust to black. He kept moving until Veyna put her hand on his forearm.

"Stop," she said.

"I am fine," Kade said.

"You are not," she said. "Under the arch."

They ducked into a narrow stone alcove where two houses leaned toward one another above the lane. The space was shadowed and smelled of old damp. A run of mortar had fallen away and left a rough pocket in the wall. The squad fanned out and took the corners without orders. Marien set himself in the mouth of the alcove and faced outward, board tucked to ribs.

Veyna cut Kade's tunic with her knife. The cut was clean and long. The skin at the edges had gone pale and hard from cold and fear and time. Blood seeped slow now, but the shirt held a clot that would not last through a fight.

"Sit," she said.

He sat. She cleaned the wound with water and cloth and a pinch of salt from her kit. He hissed at the sting. She did not pause. She threaded a bone needle and sewed in small, square stitches that held the skin without puckering. Her hands were swift and practical. She had done this before.

"Breath," she said.

"Counting," Marien said from the alley mouth. "One. Two. Three. Four."

She felt Kade's breath rise and fall under her hands. He watched her face. His eyes had the flat look of a man who has come close to dying and then walked past it. He reached for her hand and stopped halfway. She took his fingers and set them on her wrist to feel the count.

She looked at him, then at the space above his shoulder where the mortar had fallen out. It made a pocket that would take a sigil.

She stood and wrote a small, tight seal on the upper stone. "Lexeme Threshold Seal. Binder, mortar seam. Scope, alcove only. Checksum on four." The mark closed and a soft pressure settled, enough to steal the echo from footsteps in the lane. It would not stop a blade or a hard shove. It would give them a breath.

They did not speak for the next few breaths. He reached again. She did not turn away. He put his hand at her hip, slow and careful, and waited. She crowded into him with no ceremony and no debt. He tasted salt and smoke. The seal hummed under her hand where it met the stone.

Marien kept the count. He faltered once, flushed, and steadied. "One. Two. Three. Four."

They kept it brief. Time pressed in on them from both ends. She braced a hand against the stone and felt the smooth pressure of the seal change as it wore. His hands were hard where they held her. He did not try to be gentle. He did not try to take more than she gave. He came away from it breathing like a man who has climbed a long flight of stairs with a weight on his shoulder.

When it was done she tucked her shirt, fixed his bandage, and checked the stitches. He pushed his head against the wall and closed his eyes for one count. She broke the seal with a thumb and the air lifted. No vows. No words they did not mean. There was work.

Kade stood. He rolled his shoulder and tested his breath. "I can move," he said.

"You can," she said. She did not smile. She wanted to.

They stepped back into the lane. The squad fell in around them as if nothing had happened. Marien did not look at their faces. He lifted his chin.

"One. Two. Three. Four."

The Old Span rose ahead, three arches of dressed stone laid by hands that had known line and weight. The river took the arches one by one and pushed at them with a steady force that had no anger in it. Civilians crowded the bridge, pressed against parapets and bollards, trapped by the fight and the fear that if they left the middle they would be swept away by whatever was about to happen.

"Parity counts," Veyna said. "Every fourth step."

Marien called it. Kade signaled the men along the parapet to spread the instruction. The crowd began to step in a rhythm, uncertain at first, then more certain as bodies found the cadence. The bridge answered that rhythm in a way that was not sound but something under sound. The weight moved across the spans in an even wave.

Hark's men held the far parapet. They had looped a rope around the keystone of the middle arch and were feeding it through a crude pulley toward a barge below. The line was tight. Five men heaved at the barge, trying to drag the keystone enough to fracture the joint. A scribe in a dirty blue scarf crouched over the stone with a blade, tracing a blood line along the seam. He was fast. He would cut deep enough to take the keystone out of the grammar of the arch if he had time.

"Line," Kade said.

He led the push along the near parapet. Shields up. Faces set. The first sling stone hit Kade's shield and bounced into the river. A man in front of him stabbed with a spear and took a knife under his arm for his trouble. Kade stepped over him and used the rim on the knifeman's jaw. The jaw went crooked. The man folded.

Veyna climbed onto the parapet where the middle arch began. She set her compass. The stone at the top of the arch was glass-smooth from years of hands. She put her palm down and felt the grain under the polish. It was there. It ran true.

"Witness posts," she said.

Marien planted two clerks on either side of her, feet set, boards close. He drew the cadence up from his chest and made it carry.

"One. Two. Three. Four."

"Lexeme Loadshare," Veyna said. "Binder, parity count. Scope, arches one through three. Checksum on eight." For large structures she preferred a longer count to match the span.

She wrote four marks on the first arch, four on the second, four on the third, then closed the first set and moved down and closed the second set and then the third. The stones under her hands seemed to lean into the marks like animals leaning into a harness. The rope that had been tight around the keystone slackened by an inch. The barge heaved and the men on it swore and hauled and gained nothing.

The outlaw scribe in the blue scarf looked up, saw her, and bared his teeth. He had a narrow, sharp face and eyes that danced with a kind of joy that had nothing to do with happiness. He slapped his palm against the blood line to smear it, then cut again along a different angle. He meant to shear the joint rather than pry it.

"Keystone," Veyna said. "Threshold next."

Kade reached the center with three men. He took a knife on his shield and punched with the rim. He moved like a man whose limits were clear to him and nearby. He did not waste anything. He pushed the outlaw scribe off the keystone with his shoulder and the man skipped along the coping and would have fallen if he had not caught the rope.

The blue-scarf scribe swung on the rope like a boy at festival. He laughed, cut at Kade's wrist, and then turned the blade in his hand and slashed at the blood line he had drawn on the stone, trying to complete it on the fly. He was quick. He valued quickness more than correctness. It made him dangerous for one minute and dead after that.

Veyna began the keystone seal. "Lexeme Threshold Seal. Binder, keystone grain. Scope, portal only. Checksum on eight." She pulled a small dram of residue and set it into the ink. Not necessary, not yet, but good practice on a large span with a hostile rite nearby. She set the compass arms for the grain width and scribed at the inner lip of the keystone, where the curve ran into the spring of the arch.

The crowd counted. The arches breathed. The load went from one to two to three and back, even and stable, like a man stepping from stone to stone across a ford.

The outlaw scribe swung back toward the keystone and reached for the blood line again. Kade caught the rope with his off hand and yanked. The man lost his balance and his knife hand went wide. Kade kicked him in the chest. The man pinwheeled, hit the barge rail with his back, and went into the gap between barge and pier. The river took him. His knife came up once and then was gone.

A fresh rush from Hark's men tried to break the cadence. Three came at Kade together. He blocked one, took a cut on the rim from the second, and almost lost his footing when the third hooked the bottom of his shield with a spike and tugged. A levy at his shoulder put his spear into the tugger's throat and leaned his full weight on it. Kade stepped into the second man's space and they went to elbows and teeth and knees on the coping stones. Kade ended it with a headbutt that split both their brows.

"Close," Veyna said. The last marks on the keystone took. The seal settled like a weight at the pit of her stomach. The rope around the keystone loosened as if the stone had turned in its sleep and shrugged the line away.

The men on the barge pulled and swore. One let go and sat down hard, laughing in a breathless way that had no mirth in it.

"Hold the count," Marien said. His voice was raw. He held anyway. The clerks with him were crying and not leaving their posts.

Hark of the Ditch himself stood up on the far parapet then. He wore a leather coat with iron rings set into it and a cap that had once been blue and was now the color of river mud. He looked at Veyna across the span. He put two fingers to his mouth and whistled. Men who had been waiting under the far arch rushed up the steps.

"Remnant push," Kade said. "Brace."

Veyna would not be able to keep writing and live if the rush reached her. She stepped off the parapet to the inner walk and put her back to the keystone. Kade planted himself next to her, shield high, feet at a good angle on the wet stone.

"Countermark only on my call," Veyna said to the scribes. "If he brings a real binder."

Hark's rush hit like a small wall. The near line buckled and took two steps back. Then it held. Kade's shield took a mace blow that would have crushed a head. He felt the shock in his shoulder and did not let the rim dip. He punched with the lower edge, hard at a knee. Something gave. He had no time to see what.

The first outlaw to reach Veyna tried to slip a knife under her arm. Kade caught him by the collar and threw him into the parapet. The man's head hit stone. He slid down and did not get up. A second man swung at Veyna's board. She stepped back, let the blow take air, and pricked the man's palm with her bone stylus as he overreached. He flinched in surprise. Kade smashed his shield into the man's face and then stamped on his foot hard enough to break bones.

"Hold," Marien said. The breath posts along the span had picked up the count. The sound came back from the far end like footsteps in a long hall.

Hark saw it was not going to break. He spat into the river and backed away with a dozen men. He did not run. He had the sense to keep what he had left. The men on the barge cut their line and let the rope drop.

"Amnesty," Veyna said, once the last blade had cleared the rim. "Call it."

Kade lifted his chin. "Any scribe who surrenders marks and tools walks out alive," he said. "Hands up. Step away from the edges."

Two moved at once. A third hesitated, then came. A fourth turned as if to step forward, reached to his belt, and came up with a spit-damp blade instead. He scrawled fast at his own feet with a cut he made across his wrist.

Kade was there before the line could resolve. He put the man down with a simple strike that did not look like much. The man made a small sound and stopped moving. Kade toed the blade away and wiped his mouth with the back of his hand.

"Three live," he said. "Search them."

Marien's count eased. He sagged and then straightened at once as if his spine had remembered its work. Veyna checked the keystone again by touch. The seal hummed low and even. Loadshare still moved weight across the arches like a tide.

She let herself look at Kade's face. There was blood on his cheek from the headbutt. His eyes were clear. His breath was up but not ragged.

"Hold the Span," she said to him.

"I will," he said.

She turned to the surrendered scribes. They were young. One had blood to the wrist where he had made his cut and then thought better of finishing the mark. He looked sick.

"Your marks and tools," Veyna said. She held out an oiled cloth. "Lay them out. Carefully. No tricks. If you try to write in the fold of a glove or on the back of your teeth I will let him throw you off the bridge."

They laid their tools on the cloth. Bone, cheap copper compasses, a blade that had been a kitchen knife in another life. Veyna looked at the marks tattooed on their fingers and the lines on their palms.

"You can walk with us to the square," she said. "You will hand these to the Scriptorium in front of witnesses. You will give your names into the rolls. If you do that, you will live. If you run, you take your luck."

They nodded. The one with the blood to the wrist looked at Kade. Kade looked back without interest.

Mother Arel pushed through the crowd then with two clerks and a satchel. She had dirt on one cheek and a scrape on her arm where she had fallen. She did not notice.

"You have my rolls?" she asked.

"Enough of them," Veyna said. "We can proceed."

Arel stood on the inner walk and looked across the arches to the far ward, to the weir lip, to the signal tower beyond. She took in the Loadshare cadence in the bodies of the crowd and in the little changes of posture that people make when they match a rhythm without knowing it.

"Then we do it," she said. "Before the light goes."

Veyna nodded. "We do it," she said. "Marien, post the breath at the square. Kade, hold the Span with half your men and send the rest to the Counting House. I want a line from here to the door and no man walking with unsealed hands."

Kade began to divide his squad. He put the steadier men on the bridge. He sent the younger ones to the House, paired with clerks who would keep them from stupid choices. He caught Veyna's sleeve for half a second and then let go.

"Later," he said.

"Later," she said.

The sun slid toward the roofs. Smoke hung over the far ward like fog that had bad thoughts. The river took light and played it under the arches in broken bands. Veyna set her board under her arm and felt the grain of the keystone through the palm of her free hand. It was true. It would hold through the rite.

"Breath on four," Marien called from the square. His voice had carried down the street and onto the bridge. The first witnesses took the cadence at their posts. The old stones seemed to listen.

Veyna looked once more at the city they were about to write. Then she went to meet Lethrin in the square.

***

The square was already packed when Veyna arrived from the Span. Boundary stones at each corner bore old mason marks polished by years of hands. Compasses stood on tripods, copper legs braced and aligned to the carved lines. Breath posts had been chalked on the paving at even intervals, each with a clerk or apprentice in place, eyes forward. Residue jars sat in a row on a low table, wax seals unbroken, each labeled by lot and season.

Lethrin waited at the dais in a plain blue coat. He had the posture of a man who had spent most of his life standing at tables and persuading others to do what was correct. He nodded once to Veyna as she climbed the steps.

"Anchor survey complete?" he said.

"Span secured, keystone sealed. Counting House under guard. Ledgers intact enough to bind," Veyna said.

"Good," Lethrin said. "Measure residue."

She broke the first wax seal, weighed out a dram with the tin scale, and mixed it into her soot with a paddle. The ink shifted to a deeper black as the ash took. She set the vial on the table and steadied her hand. Marien lifted his board and took his place to her right.

"Witness quorum at posts," Marien called. "Breath on four."

The cadence rose from the square like a tide coming in. "One. Two. Three. Four."

Kade held his line at the east alley mouth. He had left a skeleton guard on the Span and doubled the corners of the square. His men looked tired and mean. Their shields were nicked white at the rims and spattered with smoke and blood. He rotated the worst of the wounded back to the House and placed two of Arel's clerks with every squad to keep counts and eyes on hands.

Lethrin unrolled a vellum rubric and read the standard in a voice that carried without shouting. "By authority of the Master of Standards and with consent of the Counting House, let the perimeter wards, floodworks, signal towers, and public thresholds be bound to a single Anchor Concordance. Let proper names serve as conceptual binders, breath cadence as collective binder, and witness quorum as scope assurance. Let residue be employed as stabilizer according to lot and season. Let chain of custody for referents be held under seal of the Scriptorium."

He paused. The crowd was quiet in the way that happens just before a ritual, not for love of spectacle, but because people feel when something is about to take hold.

"Proceed," he said.

Veyna went first to the north stone, the one with the deep mason's star and a chip at one edge. She placed her palm to it, felt the cold, and then scribed the first figure with the bone tip steady on the count.

"Lexeme Perimeter Bind," she said. "Binder, proper-name rolls, master set. Scope, north quarter. Checksum on eight."

Marien raised the cadence. "One. Two. Three. Four. Five. Six. Seven. Eight."

The marks closed and pulled tight like a knot under tension. A clerk read out the name rubric beside her, voice even. A second clerk traced the names as she spoke them, touching the rolls with clean hands. The stone gave a low answer that could be felt more than heard, a hum that settled behind the ears.

She moved to the west stone. Same figure, different scope. The ink took with a rich black line that dried clean and held its gloss. The copper compass legs shivered once and then stilled as if they had found their line.

At the south stone a murmur ran through the crowd. A handful of Hark's men tried to push in through the south alley, rags tied over faces, hands in sleeves where small blades hide. Kade saw them at once and moved his file without hurry. The first man swung a club at a clerk. Kade took it on the rim and broke the man's wrist with a short twist. The second reached for his belt and got a shield in the mouth. The third tried a spit-trace at knee height and got a boot on his hand before the line could close. It was ugly and short, the sort of work no one sang about or wanted to watch. The men who could still walk crawled back the way they had come.

"Hold the count," Marien called. The posts did not break.

Veyna finished the south stone and crossed to the east, where the pavement had a long crack that split the lines of the old mason's work. She adjusted the compass arms to match the grain and wrote in the gap. The figure closed with a click of bone on stone. She breathed out and felt the square answer, a pressure like a hand on the crown of the head, neither heavy nor light, simply present.

"Perimeter bound," Lethrin said. "Floodworks."

They crossed to the weir marker set into the paving near the river stair. The stone was damp and cold and tasted of iron when Veyna touched it. She measured a second dram of residue, thin this time, enough to seed acceptance without leaning. Two ferrymen in clean shirts held posts at either side and breathed with the count, eyes forward, hands still.

"Lexeme Still-Water," Veyna said. "Binder, river level mark. Scope, weir span and sluice gates. Checksum on eight."

Marien's voice lifted and spread across the river stairs. People on the steps took the count up without being asked, as if the breath had moved from one set of lungs to another through the air. Veyna wrote the spiral neatly and closed it with the stop stroke she had learned as a novice. The answer came up through the soles of her feet and into her hands where they lay on the stone. The river's skin steadied a fraction, the kind of change only men who worked the water or wrote the wards would feel.

"Signal towers," Lethrin said.

These were a sequence. Veyna placed copper compasses at the four corners of the square and a fifth on the low waterpost near the river. Marien sent runners to the base of each tower with flags to show alignment. A boy climbed the ladder of the nearest tower and sat very still with a rope looped over his wrist to ring the bell if told.

"Lexeme Concordance Signal," Veyna said. "Binder, proper-name quorum. Scope, tower sequence one through five. Checksum on eight."

She wrote the first figure on the base stone of the nearest tower and finished on the count. The boy raised his eyes when the line closed. She moved to the next, then the next, making small adjustments to compass spread to match the cut of the base stones. Lethrin walked with her and checked each closure with two fingers, not touching the ink, feeling only the pressure in the air.

At the final tower she paused to blow a bit of grit off the stone, then closed the last mark with the same neat hand she had used on the first. She did not rush. She did not speak any words that were not part of the rite.

"Final checksum," Lethrin said.

They returned to the center. Veyna set her palm flat on the dais stone. Marien took his place at her shoulder. The posts drew breath together as one, a whole square of lungs pulling the same air.

"Checksum on eight," Veyna said.

Marien counted. The crowd picked it up. The sound moved through the square like the run of a drumline before a march. "One. Two. Three. Four. Five. Six. Seven. Eight."

Veyna wrote the closing figure into the dais stone, a small seal that did not look like much. The last line met the first with a clean, almost inaudible click, the sound a good lid makes on a good jar.

The hum began at once. It came out of the stone and the river and the bridge and settled into the mortar of the walls and the old wood of the doors. It was not music and not wind. It was agreement.

Signal towers lit in sequence, lamps catching one by one from the west tower to the east. A bell tolled once, then twice, the rope lifting the boy's wrist. The weir lip took the new line like a coin laid on a table. The crowd did not cheer. They let out a long breath they had been holding all day.

Lethrin rolled his rubric closed and tied it with a leather thong. "Binding travels," he said, solemn and satisfied. "No quiver."

Veyna kept her hand on the stone until the hum settled into a baseline that felt like a heartbeat under the soles of her feet. She let go. Her fingers had a faint dust of ash on them from the residue, gray on gray. She wiped them on a rag and capped the ink.

Kade walked up with his shield over his shoulder and blood dry on his cheek. He did not mount the dais. He looked at the towers and then at the people without much change in his face.

"It holds," he said.

"It holds," Veyna said.

"Then let us do the work after the work," Lethrin said.

They counted the enemy dead in the lane behind the east posts and the alley where the granary opened. They stacked bodies in two piles and carried a smaller heap to the river where the priest with the cracked bowl said the few words that men always said at the water. A team of levies and clerks took spades to the ground outside the south gate for their own. Kade stood with them and passed water, then took a shovel for a while without being asked. He said very little. He tamped the soil with the flat of the blade when they were done.

Mother Arel came to the dais with a ledger under her arm and stood very straight. Her jaw was set. Veyna met her eyes and laid out a parchment already prepared, seals and ribbon ready.

"Edict of custody," Veyna said. "The Counting House and its rolls come under Scriptorium seal for the duration of the Concordance and for the maintenance of referents thereafter. Your clerks will be sworn keepers and paid under Scriptorium scale. Your office remains as it stands, but keys and wax pass to Standards."

Arel read it carefully, lips moving once or twice as her eyes went over clauses. She put her hand on the page and left it there. "I do not like the taste of this," she said. "But I like the taste of smoke and lost names less." She tapped the line where pay and status were guaranteed. "I will hold you to this."

"You will," Veyna said.

Arel nodded, set the ledger down to sign, and used her own seal on the copy that would stay in her desk. She handed over the key ring without drama. It felt heavier than it looked.

Lethrin pressed the Scriptorium seal into warm wax at the bottom of the edict and lifted it to cool. "Done," he said.

The dead were buried by dusk. A boy whose voice had not yet changed sang four lines his mother had taught him and forgot the fifth. No one minded. Men washed hands and faces at the pump in the square and left dark rings on the stone. The lamps took the evening.

Marien sat on the steps of the dais with a novice primer open on his knees. He sharpened a quill with a small knife, wiped the edge on his sleeve, and wrote in clean, even letters on the inside back cover where proverbs live.

Ink remembers what stone forgets.

He thought about striking the line and writing it again smaller. He left it as it was.

Kade stood at the edge of the square with two of his men and looked toward the bridge. He rolled his left shoulder and winced. Veyna came down the steps, wiped her hands one last time on the rag, and checked the residue jars. Two were empty, two half full, one untouched.

"Rest your line," she said to Kade.

"I will rotate patrols," he said. "Span, House, and square."

"Good," she said.

They did not touch. They did not need to.

Night took the Old Span by degrees. The last of the light stayed under the arches as it always does, turning the water flat and dark. Wind moved through the reeds on the far bank and made the sound reeds always make when no one is standing close to hear them.

The wards held. The breath posts took their turns through the night, counting in quiet voices that rose and fell, a low thread in the dark. Dogs stopped barking and slept with their noses on their paws. The signal towers kept their order, lamps steady and calm.

On patrol change Veyna crossed the mid-span. Kade came the other way with his shield on his back and a fresh bandage under his shirt. They paused in the middle where the keystone seal hummed softly, pressure you could feel in your teeth if you thought about it.

They looked at one another for a breath. No vows. No promises. Both knew better than to speak words they could not keep.

"Even counts," Kade said.

"Even counts," Veyna said.

They passed each other and kept walking. The city breathed on the four. The world answered because it had been correctly written.

The Ash and the Glyph

The first ash clung to the downstroke of the letter for bind.

Alreth leaned close, breath held, to see whether the darkness on the vellum was simply thickened ink. A slant of afternoon came through the violet-glass panes and turned the motes in the scriptorium to slow weather. The mark did not shine like wet ink. It matted the surface like soot.

He rubbed with the side of his thumb. The smear deadened the curve of the glyph and left his skin gray. When he lifted his hand, a faint thread of ash trailed from the vellum to the whorl of his thumb, as if reluctant to let go.

"Another botched trace?" Marien asked. Her reflection hung a ghost inside the glass. In the room itself she stood three desks away, arms full of etched vellum for first years. She wore her hair in a tight coil so ink could not find it.

"It is not ink," he said.

Marien tipped her head and did not come closer. "It will be to them. Wipe the edge clean before you teach the sequence."

He waited until she had gone. Then he lifted the vellum to the light. The ash did not fall.

He scraped the downstroke with a fine bone edge. The ash gathered at the blade and refused to leave it, as if it preferred the shape it currently held. The letter for bind is simple. Even a novice can keep the curve from collapsing into itself. Alreth had written it a thousand times from first principles, without bound phrases. The world ought to have recognized it.

That night, the ash followed him home.

It sifted from the cuffs of his robe when he reached for the latch and whisked into the seam between door and jamb. It gathered in the corner of his room, a private drift. When he shook his sleeves over the basin, the water did not darken. The ash did not wet. He went to bed with the smell of old hearths lodged in the hair near his temples.

In the morning, one of his dissolutions left a shadow.

A binding dissolved with clean lines should release its stored will and leave no trace. This one let go, then wavered as if trying to decide whether to remain. A faint afterimage hung in the air. When he looked away, the afterimage imprinted itself more deeply, as if his attention were a stylus pressing too hard.

"Stress," the master of chambers said when he reported the misfire. "Too many commissions. Take three nights of dream-sleep and walk the lower wards. Keep your eyes on ordinary things."

Alreth walked the lower wards and the ordinary things did not hold. Posters lost their letters. A chalkboard refused a rag. A student forgot the word for hinge mid-argument and called it a door-joint, as if language could be fixed with a substitute peg.

On the sixth day, while tracing Hama, the unity of cause and effect, his inner picture of the glyph broke. Not on the vellum. In the mind. The second loop would not carry weight. The arc fell into echoes. His breath stuttered. The room pulsed without sound.

When the pulse eased, ash lay in the curl of his ear.

He did not report that.

He went to the stacks no one praised.

The Kessari codices smelled of dye, copper, and unclean fire. He read until the light was blue through the violet glass. He read about heretics who claimed the First Tongue was not universal but held together by taught agreement. He read about ink cults that used ritual mispronunciations to thin the world and make it take a new impression. He read a pamphlet that warned, in a hand taught to hide its education, that the glyphs worked because the mind could resolve them, not because reality owed them obedience.

When the scriptorium closed, he went beneath it.

Below the practice rooms and the lecture halls lay a city of stone ribs and mortar, tunnels older than the College and the city both. There were alcoves where the wall plaster still held traces of letters sanded down to appease a later faith. There were rooms with fissures in the floor that breathed salt air on a tide that did not care whether it was day or night. In one such room, set like a lichen on the wall, he found a chalk mark: the letter for silence, but cut one stroke short.

The short stroke stung the eye. It promised and withheld in the same gesture. He traced it in the air with his finger. The ash in his cuffs thickened.

Marien's shadow blocked his light.

"You have not slept," she said without greeting.

"I am reading," he said.

"You are reading sideways," she said. "Your path through the stacks has started to drift. You used to move along a subject. Now you jump glyphs like stones in a stream you are eager to fall into."

He looked at her hand on the lamp. Ink had found one knuckle. He wanted to lift her hand and wipe it away. "Do you see the dust on my cuffs?"

"I see dust," she said.

"Watch," he said, and traced the letter for bind in air. The ash rose like breath in cold weather, a faint line that made the letter visible until it was gone.

Marien set the lamp down. "Do not do that again."

"You did see it."

"I saw something," she said. "That is not proof that it should be done."

He gestured toward the chalk mark. "The Kessari spoke of a glyph that refused itself. A trace that takes the mind to the place where tracing fails. There is a reference here to an orrery that taught grammar to machines. If I can find it, I can know whether what is failing is me or the tongue itself."

"Or you can teach in the morning and eat with the rest of us and sleep like a man who remembers he is made of meat," she said. "Your students do not benefit if you begin to argue with your own letters."

He tried to smile for her sake and failed. "What if the letters are arguing with me."

"Then you do not need to answer them alone," she said.

He answered them alone.

The encoded reference at the base of the chalk mark sent him into the south annex, past doors that whispered when they closed. The Orrery of Forgotten Grammar lived there among broken articulation plates and gears that once sorted vowels by taste. The orrery was the size of a summerhouse. Its rings were etched with shapes that had been letters until someone with more power than patience declared that letters should never look like that.

He stood beneath it so the shadow of a discarded alphabet fell across his face and chest. He put his palm on the lowest ring. The metal was room-cold. He felt nothing and then the faintest tremor, as if something written elsewhere had just been read aloud.

Two words arrived without walking: Resolution Horizon.

They did not sound in the ear. They stood up inside his thought as if they had always been there and had been waiting to be noticed.

He spoke them and choked, not because he could not say them, but because saying them felt like asking a question he had not earned the right to ask.

Not a storm. Not a spell. A limit. A place beyond which the mind cannot resolve the world with enough clarity to stabilize it. The glyphs work because they can be rendered by a mind that knows how to hold lines. The First Tongue is not eternal. It is useful. It is a ladder we mistake for a wall.

Alreth pressed his forehead to the ring and stayed there until his breath slowed. When he stepped back, fine gray marked the bronze where his skin had touched it. The orrery had kept his ash.

He started drawing letters the College did not teach.

The first was a curve that approached itself and never closed. The second was a box whose top refused to meet. The third was the letter for silence lacking the short stroke. He drew them in charcoal on paper at night and on the stone of his study in water that left no color. If he closed his eyes, the lines traced themselves on the inner back of his lids, and the curve of his skull ached as if it had been taught a new function that did not fit cleanly.

The day he traced the Silent Aspect in full, the dormitory across the courtyard filled with the smell of overcooked metal. Three students vomited. One of the automatons that fetched water stiffened mid-step and stood as if remembering a different task. The lamplight in the corridor did not brighten or dim. It changed its mind about what bright meant.

"He is not casting," one of the masters said. "He is channeling. Through broken symbols."

"He is sick," said another. "Or mad."

Marien went to his study and found him scrawling on the floor in charcoal, ash, and something that might have been blood if the room had smelled of iron. It did not. It smelled like copper and dye from the Kessari wing and the air inside the south annex when the orrery's rings turned in an empty room.

She knelt and took his hand. His fingers trembled like a man who has held a note too long. "Alreth," she said. "You are scaring people."

He looked at her as if from far away, through letters he could not bring to heel. "You are not scared enough."

"Then teach me why," she said.

He laughed once and the laugh caught in his mouth and became a cough. "If I teach you, I will teach the thing that is teaching me. You are sturdier than I am. You will carry it further. That would be a use. I do not think I should use you like that."

"You think you are protecting me," she said, and held on.

On the thirty-fourth day, the breach came.

He began the Silent Aspect again. His hand made the first curve. The ash streamed from his sleeves so thickly it turned the air gray. The room darkened, not from lack of light, but from a failure of the names of things to keep their edges. Desk lost its word. Wall lost its word. The door stood without reference.

Marien put her hand on the doorframe so her body could tell her where it was.

Alreth looked at her and could not find her name, only the memory of a contour she had used to carry it. He opened his mouth and nothing in particular came out. He looked at his own hand and could not remember the word hand. He remembered a letter he had once drawn to mean it, and that letter unhooked itself and drifted like a leaf in a stream without banks.

He smiled then with tears running at the same time.

Marien moved toward him slowly so the floor would remember it was a floor. "Stay with me," she said. "Not with words. With your eyes."

He tried. His eyes met hers and found purchase in the wet center where light goes to tell the mind what it has seen. He breathed, and the breath nearly became a word and then wisely decided to remain breath.

The ash poured from his sleeves like smoke from a home that looks the same from the street and is gone inside.

"Marien," he said, and this time the name arrived. It came from some-where simple, like a child. "When the line refuses to be a line, nothing is wrong with the line. The mind has reached the limit of what it can stabi-lize. If I hold harder, I break."

"You can let go without falling," she said, not sure whether it was true and deciding that saying it could make it more true.

His lips formed a letter she had never seen. For a moment he was fully himself and then he was the shape of the letter and then he was ash.

He did not burst. He did not burn. He loosened. The air filled with fine gray that moved as if remembering wind. It took the shape of his hand and then it did not. It made the curve of his name and then it refused to close.

Marien stood in the doorway with ash on her tongue and understood that if she tried to breathe him back into a form she recognized, she would lie to the world because she could not bear the truth. She did not do it.

The masters sealed his chambers and named it script-decay syndrome. They wrote two neat reports with ordinary words in ordinary order. They stored his notes in the Restricted Vault. The notes degraded into semiotic dust. The vault smelled like copper for a week.

Marien kept the page he had left on his desk.

On it was a single line: We were never reading reality. Only the story we agreed to see.

She folded the page and carried it in the inner pocket of her robe until the fold broke and the paper remembered it was pulp. Then she took the page to the place below the scriptorium where the chalk mark still hung with its short stroke missing. She held the page there until the thin air in the fissure breathed out and pulled the paper in. She let it go.

After that, she did not walk the lower wards to soothe herself. She walked the south annex when no one watched. She stood beneath the or-rery until the shadow of discarded letters brought her hands to rest at her sides. She pressed her forehead to the lowest ring and let the metal take her heat.

She did not draw the Silent Aspect. She practiced smaller refusals. The letter for door without its hinge. The letter for bind with a gap left on purpose. The letter for name where the last stroke does not close the loop, which is to say the letter that admits it is a mouth and not a coin.

When the first-year scribes asked why she left the top of her letters open a hair, she said it taught the mind to be gentle. When a chalkboard refused a rag, she did not scold the custodian. She wet the cloth, softened her own gaze, and called the board by a simpler word, and the chalk let go.

One night, she dreamed of Alreth with ash in his hair. In the dream he was tracing a curve that never closed and laughing as if someone else had told him a joke he had been trying to remember his whole life. She woke with her thumb on her own brow and the sense that she had learned where a small hinge in the bone might want to move.

In the morning she taught a lesson on Hama. She spoke the sequence and watched the second loop hold without wobble. She asked the class to set down their styluses and look at one another's hands. "The letters work," she said, "because we can hold them together. We forget that. We call them eternal. It makes us proud and dull."

"Is that heresy," asked a boy who had been taught to make questions safe by smiling when he asked them.

"It is a kind of care," she said. "It is a way to keep our pride from making us foolish."

That afternoon, beneath the orrery, she wrote a line in the dust with a wetted fingertip and waited to see whether the line would keep its edge. It did. Then she broke it with one decisive dot. The dot pulled a thread through the dust that did not show on the surface. She felt a tremor along her palm as if someone far away had just read a letter and decided not to be lonely.

She went to the chalk mark and wrote the missing short stroke in. The mark looked complete and immediately wrong. She wiped the stroke away and left the promise that did not close. The wall breathed out. The ash in her cuffs did not thicken.

That night she dreamed of the Resolution Horizon and woke before saying the words aloud. She did not need to say them. She had found their size.

When the College held its memorial for Alreth, the master of chambers spoke the ordinary sentence for a death no one knows how to name. Marien listened and did not argue because the sentence was a small net that kept people from falling into the hole of not knowing what to say. After the ceremony she went to the south annex with a basin of water and a cloth.

She washed the floor where Alreth had scrawled his refusals. The ash lifted from the stone and hung in the air in a shape that remembered a man's shoulders. It was not him. It was the way a story stands up when the person is gone. She bowed to the story and went on wiping until the stone smelled like stone.

When she finished, she sat beneath the orrery and rested her head against the ring. She felt the faint tremor again. The orrery had taught grammar to machines that no longer moved, and now it taught patience to a person who was learning to be a hinge.

"You were right not to use me," she said to the empty room. "I will use myself instead."

The air did not answer. The rings did not turn. The violet light through the south windows deepened toward evening. Somewhere above, in a corridor with a normal clock, a bell marked the hour.

Marien stood and wiped her hands on her robe. She went back to the scriptorium and taught the letter for bind. She left the top of the curve open by a hair and did not explain unless asked.

At the end of the week she found a page tucked under her desk blotter in an unfamiliar hand. On it was the letter for bind with the top strangely elegant. The student had seen what she had done and made it beautiful. Beneath the letter was a line: We were never reading reality. Only the story we agreed to see. Then a second line in a cramped hand that had not been taught to hide: We can agree to see better.

She put the page in her pocket and felt it warm against her ribs as the day wore on. In the evening she took it to the vault wall and held it there until the fissure breathed. The wall kept it. She went home and slept without ash in her hair.

In the dream that came before morning, a room pulsed without sound and a curve approached itself and never closed. A laugh arrived, then a breath. She did not try to turn either into a word.

The Wars of Name

Checkpoint at the Old Span

The bridge was three stone arches laid by dead hands that had understood weight. In calmer years the arches breathed with the city, taking the push of bodies and giving it back through the piers. Today the middle arch groaned.

A rope was strung across the span. Four men in mismatched coats had painted their shields with a crude crest: a book, a cup, a coin, all on the same field. One kept a slate. People halted under his chalk.

"Ledger form," he said to each traveler. "Say it."

An old woman with a basket said a soft temple-name the priests had given her last spring. The slate man nodded. He marked the name in a neat column and waved her through.

A butcher in a leather apron said the name that stood on his trade contracts. Another guard shook his head. "Wrong book. Speak the Scriptorium form."

"I am not Scriptorium," the butcher said.

"Then you do not cross," the guard said.

Two more voices rose behind him. A mother carrying a wrapped child. A boy with a sealed courier tube. The slate man kept marking. The line thickened.

On the coping of the middle arch a young guard knelt with a vial of black ink. He spat into it, shook it twice, and pressed his thumb over the wax seal as if that would make the lot true. He traced a fast seal on the edge stone where the parapet met the arch.

"Do not write on the parapet," a fishmonger said. "The bridge already carries a bind."

The young guard slapped the stone anyway. The mark shone with a gloss that looked too clean to be honest. For an instant the parapet felt heavier in the palm of the hand, as if a lid had been set on a jar. Then the shine went flat. The seal turned Hollow, perfect to the eye and empty to the world. The parapet shivered. People cried out and shoved. Step rhythm broke into two cadences, a temple half-count on the left and a market workbell on the right. The Loadshare that usually spread weight between arches hiccuped. The arch groaned again, lower and more tired.

Captain Jore Kadev came up the west approach with twelve men, shields worn from the week. He did not shout. He lifted his hand and the squad formed two ranks that filled the width. He walked to the rope and cut it with a short knife. One of the painted shields dropped in front of him. The man behind it swallowed and stepped back until his heels met stone.

"Lower your boards," Kadev said. "All of you. You can hold opinions without holding a crossing."

The slate man hugged the slate to his chest. "Without forms there is no order," he said.

"Without the arch there is no city," Kadev said.

Someone in the press threw a brick. It skipped across the surface of shields and hit a traveler in the face. The traveler folded and did not get up. The crowd lurched. The young guard with the bad ink reached for his vial again. Kadev took three quick steps and put his hand on the boy's wrist, not hard, not gentle. He shook his head once.

"Back," Kadev said to the crowd. "Two paces, all of you. Left side first on my count." He tapped his shield rim with his knuckles. "One. Two. Step."

Men and women obeyed because his voice sounded like work. The step-parity returned one lane at a time. The Loadshare came back in a thin thread that thickened as bodies found the count. The groan eased.

Kadev looked at the three who were not moving. Two lay twisted on the stones. One sat with blood on his face and a hand open and empty on his knee. Kadev's chalk made three quick marks in the small book he kept in his breast pocket. He did not announce the number. He did not explain it.

"Take the rope down," he said to his sergeant. "Break the chalk. Clear the parapet."

The men with the painted shields lowered their boards. One tried to speak and found he had nothing worth saying. The young guard with the vial looked at his thumb and then tucked the bad lot into his coat.

Kadev looked at the middle arch a last time. There was a fine new crack at the inner lip of the coping, hair-thin and honest. He nodded to himself and moved on.

Counting House Triage

The Counting House smelled of ink, clay, and old dust. Shelves of rolled vellum climbed the walls. Matron Arelin walked with a ledger under one arm and a chipped cup of tea in her free hand. She liked to keep something warm in her palm while she read terrible news.

"Three forms for one child," Clerk Ven said, placing the rolls on the table. "All sealed. All ceremonially valid."

Arelin set her tea down. She broke each seal and read the headers. Scriptorium blue. Temple white. Merchant red. All named the same day, the same mother, the same infant. Each claimed precedence with a clause that quoted a different charter.

"Which one came first?" she asked.

"They arrived together," Ven said. "A runner brought them in a satchel with ribbon from each registry."

Arelin put the rolls side by side so the headings touched. The air seemed to thicken. She felt the old tickle behind her eyes that announced a renderability check without instruments. She nodded to the apprentice at the weights.

"Measure R," she said.

The boy set out the little tin scales and the small bowls of salt used to test for alignment. He placed a pinch on each roll, then brought the bowls together over a marked plate and watched the shift. The salt drew into a shallow spiral and stopped. The boy frowned.

"R is lower when they are collocated," he said. "Higher if I separate them an arm's length. Higher still if I take one into the next room."

Arelin did not sigh. She had learned years ago that audible weariness taught clerks the wrong habit. "We do not separate," she said. "Separation is politics disguised as safety."

Clerk Tor leaned over the table. "We can read a unison cadence and harmonize the bind," she said. "Temple and Scriptorium in full count. Merchants on the after-beat."

Clerk Yarel shook his head. "No. We hold to the Scriptorium count and make the others answer. A chorus with two noons breaks more often than it holds."

Arelin let them argue for two breaths while she watched the rolls on the table. The salt spirals had not moved. The room felt tired.

"Enough," she said. "We are not resolving doctrine in a hallway. Lock the ledgers."

Ven brought the iron box. Arelin slid each roll inside and turned the key. She sealed the seam with wax and pressed the House crest into the pool. She could feel her hand begin to shake and was pleased to see it stop when the seal cooled.

"Send for Captain Kadev," she said. "We will escort a convoy to the Square and seat these three in the open. Call breath posts at the corners. If this city wants to fight over a newborn's name it can do it where everyone can see."

The apprentice hesitated. "The Square is crowded," he said. "There are rumors."

"There are always rumors," Arelin said. "We have a child with three names and one body. We will not fix it by pretending we did not see it."

Breath Post Collapse

Novice Chorister Pell held a small board against his chest. His knuckles were white because the board was slick with sweat. He stood at a chalk circle in a market lane where a threshold seal met the paving at a public doorway. His job was simple. Keep a witness quorum breathing on a steady four-count while the scribe inside refreshed the bind.

"Witness quorum, six," Pell said. "Breath on four."

"One. Two. Three. Four."

The market had a tone of its own. Knives on wood, coin on stone, sellers calling to buyers. The sound sat under the count like a drum under a tune. The scribe inside the doorway marked neat lines with a bone tip, ink black and just glossy.

Halfway through the figure a temple chorus appeared at the lane mouth, white scarves at their throats and a banner made of linen that caught light like water. Their cantor lifted a hand and gave a half-count that slid across Pell's rhythm like a cart wheel catching a rut.

"Do not," Pell started to say, and then he saw that was exactly the point. The cantor smiled with the careful pity of a man who is sure he is right.

The threshold bind flickered. The air went soft and strange. Sound cut in and out. A knife dropped on a board without a sound. Then sound returned too loud, all at once. Someone screamed because other people were screaming. The witness at Pell's left broke his count and ran. A second witness tripped and fell. Feet stepped on her board, then on her hand. The scribe inside the doorway looked up, startled, and the line he was drawing wavered. The seal held only when he stared directly at it. The moment he glanced at Pell the mark blurred.

"Hold the count," Pell said. He was surprised to hear his voice come out steady. He did not feel steady. He felt like a man trying to hold a pane of glass with wet fingers.

"One. Two. Three. Four."

A woman with a basket shoved through and shoved again. Someone's elbow banged Pell's ribs. He did not stop. The cantor's half-count drifted away as the chorus continued up the lane, white silk and soft feet. The bind steadied under Pell's eyes. The scribe finished the figure and lifted the bone with a small click of nail on spine.

"It holds," the scribe said, surprised.

"For now," Pell said. His mouth tasted of iron. He bent and picked up the trampled board of the fallen witness. The chalk line was smeared across its face like a bandage.

Street Rumor

By afternoon the city had found a new entertainment. Small curls of chalk appeared on doorframes and posts, little half-figures that suggested a circle without closing it. They had a way of inviting a hand to complete them. A runner brought a door plank to the Counting House with five such curls on it.

"Children tried to finish them," the runner said. "So did three grown men. One cried when we took the chalk."

Arelin studied the curls without touching. They were not innocent. They echoed a forbidden motif that had been locked in the Restricted

Stacks since before her grandmother's time. She did not open the old book often. She had opened it once. That was enough.

"Wash them," she said. "Water and a rag. No ink. No scraping. Do not give them more lines to work with."

"Will washing help?" Ven asked.

"It will remind people that wood is wood," Arelin said. "Sometimes that is enough."

The runner tucked the plank under his arm and left. At the corner of the House a boy lingered, dusty and thin, a courier's satchel too big for his bony shoulder. He watched the plank go. He watched Arelin place a small vellum scrap on the table and weigh it with the tin scale. The scrap bore one curl, drawn with a careful hand.

"Burn this," Arelin said to Ven. "In the yard. No chanting."

Ven nodded and gathered tongs and a brazier. The boy's eyes followed the scrap as if it were a coin. When no one was looking at him he eased his hand inside his satchel and touched a pocket that crinkled. The vellum there made a small sound.

Arelin turned to the ledger box on her desk. The seals along its seam caught the light. Somewhere beyond the House bells were arguing with each other, one slightly ahead of the other, both certain they were right. She pressed her palm flat to the iron and felt nothing. That was better than feeling something wrong.

"Call for Captain Kadev," she said. "Tell him we are carrying three rolls to the Square. Tell him today is going to be a long day."

Siege of the Counting House

Rain started as a mist that turned dust to paste. The Counting House door took the wet and darkened to a deeper brown. Inside, clerks sat on benches with boards against their knees. They breathed on the four.

"Witness quorum, twelve," Pell called. His voice filled the room without strain. "Breath on four."

"One. Two. Three. Four."

Arelin moved among the benches with a ledger of residue lots. Each jar had a season stamped into its wax. She signed out drams with a tin scale and marked where each went. A clerk at her elbow kept a second record in case anyone accused her later.

Outside, a choir gathered in the lane. White scarves. Calm faces. Their cantor lifted a hand. Their half-count slid into the House like water under a door.

The Threshold Seal on the jamb shivered. The weight that had settled there went light. A hairline crack ran along a grain line that had been honest for a hundred years.

"Cadence posts," Arelin said. "Louder."

Pell raised the count. The benches moved with it. Shoulders rose and fell. The seal steadied, then trembled again as a ram struck the door in rhythm with the rival chorus. The men outside had found a beat and liked the way it felt.

Kadev came at a jog with two files. Shields up. Faces tight. He took one look at the rival choir and set his men on an off count so their feet did not feed the same rhythm. The first ram blow met the rim of a shield instead of timber. The second struck air when Kadev's rank stepped back on the wrong beat for the ram and broke its swing.

"Hold," Kadev said to the line. "Do not sing."

Inside, a clerk's breath ran away from her. She gulped air and made little sounds in the back of her throat. Pell moved to her shoulder without breaking the count. He put her hand on his chest and let her feel the four.

"Match me," he said. "One. Two. Three. Four."

Arelin dipped a bone spatula into an old lot of residue, winter two years ago. The ash lay heavy in the ink. She painted a narrow reinforcement along the inner lip of the jamb where the grain showed. She did not write a new seal. She did not give the wood more geometry to argue about.

The door bowed under a synchronized shove. The inner bar moaned. The old lot took and held. The vibration changed from a sick hum to a tone that spoke of weight carried in the right direction.

A man outside shouted that they fought against mercy. A man inside wept once and then stopped. Kadev gave the word and his files drove forward with a low push that was work, not glory. The ram went sideways and fell. The rival choir faltered when a woman turned an ankle and cried out. The cadence leaked from their mouth like a taste they did not want to swallow after all.

"Seal holds," Pell said.

Arelin closed the ledger of lots and set it on the high shelf. Her hands were steady now.

"Open for Captain Kadev," she said.

Bars lifted. The door swung inward one hand's breadth. Kadev stepped through with the flat of his shield toward the lane. He smelled old dust and warm ink and nodded once to Arelin as if she had passed an inspection.

"Keep the door," he said. "We will keep the lane."

The Bridge Pogrom

Night took the water. Torches flared along the Old Span. Militia in mismatched caps had tied strips of color to their sleeves. Red for contract names. White for temple names. Blue for the book.

"Speak your form," a man said to a trader who had three seals on his contract tube. "Speak the right one."

The trader tried to laugh. He failed. "I am one man," he said. "I have one mother."

"You have three ledgers," the man said. "Speak one."

The trader chose the wrong roll. Hands took him by the arms. He struggled and pleaded and called the other names, all of them, fast and earnest. It did not matter. He went over the parapet with a sound like a broken bell.

Kadev's boots rang on the stones. He had run from the House. He did not speak until he was at the center. Then he stood with his back to the parapet and his shield hung on his arm so his hands were empty.

"Everyone backs up," he said. "For the next ten breaths you look at me, not each other."

He counted. People hate to be told. They obeyed because his count was work. Red stepped back. White stepped back. Blue stepped back. The men who had thrown the trader tried to leave. Kadev's sergeant took two by the collars. The third ran. He struck the coping with his shin and fell but caught a gap with his fingers and hung there, sobbing. No one helped him up.

Kadev walked the coping. Chalk marks curled at the keystone like small, innocent horns. Each arrow pointed to the inner lip of the arch. The curls had the same wrong invitation Arelin had seen on doorframes.

"Scour," he said. "No scrapes. Wet cloth only."

A levy knelt and wiped. The chalk smeared like dead skin. The curls lightened and thinned until they were gone.

"No more spoken forms on my bridge," Kadev said. "You cross or you do not. You do not pass judgment here."

A man in red opened his mouth. Kadev looked at him. The man closed his mouth.

Kadev stood there long enough for three torches to burn down to black ends that smelled like rancid oil. The river pushed under the arches with its old iron sound. He logged one death, two arrests, one escape. He did not write the name of the man in the water because no one on the span could agree on what it was.

Council in the Square

By morning the Square had a table with four chairs and a fifth that no one sat in. Lethrin's old rubric lay open under a weight. The signal towers stood by like tall, patient men who did not intend to help.

Arelin came with two clerks and the iron box that held the newborn's three rolls. Kadev stood with his sergeant and left his shield leaning against the steps. Magister Boras arrived in Scriptorium blue with a mouth that looked like it knew how to say no. Prelate Sahvi wore white and smelled of clean linen and smoke. Guild Prefect Irado had coin grease on his fingers and a habit of tapping.

"We cannot run a city on three sets of names," Boras said.

"We cannot run a city on one set of names chosen by you," Sahvi said.

Irado tapped. "Contracts must survive the people who write them," he said. "Trade dies when names float."

"Trade dies when bridges break," Kadev said. He did not sit. "Last night men threw a traveler into the river because he picked the wrong line to speak first."

Sahvi folded her hands. "The temple does not condone murder," she said.

"You condone your noon," Kadev said. "Then you send choirs to other people's doors."

Arelin set the iron box on the table and turned it so the seals faced the others. "We have one body with three valid rolls," she said. "Standing here shouting about principle will not make that smaller."

"Then what," Irado said. "A lottery."

"A Grand Recount," Arelin said. "Bells tied to one line. Breath posts every fifty paces. The Square set for a day of names read aloud. We seat these three rolls in the open and we bind them into one picture while the whole city watches."

Boras made a sound with his tongue. "Under Scriptorium custody," he said. "Chain of custody is a mechanical requirement. You know this."

Sahvi lifted her chin. "Witness quorum by temple measure," she said. "We will not submit sacred names to a dry count."

Irado tapped faster. "Contracts keep their red seals," he said. "You can read until you drop. The market will still call what it must call."

Arelin held up a hand. "One day," she said. "One line for bells. One cadence. One reading. One custody for the rolls while the rite runs. After that you can all write charters and counter-charters until you die. We will at least know what fails."

Kadev looked at the four chairs and at the fifth one none of them had taken. He thought of the men on the bridge who had shouted themselves brave and then thrown a stranger into the river.

"I will hold the streets," he said. "No colors at chokepoints. No chalk near keystones. Any choir that comes to spoil the count will sing in a cell."

Boras touched the iron box with two fingers and then wiped his fingers on a cloth as if the box had burned him. "One day," he said.

"Today," Arelin said.

The Ash Market

The market under the old aqueduct woke at dusk. Lamps hung on ropes from post to post. A narrow aisle wound between tables covered with broken brass, old tools, and glass jars with gray dust in them. Men and women spoke softly, names low.

Pell followed two runners through the crowd. They moved as if they had a reason for being anywhere they pleased. The runners stopped at a stall draped with blue cloth. The woman behind the table had hair the color of soot and hands that did not tremble. She smiled at Pell as if she had been expecting him.

"Quartermaster," she said, though he wore no badge. "Looking for memory."

"I am a chorister," Pell said. "Not a quartermaster."

"Tonight you are both," the woman said. She tapped one jar. "Winter ash, good lot, sings when you shake it." She tapped another jar. "Cut with chimney soot. Shines on the line, fails on the world. Cheaper."

"What is your name," Pell said.

"Viska," she said, and smiled again.

Kadev came out of the dark with two levies. The lamps caught his face and made it older. He looked at the jars and then at Viska's hands.

"Market is closed," he said.

"Everything is closed," Viska said. "Everything is open. It depends on the ledger you carry."

Kadev lifted the blue cloth. A ledger lay under the table, bound in oiled leather, tidy and thoughtful. Names filled its pages in clean hand. Buyers. Amounts. Lots.

"You keep good records," Kadev said.

"It is a public service," Viska said. "No one can accuse me of hiding stock."

He took the ledger and tucked it into his coat. "You can accuse yourself later," he said. "Go home."

She laughed. She had a good laugh for a market at night. She slipped into the crowd and was gone before a levy decided which arm to hold.

Pell picked up one of the jars. The ash inside was light and fine. It looked like memory should look if memory were ground to dust. He shook it and listened. Nothing.

"Counterfeit," Kadev said.

Pell set the jar down with care, as if it might still be part of something worth respect. When they left the stall he realized his hand had found the ledger in Kadev's coat and then let go. He did not know why he had wanted to hold it. He did not know why he still wanted to.

Processions of Authority

The city gathered three caravans at the hour when lamps were just lamps and not yet stars. Scriptorium blue came from the north gate with compasses on poles and clerks in clean coats. Temple white came from the river quarter with scarves and a bell that carried sweet and far. Merchant red came from the grain road with banners and boys who could run.

The route for the recount had been chalked at noon. Narrow lines marked a path around the Square and out to the boundary stones. Blue chalk. White chalk. Red chalk. Someone had added arrows at corners. Someone had scuffed feet through sections and made dust.

The first trouble came when a red bearer stepped on a blue line and the chalk smeared across his boot. A woman in blue struck his shoulder with a baton. He pushed her away and fell into a man in white who had been looking up at the bell. The baton fell. A torch dipped. Linen caught.

"Do not write on it," Arelin said at once. "No seals. No marks. Put it out with wet cloth."

Clerks ran with buckets. Boys pulled down banners and shoved them into troughs. The fire coughed and sulked and then died, leaving a scorched smell that made the throat itch. People shouted the names they preferred as if that would fix smoke.

Kadev stood on the edge of the Square and watched the caravans ground their banners as ordered. He sent runners to clear the Old Span of color and to post men at alleys where choirs like to enter. He rubbed the back of his neck and felt grit under his fingers.

Pell climbed the dais steps and looked out over the three colors and the three sets of faces. He put two fingers against the pulse in his throat. He knew his count. He believed it mattered. He believed it would be enough to carry one day.

"Bells tie at dawn," Arelin said to him. "Your voice first. Hold the four."

"I will," he said.

The signal towers stood like tall men in a doorway. The night settled around their bases. The city exhaled the day and pulled the dark into its lungs. Somewhere in the lanes a chalk curl waited on a post for a hand to finish it. Somewhere in a house a jar of ash that looked honest and was not sat ready for a scribe who would press a thumb to its wax and hope.

Arelin checked the seal on the iron box with the three infant rolls. It was still cool and firm. She did not let herself imagine the child who wore those names. She did not let herself imagine the mother's face.

"Dawn," Kadev said. He did not look at anyone when he said it. He looked at the stones. "We hold the streets at dawn."

Breath Lattice

Dawn took the color out of the streets. Chalk circles glowed faint on damp stone. Every fifty paces a breath post stood with a board, a clerk, and a small flag tied to a bellline that ran along the eaves like a string drawn across the city.

Pell stood on the dais step, two fingers at his throat. The bell master gave him a nod and pulled once on the master rope. The line went tight from tower to tower. The city seemed to draw itself up to listen.

"Witness quorums at posts," Pell called. "Breath on four."

His voice carried without strain. It found the first rank of clerks and moved down the streets like water. "One. Two. Three. Four."

Kadev had placed squads at chokepoints before the light came full. Two at the Old Span. One at the grain road. Three small files at lanes where choirs liked to enter late and loud. He checked shields, checked faces, and sent a runner with a quiet instruction: no colors at crossings, no chanting within ear of a post.

Arelin rode the route in a narrow cart with a ledger on her knees and a box of residue at her feet. Each jar had a season stamped into its wax. She signed out measured drams with a tin scale, handed them to clerks who held them like small, breakable favors, and marked each lot on her page. The cart wheels made a dry sound over the chalk.

The first tower bell answered the line with a single clean note. The second took the same note and set it beside the first. The breath posts lifted and fell as one on the count. For a moment the city felt like a body that had remembered to breathe.

Perimeter Bind Reboot

The north boundary stone had a mason's star cut so deep a thumb could sit inside it. A clerk in blue read names from the master roll while Magister Boras bent to the stone and re-inscribed the old standard figure first laid down generations ago by a binder-captain whose name the Scriptorium taught and the streets had forgotten.

"Lexeme Perimeter Bind," Boras said. "Binder, master proper names. Scope, north quarter. Checksum on eight."

Pell raised the count. "One. Two. Three. Four. Five. Six. Seven. Eight."

Boras's hand was stiff now, but exact. The bone tip met the stone with the small click that says the cut is honest. The line closed and the hum settled behind the ears. People near the corner exhaled without knowing why they had been holding their breath.

They moved to the west stone. Same figure. Same clean closure. Two women laughed quietly, the kind of laugh people make when fear loosens its fingers. A boy tugged his mother's sleeve and said he could feel the ground listening.

At the south stone a man crossed himself and stepped back twice, not out of contempt, but to give room to something that was working. The hum gathered weight without getting louder. It felt like a door leaning into its hinges the right way.

First Interference

The east stone sat near a small plaza where the temple likes to sing. Pell could see white scarves at the end of the street before he heard the voice. The cantor came late by half a count. His noon had been taught to him by men who believed noon could be made new.

The cantor's half-count laid itself across Pell's four. It was not hostile. It was simply certain. The bind at the stone completed under Boras's bone and held while every eye watched it. When the scribe stood and looked to the next corner, the line lost color and went soft at the edges as if the stone were remembering a drawing it liked but could not keep in mind.

"Split the choir," Pell said. "Half hold the master four. Half follow the cantor for one cycle and return."

They did it. The stone held. They tried the same trick at the next corner. A merchant bell tolled the work hour from the grain road with a fashionable downbeat that had caught on in the last year. The sound ran through the plaza like a ripple on a cistern. Pell's split held for two beats and then slid. The bind wavered again when backs turned.

"Posts, eyes on lines until relief," Pell said. His voice did not break. His mouth tasted of iron.

Anchor Oscillation on the Span

On the Old Span the crowd had been held back from the parapet. Kadev stood on the coping where he could see both approaches. The keystone seal hummed as it always had, a low pressure that sits in the teeth when you think about it.

A clerk read three forms of a woman's name in sequence, blue, white, red. The Loadshare binder took the first, gripped, and spread weight across the three arches. It released on the second, as polite as a host stepping aside. It gripped again on the third with less enthusiasm than the first, as if the arches were willing to do the work but unsure who had asked them.

Civilians swayed as if they were on a deck in choppy water. A woman put a hand out to the parapet and left it there until her stomach settled.

"No cadence on the Span," Kadev said. "Silence."

He posted his men with shields and shut their mouths with a look. He did not want a fourth rhythm to confuse the stone. He watched the clerk finish the names and make a chalk mark on the coping to log the closure.

The chalk line looked plain. That was good. Plain lines do not invite a hand to finish them. They are already finished.

Counterfeit Closures

Two streets south of the Square a district captain with a torn coat and a face drawn tight with exhaustion shook a jar from the night market and pressed his thumb to its wax as if a thumb could make history honest. He spooned a measure into his ink and drew a Threshold Seal across a failing balcony beam where a dozen people waited for the recount to pass.

The figure was perfect. The geometry shone with the gloss Bad Lots like to wear, a gloss that promises forever to the eye. People beneath it sighed as if they had stepped under a good roof.

Five minutes later the gloss flattened. The mark held its shape and lost the world. The seal turned Hollow. The beam made a soft sound like a sigh. Then it cracked. The balcony tilted, broke free, and came down in a short rain of wood and lime.

Kadev reached the street after the first shout. He did not speak. He moved debris with two men and his hands. He pulled a girl from under a piece of railing and then a boy whose face was white with dust but whose eyes were clear. He placed them gently beside a wall and nodded to the woman who crouched there and counted their breaths.

He picked up the broken board with the beautiful empty figure and looked at it for the space of one count. He set it down without anger.

Recursion Leak

By midmorning chalk curls began to appear inside the recount figures as they were laid down. They were small. They were placed where only a scribe would see them. They looked like nothing and exactly like something a hand would finish without thinking.

Pell reached for one before he knew he was reaching. He slapped his own wrist without ceremony and heard the sharp sound of skin on skin. He held up the chalk for a runner to take.

"Confiscate chalk at all posts," he said. "No exceptions."

Arelin saw the same curls inside a closure on the Square and felt the small, unkind invitation she had felt on doorframes. She order runners to burn marginal scraps in the yard. They did. Ash lifted in a gray billow and made people cough. A dozen voices accused her of burning names the way enemies had burned rolls in other years. She wanted to say that sometimes wood is wood and must be kept wood. She did not say it. She gave the order again in a flat voice.

At the edge of the crowd a boy with a courier's satchel watched a scrap catch. He worried a vellum edge between two fingers inside his pocket until it softened.

The Counting of Names

Noon. The bellline had held long enough to make a shape out of the morning. The Square breathed on four. Three registries stood shoulder to shoulder with the master concordance unrolled across two tables. The script on the vellum looked clean enough to eat.

Pell lifted his hand and the breath went quiet in the way breath goes quiet when many people hold it together. He gave the four. The first reader in blue spoke the names that began with A. The white reader picked up the same names and added the sacred forms where tradition expects them. The red reader followed with the market styles used on contracts. For a long minute it felt like the city could stand this. People who had been waiting all day let their shoulders drop.

Then a bell drifted. Not far. A half beat and a fashion. The grain road workbell liked to land late because men like to think they are outside the rule for a moment before they fall into it again. A choir near the fountain took the downbeat because it was pleasing in the mouth. The master four continued at the posts. The temple noon stood where it always stands. For three breaths all three sat inside the same space and canceled into a hush that spread like a ring down four streets.

Inside the hush the readers' mouths moved without sound. The crowd felt the shapes of words without hearing them. The line on the vellum continued to the end of the sentence. Boras's hand made the closing stroke with care. The seal clicked with the clean note a good lid makes on a good jar.

The Square stood in silence. It was not reverence. It was subtraction.

The hush passed. Sound returned too bright. Someone cheered out of habit. Someone wept and did not know for whom. Pell lowered his hand. He had not noticed that he had been holding it in the air.

"Next names," Boras said, because a page does not know how to stop when a street stops. He did not look up.

Pell looked at Arelin. Arelin looked at Kadev. Kadev looked at the stones under his boots. He could feel the hum in them. It was there. It was thinner than it should be. He lifted his book and made one small mark that meant three injured, none dead, balcony failure, counterfeit lot.

He did not add a line that explained why the closure on the page had been perfect while the world had refused to answer. There was no line for that.

Paper Victory, World Loss

Magister Boras dried the seal with the care of a man cooling a blade. Wax cooled, impression flawless, ribbon straight. The rubric sheets lay flat on the table, columns aligned, signatures crisp, the concordance copied in three clean hands and cross-checked line by line. If a city could live inside paper, this would have been enough.

"Entered," Boras said, more to the vellum than to anyone listening. He tapped the margin where closures were logged. "Renderability is total on the page."

No wind moved in the Square. The signal towers cast long morning shadows across the stones. Far off, two bells agreed by accident for a few beats and then forgot each other again.

In the lanes the world began to show its own opinion. A doorway seal stayed firm while the scribe's eyes were on it and softened when he turned to speak to a neighbor. A ward drawn clean across a shop threshold hummed until the clerk went to the back room; by the time she returned, dust had gathered in the strokes as if the lines had been chalk all along. A boundary stone held north for one patrol, east for the next. Neighbors corrected one another's names with the stubbornness of hunger.

"Hold still," a woman told her husband, "you're Yal in the book."

"I am Hesh to my mother," he said, and said it again like a charm against theft.

Echo became a kind of weather. People learned where to look and when, and what to say to keep the lines from fading while they crossed. The learned skill made them proud for a day. By the second day it felt like carrying water in a sieve.

Boras stamped another copy and set it on the pile without looking up. The pages looked immortal. The streets did not.

Custody and Cost

Arelin sat with her ledgers and a sheet already prepared. She read each clause aloud to her clerks, chain of custody; seal authority; the rights of sworn keepers to remain at their posts; the penalties for tampering. The words were old, precise, more carpenter than poet. She signed her name and pressed the Scriptorium signet into the wax. The act had a neatness to it that comforted the hand and hurt the heart.

"Affixed," she said. Her voice wavered, and then steadied. "Post copies at the House and the Square."

By afternoon people called it a coup. They said the Matron of the Counting House had married herself to Standards and sold the names for painted seals. A priest with soot on his stole stood on the fountain rim and declared the recount void in the world that mattered. He did not name Arelin or Boras. He did not need to. People understood where to point.

Merchants watched the argument settle like dust and then wrote a private standard in red: contract names first, all others acknowledgments only, disputes to guild juries. They hired boys to carry the decision to market stalls and to collect signatures in neat rows. You could count the city's truths then with two hands, blue in the House, white at the altar, red at the stall, and find no single one that could be called a lie without also reaching for a knife.

Arelin stood in the Counting House doorway with the edict nailed to the jamb at eye height. She watched a woman read the lines and then look up with a tired fury that had more years in it than this morning.

"You took our names," the woman said.

"We are keeping them," Arelin said.

"It feels the same," the woman said, and then went away because argument required breath she had already spent.

Arelin locked the House and sat at the big table with her hands on the wood. The grain ran true under her palms. She knew how to feel that. She did not know how to feel a city she could not hold still.

Kadev's Last Patrol

On the Span, Kadev put his files side by side, shields half-sloped, a posture that said ready without saying threat. He rubbed the chalk scar on the coping with his thumb until it didn't catch.

"No more spoken forms," he told his men. "Not here. Look at faces, not ledgers. If you don't know, ask for a neighbor. If they say two names, let them pass."

A sergeant frowned. "Orders will be challenged," he said.

"By whom," Kadev said. "The river?"

They held the bridge that way for a day. It was not elegant. It was quiet. Old women took baskets across with their mouths set like door bolts; men nodded at the guards and did not flinch. A boy who had carried three contracts yesterday carried none today and waved at Kadev with all his fingers, not just the two you wave when you are not sure if a man should see you.

Then a new captain came from the north precinct with fresh lacquer on his board and a voice that broke when he shouted. He unrolled a set of instructions written by someone who had never walked the parapet in rain. Spoken forms were required again, as if the river loved a column more than a man.

"Not my command," Kadev said, which was the truth. He walked the bridge one more time before the changeover. He put a palm on the keystone and felt the low hum that had always been there. It was thinner now, like a string tuned down a cent, nearly right if you did not have a memory for pitch.

He went down to the bank and walked along the reeds. He stood where the wind made the same sound it had made when he was a boy and a levy and a man who believed that craft plus will could keep a square livable. The reeds did their old song. He listened until he knew he could not reenlist without lying to a younger version of himself.

When he turned back, a heron lifted and moved upstream the way a slow thought moves across a tired mind.

Pell's Choice

The breath posts had been collected, boards stacked in a dry room like shields after a festival. Pell took one at dusk without writing his name on the loan sheet. He carried it to the small market lane where the threshold seal had flickered under the temple half-count. No clerks waited there now. A woman swept her step. She waved without looking at his face.

"Witness quorum, one," Pell said, to the air. "Breath on four."

"One," he said to himself. "Two. Three. Four."

His voice did not have to carry. It had to be honest in his own chest. He felt silly for a moment, and then less silly, and then something like grief. He had believed that one day of perfect counting could hold when the rest could not. It was not a foolish belief. It was a young one.

He took from his belt pouch the novice primer he had carried since training, thin now, the leather dark with the oils of his hands. On the inside back cover proverbs live. There were already two that somebody older had written in a clean hand when the world was less complicated. Pell sharpened a quill with a small knife and wrote in letters that were almost too neat: The page remembers what the street will not.

He stared at the words until their edges softened. He felt shame rise, a useless, clean shame that attached itself to no one else and changed nothing. He tore the page out carefully along the stitch holes and slid it inside his coat.

The wind in the lane shifted a little. The door across from him stood between open and shut. He wanted to say the right word and watch the wood answer. He counted instead. "One. Two. Three. Four." It helped as much as counting can help.

***

Morning came with the particular square light that makes chalk look important. Map chalkers went to work, blue from the north, white from the river, red from the grain road. They redrew the city as they knew it should be: wards in loops and ribs, alleys in threads, names in careful letters at corners. Each line was a promise and a claim. By noon the lines overlapped until the paving stones held more color than decision, the gray of mixture spreading from block to block.

Children played a game that had no name. They ran along the chalk, jumped small gaps, and stepped around boundary stones without knowing why their feet would not step on them. A boy with a satchel watched and joined in, careful with his pockets.

The signal towers lit in order, west to east, old habit standing. The bells answered late on one side and early on the other. People looked up because bodies are animals that still love a sequence of lights at dusk. The hum traveled through masonry and river and stopped short of comfort. If you had a memory for pitch, you would say it was one cent flatter than last century; if you did not, you would call it almost right and feel tired for reasons you could not give a name.

Arelin locked the Counting House and stood with her key ring heavy in her hand. Kadev, already a civilian in practice, crossed the Square with a roll of bandage in his pocket because pockets learn habits slowly. Pell counted under his breath because breath will be there after words go missing.

The city breathed. Not together. Not yet. Perhaps not again. The lines on paper were beautiful, and the world, stubborn, plural, unshamed, refused to live inside them for longer than a look.

Cycle IV
The Divergent Eye

She dreamt that the sun moved.

Not in a neat circle, not in a way a hunter could mark with a cairn and say, from this stone to that, but with the patient inevitability of a bead of water sliding down a pane of glass. In the dream, shadows lengthened like slow knives, reversed, then lengthened again. The blue above her changed tone without her sensing the moment of change, as if color itself were something that traveled.

She woke with her pulse beating inside her fingertips. The dream had not ended. There was a brightness in the corner of the alcove mouth where no brightness had been before. It made a thin wedge along the stone floor, as if the light had remembered how to turn.

She lay still long enough to count her breaths. The alcove was cut from the mountain's flank, one in a honeycomb of sleeping hollows that opened onto the terraced slopes below. From here she could see the valley, the terraces like ribbed balconies, the swarm in its morning posture. Figures stood at even intervals, hands at their sides, faces lifted toward the horizon. In the half light their stillness had a dignity that always moved her. They were a wall of attention. They were a net of sight.

She pulled on a hunter's tunic and stepped out into the air. The hum of the field met her skin and soaked into it. It was the hum of shared looking, of ten thousand eyes braided into one. The field smoothed the serrations of thought. The field had kept the valley whole for longer than the clan's memory. In the field, the mountains did not crumble and clouds did not wander and the great sun sat level with its stone cradle and shone with affection upon its people. Children were taught to enter the field by degrees, the way one entered cold water. She had entered it that way and, until the dream, felt only relief.

The hum collected in the hollows above her ears, the way a shell collects the sound of the sea. She lifted her gaze to the horizon and let her focus widen until it softened. The trick was to let the eyes see without seizing. When done together, the weave of sight was seamless. When seamless, the world did not slip.

The sun had slipped.

Only a fraction. Only enough to lengthen the shadow of the western ridge by the breadth of a hand across the far slope. It was enough. Her throat closed on air.

"Are you ill?" said Maret.

He stood at her left, as he had since they were children. Maret had broad wrists and a soft voice and could still a goat with his palm to its forehead. He did not turn to look at her. One did not turn in the field. But she heard the tension in the words.

"My sight is not steady," she said.

"Lean into the hum," he said. "Breathe with it. Let the valley hold you."

She tried. The hum rose, cool and heavy as clay, and for a moment she felt it take her weight. The wedge of brightness in the alcove floor retreated. The ridge's shadow resumed its old place. Relief uncoiled in her ribs.

But the dream waited inside the relief like a seed. She lifted one eyelid the smallest measure. The sun had crept again. The air above the terraces trembled. A thread in the field quivered and sang out of tune.

Maret's knuckles whitened on the railing before him. "Do you feel it?"

"Yes."

"Then do not feed it." His hand opened and closed once, as if he were crushing a gnat that was not there. "If you do not feed it, it starves."

She closed her eyes. The hum sealed her like a jar. She breathed through the sealing and tried not to think of the wedge of light that had crawled along the stone of the alcove floor and would be crawling still.

Later, the Overseer came.

The Overseer walked the terraces with her eyes closed, for her task was not to add her sight to the weave but to tend it. Her cloak was white, not in defiance of the dust but as a promise that dust would not cling. The

Overseer stood at the lip of the alcove, head slightly bowed, hands folded at her waist.

"You felt motion," the Overseer said. It was not a question.

"Yes."

"Was it outside you or inside you?"

"Both." The word surprised her. She had meant to say she did not know.

The Overseer nodded, as if the answer had been expected. "You must choose to return your gaze to the field or to walk apart and let your sight find its own braid. If you return now, the swarm will hold. If you walk apart and keep looking, the weave will loosen. If the weave loosens, change will find its way into the stones."

"What is the worst that can happen?" she asked, and then felt foolish. The field was built to prevent what was worse than worst.

The Overseer's mouth did something like a smile. "Inside the weave, that question has no meaning. Outside it, the answers multiply."

"Has anyone kept looking before?"

"There are stories," the Overseer said, and for the first time she opened her eyes. They were gray and clear. "None told by those who stayed."

That night she dreamed again. The sun moved. It moved across the sky, and with it moved a herd of lights in a black pasture. The lights walked in patterns that were almost letters. She woke to a thin ache in the center of her forehead, as if something had pressed there.

She did not go to her place on the terrace. She climbed.

The ridge above the terraces was a long back of stone with thorn-scrub and tiny pink flowers like eyes. She walked until the hum thinned and then felt it snap. The silence after it was so sudden she staggered. The valley below her was a slate image. The still figures of the swarm were marks etched in rows.

She opened her eyes to the edges. She opened both, fully, as if taking off a bandage. The sun was not where she had left it. It had slid a finger's width. The light fell at a new angle. Tiny shadows appeared beneath the flowers where there had not been shadows. A thin stream flashed where rock had been dull.

For a heartbeat she saw both worlds. The one where the sun was fixed and the one where it moved. The one etched in slate, the one inked anew.

In one, the valley held the swarm like writing. In the other, the valley looked up at her.

A low sound made her turn. Maret had followed her. He climbed the last meters on his hands and knees, then rose and stood a little distance away, chest heaving. His eyes, for once, did not watch the horizon. They watched her.

"Do you feel what you are doing?" he asked. "Do you feel it in your skin? The hum does not reach here. Your sight is loose. It slips into the cracks and pries."

"If the sun moves, it moves whether I look or not."

"If the sun moves and no one sees it, the world stays."

"That is not staying. That is not knowing."

"Staying is what kept your mother and mine alive long enough to give us names," Maret said. "Staying is why we have terraces. Staying is how the mountain learned our weight and decided not to shiver us off."

She felt heat in her face. "Do you believe the mountain loves us?"

"I believe the mountain does not notice us," Maret said. "The swarm notices for it. That is what the field is. We lend the world our noticing. In return, the world lends us its calm."

She turned away. The sun had moved again. The ache at her brow sharpened until it was a clear point. A hawk's shadow cut the slope and then, impossibly, went back the way it had come. The smell of the thorn-scrub changed from sap to something like iron.

She did not sleep that night. She lay on the ridge and watched the stars. They were not as still as she had been told. They heaved like a breathing chest. Once, as the ache at her brow pulsed with her heartbeat, she saw two skies at once. One held a bowl of motionless fire-seeds. The other was a turning wheel. At the center of the wheel was a dark where no stars shone, a hole so pure it made her teeth hurt. It was the kind of dark that felt like a mouth.

In the morning she returned to the terraces. The swarm stood in its ranks. The hum lifted and fell like the sea. Children were shown where to place their feet, how to soften their eyes. She took her place beside Maret and eased her breath into the rhythm. The sun sat a little to the right of where it should have been.

"This is not kindness," Maret said without moving his lips.

"What?"

"Coming back and tugging at the weave from inside it," he said. "Choose outside, or choose here. But choose."

She tried to choose. She closed her eyes and tried to let the hum fill the ache in her brow. The hum flowed around the ache like water around a stone.

Near midday, the Overseer came walking along the row. She did not need to open her eyes to find the places where the weave thinned. She stopped behind them.

"Walk with me," the Overseer said, and they followed her out of the line and along a narrow path that led beneath an overhang of rock. The hum dimmed. The air was cooler. A spring dripped from the stone into a basin. The Overseer wet her fingers and pressed them to the center of the hunter's brow. The ache flickered.

"Do you want to belong?" the Overseer asked.

"Yes," the hunter said. "But not to a lie."

"What you call a lie is a net," the Overseer said. "You can fish with it or drown in it or cut it and watch the fish scatter. There are small fish that need the net to know what water is."

"Are we small?"

"We were small when the first freeze came," the Overseer said. "When storms moved the sky by inches each day and whole hills went wandering. There was a time when the sun could not be trusted and the ground shifted like a sleepwalker. The swarm learned a way to hold the world still enough to plant a child in it and know the child would not fall through. That is the story. Then there are the other stories."

"Tell me one."

The Overseer's gray eyes opened very slightly, as if to let in a measured light. "There is a story that the field does not hold the world still. It holds us together. It makes our eyes agree. It is not the mountains we fix. It is our position relative to one another. The mountains look stable because we are tied to each other tightly. When one eye looks away, the knot around that eye loosens. If enough loosen, there is not a swarm, there are only people with eyes, and the mountain has never promised anything to a person."

"Then why have a field at all?"

"Because it is hard to be a person," the Overseer said, and the words were very soft.

Maret made a sound then that was almost a laugh, almost a sob. "You speak as if you have stood outside it."

The Overseer did not answer. She took the hunter's hand between both of hers. The hands were warm and dry and held for exactly as long as the hunter allowed it. When the hunter did not pull away, the Overseer let the touch remain.

"You are a hunter," the Overseer said. "You know the taste of the world's edges. You know what it means to follow a trail no one else can see. If you choose to keep looking, take what the field gave you and go further. Do not tear the weave to prove there is a sky on the other side. Walk out from it and find out. But go knowing you will not come back to what is."

"If I go," the hunter said, "what happens to those who stay?"

"They will feel the looseness and pull their knots tighter," the Overseer said. "The hum may rise like a warning. There may be a shudder in the terraces. Perhaps a wall will crack. They will mend it. Your name will be spoken and then spoken less. This is not cruelty. This is how the swarm remains a swarm."

Maret's profile in the cool shadow was a study of tension. "If you go, I will feel it," he said. "Every morning I will feel it and not look. I will stand in the net and remember there was a time you made a hole and I did not go through."

She looked at him and loved him for saying it. She looked at the Overseer and loved her for not pretending love would make the choice lighter.

That night she lay awake again. The ache in her brow pulsed. She pressed her thumb to it. When she did, she felt something like a joint shift beneath the skin, as if her skull had a hinge and it had found its motion. She sat up with a small sound and the alcove seemed to lengthen in front of her like a hall. She reached her hand into the air and the air felt not empty but braided, as if threads ran through it in patterns that had been invisible and were now only barely seen.

This is what it is to be outside, she thought. Not to be alone, but to be among other braids that do not know your name.

She chose in the hour before dawn. She did not speak the choice aloud. She put on the pack that had always hung ready for a hunt, took water and a strip of dried meat and a coil of rope. She stood at the mouth of the alcove and watched the swarm's first stirrings, the way the hum gathered like bees at the edge of hearing. She placed her palm against the stone of the alcove mouth, as if to leave the print of her heat there. When she turned, Maret was standing in the path.

No words. He was holding something wrapped in cloth. He set it on the floor at her feet. She unwrapped it and found his knife. The bone handle had been polished by his hand. It was the kind of knife that could split a fish or carve a letter in bark.

"I will not ask you to stay," he said. "I ask you to bring back a word that means more than staying."

"If such a word exists," she said, "I will bring its shadow for you to taste."

He closed his eyes and let his breath move in and out once. "Walk well, little hunter."

She walked.

The first thing that changed was how distance behaved. On the terraces, distance was a series of agreed textures: gravel here, earth there, moss on that rock, the step down that always matched the length of a leg. Outside, distance loosened. A ridge that seemed a few breaths away became an hour. A turn in the path offered two different turns. She found that if she did not grip one too hard, both could be walked a little. She would go to the right and feel, almost like a pressure on the cheek, how it would be to go left. Neither path was a lie. One she took with her feet. One she took with a new kind of attention that tired her in a way muscles do not.

The second thing that changed was time. At first it was small. The shadow of a thorn bush reached toward a stone and then pulled away like a tide. Her own shadow shortened and lengthened by measures smaller than a finger. Then the changes grew. The sun's angle did not hold itself steady when a cloud thinned. The morning felt slightly longer. The ache at her brow relented as the sun moved, as if some inward muscle were no longer clenching.

On the third day she met another.

It would be truer to say that she encountered a braid that crossed her own. The path narrowed between stones. A figure stood at the far end of the narrow, watching her as if she were a deer. The figure had a cloak of woven grasses and a staff with a ring on its end. When the figure moved, the air around it seemed to catch and ripple, as if the figure pulled threads deliberately, the way a musician plucks.

"Your brow knows how to open," the stranger said. The voice was neither man nor woman, or else it was both with ease.

The hunter put her hand to her head without meaning to. "I am learning."

"You are unbraided from your swarm," the stranger said. "The taste of clay is still in your breath."

"Clay?"

"The field is like clay. It takes an impression. It holds a shape. It is useful. It dulls a knife. May I walk with you for a span?"

"Who are you?"

"A name from a different knot," the stranger said, and smiled. "I was once called a Severer. I am called other things now. I prefer Traveler."

"Walk, then," the hunter said.

They walked until the path opened into a saddle between two slopes. From there the valley was another valley. She could see the terraces in outline. She could almost feel the hum from this far, a low murmur under the skin like a memory of bees.

"You think your looking makes the sun move," the Traveler said.

"I think my looking lets me see that it does."

The Traveler nodded. "Both are toys of language. The world does not require your permission to change. But it is true that looking has the power to prefer one change over another. It is also true that when many eyes prefer the same thing together, that preference builds a scaffold that feels like law."

"Then the field was a kind of law."

"A kind and stern law. The kind a people make when the outside is too large to face without armor. The kind that saved children. The kind that eats the unwary. There are other laws. Some are made by looking. Some are made by refusal to look. Some are made by things that have never had eyes."

"What are those?"

"Wait until a night with no clouds," the Traveler said. "And do not be afraid when the dark at the center of the wheel looks back."

They made camp and ate in companionable silence. The Traveler's staff made a low tone when struck against a rock. The tone quivered in the new way she had begun to notice, which was not through the ears alone. It was like feeling a thread vibrate between teeth.

"Tell me a story," she said.

The Traveler obliged. "There was once a village on the edge of a salt plain. The plain was white and flat and the sky was hard and the sun was a coin pressed into the sky by a god with a steady thumb. The people learned to stand so that the god would not tilt its hand. They stood that way so long that their bones remembered the posture. Children were born with the posture already in them. One day a girl blinked an extra blink that had never been blinked. When she opened her eye, the coin had rolled a little. She laughed and the plain buckled. Her people scolded her and gave her water and taught her the posture anew. She learned. She forgot the extra blink. She grew and had children and they stood very still. Fifty years later, in the hour before her death, her eye blinked the extra blink again. The coin rolled. She laughed again, and the plain made a small sound, and the salt that had been flat for a hundred years shattered into a hundred thousand blades. The people bled but did not die. The wind came. The plain was never quite the same. This is not a parable. It is a record."

"Who recorded it?"

"Those of us who walk outside the clay," the Traveler said. "We tell the stories of the first blinks. There are more than you would think. There are fewer than are needed."

She slept with that sentence in her mouth like a pebble. She dreamed of a wheel of lights turning, of a hole in the center like a mouth, of a sound that was not a sound but a pressure, as if the world were a drum and something beneath it had struck once and was waiting for the echo to come home.

In the morning the Traveler was gone. The staff had left a circle of soot on the rock where it had rested. She stepped over it and felt the circle in her skin. A small, patient beat had joined her pulse.

She walked on. The land did not repeat itself as it had on the terraces. There were stones shaped like the backs of sleeping beasts and stones like broken teeth. There were flowers that turned their faces and seemed to whisper. There were runnels of water where she expected dry and dry where she expected spring. The ache at her brow was almost comfortable now, like a muscle used in a new way that promised strength.

On the seventh day she came to a place where the ground ended. Not in a cliff. Not in a fall. It ended in a thinness, like the place where a woven mat frays. Beyond the thinness was a slope of black where no light clung. The black did not absorb. It discarded. It was the kind of dark that made the air bright around it by contrast.

She crouched and touched the thin place with her fingers. It was cool. It vibrated very slightly. She pressed her palm and felt that if she leaned her weight she could make an opening. She sat back on her heels and laughed, and her laughter came back to her the way a metal bowl sings when struck.

"Do not do this alone," said a voice.

It was the Overseer.

She stood a little distance away, without her white cloak, dressed like a traveler in a garment the color of dust. Her eyes were open. They were gray and direct. She looked smaller without the hum surrounding her.

"How did you find me?"

"You are not hard to find," the Overseer said. "The places that fray like this attend to those who can attend to them. I have walked to several and looked. This is the one that looks back when you look. So here I am."

"Did you leave the swarm?"

"I never fully stood in it," the Overseer said, and the honesty of it made the hunter wince. "I tend the net. It is my task to feel its tensions, to repair its knots. That is a different standing."

"Will they be safe without you?"

"They will be safer without me if I must lie to them to keep them safe," the Overseer said. "Maret will stand in the field and hold it as if it were his own ribs. Others will follow him. The hum will be a little harsher for a while. It will smooth. And you, little hunter, will either come back with a word that is more than staying or you will step through and be a story. Both are a kind of help."

"Why come if you think I might step through?"

"To ask if you want a hand," the Overseer said.

They sat together at the fray. The black slope beyond looked patient and bottomless. It was not a pit. It was an opening whose direction did not obey up and down. The hunter closed her eyes and felt the threads in the thin place sing very softly. The Overseer took her hand as she had at the spring and set the hunter's palm flat to the thinness.

"Listen," the Overseer said.

The hum of the swarm was a memory now. Beneath it were other sounds. A rushing like sand. A tick like the crack of ice in spring. A distant longing like wind looking for a door. Under all of it a throb that did not come at regular intervals. It came when it wanted.

"What is it?" the hunter whispered.

"Names are nets," the Overseer said. "This one shreds nets. I have called it Mouth because of how it feels to be near it. The Traveler you met calls it Wheel. Others call it Seed. People who fear it call it End. People who swallow their fear call it Beginning."

"What do you call it?"

"Invitation," the Overseer said.

The hunter laughed again, softly. "Maret would say that not every invitation should be accepted."

"Maret is not wrong," the Overseer said. "But Maret does not have the hinge in his brow that you have. We are given our doors."

They did not speak for a time. The black slope did not move. The thinness vibrated. The hunter put her forehead to it, then her chest, then stood with her whole body against it as if the fray were a friend she had not embraced in years. She felt something shift inside her, the way a flock turns when one bird moves and the shape that is not the birds moves with them. She stepped back, breathing fast.

"If I go," she said, "I will not come back to what is."

"No," the Overseer said. "You will not."

"If I go and find nothing but hunger?"

"Then you will have met hunger, which is more than most meet when they stand still and insist the world does not move."

"If I go and find a way to hold what moves without making a net that kills the movement, I will have a word to bring."

"You will."

"What if the word is not a word," the hunter said, "but a practice?"

"Then you will teach it by doing it," the Overseer said.

The hunter thought of Maret's knife wrapped in cloth. She thought of the way his voice had held on to her name. She thought of the children placed at the terraces, shown how to widen their gaze until it softened. She thought of the hum like bees. She thought of the ache in her brow and the wheel of lights and the hole at its center that was not a hole but an opening. She thought of the story of the salt plain. She thought of the Traveler's staff singing on rock. She thought of the Overseer's hand around her wrist, warm and patient. She thought of the sun moving because it had always moved.

She stood. She put Maret's knife in her belt. She took the Overseer's hand. Together they pressed their palms into the thinness and leaned until it parted. It did not tear like cloth. It opened like lips.

The dark beyond was not absence. It was a medium. It felt like water that had never met light. It took their weight and cradled it and then, very gently, let it fall sideways. They did not fall downward. The world turned and they went with it. The sensation did not make her stomach lurch the way a cliff makes a stomach lurch. It made her chest open the way a laugh opens a chest.

They came to rest not on ground but on a web of something like ground. It was springy. It did not care what feet were. It held them the way a word holds a thought. Above them was a sky with no color she had known, and yet all colors were variations of it. In that sky moved not one sun but many, and some were not suns but wounds that bled brightness, and some were not wounds but eyes, and some were not eyes but ideas that had not yet chosen a shape.

The Overseer knelt and touched the web. It vibrated and made a sound like a chorus of low bells. The sound carried into the hunter's bones and found places there that had been empty and put something in them. She felt the ache at her brow become a line of clarity, like the edge of a blade.

"Look," the Overseer said.

The hunter looked, and as she did she saw the weave behind the weave. She saw that each light moved, and that each movement was not only itself but an agreement among other movements. She saw that nothing stood alone. Everything moved with at least one other thing and, in moving, made a pact that had the texture of law. Not a law that pinned. A law that obliged. She saw what it would mean to prefer a change without coercion. She saw how to watch without fixing.

"We can die here," the Overseer said, as if remarking on weather.

"We can die anywhere," the hunter said, and her voice was steadier than she expected. "Here we can die learning something useful."

The Overseer smiled with her eyes. "Spoken like one who has walked out of clay."

They walked in that place for a measure that could not be counted by the shadows of a ridge. They met others there. They met a woman whose hands smoked when she clapped them and whose laughter opened flowers that did not have stems. They met a person whose head was a cage of wires that sang when the lights passed through, and the song told of shores where time piled like driftwood. They met a being made of small mirror facets that changed reflection each time the hunter blinked. Some spoke in words. Some in tastes and pressures. Some in threads drawn across skin and tied in bows.

From each the hunter learned a small practice. How to press her thumb into the air and make a knot that could be pulled if something needed anchoring. How to open the hinge at her brow more gently so that the thin places opened without tearing. How to listen for the throb that came when it wanted and let her own breath match it without chasing. How to prefer a change that did not require denial. How to leave a path she could follow back if she needed to fetch someone else.

At the center of that place was the Mouth. She walked to its edge and felt her teeth hum and her bones ring. The Mouth did not eat. It invited. In its presence, practice felt like prayer and prayer felt like practice. She stood there with the Overseer and they did not speak because words would have made the invitation smaller.

When she had learned enough to know she would never be done, she turned to the Overseer and said, "I have a word."

"What is it?"

"Turning," she said. "Not the kind that betrays, the kind that attends. The kind hawks do. The kind wheels do. The kind rivers do when they find a new bed. The kind eyes do when they learn a second blink."

"That is a good word," the Overseer said. "It is a practice also."

"I will bring the practice."

"You will not be welcomed."

"I do not need welcome. I need Maret."

They returned through a thin place that opened when they pressed their palms to it. The terraces were as terraces are. The hum was there, but it was different to ears that had heard bells beneath bone. The swarm stood. Children watched their teachers widen their gaze. The sun sat. The ridge kept its distance. On the far end of the long slope, a wall that had always been sound had cracked, and a line of people were packing clay into the crack with careful hands.

Maret was standing near the crack, directing the packing. He turned before she called his name. He turned because he felt the loose place that was her, nearer now, and because his knots remembered a certain pattern of tension that belonged to her.

He walked to her and did not stop, and she put her forehead against his and felt the swarm's hum and the Mouth's throb make a braid that did not strangle.

"I brought a word," she said into his skin.

"Say it."

"Turning."

He closed his eyes and the lids trembled once. "Show me."

She did not lead him to a fray. She did not tell him to leave. She put his hand on her brow where the hinge had learned to move and she guided his finger to the place and pressed very gently until she felt his skin learn. His breath changed. He made a sound a child makes when wading into cold water and realizing that cold is another kind of alive.

"Now look at the sun," she said.

He looked. It moved. He did not pull away. His stomach tightened as if expecting to fall. He did not fall. The hum around them rose, then steadied. The crack in the wall made a different sound as clay settled deeper. A woman in the line packing the crack turned her head slightly in surprise and then resumed packing, but with a new measure, as if she had felt a different beat and chosen it without fear.

"What do we do?" he asked.

"We look together," she said. "We hold each other and look. We prefer change without lying. We make a net that flexes. We teach the children how to blink twice."

He laughed then, and the laugh met the hum and did not break it. He touched the knife at her belt, his knife, and she placed her hand over his hand.

"Will the mountain love us?" he said, because he was still Maret.

"The mountain will not notice us," she said, because she was still herself. "But we will notice it more truly. That is enough."

Not everyone chose the practice. Some pulled their knots tighter and made the hum ring like metal. Some looked once and grew sick and went to their sleeping hollows and spoke to no one for a day. Some learned to blink twice and found they could not stop. Some did not learn but did not forbid. The Overseer returned to her paths and tended a different net than before. The Traveler came to the ridge and stood at the edge of the terraces and struck the staff against stone and let the tone bring those who were ready.

The sun moved. It was not a disaster. It was the beginning of a long apprenticeship. The terraces shifted their step by a fraction. Plants learned to lean and then learned to grow in arcs. The goats found new shade. The wall cracked and was mended and cracked again along a different line that made more sense. A child fell and did not break a bone because the child's mother turned at the right moment and caught a forearm. The hum became a different song, not a choir holding one note because it feared silence, but a chord made of notes that knew how to arrive and leave.

Years later, when the hunter's hair showed threads of white and Maret's hands had the faint tremor of a man who has held too much and let it go, a young one came running to the ridge with eyes too wide. The young one had dreamt that the sun had stopped. The young one was afraid because stopping now felt like death.

The hunter knelt and pressed her thumb to the young one's brow where the hinge lived. The young one's breath steadied. They looked together at the sky. The sun was paused behind a cloud's edge and then it slid free.

"Sometimes not moving is a kind of movement," the hunter said. "We learn that too."

The young one laughed the small, proud laugh of someone who has grasped a new tool. The hunter watched the laugh pour into the hum and make it glow for an instant the way iron glows when it has learned a new shape.

In the quiet that followed, she looked past the valley. The thin places were there. They always had been. She could see them now the way a fisher sees the heavy shine of a school beneath the surface. She knew she would walk again. She would return with other words. She would discover that each word was smaller than the practice it named. She would die one day, perhaps at the edge of a fray with her palm across an opening and her cheek against the fabric that vibrated to a beat that did not count itself. Maret would die perhaps standing, perhaps sitting on the terrace with his eyes open and his gaze softened, perhaps with his hand on a child's wrist teaching the gentle pressure that shows where the hinge is.

The mountain would not notice either passing.

The sun would move.

The swarm would stand and would turn and would learn how to be a swarm that turned without dissolving, how to hold without pinning, how to prefer without lying. They would teach the children both blinks. They would say, this is how we stayed alive when the world was too large and our fear was too loud. They would say, this is how we got larger than our fear.

And somewhere beyond the ridge, the Mouth would open and close as it pleased. Somewhere in a sky she could not yet name, a wheel of lights would turn and each turn would be an invitation and each invitation would cut a new hole in a net and the nets would not be wasted, because nets are only cruel when they cannot be unknotted.

The hunter stood and put her palm to the stone of the alcove mouth as she had on the morning of her leaving, not to leave her heat in it now but to feel how it held heat differently. She pressed her thumb to her brow and then to Maret's and then to the child's, a blessing that was not a prayer but a practice.

"Look," she said, and all three of them did, and the sun moved, and the valley moved with it, and nothing broke that could not be mended by hands that had learned how to turn.

The Knot Garden

The terraces woke to breath.

They rose in steps against the slope, bands of stone and earth edged with dew. Water slid along the channels with a sound like quiet cloth. In the half light the cabbage leaves held round beads that made the rows look jewelled. Goats stood tethered at rope length along the upper wall. Their ears flicked at gnats, then went still again as the first bell rang.

Sera lifted the striker and touched it to the frame. The bell was no bigger than her palm, a thin disc strung in a wooden yoke, yet the tone it gave reached across the terraces and softened the eyes of those who heard it. People turned toward one another, not to focus, but to rest their gazes, to let seeing be a place to stand. Breath in fours. In, hold, out, rest. The sound cupped the morning, and the morning held.

Stilling was the word they used. It was not sleep and not prayer. It was the way the habitat kept itself smooth when the world wanted to pull it apart. Stilling brought many eyes together so that the place did not slip or snag. When the eyes were together, the air felt honest. When they were not, it felt thin at the edges and sharp in the middle.

Sera walked the nearest terrace while the breath counted itself. Her bare feet knew the good stones from the greedy ones. The soil held a faint cool through the soles. She set her hand to a resonance post at the row's end. Each post was a rib of seasoned wood set into the bed, banded with ring-iron. When she leaned in, cheek to grain, she could hear the line of the terrace, a thin hum behind the wind, the way a string sounds through a table.

The hum was even today. A good sign. She rested her fingers on the iron bands and felt them answer the bell. Parity, she thought. The word meant the way one tone lays within another without sanding it flat. Parity meant the breath and the bell and the line of stones agreed enough to keep the place gentle.

She moved on. A child coughed near the lower channel, then kept the count. The goats swallowed and stood. The first sun struck the far ridge, turning the rocks to a white that looked like water. In their pens, bees made a soft body of sound. Sera crouched at a gap where the channel lip had taken a nibble from a recent rain. She pressed the edge back into shape with her thumb and a flat stone. Water ran true.

At the third bed she saw it. To the eye, the cabbages were full. Leaves like outstretched hands, the soft gray green of a morning lake. Yet when she listened with her fingers to the post at the bed's head, the hum gave a little drag. Not broken, not even sour. Off by a tooth. She watched the leaves again and saw the pulse. The row breathed slightly against the cadence, a fraction of a count late.

Sera did not frown. She pressed the post again, then looked to the water. Nothing blocked the channel. The soil held moisture the way a good cloth holds dye. She took the little chalk from the pouch at her hip and made a single dot on the post. The chalk was ground with a shaving of bell metal. It left a pale mark that only startled when the hum grew thin. The dot stayed quiet. She tapped the bell yoke once to ease her mind. The tone came true.

"Later," she said under her breath. She flagged the misalignment in her head and kept walking.

Along the upper terrace the goat herder raised a hand without looking up. It was enough. Sera returned the gesture. His herd, rope-quiet, blinked in the soft way that told her the stilling held. Farther downslope, a midwife stood at a doorway with her palms open to the air, letting the first light fall across the lines of her hands. The air smelled of wet earth and the sharp green of crushed weeds.

Sera crossed to the bell-frame again and pulled the striker gently along its rim until the tone lifted and softened. The breath shifted with it. In, hold, out, rest. The counts rolled on, smoothing as they went. She walked to the next resonance post and laid her cheek against the wood. Behind the wind, behind the little noises of the waking place, the faint thread again. The thread said why. If the thread pulled tight and thin, the stone would want to crack along it. If it deepened, soft as a river pool, the terrace would take weight and pass it on without complaint.

A hand touched her elbow. She did not start. Tamar did not speak, either. He had a talent for not scraping the air with words before the bell settled the morning. He lifted the chalk pouch from her belt, shook it, and nodded. Enough for the walk. He pointed with his chin at the cabbage bed she had marked in her thoughts. She nodded back, a small tilt. Later.

The stilling drew down to its rest. People let their eyes sharpen again. Hands returned to tools. The goats stepped and tested the rope's reach, then took their first mouthfuls. The bell's last tone thinned and went, leaving only the run of water for a moment. Sera felt the absence like the removal of a weight. The habit of listening did not stop when the sound did. It just changed how it lived in her.

"Yield is up," Tamar said at last. His voice was low. He did not need to say it loud. The terraces told it for him. "Elder Pell will like the numbers."

"She will like the look of it," Sera said. "Numbers have voices. They sing truer than faces."

He smiled. "You are the only one who hears them sing."

"You hear them too. You just call it something else."

The goat herder laughed at his pen. Someone had stepped into a puddle and enlisted the good humor of the others to hide the wet footprints before the midday heat found them. Water clinked against the channel stones. The sky lost its pink. The light grew practical.

They heard the Stilling Circle before they saw the white of their cloaks. The bells the elders carried did not ring. The elders let the cloth speak for them. Three figures came along the upper path, heads uncovered, faces careful. They paused at the line of goats, hands folded, eyes resting in a practiced way that did not feel like rest at all.

Sera met them at the bend where the path stepped down. She did not bow. She touched her fingers to the post beside her, then to her chest. Welcome. The elders copied the gesture.

"Good water," said the first. Her hair was a pale braid that lay along her shoulder like a rope. "Good yield."

"Good breath," said the second. His voice had a trained evenness. "I felt no sand in the count."

The third elder said nothing. He stood with his hands inside his sleeves and looked over the beds with eyes that took in the edge of everything.

"Thank you," Sera said. "We tuned yesterday at second light. The wind was kind. A child had a cough at stilling. The count did not break."

"You have done careful work," said the first.

"Care speaks," the second added. "It is plain to anyone who listens."

The third elder finally looked at Sera, not past her, not through her. "Care is a wall until it is a door," he said. "See that it does not become a wall."

Sera waited. The words wanted to be three things at once. Praise. Warning. The shape of policy. The goats breathed and chewed. A bee landed on her sleeve, walked a moment, and continued.

"We had a thought," the first elder continued. "There is talk of wandering eyes."

The phrase was old. It meant people who let their gaze harden when the place asked for softness. It meant private attention kept when the habit asked for shared attention. It meant the kind of looking that could snag the hum and make the air thin.

Sera kept her face gentle. "I have walked most lines each day," she said. "The breath holds. The hum answers. A cabbage bed is a fraction off cadence. I will correct it."

The second elder tilted his head. "A fraction is where cracks begin."

"I have marked it for later," Sera said. "It is not the kind of error that comes from hard eyes. It is a small slip. Soil took more water in one place. The bed will balance."

The third elder's gaze slid to the chalk pouch at her hip. "We have seen chalk maps become superstition," he said. "A dot turns into a story. A story turns into a fear."

"The chalk is for my hand," Sera said. "Not for a story."

"Keep it so," the first elder said. "We will hear if anyone speaks of other dots."

The second elder turned his eyes toward the lower terraces, where market stalls would later set out baskets of greens and jars of honey. "The city is calm this week," he said. "Refugees have passed on to the next valley. There is no cause to squint at the wind and call it weather."

The third elder took a step down the path and touched a resonance post. He did not lean his cheek to the grain. He did not need to. He had the kind of hearing that turned inward first.

"The net holds," he said at length. "Do not pick at it."

Sera inclined her head. It was not assent. It was the shape of the moment. "We will keep yield and breath together," she said. "We will not pick."

The elders were not unkind. They were careful in their way, which was a way of protecting the names for things so the things would stay. They walked on, white cloth moving like a slow cloud across stone. As they passed the goat line, the animals lifted their chins for a heartbeat, then dropped them again. The elders' bells did not ring.

Tamar exhaled a breath he may have been holding. "They praised you," he said.

"They praised the garden," Sera said. "Then they warned the gardener."

He pointed his chin toward the cabbage bed. "Now or later?"

"Later," she said. "When the market stilling begins. I want to hear it with the place awake."

She tied the chalk pouch tight at her belt and lifted the bell striker again. The tone she coaxed from the disc was a shade lower now, made to sit under the day rather than lift it. People set to work with a rhythm that felt both human and fitted to stone. Sera turned the striker between her fingers, feeling the little pits in the wood where it had been held a thousand times. She looked once at the bed with the late-breath cabbages, then away.

The terraces held. The morning went on. The brittle places, if they were there, were still beneath the gloss, patient as hairline frost.

***

By midday the terraces were a market. Shade cloths had gone up along the lower paths, pale strips on ropes that made soft squares of cool. Jars of honey glowed where sun slipped through. Loaves sat under woven covers that smelled faintly of smoke. Someone played a low reed, barely a tune, more like a held breath with notes.

The bell for market stilling hung at the central post. People came to it with their chatter trailing, hands still dusted with flour or dirt, eyes ready to soften. Sera stood with her palm on the post, listening to the run of sound that was not yet lined up. Tamar stood at her side, chalk pouch tied and ready.

The first tone was lifted. It spread like a bowl turned right side up. Heads tipped. Eyes rested in that quiet way that is not blankness, but a relief from it. Breath in fours. In, hold, out, rest. The market eased into

235

the count. The reed stopped. A child reached for a plum and then did not. Two arguing cousins placed their hands over one another's, not as apology, but as a way to stall heat.

The seam came in the second hold.

It was not loud. It was not a crack by sound. It was a feeling like metal on the tongue. The air went bright and thin for a heartbeat. The hum behind it caught and grated, then smoothed again because so many eyes were resting.

The goats felt it first. Up on the upper terrace they stiffened as one. Legs braced. Eyes wide. Not a bleat. The ropes took their weight. For an instant the animals looked wrong inside the stillness, like drawings on a sheet that had been tugged from underneath.

Sera did not move her hand from the post. She let the count finish. When the breath released, she lifted the striker and pulled the tone back down a shade, making a little nest for the air to climb into. The goats stayed locked another two counts, then stepped forward and shook their ears.

She looked at Tamar. He had already untied the chalk pouch.

"Frost," he said, low.

"Frost," she agreed.

They did not ask the elders. The Circle had gone elsewhere after their rounds, white cloth a small waterfall up the path. This was craft. It belonged to the hands that held the posts, the bell, the chalk. Sera and Tamar started at the market's clean edge, where the stone path met packed earth, and worked outward.

Sera touched the bell with the back of her finger to call a traveling tone, soft and thin, just above the noise of the day. Tamar walked with the pouch and the stick of chalk between his fingers. Where Sera laid her palm to stone or wood, he listened with her and watched her hand. When the hum was even, he did nothing. When it caught, he marked with a whisper of gray-white that had a shine at the core.

The chalk was not magic. It held a shaving of the same metal as the bell, so it woke when the hum thinned. In good light the lines they drew were almost nothing. But when the air went metallic, the chalk let them see what would otherwise only be felt.

At the first bend, a thread of frost showed itself. Not on the wall line, not on the drainage break. It ran down the short cut between a baker's stall and the midwife's courtyard. You would not see it if you watched for straight things. It had the shape of footsteps that no one wanted to take. Sera and Tamar looked at it in the same instant.

"Here," Sera said.

She did not step on it. She stood with her heels just clear. She raised her hand and the little traveling tone deepened a finger's width. The hum around them pulled, resisted, then settled. The chalk brightened along the thread, thin light like winter in a hair.

People noticed the two of them, but did not crowd. The market knew Sera's work. It was the sort of attention that waited, that did not poke until asked. The midwife stood under her awning. The baker set his hands on a board to feel its flatness and kept them there, as if to keep himself from speaking too fast.

Sera looked to the midwife. The woman's mouth was a straight line that was not anger. Sera nodded, once, in a way that was not a request and not exactly permission either.

"Gentle," Tamar said.

Sera drew a breath and softened her eyes. She did not close them. The world was present, it simply became less sharp. She pressed her palm to the resonance of the path in front of her. Not stone, not wood, but a place worn by feet until it held a kind of tone. She waited until she could hear the market beneath the market. The reed came back in, a few notes. A goat coughed. A child's sandals squeaked. Behind those, the hum, and within the hum, the catch.

She lifted her other hand, palm up, and those closest mirrored her without talking. It was not formal. It was habit from other mornings. The two-blink cadence moved through the group like a ripple. In, hold, blink, blink, out. Sera let the second blink be late, barely so, just enough to see if the net would flex.

The ground did not move. The tone did. The thinness let go of its edge and slid back half a finger. The chalk line dulled.

Someone exhaled. It was not the sound of relief that comes from fear's end. It was the sound a person makes when a thing they have been holding finally says its own name out loud.

The woman under the awning stepped forward, then stopped, then came the rest of the way as if she had made the decision yesterday and only remembered it now.

"I have not gone to Bera's door," she said. Her voice did not tremble. "Since the loss. I walk around the back lanes, even when I carry herbs to the birth house. I have done this for three months."

She looked at the midwife as she spoke, not at the ground. Her hands were not empty. She had been threading a line through a row of little bells for a crib and the line still ran through her fingers like a river through reeds. The midwife listened with her whole face. She did not step forward. She did not soften or harden. She let the words pass, then she nodded once in a way that meant both I heard you and I am still here.

The chalk mark went dull where the path crossed between them. The frost thinned and broke into harmless shards that the next breeze would take.

Sera lowered her hands. She did not say thank you for the confession. It was not something that had been given to her. It belonged to the two women and to the place where it had landed. She touched the bell with the striker with the lightest stroke and brought the little traveling tone back to level.

They worked outward. Every time the chalk brightened, they noted where it ran. It refused to behave like a wall fracture. It followed the memory of arguments, the habit of avoidance, the quiet ways people had adjusted their days to step around one another. Lines curled around the back of the water jars where two brothers exchanged them to keep from speaking. A thin thread ran between a mason's bench and the shade where he used to sit with his father. It veered away from the bench as if embarrassed.

Tamar kept count in his way. Not numbers on a page, but tones in his mouth, barely voiced. Two long, one short. One held longer where the chalk flared wider. Sera listened for parity and made small adjustments. Sometimes it took nothing but a hand laid flat and a breath in twos. Sometimes it asked for the two-blink to pass through a dozen people at once, a little wave that made the market sway as if wind had found it.

Near the cabbage bed, the chalk did not flare. It stayed quiet as Sera had expected. The misalignment there was work for water and soil and hands. It was not a knot. They left it.

By the third pass, the map looked like a frost that only a winter in memory could make. Delicate, unavoidable, beautiful in a way that no one would admit while it was still dangerous. Sera stood back and pressed the chalk stick between her fingers until a faint powder coated her thumb. She tasted iron.

"We will need a ledger," Tamar said. He kept his eyes on the lines, not on her.

"Not here," Sera said. "Not yet."

"Night then."

"Night."

They turned a final corner and found the goat herder standing at the end of his rope lines, not holding them, just standing so the animals could see him. His goats had softened again, chewing with the simple wisdom of things that know how to be in a place. He gave Sera and Tamar a look that asked if this was a craft matter or a danger matter. Sera tipped her head toward the chalk map and then touched her chest. Craft, for now.

He grunted and scratched a goat between the horns. "Felt it on my teeth," he said.

"We all did," Tamar answered.

The sun shifted. The shade squares moved. Trade began again, not louder, but looser. The woman with the crib bells took a step toward the midwife's table and set her basket down on it, palms open. The midwife set her own palms open beside it. A small bell rolled to the edge and stopped with a sound like a smile.

Sera and Tamar returned to the central post. The chalk on Sera's fingers had lost its shine. She brushed her hands together and watched the powder fall into the seams between stones.

"Hidden knots," Tamar said.

"Not hidden," Sera said. "Only unsaid."

He looked at the map once more. "The Circle will not like this."

"They like yields," she said, and lifted the striker to draw the afternoon tone. "We will give them yields."

She set the tone delicately, a thread that could be carried with a person as they walked from stall to stall. The market breathed. The hum found its level. Underneath it, the frost lines held their shape, less bright now, but there. Sera felt both the beauty and the brittleness at once and knew it would not be enough, in time, to keep walking around such lines and pretend the stone was smooth.

***

Afternoon stretched, then folded into itself as Sera and Tamar walked the lines. They moved like a tide, two people in a pattern that had learned their feet. Palm to post, chalk to stone, tone to breath. Sera called a note low enough to hide under talk. Tamar kept his count the way he always did, a murmur in the mouth that never turned into numbers on a page.

Where the hum snagged, the chalk woke.

They found it behind the baker's stall where the back path, quicker, less seen, curved away from the midwife's courtyard. They found it at the edge of the mason's bench, the place where his chisel sang a thinner song since the tremor began in his hand. The chalk traced a thread from there to the shade where his father used to sit, a curve that did not touch either spot, as if it could not decide which was the memory and which was the ache.

A child had stopped singing in the mornings. Not a refusal, more like a tone that would not leave the throat. The chalk brightened along the path from her doorway to the school post, then dimmed at the point where she usually forgot and began to hum again. Sera knelt at that spot, pressed her palm to the warmed stone, and gave the bell a small lift. The child tried two notes, then smiled without looking at anyone, and the chalk cooled.

They watched a trader veer a little too wide to avoid a friend. Sera and Tamar marked the arc his steps drew. Later, when the trader brought bread to the friend's stall after closing, the line dulled like dew drying.

Sometimes the frost lit in places that had no story Sera could hear. She did not chase them. The chalk taught patience when it could not teach clarity.

At a bend where the terraces narrowed, Tamar's hand passed close to Sera's cheek and left a soft streak of gray. She closed one eye, felt the smear pull when she smiled. He reached to brush it away. She caught his wrist for a second and pressed his palm to a post instead. They listened together, skin to grain. A ripple passed through their hands at the same moment. The hum and their touch agreed. They laughed under their breath, quick, like birds.

By late light the map ran like frost caught in a spider web. Not on the walls, not along the water breaks, but over paths where people chose and chose again. Sera stood back to see it whole. She tasted iron again, faint on the tongue.

"Someone will have to keep this," Tamar said. He did not mean the chalk. He meant the practice.

Sera nodded, once. The word for what it needed came to her before the name did.

They climbed to the ridge above the upper terrace where a breeze kept the gnats from their eyes. From there the market looked like a single woven thing, roofs tied to paths tied to water strings. The sun was lower now, the white ridge beyond turned to a color between stone and milk.

The Overseer stood already on the ridge, not in white, not in cloth meant for notice, but in clothes that could have belonged to anyone who worked. He had a staff in his hand, the kind that took a tone if tapped at the right point, and a face that could listen without pulling words out of people.

"You have been walking," he said.

"Walking," Sera answered.

They did not bow. They stood near and looked in the same direction for a breath, so the talk would have a place to sit.

"The net holds," the Overseer said. "For now."

"It holds," Tamar said. "It snags."

The Overseer's eyes moved across the terraces as if he could see the chalk from here. Perhaps he could. He turned the staff a little in his fingers and brought it down with a soft touch on the rock at his feet. The tone was simple, clean. The air steadied around it.

"I have seen nets made to hold rock," he said. "Such nets do not know what to do with a person. They make a shape strong, then leave no room to untie anything without tearing it all. Nets that cannot be unknotted become cruel."

Sera kept her gaze on the terraces. "We found where it snags," she said. "Not on stones."

"On lives," Tamar added.

The Overseer nodded. "Then your work is listening, not tightening. You will need a place where small truths can be laid down without breaking the whole."

"A ledger," Sera said, surprised to hear the word so quickly. "One knot at a time, spoken and held."

"A Knot Ledger," the Overseer said, and the phrase settled between them as if it had been waiting at their feet. "Sanction a place to speak one thing each night. Not confession, not tally. A token to mark a truth. The map will loosen where it should. The net will learn how to breathe."

"Sanctioned," Tamar repeated. "The Circle will want to name it before it is even wood on stone."

"They can name it," the Overseer said, "if they will also let it be used."

Sera felt her jaw tighten, not at him, at herself. The word ledger had reached for something inside her. A name pressed behind her teeth, the one she had not said in a year of mornings. She swallowed and the name stayed where it was, waiting like a hand on a doorframe. She put her palm on the ridge rock and listened for the faint thread behind the wind until her breath steadied.

"We can try it at the lower terrace," she said. "After work, when there is time to stand without breaking someone's day."

The Overseer's mouth curved at the corner. Not quite a smile. An assent.

They did not hear the Stilling Circle approach, only the soft stop of their steps when the elders reached the ridge. White cloth makes its own tone. The three stood a little apart from the Overseer, as if they had climbed a different ridge and only arrived at the same stone by accident.

"We have heard talk," said the first elder, her braid dark against the pale of her shoulder. "Of chalk maps and private lines."

"We walk the lines to know where the hum snags," Sera said. "So we can loosen them."

"Or tighten them properly," said the second, voice even as ever.

The third elder looked past them to the terraces that had begun to take on the colors of late day. "You will not start a fashion of tokens and stories," he said. "Stories collect weight. They tip a place."

"We are considering a ledger," Tamar said. The word was deliberate now. If they were going to be named as doing something, he preferred to name it himself.

"No," said the first elder, gentle in a way that made the word heavier. "We issue an edict. Smooth all deviations, remove personal knots. Your work is to keep the hum even, not to invite it to speak back. If this chalk practice continues, we will remove work from those who persist."

Work removal meant you kept your hands, but you did not get to use them where you knew how. It meant someone else came to your post and set the bell for you. It meant the place kept breathing and left you out of the count. Sera felt the heat of that threat in her chest.

"The frost lines run along people," Tamar said, soft.

"People will learn to keep their eyes," the second elder replied. "They will stop wandering."

The Overseer watched the elders the way a person watches a bend in a river they have crossed many times, knowing both the quiet water and the sudden drop live a few paces apart. He tapped the staff once on the ridge rock, low.

"Nets that cannot be unknotted become cruel," he said, still looking at the terraces, not at the elders. "A ledger is a way to untie without tearing. One truth, one token, each night. You may sanction it or forbid it. The place will decide which one holds."

The elders did not turn toward him. They were careful not to make the talk into a contest. The first elder lifted her hand and let it fall again, the way a person resettles a thought in their lap.

"Keep the counts clean," she said to Sera. "Erase the chalk at dusk. We will speak again when the week is out."

They went down the path in their slow, deliberate way. The goats watched them pass and did not move. The elders' bells did not ring.

Sera watched the backs of their cloaks until the white was only a pale idea against the stone. She rubbed her thumb across the chalk on her finger and left a streak on her palm that looked like a thin cloud.

"We could leave the lines," Tamar said. "And still not forget where they are."

Sera did not answer. The knot behind her teeth pressed harder, not to choke, but to be known. It had weight. It had a sound she could hear when she put her cheek to wood. She touched the ridge rock again and listened to the faint thread behind the wind until the urge to speak eased. It did not pass. It settled, the way a hand settles on a doorknob and rests there before the turn.

"Night," she said at last. "Lower terrace."

"Night," Tamar echoed.

The Overseer gave the staff a small lift and the tone it made seemed to go down into the stone instead of out into the air.

"I will stand with you," he said. "Whatever the Circle names this, the place will know what it is."

They stayed on the ridge until the day thinned and the bees' hum turned to a low saw by the pens. Below, the frost map held faintly in the last light. Sera tucked the chalk away and felt her mouth shape the first letter of a name. She did not let it out. Not yet. She turned and took the path down into the woven thing that was their home, the net holding, the knots waiting to be loosened one by one.

***

Noon brought the heat in a sheet.

Shade cloths went pale and tight. The water in the channels slowed as if even it had to take a breath before crossing the open. Bees kept close to the hive mouths. The bell at the central post was quiet, waiting.

The Stilling Circle gathered on the upper path. White cloth caught the light and threw it back. The elders did not descend. They stood where the terraces could see them all at once. The first elder lifted a hand. The second set his gaze on the market without blinking, the way a teacher sets a lesson in the air. The third touched the central post with two fingers and left them there.

"Hold," the first elder called. The voice was not loud. It did not need to be. "Eyes wide. Breath to four. Do not move your gaze."

People obeyed. They had learned to keep a place smooth on less.

Sera and Tamar took their usual positions near the bell. Sera let her eyes soften, then stopped herself and kept them open as ordered. The count began. In, hold, out, rest. The elders made no tone. The silence above the breath felt clean in the first measure, then became a polished surface in the second.

The hum went glassy.

Sera felt it under her palm before she could name it in her head. The resonance did not settle into the stone. It skated across. Faces looked peaceful, but the peace had no depth. The goats on the upper line set their legs and stared. A child smiled too wide and kept smiling as if the expression had been set there.

Perfect. For a count or two, it was perfect. The terraces looked like a drawing. Every line behaved.

Then the glass broke.

The break had no sound she could point to. It lived at the back of the teeth and the base of the skull. The air turned metallic. Light bent thin along the edges of things. The hum hooked in the middle and tore along a line no wall had made.

Sera knew the path as soon as it cracked. It was the route between two families who had stopped visiting after a quarrel at a birth. The walkway between their doors crazed, a fine web of lines racing ahead of any foot that might step there. The wall beside it kept its calm.

Someone's basket fell and rolled. The goats locked their legs, then tried to step and found the ropes more real than the ground. A stall post quivered like a reed in shallow water.

Sera dropped the elder's instruction out of her body. She raised both hands in the signal the children used when they played the two-blink game. Palms up. Eyes soft. She did not ring the bell. The air could not hold a strong tone. She turned to Tamar.

He was already counting, not numbers, the mouth-shape of tones, low. He took her wrists and steadied her hands. She nodded once. The Overseer stepped into the open space by the central post and lifted his staff a finger's width. He did not strike it. He set its tip where it would be seen.

The first wave went through the market like a fold in cloth. In, hold, blink, blink, out. Not hard. Not sharp. Sera let the second blink lag a breath and felt the net flex. The glass edges around the crazed path softened. A crack that had been running paused, as if to look back at itself.

"Left," Tamar murmured. He meant the direction of the next wave.

Sera sent it. Palms shifted a fraction. Shoulders set, then eased. The goats took a step and did not fight the rope. On the upper path a jar tipped and did not break. The walkway held its fine lines and did not shatter into a fall.

The consensus storm rolled. It had a shape like heat on stone. It found every brittle place Sera and Tamar had mapped and pressed there, not to break bodies, but to test what the net could bear. People stayed in place and breathed to the hand, not to the elder's fixed count. The two-blink passed through them again, this time from the edges inward. The hum did not become soft. It became deep enough to contain what pressed at it.

Sera felt her hands start to tremble. Tamar's fingers closed over her wrists for a heartbeat, then let go so he could signal the next team down the row. The Overseer's staff pointed at the high terrace. A child caught the glance and threw the signal to her mother without words. The mother passed it to a neighbor. The wave climbed.

Light kept its thinness for another count. Then it thickened, not in weight, but in the way water thickens when it settles in a bowl. The metallic taste faded. The hum loosened. The crazing on the walkway stayed, a memory of the break, but it did not open.

The storm passed through the lower beds. A cabbages row held true without help. The frost lines Sera had traced at the market edge dulled a shade. The goats shook themselves and made the small sound that means a discomfort has left.

Silence came back first, then sound. Someone laughed once, too loud, then put a hand over their mouth. The baskets sat where they had fallen. The reed player did not move to lift the instrument.

The elders waited until the square had settled into the usual shape of noon. Then they came down the path. The white of their cloaks made a clean line through the air, as if they could draw straightness by walking.

"Well contained," said the first elder. Her face did not show relief. It showed confirmation.

"The hum was thin," the second said. "Something wandered."

The third elder stood directly in front of Sera and looked not at her hands, which still held a little tremor, but at her eyes.

"You called a wave," he said. "You broke the count."

Sera wiped chalk from her fingers onto her skirt. "The count was breaking," she said. "We flexed the net."

The second elder's mouth tightened. "Blinking breeds blinking. You teach people to keep their attention private, they will do it when the hum needs them most."

"We moved together," Tamar said, tone even. "No one fell."

"Not this time," the second elder replied.

The first elder turned her gaze to the crazed walkway. The fine lines looked like frost caught on stone. Two doorways faced one another across it, both shut. "This was not a wall," she said. "Someone turned their eyes the wrong way."

"Two someones," Sera said. She kept her voice gentle. "They will need a night to stand and say one thing. Then this will ease."

"The ledger you are planning," the third elder said. It was not a question.

Sera did not look away. "A place to lay one knot down each night. One token. Sanctioned. Small truths loosen small stress."

"No," the second elder said. "We will not encourage private knots to become public weight. Erase your chalk. Keep your eyes wide in stilling. Smooth the count. If waves must be called again, the Circle will call them."

Sera felt Tamar shift beside her, not to argue, but to warn her with a breath that said not now. She nodded once to the elders. It read as assent. It was the shape of what she could do in that moment without tearing something that could be unknotted later.

The elders turned and walked the length of the market, touching posts, letting their cloth be seen. People made way for them. No one bowed.

When they were gone, the Overseer lowered the staff and let it rest against the post. He did not speak. He looked at the walkway and then at Sera and Tamar. The three stood in a small triangle of shade that felt like shelter made of attention.

Sera let herself breathe all the way out. She felt where the tremor had settled in her forearms and shook it into her hands, two small flicks that looked like a bird setting its wings. Tamar took her hands as if to check the hum through her skin. She let him, and their breath found the same pace without counting.

"We did not fall," he said.

"Not today," she answered. She looked at the walkway again. "The crack is a map. We will not plaster it."

"Night," Tamar said.

"Night," Sera agreed.

Around them, market life began to climb back into itself. Someone set the reed to their mouth and let out a thin note, then a second, then found the tune again. The goats shook dust from their coats. Two doors across the crazed path opened a hand's width and stayed there.

Sera lifted the striker and brought the bell to a tone meant for afternoon work. It sat under voices like a quiet floor. People heard it without looking up. The net held. It did not forget what had moved through it.

***

Late light turned the chalk to ash.

Sera and Tamar laid the map flat across the central stones, a lace of pale lines that looked like winter laid over summer. The day's warmth rose through it as if memory could have temperature. The crazed walkway between the two doorways showed as a skirt of fine crackle. The arc behind the mason's bench curved like the white of a nail. Threads from the baker's stall touched the midwife's step and faded at the place where the woman with the crib bells had stood.

Tamar set the bell-frame at the edge of the map and tuned it low, so the tone would nest in the stone and not float into the air. He did not ring it. He slid a finger around the rim until the frame hummed to itself. Then he began to count in the way he counted when the counts mattered. He did not speak numbers. He spoke tone shapes.

Long, long, short. Hold. Long, short, short, rest.

He traced one path with his fingertip and set a soft pitch to it. The chalk brightened and dimmed as if it could remember where the hum had snagged. He traced another and let a second pitch lay across the first. Where they crossed, he held both a fraction longer. The two pitches did not cancel. They made a third tone that neither one held alone.

"The stilling count misses this," he said. "It is square. The place is not."

Sera listened with her head tilted a little, so the world and the map could share her ear. Tamar moved his hand again, overlaying the chalk with tally tones only he could keep that steady without a drum. A rhythm appeared that the bell did not call. It lived between. It wanted steps.

Children drifted to the edge of the square. They pretended not to watch. One had a reed. One had a little bell on a string at her wrist. Ilen stood with his weight forward, as if the ground could start any moment and he would follow it.

"Do you hear it," Tamar said, not quite a question.

Sera did not answer at once. She closed her eyes and opened them again. Two blinks. The rhythm waited for the second. It was late by half a breath, then early by a sliver, then late again. Not lazy. Not careless. Human.

"The adolescents are already moving on it," Tamar said. "Watch their shoulders."

He did not mean it for flattery to the young. He meant it because their bodies had not been taught to iron the world. Ilen lifted his heels and lowered them without thinking. The girl with the wrist bell did not ring it. She let it sway. It caught the light on a beat Sera could not have written if she tried.

Sera let out a breath she had been holding since noon. The metallic taste had gone. The smell of evening water took its place. The frost map sang back to them. It asked to be danced, not erased.

"You can keep the counts square," Tamar said, softer now, feeling where she was standing in herself. "Or you can set the frame to what the place already is."

Sera thought of the elders on the ridge, the word edict on their tongues. Smooth all deviations. She thought of the walkway that had crazed and held when the market flexed together. She thought of the woman with the crib bells and the sound her basket had made when it rolled to the edge and stopped like a small laugh. The knot in her mouth pressed at her teeth, not to choke, but to remind her it had a right to air.

The Overseer came without fuss, as he always did. He did not look at the map first. He looked at their faces to know what he was walking into.

"You found it," he said.

"Tamar heard it," Sera answered. "I only agreed."

The Overseer smiled with his eyes. "That is often the work."

Sera knelt and placed her palm on the chalk where three threads crossed. She felt the bell-frame's low hum through the stone. She felt the tally tones through Tamar's breath. She felt the map answer, a line of quiet that held. It was not flat. It was layered. Like soil that grows things.

She stood and brushed chalk from her knees. She looked toward the lower terrace where the last of the shade was gathering. Beyond that bend the Circle's eyes did not reach unless they came down among the stalls and stayed.

"Night," she said.

The Overseer tipped his head. "Night."

"Tamar," she said without looking at him, so the words would not make him carry more than his share. "We will pilot the ledger at lower terrace. One truth. One token. Those who come will stand in two blinks. We will not call it against the elders. We will call it for the place."

"For the place," he echoed.

Ilen had edged closer, the way children do when they know they are about to be allowed into something adults think is theirs. He balanced on the balls of his feet. The girl with the wrist bell tucked her hand into her shirt to stop it from betraying her interest.

Sera straightened and turned to them. "You can help," she said. "Not as game. As teaching. The two-blink is the door. Some will need your bodies to show them how it opens."

Ilen tried not to grin and failed. He put his palms together and then opened them in the slow hinge that made the blink visible without making it a trick. The girl took her hand from her shirt and let the bell turn once. It did not ring. It flashed. It was enough.

Tamar looked at Sera. "If the Circle hears," he said.

"They will," she said. "Later. After the place has felt what it is like to loosen. The elders can forbid a word. They cannot forbid a breath."

She went to the bell-frame and tuned it down another hair until the tone matched the angle of the sun. Then she lifted the striker and called a single note to catch the end of the day. Not the stilling tone. A call to gather.

People looked up from their tasks. The sound did not ask for heads bowed or eyes wide. It asked for presence and patience. Sera made a sign toward the lower terrace with her hand, not secretive, not grand.

"After work," she called, voice easy. "Before full dark. Bring a small token. A button, a seed, a bit of wire. One truth only. We will keep the place steady and let it breathe."

No one applauded. That was not how things were asked for here. A mother nodded without looking at her child. The child hopped once and tried to turn it into a step. The mason, who had learned to hold his chisel with his other hand, lifted it in salute. The midwife touched the table and then her chest.

"Ledger stone," Tamar said. "Where?"

"Lower terrace," Sera said. "At the old watering trough. It holds tone and does not shout."

The Overseer set his staff tip on the map so lightly the chalk did not smear. "Sanction comes in two kinds," he said. "Paper and doing. Tonight you will have the kind that makes tomorrow possible, even if the first takes longer."

"Will you stand with us," Sera asked.

"I will stand," he said. "I will not speak unless asked. This is your work."

Sera picked up the chalk and drew a small open circle at the lower edge of the map where the trough would be. She did not need to. She wanted to. It felt like setting a bowl under a drip.

The adolescents had already started moving. Not toward the trough. Toward each other. The two-blink passed between them as easily as a joke. Quick, soft, exact. A new rhythm laid itself over the square like a transparent cloth. The reed player found it by accident and then pretended it had always been the tune.

Sera watched until she could feel the beat in the skin on her forearms. She let herself imagine, for the space of a breath, what it would be like to step into the ledger's circle and say the name that had sat in her mouth all year. Not confession. A truth, set down so the map could loosen where it must. The thought lifted and settled without breaking her.

"The Circle will call this wandering," Tamar said, quiet.

"They can name it as they like," Sera said. "We will name it listening."

She took the bell-frame in both hands and carried it to the lower terrace. Tamar gathered the chalk and the small bowl that would hold tokens.

Ilen ran ahead and cleared pebbles from the trough mouth, the way he would before a game. The girl with the wrist bell walked slowly, close behind Sera, so the bell would learn the path.

Evening came on. The map stayed on the stones behind them, singing in its soft way. The place did not forget its snags. It did not forgive them either. It allowed for them. Sera felt the turn inside herself as clearly as any tone she had ever set. The decision had weight and it made the ground steadier under her feet.

***

Night came down the terraces as small lights.

Candles stood in clay cups along the rows, one at the end of each bed, the wicks giving a calm, steady flame. The old watering trough on the lower terrace had been scrubbed and pushed up onto flat stones to make a table. The bell-frame rested there, tuned so soft the note only lived in the wood. A shallow bowl sat beside it. Someone had lined the bowl with a strip of cloth, so the tokens would not click like coins.

Adults gathered in ones and twos, the way people do when they want to be present but not be seen arriving. Children came as rivers do, in small currents that merge. They peered around legs, whispering, then went quiet when they saw the candles and the bowl. Ilen stood to the side with the girl whose wrist bell had learned the new rhythm. The Overseer took a place at the edge of the circle, staff grounded, eyes easy. He gave Sera a small nod and then let his face become ordinary.

Sera lifted her hands. Palms together, then open. A hinge. The two-blink cadence began at a hum low enough to sit under the night. In, hold, blink, blink, out. The first rounds were slow. Adults looked at their hands as if they were new tools that might not work. Children copied Sera and then copied one another, palms pressed, fingers lined up, shoulders loosened. The breath found them. It felt like setting down a weight you did not know you were carrying until you let it go.

"The ledger is simple," Sera said, when the cadence had settled. "One truth, one token. Not a story. Not a plea. We set one knot down so the map can loosen. The bowl will hold them. The place will do the rest."

No one moved. That was right. The first step in any rite is the moment where nothing happens and everyone decides whether they are truly there. The bell-frame's soft tone held the space between. A moth passed through the candlelight and left no scorch.

The first to step forward was the woman who had strung crib bells. She carried a small seed in her palm, thumb over it as if it might fly. She set her other hand on the trough stone, closed her eyes once, opened them, then spoke.

"I have not said her name at the door," she said. "I will say it here. Lera."

She placed the seed in the bowl. The cloth caught it with the faintest sound. The chalk frost along the nearest bed dulled by a shade, as if someone had breathed on cold glass. The midwife stood three steps away. She lifted a hand and set it open on the stone beside the bowl. She did not reach for the woman. She let her be within reach.

A mason came next. He put down a washer of bent wire and kept his eyes on his hands. "I have a tremor in the hand I use," he said. "I have hoped no one noticed. People have noticed."

He let the wire go. The chalk along the path between his bench and the shade where his father used to sit lost its thin shine. He did not look toward the shade. He stood another breath, then nodded to no one and stepped back.

The trader who had walked around a friend's stall stepped forward with a button that had lost its backing thread. He held it between finger and thumb. "I owe for bread," he said. "Two loaves. I avoided paying because the numbers I keep are a mess I do not want to show. I will pay tomorrow. I will show the mess."

He set the button down. The arc that had traced his avoidance dimmed until it was only memory. Across the square, his friend lifted his eyebrows once in the shape of a yes, and returned to stillness.

A girl spoke from the edge. She did not come to the bowl. She kept her feet where they were and raised her voice just enough. "I stopped singing, not because I could not, but because when I sing my brother cries, and I did not want to make him cry." She blushed, then smiled at her own simple logic. "I will sing when he sleeps."

Sera gestured with two fingers toward the bowl. The girl ran to it and dropped in a bead with a chipped blue glaze. The chalk on the path to the school post cooled to its ordinary gray.

A man Sera did not know well placed a piece of smooth glass. "I will not take the ridge path alone this month," he said. "I pretend I like its view, but I am afraid of how the wind takes me there."

Each truth had the weight of a stone small enough to carry, large enough to feel. No one made a speech. No one asked for pardon. They set one thing down and made room for the next. The bowl began to fill with the humble inventory of a life: a nail without a head, a strip of cloth with a knot tied in it, a curl of shaving from a newly dressed post, a single bell clapper without its bell.

Between each step, the two-blink moved. The children carried it, then handed it back to the adults without fuss. In the candlelight the hinge of many hands looked like a flock of small birds opening their wings.

Sera recorded each token in a thin hand on a strip of bark. Not names of people, names of truths. Tremor. Ridge. Bread. Lera. She did not look up when she wrote. She let her ear keep the place in her body where words belong.

Tamar kept the tone under the rite. He did not strike the bell-frame. He ran his finger along the rim in slow ovals so the wood would remember being asked, not commanded. Every so often he glanced up at the chalk marks on the nearby posts. With each truth, the faint frost receded a touch, the shine leaving, the wood becoming only wood again.

At last the movement thinned. The bowl was not full, but it had a shape now that did not look temporary. People stood in a circle wider than at the start. They breathed in twos without thinking. A baby made a soft sound and fell back to sleep against a shoulder. Far up on the upper terrace, a goat sneezed and then decided not to sneeze again.

Sera let the cadence slow. She closed her palms and opened them once more, then set her hands down on the ledger stone. "Thank you," she said. "We will keep the bowl here overnight. If a truth comes, set a token without words. Morning will hold it just the same."

People did not applaud. They did the older thing. They stood a moment longer than they needed to, then left by slow paths that allowed for small encounters to become small repairs. At the edge of the square the woman with the crib bells and the midwife stopped, faced one another full, and did not speak. They did not need to.

The candles burned lower. The Overseer lifted his staff, left a small touch of wood on stone to mark that he had stood with them, then walked away without a scrape of his steps. Ilen collected wax drips with a child's attention to treasure. The girl with the wrist bell tied it off so it would not ring in her sleep.

Sera stayed to close the bell-frame. Tamar stayed with her. They said nothing until the square was mostly theirs.

"Good work," he said at last, voice a thread under the air.

"It felt like right work," she said.

They sat on the low edge of the trough, hips almost touching, shoulders warmed where the candle heat had soaked the stone. Sera turned to him and rested her forehead against his. He leaned in without surprise. Their breath found the same count without being told. In, hold, out, rest. She let the two-blink settle between them, a small hinge that did not need to open all the way to be understood.

She reached into her pocket and brought out a small smooth disc of clay. It was unmarked. Most people press a line or a seed into such discs before they keep them. She had kept this one blank since the day she made it. She set it on the ledger stone between them, not in the bowl, not yet.

"I cannot speak it," she said, almost a whisper. "Not tonight."

"I know," he said.

"This is a promise that I will."

He covered the disc with his fingers, then lifted his hand away so that it was visible again. "I will be here when you do," he said. "The place will be here too."

They stayed a while longer, listening to the low run of water in the dark. Sera closed the bell-frame by running her finger around it once more and letting the tone go back into the wood. The candles dwindled to a few soft cups. Somewhere a night bird gave a single call and then thought better of it.

They stood and gathered the bowl and the strip of bark with its clean list of truths. Sera left the blank token on the stone where the first light would find it. She pressed her palm to the trough edge and felt the hum in the stone settle as if a hand had smoothed a wrinkle from cloth.

"Tomorrow," Tamar said.

"Tomorrow," Sera echoed.

They walked out together into the dark that was not empty, the map easier by a degree around them, the knots a little looser, the place learning how to breathe.

***

The edict came in white.

At first light the Stilling Circle walked the upper path and read from a strip of bark held between careful fingers. Their cloaks caught the day like clouds that had chosen to be rectangles. People paused along the terraces, not out of deference, but because the sound of law has a way of asking for space.

"Ledger gatherings are forbidden," the first elder read. "Erase chalk from posts and paths. Stilling is to be kept in the count, eyes wide, without variation. Those who convene unsanctioned rites will be removed from work."

The second elder folded the bark and placed it in the sleeve of his robe. The third touched the central post, not with the affection of a hand that knows wood, but with the weight of a seal.

Sera stood by the old trough, the bowl of tokens under a cloth, the bell-frame with its note asleep. She said nothing. The Overseer watched from the lower terrace with a stillness that had its own tone. Tamar stood beside Sera, hands open at his sides, chalk pouch tied and visible.

People looked from the elders to the trough and back again. No one argued. Arguments turn air thin. The elders departed in their measured way, white slipping behind stone and reappearing along the next path.

The council met at midday in the long house that faced the square. The long house held cool even in heat. Banners of woven reed hung between its posts and made the light into quiet bands. The Stilling Circle sat at one end. The Overseer stood rather than take a seat. Sera and Tamar took places near the middle, close enough to be called on, far enough not to make the meeting about their bodies.

"The ledger invites wandering," the second elder said. "It substitutes private weight for public duty."

"The ledger invites speaking," the Overseer answered. "It loosens where the net snags. A knot that cannot be set down becomes a hard eye later."

"We hold together by sameness," said the first elder. "The count is the measure."

"The count is a frame," the Overseer said. "The place has a rhythm underneath it. We heard it when the walkway crazed and did not break. Sanction a small rite. One truth, one token, each night. Keep it near the frame. Do not drive it into shadow."

Murmurs moved along the posts like a low wind. People who had stood at the trough the night before did not speak, and it was not silence. It was a kind of consent that waits for a shape to hold it. A mason lifted his left hand, the one that did not tremble, and asked to put words in the room.

"I would prefer to say my one thing where others can stand with me," he said. "If I cannot say it where it belongs, I will still have it. It will not leave me if I pretend it is not there."

A midwife added, "When a name is said, breath returns to the door. It is a small thing. It keeps the house."

The third elder tapped his fingers on the bench as if to count without letting the sound be known. "We cannot permit a fashion. It will grow like vine over stones."

"Then trim it," the Overseer said. "Do not salt the soil. If you forbid the two-blink, children will carry it anyway. If you forbid the ledger, truths will seek a poorer vessel and spill in worse places."

The council did not decide. It split. By afternoon, work on the upper terraces slowed, then stopped where people were not certain whether they would be punished for stepping along chalk. Water channels, left without their usual small corrections, began to overfill at a bend and send a thin sheet across a path. Goats, unhappy with wet hooves, pulled their ropes and complained to anyone who would listen. Sera and Tamar moved to trim the channel lip and hesitated, not at the labor, but at the way the act might be read.

"Do we work," Tamar asked, "or do we stand still to make their stop a fact?"

"Work," Sera said. "The channel does not know edicts." They shaped the lip with flat stones until the water ran true again. Two elders watched from the ridge and said nothing.

By late day a new sound traveled the square. Not the reed, not the bell. Laughter with a beat in it. Children had made the two-blink into a game. They stood in a ring and passed the hinge in a ripple, palms pressed, eyes soft, then open, then soft again. Ilen called the changes with his hands, not his mouth, so the elders could not say he had given a command. The girl with the wrist bell had tied it so that it flashed when the second blink came, quick silver at the edge of vision.

At first adults frowned, because frowning is a habit when law is near. Then they did the older thing. They watched without stopping it. Two women on their way to the well paused as the ripple reached them. They let it pass through their chests and found themselves breathing steadier after. A man on a ladder fixing a shade cloth matched the blink without climbing down and later could not have said when he had learned it.

In the quiet between chores, Sera and Tamar unrolled the chalk map in their workroom and set a small lamp beside it. The room was little more than walls around a table, a window without glass, a shelf with tools lined like simple bones. The lamp made a small lake of light. Outside, voices dimmed to evening shapes.

Sera's hands shook. Not with fear exactly. With the residue of being looked at by white cloth. She lifted the chalk and found she could not set it down where she meant. The line did not care about law. It cared about touch. Her touch had become a little less sure.

Tamar came around the table and set his hand over her wrist, not to stop it, to lend it weight. He guided the chalk to the place where the frost had been brightest at noon and pulled a thin crescent that did not double itself. The chalk took, even pressure, even shine.

"I am afraid of losing tempo," he said. He did not hesitate, as if he had saved the sentence for the right simple moment. "When I am counted at, I can keep any beat. When I hear the place and must answer without a mark, I think I will falter. I do not want to falter with you watching."

Sera set the chalk down and turned her hand under his so their palms met. She did not hurry her answer. "I am afraid of speaking the one thing I need to say," she said. "I carry it like a stone in my mouth. I do not want to drop it on the map where it might break the table."

He smiled without humor and pressed their hands together until the tremor in hers found a place to live. "We will fail on small things, here, where it is safe," he said. "Then we will step out there and fail less. Or fail better."

"Keep mapping," she said.

They did. By lamplight they traced the lines the storm had woken. Tamar's mouth formed tones under his breath to keep their hands steady. Sera's touch became sure again. They left the map rolled at the edge of the table where the lamp's soot would not smudge it and put the chalk to sleep in its pouch.

The night carried the game of blinks into courtyards and doorways. Children taught adults the way only children can, by not naming what they were doing as teaching. The edict held on the ridge in white language. It did not hold at the level of small hands. The place learned the hinge by repetition until it ceased to be separate from how people stood near one another.

Near midnight the water in the channels told Sera what she needed to know. It had its usual voice again. Overflow had settled back into line where neighbors had nudged lips with a flat stone on their way home from the square. No one asked if they were allowed.

In the morning, the elders would make the edict again. In the morning, the council might call a vote. Between those times the ledger bowl would sit under its cloth at the trough and collect a couple of tokens set down without witness. The map would keep its memory of frost without the brightness of fear. Sera and Tamar lay down for a few hours with work still in their hands, a shared rhythm under their ribs, and a decision they had already made. They would keep mapping. They would keep listening.

***

Morning brought a working quiet.

Sera spread the chalk map across the central stones and weighted the corners with flat rocks. The frost lines were a memory now, not bright, but present. She set a basket of markers beside the map: red cloth strips for slump zones, thin willow wands for bracing, a handful of smooth stones to mark catch basins where water would pool.

"We plan for safe failure," she said to the small circle around her. "We do not pretend nothing will give."

The circle was mixed. Tamar and the Overseer. Ilen and three other adolescents who had learned to throw the two-blink like a ripple. The goat herder. A mason who could build quick and true even with the tremor. Two market women who held a street with a look. The midwife. A pair of elders who were not of the Circle and wore their age like a tool.

Sera touched the map.

"Slump zones here and here," she said. "The beds are heavy. If the hum hardens, they will want to move. We give them a place to settle without taking anyone with them."

They tied red cloth at the ends of those beds and piled loose soil into low troughs to catch the slide. Children carried buckets. The mason set small wedges where the wall stones could give without jumping. Every so often he stopped, shook his working hand loose, and went on.

"Walkways," Sera said. She laid willow wands across the chalk where paths crossed the heaviest social lines. "Brace these spans. Rope lattices.

Spare planks. If the air goes thin, feet will try to hurry. Hurrying makes breaks. We make sure a misstep lands on something that can take it."

Tamar and the goat herder hauled planks that had been sunning against a wall since last season. The women wove rope between posts with a speed that came from years of tying loads that must not spill. Ilen ran messages and came back without panting.

"Water," Sera said. "Catch basins here." She set the smooth stones down on the map as if placing drops that would later be real. "We lower the small gates upstream to overfill the basins by a hand, not more. If a bed slumps, the water takes weight and slows a slide. Ready to be let go when the storm passes."

Two boys ran for the gates, too eager, then slowed under Sera's raised palm. "Not yet," she said. "When I call. The channels remember better if we ask what we need from them at the right time."

Tamar tuned the bell-frame low on the ledger stone. He did not ring it yet. He marked the map in tones. Each terrace received a note, gently different from its neighbor, so that a wave could be called along or across without confusion. He assigned hands to notes: palms high for the top tone, waist level for the middle, near the knee for the low. He showed the teams how to mirror the signals so a wave could travel in both directions.

"Team one," he said, "takes the high path and watches for goat lines. Team two braces the market edge. Team three holds the bridge by the crazed walkway. Team four runs messages to Sera and returns. No one is a hero. Everyone keeps a breath that someone else can borrow."

The Overseer moved through the preparations without taking charge. He spoke with the two older townsfolk apart from the others. Sera caught the drift: witnesses, a quiet duty. If the storm came as they expected and passed as they hoped, there would be a first moment when the ledger could be sanctioned by deed, not word. They would stand at the trough with bark and ink and record the first entries of the ledger under watch, because living through the storm would grant them the right to mark what it had taught.

"If we live," one of them said, not dramatic, just honest.

"If we live," the Overseer echoed, and touched his staff to the trough stone with a sound that felt like a hand on a shoulder.

Training began.

In small groups Sera walked teams through the two-blink under motion. Not in place. Along paths. Up steps. Over braced walkways. She called a blink with her fingers and let the wave cross them at different angles, so they would know that the body can hold a door open from more than one side. Ilen taught the children to throw the signal without making a game of it now, though he could not help smiling when an entire row of neighbors caught the hinge and made it theirs.

Tamar drilled the tone map. High note left, low note right, middle down the center. He sang the intervals soft so the ear could learn them as distance, not just sound. The teams repeated them back until the tones belonged to them. He pressed chalk on volunteer wrists in small circles that would remind them, when the air went metallic, that the body still knew what to do.

Sera walked the slump zones and felt the weight of what she was asking the place to do. Beds would move. There would be cracks that could not be smoothed after. She set her palm to one red-marked bed and leaned her cheek to the wood of the post at its end. The hum behind the wind said it would bear it if the people did.

Near noon she found Tamar alone by the ledger stone. He had finished marking the assignments and was rubbing the ink from his fingers with a rag. The square was noisy in the way work is noisy. The noise made a good cover for quiet things.

"Sera," he said, without looking up.

She set both hands on the edge of the stone and felt the cool through her skin. The blank of last night's token waited in her pocket. The knot in her mouth had stopped pressing like a fist. It had become a small warm weight. She took the disc out and held it between her thumb and forefinger, then set it on the stone in the same place she had the night before.

"Listen," she said. It was not a command. It was a request to herself. She closed her eyes once, opened them, and let the name out.

"Rion."

The breath that followed was not hard. It was not relief, exactly. It was the right thing after the right word. Tamar's hand found hers without looking. He did not squeeze. He accompanied.

"My brother," she said. "He went on the ridge in a wind that was not kind. We did not say his name at doors because the wind seemed to lift when it heard it. I have been quiet for a year. Quiet does not hold a place. I know that. I know it now in my mouth."

Tamar turned her palm over and set the blank disc in it, then covered it with his hand and lifted both to the bowl. He did not drop the token.

He waited until she nodded. She nodded, and they let it go together. The cloth in the bowl took the weight and the sound did not travel.

"My knot is fear," he said. His voice did not waver. He had been saying parts of this for days. "I fear losing tempo when no one calls it. I fear the count in my mouth will slip when the storm asks for steadiness. I do not want to make a mistake where you can see it. I do not want to make a mistake where the place can feel it."

Sera slid her fingers between his and held them. "You already told me," she said. "Tell the place."

He took a thin washer from his pocket, plain, the kind a person keeps because they know it will be useful one day. He set it in the bowl and the ring lay next to the disc like two notes that made a chord.

They did not kiss. They pressed their foreheads together for a breath and let the two-blink pass between them. It was enough. The Overseer approached and stopped at a distance where words could reach without touching.

"I heard," he said, quietly. "Not the names. The sound of two knots set down. Thank you."

Sera lifted her head and met his eyes. "We will need your witnesses," she said.

"They are ready," he answered. "They will stand at the ledger when the air is thin. If we endure, they write. If we do not, the stone will remember our hands."

Work resumed with a new steadiness. Teams moved to their positions. The rope lattices looked like nets that knew they might have to hold a person, not a load. The catch basins along the channels sat like quiet bowls ready to be useful. The red ties on the slump zones lifted a little in the light wind and fluttered as if they were saying what they were for.

Tamar stood at the bell-frame and ran a fingertip along its rim. He called each team's tone once. The notes did not carry far. They sat under the air, a plan you could feel through your feet if you had learned how. The adolescents took their places at the edges to throw signals where the tones would not reach.

Sera walked the length of the square and felt where her fear had been. It had thinned. Not gone. Honest. She checked the braces at the crazed walkway. She spoke softly to the goats, who met her eyes and then looked past her, which is the way animals show trust. She placed her hand on the central post and listened for the thread behind the wind. It held true.

"Lower the gates a hand," she called. Two small figures at the channel handles obeyed. Water lifted into the basins and made a low sound like someone pouring from a clay jug. "Hold there," she said, and they held.

The Overseer made one more round with the two witnesses. He showed them where the bark and ink lay and where to stand so they would not be in the way when the wave moved. He did not bless them. He did not need to. He set the end of his staff on the stone and left the smallest mark, a circle no bigger than a coin, a sign that someone had planned for after.

They gathered at the center once more, not for stilling, for alignment. Sera raised her hands and the teams mirrored her. Palms up, then down. Two blinks passed through them to test the hinge. Tamar nodded to the bell-frame and the tones answered in order, high to low. The adolescents threw a wave across the terraces and caught it coming back.

"This is the plan," Sera said. "We accept what must give and keep each other from falling. We speak when we must, we signal when we can, we stay in reach."

The day did not darken yet. It changed shape. Heat eased. A hush not of silence, but of preparedness settled. The map lay on the stones, marked and understood. The ledger bowl held two more tokens. The basins waited. The nets of rope shone a little. The count in Tamar's mouth stayed true.

Sera looked to the ridge. Clouds gathered in a thin line there, a sign without a promise. She lifted the striker. She did not ring the bell. Not yet. She set it back in the yoke and felt its weight. Then she took her place at the ledger stone and put her hand on the trough as if it were the back of a living thing, and waited for the air to choose.

***

The wind went out like a held breath.

Leaves that had been whispering went flat. Shade cloths eased their snapping and hung still. The hum rose, high and thin, the way a string sounds when it is turned past what it wants. Sera felt the tone pick up behind her teeth. The hairs on her forearms lifted. Goats along the upper line set their legs and stared, ropes taut. Frost lines the chalk had left as memory woke and burned pale along paths and posts.

The air tasted metallic.

Sera lifted both hands. Palms up, then out. The first signal. Ilen caught it and threw it along the row of children. The two-blink started in bodies that could learn a rhythm by playing it. In, hold, blink, blink, out. The wave moved to the adults as water finds the bed it has always known. The market stood where it was and flexed.

Tamar tuned the bell-frame with his fingertip. He did not strike. He called the tones that mapped the terraces. High to the ridge, low to the market edge, middle down the spine. Teams answered with hands at height. Palms shown for high, waist for middle, low near knees. The Overseer set his staff tip where witnesses could see it and lifted his chin to the two elders who had agreed to stand and write if breath allowed.

The first impact came along the crazed walkway between two doors. Light bent thin as paper. The fine crackle from before brightened and tried to widen. Sera sent the wave left, then back, lagging the second blink by a sliver so the net would stretch instead of snap. The rope lattice took weight from a boot that slipped and put it safely down. A jar tipped and stopped, resting against the rope as if it had found a seat.

"High," Tamar murmured. He meant the ridge.

Sera threw the signal. Palms up. The children mirrored her. The wave climbed. On the ridge path the goats fought their ropes for one count, then let the net catch them. The goat herder set a hand to a horn and spoke without words. The animals blinked slow and steadied.

Water in the basins lifted to the lips. Sera saw it with the edge of her eye. "Now," she called, and two small figures at the channel gates eased them open a thumb. The first surge spread into the bowls and made a sound like someone pouring a full cup into another full cup without spilling.

The beds moved.

They did not slide as disaster slides. They slumped as planned. A red-marked bed on the upper terrace settled into its trough with a low sound and a lean. Soil mounded against the catch and broke like a field after rain. A woman stepped back into a braced span without flinging her weight. A child put a hand to the ground and laughed once because the world under her palm felt like a sleeping animal turning.

Tamar's tones ran along the map. He marked the right side with low, the left with high, and sent the mid tone down the center to hold. He stood close to Sera without crowding her, his breath counting in his mouth so she could borrow it if hers missed.

A facade along the market edge cracked in a line that no builder had placed. Not mortar or seam. A social line made visible. The plaster opened as if it had been waiting to be honest. It did not collapse. It left a visible truth. Sera wanted to cover it and did not. She let it be.

"Middle," Tamar said, low. Sera signaled with a hand close to her chest. The nearby team took it and passed it down the row through bodies that already knew how to listen. The air around the ledger stone trembled.

Sera stepped to the trough.

The witnesses held bark and ink, hands steady, eyes soft. The Overseer moved his staff enough to set a ringed shadow on the stone. Tamar touched Sera's shoulder, not to turn her, to set an anchor. The two-blink trembled at the edge of her vision and then steadied. She reached into the bowl, found the blank disc she had set that morning, and lifted it into the light.

She closed her eyes once. She opened them. When she spoke, the name had weight, not sharpness.

"Rion."

The sound of it landed on the taut string of the hum and took the strain down. The high tone in the air found a place to sit. The market felt the drop like rain after a long dry, not relief exactly, the right next thing. The witnesses wrote without looking up. The Overseer whispered thank you to no one in particular.

The storm flared again.

A trough on the opposite side collapsed into itself as planned, the soil giving way, not grabbing. The wave got noisy. Voices lifted without meaning to. Sera's hands shook. Tamar moved close and set his palm at her shoulder. He did not squeeze. He pressed enough that their bodies shared a count. His mouth shaped the tones for team three at the bridge. Middle, low, low. Sera matched his breath and lifted her hands. The team saw them. The signal traveled.

The two-blink chorus thickened. Children called it first, then adults carried it. The net flexed in visible waves. People leaned toward one another without clutching. Hands went out palm to palm, then down as the blink passed. Goats breathed slow in their strange way, as if they had caught the rule without knowing the words.

The second slump zone took its weight. The catch basins filled and held. Mud pushed against the braces and then calmed. A plank bent, then settled. The rope lattice creaked and did not fail. A bowl fell and landed on cloth instead of stone. The reed player lifted the instrument and put it down because the air was too thin for notes.

At the ledger stone, Sera set the blank disc back in the bowl. The witnesses added a mark to the list. Tamar's fingers stayed at her shoulder long enough to be felt, then left so he could point a team to the lower gate.

"Let it go a thumb," he called. The boys at the handles obeyed. Water ran out of the basins and back into the channels with a low sound of relief. The mud lost its shine and kept its shape.

The light stayed thin at the edges for one more count. Then it thickened into its proper weight. The metallic taste faded. The hum lowered and spread, not flat, deep. The frost lines dulled. The crack in the market facade stayed visible like a healed line on skin.

Silence arrived as a visitor and sat for a breath. Then sound returned in clean pieces. The goat herder let out a breath that had been serving as a piece of rope. Someone laughed once at nothing and then another person did because laughter can be a map back to ordinary.

No one fell.

Sera stood with her hand on the trough and felt her body register what had been prevented. Her knees wanted to go soft. She let them a little and found the ground willing to meet her there. She looked at Tamar. He nodded, mouth still shaping tones because the habit would take a while to let go. She smiled without trying and put her forehead to his for half a breath. It was not the time to be long. It was the right amount.

The Overseer raised the staff an inch and set it down. The witnesses, who had kept their place with the discipline of people who have lived through worse, made a final mark and lowered the bark to their laps.

Sera lifted her hands, palms open to show empty. The signal for rest. The chorus eased. Bodies shook out tension in the small ways that do not insult what has just been done. Someone righted a basket. Someone tied a cloth back to its post.

She walked to the cracked facade and put her palm on the line. The plaster felt like bone under skin. She left it unplastered. A child traced the line with a fingertip and then walked away as if she had been told a story that required no extra words.

Teams checked braces and ropes. People retied what had loosened. The basins lowered to their ordinary level. The red cloth at the slump beds hung limp with honest dust on it. The goats shook and turned their heads toward the ridge as if to say the same thing Sera felt. The place had taken a weight and learned something in the taking.

The bell-frame sat quiet on the trough. Sera ran a finger along it once to thank it and did not ask it to sing. The hum did not need a tone over it. It had its own.

The elders of the Stilling Circle appeared along the upper path, white against stone, faces careful. They looked for failure that would let them count the cost and name fault. They did not find bodies on the ground. They found planned slumps, a visible crack, rope lattices that had held, and a ledger bowl with a new weight.

They did not praise. They did not scold. They watched.

Sera met their eyes and then looked past them to the people who had carried the wave. She touched the ledger stone. The two elders who were not of the Circle raised the bark and the ink for all to see. The first sanctioned entries waited to be read aloud when the time was right.

"Rest," Sera said to the square. "Then we clean. Then we leave what should be left."

The wind returned in a small way and moved the red cloth. It sounded like a sigh that belonged to the terraces themselves. The storm had pressed. The net had flexed. The map had changed and so had the people who held it. The day did not go back to what it had been. It carried forward with a new chord under every step.

***

Morning made a simple inventory.

The slumps lay where they were meant to be, soil mounded in the troughs, edges tidy where hands had trimmed them after the wave. The crack along the market facade stayed visible, clean, a line you could trace without flinching. The rope lattices hung slack. The basins sat at their ordinary level. Nothing had fallen that should not have. The city stood.

The Knot Ledger sat open on a stone by the old trough. No one rang a bell. People came before work and added tokens without being called. A washer with a nick where it had once been forced. A curl of goat hair twined to string. A splinter of blue glaze. One bean from a jar meant for winter. Each person spoke a word, not loud. Sometimes only a name, sometimes a shape like debt or ridge or tremor. The bowl took them. The cloth muffled their small sounds. The chalk frost on the nearest posts had already lost its shine.

By midmorning a strip of bark went up at the long house. The clerk pinned it with two slivers and read it once, plain. The council rescinded the blanket edict. Ledger practice sanctioned at dusk. One truth, one token. The Circle to give guidance on placement and crowding. The words did not cheer. They did not need to.

The Stilling Circle came down in their white, smaller than before. The first elder placed a hand on the ledger stone and left it there for a breath. The second walked the planned slumps and nodded when he saw where a bed had settled and spared a walkway. The third stopped at the cracked facade and did not call for plaster. He traced the line with a fingertip and let his hand fall empty.

"Guidance," said the first elder to Sera. She meant it as an offer and a boundary both.

"Guidance," Sera agreed.

Tamar worked at a table under the shade of a fig. He copied the bell-tone map onto a travel frame, a small hoop of bent wood with three thin bars set across it. He tapped each bar and wrote a mark so that a high note meant ridge, a low meant edge, a middle meant spine. He strung a narrow strap so the frame could hang from a shoulder without singing when it should not. When he was done he ran a finger along the rim. The hoop held a soft memory of tone. He smiled without looking up, the smile of someone who knows an object can carry a practice if the practice is light enough.

Ilen led a first class of adults outside the terraces. They stood on the path by the scrub where the wind came unasked. He showed them the two-blink with his hands. He walked them into it with the patience usually saved for the very young. A mason with a brace on his wrist copied the hinge and laughed when he found he could learn new muscle without the old trembling. The goat herder watched from a rock and blinked on the second as if it had been his idea. The midwife learned with the steadiness of someone who has taught bodies to do hard things before.

Sera walked the square and checked what needed checking. Braces that could come down. Posts that wanted a new band. The ledger bowl's weight. The map on the central stones, now dulled and useful. People waved to her with chalk on their fingers. Children stepped aside without being told because they could read a plan underfoot when they saw one. The air felt easier between buildings.

At noon there was stillness, but not the fixed kind. Eyes softened, not sharpened. Breath counted itself. The hum sat lower in the body of the terraces. You could feel it in the palms more than the teeth. It made space without becoming thin.

In the late day the council gathered at the trough to hear the first sanctioned entries read aloud. The two witnesses stood with bark and a reed. They kept their voices clean. Tremor. Ridge. Bread. Lera. Rion. Each word fell and made a little room. No one applauded. Work resumed in the way that tells you a place is mending while it keeps moving.

At last the sun drew a white edge along the far ridge. The square let itself be ordinary. Tools were hung. Cloths were rolled and tied. The ledger bowl was covered with its strip of fabric and placed inside the trough's shadow. Tamar handed the travel frame to Sera and then took it back and adjusted the strap so it would sit where she liked it. They smiled at their clumsy care and stepped out along the upper path.

The Overseer waited on the ridge where the wind moved again. He had his staff, though he did not lean on it. They stood together with the slope falling quiet under them and listened. The hum held, wide. It had air in it. Not looseness. Space.

"Nets that can be unknotted do not choke," he said.

"They also show their seams," Sera said.

"They do," he answered. "That is how you know where to mend."

They said nothing for a while. The goats shifted below and made their small satisfied sounds. Someone laughed in a courtyard and then went on with the simple work of evening. A child's wrist bell flashed once and stilled.

Sera lifted the travel frame and ran a fingertip along its rim. It did not sing. It remembered. Tamar stood close enough that his shoulder brushed hers when the wind turned. The Overseer looked toward the farther valleys, as if sound could carry to a place he had not walked yet.

"We will leave the crack unplastered," Sera said.

"Good," the Overseer said. "Let it be true in daylight."

They stood until the light changed one last time. Then they turned back toward the terraces, where a ledger and a frame and a practice waited for another day. The hum went with them, deeper now, not a wall, not a chain, a net that could be held by many hands and loosened by one spoken thing.

The Empty Bowl Night

Morning made the stone honest. It kept the night's cool the way a jar keeps water. Nema set the Keeping Bowl on it, thumb finding the worn place at the rim where two centuries of mornings had taught the metal to feel like skin. The unplastered crack in the market wall caught a blade of early light. Someone long ago had set a small plaque above it. The words were simple: leave daylight a line.

The square lifted itself without hurry. Shade cloths still slept on their ropes. Doors stood half, letting first air move through rooms that had belonged to other names and would belong to more. Tone hoops hung in a few doorways, quiet as rings in a lake. Far up the path the goat line pulled a single soft clink from a pin and then went still again, as if the animals had remembered the morning before they were asked.

People came in pairs, in threes, then stood as if they had arrived alone. A broom finished crossing a step. A reed was set down without its tune. Hands settled at the belly or at the sides. Eyes softened the way you do when you are done reading small print and want to see a face again. No one announced anything. The air had already agreed.

Nema drew a low note from wood, not air, and let it sit under the square. The sound was more feeling than music, a shape for the ribs to follow. Breath in fours. In, hold, out, rest. The goats along the upper path watched and did not chew for a few heartbeats. Then they did. That was how a place agreed with a morning.

"One truth, one token," Nema said. She did not raise her voice. She did not need to. "We set a knot down. The bowl will hold it. The place will loosen where it should."

A man from the west lane laid a little washer into the bowl. He spoke no name, only a shape. "Debt." He said it with a steadiness that made the word a brick rather than sand. A woman placed a sliver of blue glaze and said, "Ridge." A child came with empty hands and said, "I am angry at nothing," and people smiled, because anger at nothing has a way of finding a thing if you do not name it first. A girl, hair still plaited from sleep, sang a single line she had learned as a game, the way small songs slip out when rooms are quiet: second and second, then see. Her mother touched her shoulder. The girl hushed, pleased with herself without needing to be told so.

Nema wrote on a strip of bark: debt, ridge, nothing. The words looked clean in her hand. She kept the letters narrow, so the list could carry more of the day. When a person had no token and no word, she let them set a fingertip on the rim and breathe there. The bowl noticed. It always had. Old bowls know skin.

Beside her, Bren listened with his fingers. He held a reed hoop he had bound himself, three thin bars stretched across it. He had learned to hear when a token had been set with breath rather than with clever timing. A faint charge stayed in the bowl for a while after a truth landed. Charges gathered at the rim like sips of heat around a kettle. Bren touched there and nodded. "These sing," he whispered.

Nema did not look up. "Good."

A baker with flour on both wrists placed a loop of twine. "I will stop ending loaves early. My hands rush. My neighbors taste it." A young mason, careful not to show the left hand that sometimes trembled, set down a nail with a bent head and said, "Wall at south bend is honest. My temper there was not." A midwife laid a small curl of goat hair into the bowl. "I feared a name. I was wrong. I will go to that door this morning."

Bren touched the rim again, then the hoop's crossbars, listening for the faint hum that follows a spoken thing. "Four," he said, meaning four tokens had sung in a row. "Five." He smiled the small smile he used when his ear and the bowl had agreed.

A courier stood a little apart with courteous hands. No white, only tidy cloth and good sandals. He watched the way Nema's palm moved when she wrote. He watched the way Bren held the hoop. He could have been anyone doing any errand at dawn. He was not. He made a note on a strip of bark and put the strip away. He kept his face arranged in the shape of a person who respects a rite without needing to understand it.

A boy stepped forward with a bead of gray clay. "I speak for my brother," he said, eyes on the bowl, then on Nema. "He will not come to the square. He says the count scratches his teeth. He bites his lip to stop the scratch. He is tired of blood. I want that to be over." The bead rolled into the cloth and stayed. Somewhere on the upper path a goat sneezed and decided not to sneeze again.

A traveler's pair, dusty to the knees, came like people who did not intend to stay. The elder set down a strip of reed with a knot in it. "We used the wrong path," she said. "We called it a shortcut. We did not ask the ridge. We will ask next time." The younger did not set a token. He touched the rim with two fingers and breathed as if his breath had been carrying another's weight for a while and was glad to find a place to set it.

Nema wrote quickly, her hand finding its pace. She paused once to push a small chip of grit from the cloth so the tokens would not wobble. The bowl's metal had a soft burr at one point where a thumb had polished away the last of a casting line. Her own thumb found it and rested there when she needed to steady a word.

The bell on the frame offered a little climb, then settled. Breath in fours carried itself now, without the sound. People as a group are clever at remembering rhythms that make them kinder.

At the edge of the square, a pair of Index Wardens passed without stopping, white cloth drawing a clean seam through the morning. They did not look in. They did not need to. Their business was the hour when cloths were bright and the day was set to order. Dawn belonged to bowls.

Bren shifted his weight and set the hoop on its edge so it would not touch the stone. "Two of these carry the long charge," he murmured, meaning that two knots would keep singing until noon. "You can hear it if you try."

Nema did not try. She trusted his ear the way he trusted her hand. "Good," she said again. It meant more than agreement. It meant a place had done what a place should do.

A woman at the back of the gathering kept her hands tight. She wore a ribbon at her wrist that had been someone's before her. She did not step forward. She looked at the plaque above the crack and looked away. Nema saw her and did not mark the seeing. Not everyone brought a thing the same day they noticed it.

A boy with a reed made a sound that was almost a note and then decided against it. The little silence he left behind was pleasant. A man coughed, once, then put his knuckles to his mouth and caught the second cough before it scattered the count. On the upper path a goat stepped, tested the rope, found the length of it, returned to chewing. Small confirmations, all of them.

When the round had made its circle, Nema lifted her palm, then lowered it. The sign for done. No one clapped. That belongs to other kinds of mornings. People stood a moment longer than needed, then went their ways as people do when they have done a hard small thing and intend to do another. Shade cloths woke. Doors widened. Someone laughed and then caught the laugh and kept it, to use somewhere quieter.

Nema covered the bowl and tied the cloth. The knot she used was the easy one that holds and comes free with a thumb. She set the strip of bark beneath the rim and pressed the edge flat so the list would not curl. Bren leaned the hoop against the stone and checked that the crossbars were firm. He smiled the careful smile he used when a task had gone properly but might not tomorrow.

"Leave daylight a line," he said, tapping the plaque with a knuckle. The metal made a tiny honest sound.

"We will," Nema said. "Until someone paints it over again."

"Or until the paint learns to crack," Bren said, and it was not a joke. Paint does that when a wall wants to tell the truth.

Above them the goats shook their heads and went back to the day. The square took up its work with a rhythm that felt both human and fitted to stone. The bowl sat under its cloth like a heart resting between beats. The crack on the market wall held its thin bright and did not ask to be hidden. The morning, having done its part, moved on.

***

They met at noon in the long house with the reed banners. The room cooled the air without asking anyone to name why. Bare feet on smoothed planks made small sounds that did not echo. Smoke from the cook yards rose in the square and braided itself thinly through the rafters, polite as a guest.

Index Wardens stood under the lintel in their white with clean edges. They had the posture of people who knew where to place a hand on any door. The Auditor did not wear white. He wore tidy gray, patience at the corners of the mouth, the kind of stillness that looks like strength from far away and like practiced waiting up close.

"The Sympathy Index is a way to share load across valleys," he said. His voice made no promises. It stated shapes. "Standard tokens, standard scripts, a synchronized dusk. Your bowl read at the same breath as the bowls in Cliffmouth, Saltspan, and the two small towns between. Need will rise where it is greatest. Aid will flow there without waste."

He gestured and a Warden unrolled a strip of bark almost the height of a person. Lines and small hand marks showed where hands should be held and where eyes should rest during reading. The script had the clean logic of something made on a table that never saw dust. The Warden pinned it to a post with a sliver of bone.

"Variance breeds failure," the Warden said. "Children's games. Off beats. Wandering seconds. All removed for safety."

Nema watched the council watch the man. Order has a smell when you have lived with wind. It smells like clean cloth and a floor with no dust. People love that smell until they remember what dust does for a field. She felt the room lean toward relief. Relief can be a good first step. It makes a bad foundation when the wind turns.

Another Warden lifted a shallow tray. "Standard tokens," she said. "Three weights. Reed, clay, metal. Each with a mark on the edge so stewards cannot be fooled. One knot, one token. No substitutions. No household tokens that carry private meanings. The Index will supply strings monthly."

A trader from the east row raised two fingers. "If we read together," he said, "and wagons set out at once, we will halve the time to get flour to a flooded place. I have seen corridors empty as a polished gourd. A standard that fills them could save lives."

A midwife touched the bench in front of her with the flat of her hand. "And if our keeping leans," she said, "who listens for the door that breath forgot to visit yesterday. Who notices when a name is kept too long. I am not against help. I am against forgetting the size of a room."

The Old Overseer touched his staff to the post and left no mark. "Invite, do not command," he said. "Let the bowl hold truth and the place will flex. Synchronized breath at distance risks thinness. You will not know which seam you polished thin until it tears."

"Precedent," the Auditor replied. "The Fifty Valley Concord held three dust seasons with synchronized stillings. Let us add keeping to the frame. You have seen drift years. You know how quickly rumor empties a road toward news that was never true. With the Index, attention is measured. Care is sent where it belongs."

He turned to Nema with courtesy that did not press. "You will keep your bowl better than most. Your keeping will help those with less. Your neighbors will stand taller because you stood first."

Nema could not argue with helping. She could argue with the way the help was asked to be held. "Our frames carry local weight," she said. "We do not face the same wind as the cliff. We tune for goat lines. Cliffmouth tunes for stairs that want to shed themselves."

"We are not forbidding local work," a Warden said. "We are aligning the moment when care is named. The rest of the day is yours. The dusk is ours. For one count."

The scribe at the end table sharpened a reed and waited. His job was to write a decision that would look good on bark at the door. He could write either way. His face already held the relief of knowing what he would copy by evening.

The Auditor tapped the tray of tokens with a finger that did not make a sound. "Fraud is a pressure," he said. "A person might place a token without breath to pull sympathy toward a corner that is not hurt. Standard weights and edges reduce such noise. Synchronized reading reduces timing tricks. If your bowl sings and another's does not, your song will carry."

Bren kept his eyes on the tray. He watched the edge marks, neat little bites. They would be easy to copy if a person had a file and patience, easier still if they had authority. He did not speak. He imagined setting his reed hoop on those tokens and hearing nothing. He imagined the way a room feels when a tone is right and someone calls it noise.

A young guard from the river gate asked a question no one else had wanted to carry. "If our dusk is their dusk," she said, "who holds the gate. We have had trouble at dusk."

A Warden answered without looking at her. "Scripts provide for a fraction of bodies to hold posts during keeping. The fraction is printed here." He pointed to a column of small marks. They were tidy. They did not look like people standing in the heat while others breathed in a room.

A potter rubbed a thumb on her apron. "What happens if a token is placed with breath at a time not printed," she asked. "A grief does not look at the sun and choose the right window. If a person sets a word at noon, will the Index count it."

"The bowl will hold it," the Auditor said. "The Index will count at dusk. It is a ledger, not a sky."

The Old Overseer's mouth bent at one corner, not in disdain, in recognition. "A ledger is a sky for some," he said, softer. "When you standardize skies you get beautiful maps and more lost people."

Nema looked at the reed banners. Wind passed through them and did not shred them because the weave left spaces, on purpose. "Our seconds," she said, meaning the hinge rhythm the children played, "sit under the count and keep people soft when the count goes hard. Will the Index write against them."

"Children's games," the Warden repeated, kindly this time, as if explaining that a beloved habit could live in a different room. "We do not erase play. We remove it from keeping."

She pictured Savi flicking a wrist bell in an alley, head tipped, figuring the shape of a rhythm with no name on it. Savi would learn either way. The question was what would be called wandering in the square and what would be called learning in the shade.

The Auditor opened his hands, palms visible, as if to show that nothing was hidden there. "It is hard to give up private measures," he said. "But private measures are how we get roads full of wagons that arrive where no one waited."

"We also get roads that reach houses by mistake and find a person who needed them anyway," the midwife said, and did not soften her voice.

The council liked both sentences and chose the one that made the room feel clean. They voted with the pleasant relief of having done something that could be written on bark at the door. Dusk would be synchronized across five towns in two days. Index Wardens would oversee the scripts. Standard tokens would be issued. Variants would be called noise for a time.

The scribe wrote quickly. The Warden pressed a seal at the bottom that made a neat circle with a little hinge inside it, a symbol stolen from children and made to look like order. The Auditor thanked the room for its trust. Trust is a word that wears many coats. Today it wore tidy gray.

As people stood, the Old Overseer leaned toward Nema. "Prepare for thinness," he said. "Design for safe failure. Leave daylight more than one line."

"I will," she said. She did not say how. The how would start before dinner.

Outside, afternoon heat draped itself over the square. A child flicked a wrist bell to catch the sun and did not ring it. Savi watched from a wall and learned more from the flick than from any speech. A goat shook dust from its coat and blinked, second and second, then saw. The plaque on the cracked wall held its light and kept the plain words plain.

***

Dusk gathered like water in a bowl. Shade cloths let go of the day an inch at a time. The bell tone was the same in Riverplain and in Cliffmouth and in Saltspan and at two small places that had always borrowed names from bigger ones. That sameness had a shine to it. People liked how it felt against their ribs. Hands rose when the script said hands. Heads turned where the script had drawn arrows. A Warden stood by each door with a strip of bark rolled in a fist, not to threaten, to make the room look like a promise.

Nema set the cloth aside and opened the Keeping Bowl. The rim caught the last of the light. She felt for the familiar burr with her thumb and found it. She said the words the way you say words a bowl already knows.

"Tremor," she said. The mason who had placed that token kept his eyes on the floor and breathed once, evenly.

"Birth," she said. The midwife's mouth softened by a hair. "Trail," she said. The river guard stood taller without moving.

Her voice did not go far. It did not need to. The bowl was near and that was what mattered.

Bren held his reed hoop with both hands. He had washed the dust from the bars so the faintest hum would not snag on grit. He touched the hoop to the rim in a place no one could see. Charges collect there for a while, like warmth near a kettle. He listened with the skin of his fingers, not his ears. The first three tokens sang, small but clean.

The script asked for facing. Most faces turned toward the ridge. The ridge is beautiful. Beauty is not a need. Nema noted the angle against the habit of the room. It was a degree off where the bowl usually liked to sit. She moved the bowl a finger's width toward the crack in the market wall, out of courtesy to the bowl more than to the script. The Warden at the door saw and did not mark it down. Courtesy is hard to outlaw on a first day.

Another token. "Gate." A child. "Brother."

"Debt delayed," said a trader who would have preferred to say nothing. "Bread," said the baker, as if the word could mend crust.

The bowl leaned.

It was not a thing the eye could track. It was a thing the body feels when a table is not level and you pretend it is. Sympathy slid sideways in the count. Attention thinned locally and settled into a corridor that had nothing to do with Riverplain's paths. Nema did not see it; she felt people's shoulders tip. Bren did not see it; his fingers lost the whisper of charge a breath too early. The script had drawn a facing that put most bodies toward the ridge. The ridge pulls eyes the way a clean door pulls a hand.

Frost flared along a lane that had been calm all week. It lit where two cousins lived door across and had learned to stand near each other without speaking. They flinched at the same instant, not at sound, at the bright thinness that comes when a room looks right and is wrong underneath. The goats on the upper path lifted their chins and then set them again, undecided.

Nema kept reading, because stopping is its own kind of order.

"Stairs."

"Milk."

"Lera," said the woman who last week had only said ridge, and the sound of the name landed like a weight taken off a taut string. The frost by the midwife's step dulled. Not all the frost. Enough to be called honest.

Bren touched the rim and frowned without meaning to. "These are quiet," he said of two tokens that sat among the rest like clever stones. He did not lift his voice. He spoke along the edge of Nema's shoulder.

"Hollow?" she asked, softly.

"Or tired," Bren said, because doubt is a craft. He wanted to be wrong more than he wanted to be right.

The Warden by the door shifted weight and looked anywhere but at the bowl. He had been told to watch hands. He had not been told what to think with his hands when a rim stopped answering skin.

Outside, the corridor the Index had named lit up the way a swept floor looks brighter than the rest of a room. Teamsters saw it without being told to call it a corridor. They stacked sacks the neat way people do when they expect to be praised for the shape of a thing. Wagons were loaded after the rite and set on that brightness. No one really knew who had asked for help at its end. The Index placard said flood in a tidy hand. The river had not risen in Riverplain. A woman noted to herself that tidy hands do not always know wet feet.

"Keep," Nema said, finishing the round. She covered the bowl with cloth and set the bark list under the rim with a press of thumb that made the strip lie flat. People let their hands fall and stood a breath longer than the script wrote for. The habit of rooms does not leave with one order.

Savi slid off the wall outside and walked as if she had a different errand. She watched which wagons took the clean corridor and who rode on the tailboards with their legs swinging. She watched which child ran alongside and then stopped running because the road had learned to be long. She flicked a wrist bell once to catch light and tucked it back into her sleeve.

Bren did not leave with the crowd. He set the hoop on the bowl's cloth, then lifted it and listened again for charges left from a true setting. He heard a faint hum where Lera had landed. He heard nothing where one of the clever stones lay. He tilted the hoop and tried the crossbar. Nothing again. He met Nema's eyes.

"Tired?" she said.

"Maybe," he said. "Or an object that wants to be a truth."

"Someone will sleep on it," she said. "Bring it back in a better state."

"Maybe," he said again. He did not like saying maybe twice.

The Warden with the strip of bark made a neat circle at the bottom of a page and called it done. He had a tidy mind. He believed tidy minds help other people. He believed it with a kind of goodness that is hard to argue with and still keep friends.

At the counting room, the courier who had watched at dawn worked the night shift. He washed his hands before touching the string of tokens, carefully, fingertips, palms, between each finger. He made polite notes again while he traded a string behind a screen for another string wrapped in nice cloth. The trade was not theft the way a thief takes a loaf. It was a shift of weight from one pocket to another. He told himself he was helping the Index remove noise. His hand shook once when he sealed the pouch and then did not shake again.

Back at the square, the last wagons rolled onto the clean corridor. The ridge caught dusk on its edge and made the day look like a bowl tipped to pour. Two cousins who had not spoken since a winter argument stood at their doorways and watched the road pull the town's attention the way tide pulls at a shallow shore. They did not speak now either. Their shoulders loosened by a hair when the wagons finally turned the bend and the air thickened a little.

Nema lifted the cloth to check the bowl once more before taking it in. The rim was cool. The charges were fading at the right rate for truths that had been spoken with breath. She could tell by touch. She could not tell where sympathy had gone that did not belong to the square. She tied the cloth with the easy knot and held the bowl against her hip the way a person holds a sleeping child who might wake if the room asks the wrong question.

Outside, the corridor's brightness thinned as dust rose and turned it into ordinary road. The script posted at the door curled at the edge where heat found it. Bren carried the hoop with both hands and did not look at the ridge. He looked at the crack in the market wall and at the plaque above it, at the few words that never learned how to look grand: leave daylight a line. He touched the hoop to the stone beside the crack and felt steadiness there. It would have to be enough, for this dusk. For the next, he did not make any promises to himself. He preferred shapes. Shapes do not lie.

***

They walked bowls the way other people walk fields.

In Riverplain they moved from house to house where pocket bowls lived on shelves beside water jars. Nema asked for a word, not a story. A person spoke, set a token, and Bren listened at the rim with his reed hoop, fingers resting on the crossbars. Real tokens hummed the way embers do under ash. The hum stayed for a count, then thinned in the right way. Twice the hoop heard nothing. The tokens were clever by weight and edge mark. They were dead.

They crossed to Cliffmouth at first light. Wind there had cliff in it, thin and quick. The plaza floor was an old wheel laid flat. Wood filled the spaces between stone spokes. Children traced hinges between the spokes with their palms, then pretended not to be doing anything worth noticing when adults looked. The Keeping Bowl sat near the hub on a low table that had learned many mornings.

Nema asked for a round with the local steward's leave. Cliffmouth folk were proud of the wheel. Pride is good for care and bad for listening. The steward nodded anyway. "If it helps the belt," he said, meaning if it helps the five towns all at once.

A woman set a chip of red clay. "Brother," she said. The hoop heard the ember hum. A man set a length of twine. "Gate," he said, and the hoop heard it. Three tokens later a bead of neat glass met the cloth with no sound in the field at all. Bren did not look up. He tilted the hoop and tested the crossbar. Nothing. He marked the glass with his eye and said nothing to the man who had placed it. There was no use in shame.

They moved along the rim and heard a pattern. Truth, truth, quiet. Truth, quiet, quiet. The quiet ones matched the Index's tray weights well enough to fool a scale. They did not fool a bowl that had learned breath the long way.

Savi did not stand at the wheel. She stood where couriers pass. She let her body carry the look of a person late for someone else's errand and drifted when a man in tidy cloth left the steward's lodge with a pouch that sat too square at his belt. He took back lanes that knew how to avoid being seen. The counting room smelled like bark and wax. The man at the table had a habit of turning his head when he put things down so that his hands did not have to answer to his eyes. Savi learned the habit and the trick inside it. Strings could be swapped if you looked away at the right beat. A tidy swap needs a tidy room.

She did not touch anything. She counted the heartbeats between head turn and hand. She watched where the seal slivers were kept. She memorized a stain on the cloth that covered a hook. She left by a different door and returned to the square as if she had been fetching water.

Nema and Bren finished their round at the wheel and thanked the steward. They did not accuse. They named only what the hoop knew. "Some tokens here do not carry breath," Nema said. "Listen with your own hand when you have quiet." She showed him where on the rim the charge gathers longest. He tried, felt nothing, frowned, tried again. The second time there was a faint hum and he blinked, surprised, then embarrassed by the surprise.

Saltspan lay another day away. They did not go there. They sent a runner with a short bark in Nema's hand: listen for quiet stones, stagger your dusk, do not face the wind because a script says face the wind. The runner carried a tone hoop looped over one shoulder like a small yoke.

Back in Riverplain, afternoon put heat on the long house. The council called the Auditor into shade. He accepted their concern as if accepting a gift you do not want. He set it down with care.

"People lie with tokens," he said. "People have always done that. Standardization will reduce such noise. Synchronized reading makes fraud less likely, not more."

"Tone is not fraud," Bren said. "Tone is breath."

"Breath is counted," the Auditor said, pleasant as a flat stone. "We will count it."

Nema kept her eyes on the bark script pinned to the post. The marks for facing were arrows that did not know the square. The column for gate holders looked fine until you thought of a sick child at the hour when the gate must be held and the keeping must be read and a person cannot be two bodies. "Your counts look tidy," she said. "Tidy is not wrong. Tidy forgets."

A Warden lifted the tray of standard tokens a little higher. "Edge marks," he said. "Three weights. We have thought of the tricks you are naming."

Bren tapped the tray with a finger, very light. "A dead stone wears an edge mark well," he said. "A bowl wears breath better."

The Auditor's patience held. "We cannot have five towns reading as they like," he said. "We will never learn which places need care most. We will never move in time."

"Then let the towns answer in different ways and keep the dusk from being one long rope," the Old Overseer said from the doorway. His voice did not ask to be the room. It asked to be heard. "Variance is not failure. It is how a field finds rain instead of glass."

The Auditor inclined his head, a gesture that can mean respect or can mean I have heard a version of this and the decision is already written. "We hold the Great Keeping in two days," he said. "We will look at your notes after."

After can be too late when what you are measuring is the strength of a bowl and a way of seeing. Nema saw it. Bren heard it. Savi, on the wall outside, rolled a wrist bell along her palm and set the second in her own bones again, quiet, so it would be there when orders made air thin.

***

The wardens posted more scripts.

They came with bark strips rolled tight and bone slivers already set to pin. Hands at shoulder height, not higher. Turn on the third count, not the second. No palms to palms except to carry a bowl. Dusk windows narrowed to a single mark you could cover with a thumb. The white circles on the posts multiplied until even the shade looked regulated.

A clerk followed with a tray of standard tokens, reed, clay, metal, each edge nicked to match a diagram. "Household tokens may be retained," he read, "but unsanctioned objects placed at dusk will not be counted." He smiled the smile of a man who believed clarity was mercy.

The council scheduled a five-hub Great Keeping for the end of the week to prove what could be proven. A scribe wrote the notice large and neat so travelers would see it and carry the news uphill and downriver. Index Wardens promised to stand at every bowl, to straighten hands that wandered, to correct facing so five valleys would wear the same posture at the same breath.

In the alleys, children made the second because bodies teach themselves what rooms forget. They flicked wrist bells for flash and rhythm, not for sound, and passed the hinge between them with a pleasure that did not ask permission. Adults copied without looking like they were copying, shoulders loosening a hair, breath catching the hinge under the count the way water finds old channels under new banks.

A woman asked at market, "Can I place a token at noon if noon is when the knot arrives?" A Warden told her yes, the bowl would keep it; the Index would count it later. She looked relieved and not relieved, both at once. Another asked if she could lean her head to another's during keeping. "That is not in the script," the Warden said, kindly enough, which is a way to end a thing without calling it ended.

Bren tried the hoop on the rim after a training drill and a Warden cleared his throat the way a person clears a path without touching you. "Auxiliary instruments are not part of the dusk," he said. "They introduce variance." Bren nodded and lifted his hands from the bowl as if from the back of an animal that had decided it was done with him.

The long house hosted a practice of posture. People stood in rows and learned to breathe at a pace set by a bell that lived in the next room. The bell did not sing. It ticked, a small, perfect sound that felt like duty from the first note. Some liked it. Some did not. All could repeat it by evening.

The Old Overseer came to Nema's table at dusk and put his hands on the wood as if it could hear him. The table had learned a thousand small truths. It was a good listener.

"Do your work," he said. "Prepare for a day when the clean count makes a thin field. You always told truth to stone. Tell it now."

Nema looked at the plaque above the crack. Leave daylight a line. She had repeated the words so often they had become muscle. Today they felt like a tool she had not yet used correctly. She touched the Keeping Bowl's rim and found the burr with her thumb, the place where many hands had agreed on the shape of morning.

"We will leave more than a line," she said. "We will leave a way out."

Bren stood at her shoulder without touching. "Red cloth?" he asked, meaning slump ties. "Rope?" meaning lattices. "Water?" meaning catch basins.

"Soon," Nema said. "Quietly."

Outside, a child ran the second across a courtyard and two elders caught it without knowing who had thrown it first. A warden stopped to watch and then pretended he had stopped for shade. The notice at the door curled at one corner where heat found it. The clean count waited like a knife laid carefully on a table. Nema looked at the knife, then at the bread, then at the hands that would have to keep eating either way. She began to make a list, not of arguments, but of places that could give without taking a person with them.

***

Savi lifted a pouch from a belt in a crowd without ever touching the belt.

It was market-close, a knot of bodies moving as one long creature around a cart of early figs. She stepped into the hinge between two turns, let a sleeve brush a sleeve, and transferred weight from one loop to her own waistband with the same care she used to pass the second in an alley. No one felt lighter. She felt heavier by the size of a hand.

She did not run. Running is a language. She walked the bend behind the long house where the fig made its patch of shade and set the pouch on Nema's table as if she had brought a handful of leaves.

Nema and Bren untied the neat knot. The pouch had been sealed with a sliver of bone pressed into wax, ring-shaped with a tiny hinge inside it, the Wardens' new mark. Inside: strings of tokens arranged by weight and color the way someone arranges tools before fixing a gate. Reed, clay, metal. A glass bead the size of a lentil. A washer with the right nick. Each object plausible. Each wrapped in clean cloth so it would arrive polite.

Beneath the strings lay scripts written in a hand that did not tire. Arrows for facing. Small marks for hand height. A grid for pacing the breath: four narrow boxes repeated five times with a diagonal stroke through the third box in each row. Notes in the margin: align east in Riverplain; south-by-east in Cliffmouth; align to water in Saltspan. A line at the bottom: bowls to be turned on count two to catch drift.

Bren spread a page flat with two fingers. "Which hand to lift on which count," he said, measuring without meaning to. "Even the angle of the wrist." He hovered his palm over the little drawing and felt his body try to mimic it.

Nema read every line as if it might cut. The scripts were careful in a way that sent a prickle along the back of her neck. Care is a virtue. When care forgets people, it becomes something else. She turned a page and found a diagram of the square with a dotted corridor drawn through it as if a road could be pulled out of air by posture.

"It is the read," Nema said. "Not the tokens alone. The read will pull us into a long rope and we will take each other's air."

Savi leaned in and tapped the margin where time marks lived. "They want the breath to land at the same blink in five bowls," she said, pleased and appalled in one breath at the trick of it. "If we're late by a hair, the script tells us how to turn the bowl to catch up."

"Pace correction," Bren said, a little sick at how pretty the words made the thing. He lifted one of the stringed sets and let it lie in his palm. "These will pass edge-checks." He touched the reed hoop to the pouch's cloth and listened without putting the bar on the tokens themselves. He heard nothing, which was not proof, not yet, but it made his mouth feel dry.

Nema traced a finger along the dotted corridor. "A clean path that serves no one," she said. "And it will look like cooperation when we're pulled."

Bren sat back on the bench and looked at the fig leaves trembling in a wind that did not reach the ground. "We cannot cancel," he said. He said it the way people name a wall before they walk around it. "The Great Keeping is written and pinned. If we try to pull our dusk away, the Wardens will call it refusal and post more scripts."

"No," Nema said. Her hand rested where the table knew her. "We can fail without falling."

Savi's eyes sharpened the way a child's eyes do when a game becomes a job. "What do we move," she asked. "Beds? Water? People?"

"Some of all," Nema said. She stacked the scripts back into a neat pile and tied them with the same cord they had arrived with. It felt right to let order carry its own weight. "We mark where stone can give. We brace where feet will hurry. We set deed-tokens at places the scripts cannot see. We teach the second where no one is counting."

Bren turned the pouch inside out and shook it. A last strip fell, a schedule of sealings and the names of stewards assigned to read aloud at each bowl. His finger found Nema's name. He did not show her. She knew without seeing.

"Leave daylight a line," Nema said, not to the plaque on the cracked wall this time, but to the air under the fig. "And leave another beside it."

Savi slipped the pouch into the cook pit and tucked ash over it with the back of her hand. "I can return it to a belt that looks the same as the first belt," she offered.

"Do," Nema said. "Let it be exactly where someone expects it to be. We will be elsewhere, doing the work that is not on their page."

***

They did not announce. They did.

Red cloth went up at beds that would be allowed to slump. Not flags, ties at the posts, two fingers wide, the kind of red you make from brick dust and vinegar. The ties fluttered when wind remembered to visit and lay quiet when the air forgot itself. Rope lattices crossed spans where people would try to hurry: the short cut behind the ovens, the step by the cracked facade, the plank over the ditch that everyone swore they never used and used daily. The mason wedged shims under two wall runs so the stones could give without leaping. He used his steady hand for the fine work and his trembling one to test if a brace would sing under weight. When it did, he smiled like a person who had fixed a small truth.

Catch basins along the channels were filled a hand higher than usual. Two children worked the little gates with their whole bodies, leaning back to lift, forward to lower, careful to stop when Nema lifted her palm. Water thickened in the bowls and made the sound of someone pouring from a full jar into another full jar without spilling. At the upstream bend, a tethered goat took a drink and blinked as if recognizing an old practice in new clothes.

Deed-linked tokens were placed at stress points: one truth, one token, one act. A mended gate received the bent nail that had lost its temper, hammered straight and useful now. A repaired step got the shard that had cut two heels last month. A shared meal crossed a line between cousins; the chip of glaze from the bowl they ate from went into the keeping. Bren touched each rim with his hoop. The tokens hummed the way bees hum in evening, small, patient, impossible to fake.

Pulsed consensus was taught to market crews outside the Index window. Nema called no class. She asked for help moving a table, then let the **second** carry through hands and shoulders as the table "accidentally" turned on a late beat. People laughed at themselves for standing steadier afterward. Savi showed, then stepped back so others could show. A fishmonger who had never taught anything but knives taught the hinge to three neighbors without naming it teaching. A weaver learned to toss the second through a rolled carpet and have it come out the other end at the right blink.

Wardens passed and pretended not to see. It is hard to forbid something that looks like kindness and looks like lifting a box.

The Overseer found two people with good backs and level writing and asked them to witness. He did it in a doorway with one foot already out, so saying yes felt like walking rather than kneeling. "If we live," he said, not as drama. As truth. He showed them where to stand so they would not be in the way when the wave moved, and where the bark and ink would be, and how to keep their faces ordinary when someone said a name that would wake the whole square.

Bren copied tones to portable hoops under the fig. He tuned by breath instead of by bell, rounding splinters with a knife until the bars did not catch a sleeve. He greeted his fear like a neighbor rather than an enemy. "If I lose tempo," he told Nema, "you take it. If you lose tempo, we let Savi take it. If Savi loses it, we rest and take breath anyway."

"Leave daylight a line," Nema said, and he smiled at the plaque without looking up.

They walked the routes twice: where to step back when a rope takes weight, where to lean a shoulder when a plank bows, where a child should stand to be seen by three adults at once. Nema marked two quiet places where a person could sit down and cry without being in the way. "Order needs rooms," she said. "So does grief."

By late light the square looked unchanged to anyone who loved tidy. To anyone who had learned to see plans under dust, it was different. Red ties waited like sentences not yet spoken. Ropes lay slack in friendly shapes. Water held its patience in bowls that wished to be useful. The wardens' scripts hung on posts and curled at their corners, busy with what paper does in heat.

Savi ran the second once along the edge of the market and handed it to a child with a nod that said: keep it moving, quietly. The child understood. Children usually do. The day thinned. The plan held. They went home not to sleep but to set their hands where their bodies would remember them in the dark.

***

Five bells called five dusks that were the same dusk.

From the ridge to the salt, the sound stepped across valleys as if on flat boards. Bowls were uncovered. Scripts were held at the edge of sight. Hands rose together and turned where the lines said turn. The Wardens positioned themselves at lintels and corners, strips of bark rolled tight in their fists. The Auditor stood where he could see faces align like a field of grain turned by one wind.

Nema felt for the burr on the Keeping Bowl's rim and found it. She set the bowl a finger's width toward the crack in the market wall, not disobedience, courtesy. Bren cleaned the dust from his reed hoop with the heel of his hand and kept it low, out of any Warden's line of attention. The two witnesses took their places by the ledger stone, bark and ink ready, faces ordinary.

Words were read that belonged to real lives and words were read that belonged to no one.

"Tremor," said the mason.

"Lera," said the woman who had learned to say her daughter's name.

"Trail," said the gate guard.

"Salt," said a trader, and the word had the shape of an inventory, not a knot.

A glass bead settled without sound. A washer with the right nick followed it like a polite cousin. On Bren's fingers the faint charges gathered and thinned in the right way, then vanished a fraction too soon. He did not raise his head. He adjusted the hoop as if the shift belonged to his tool and not to the air.

Across the belt, the same breath. In Cliffmouth, the bowl sat on the hub of the flat wheel; children stood back with their hands pressed together to keep from imitating what bodies imitate. In Saltspan, the causeway bowl faced the long water as the script drew, its rim faintly salt-streaked from a century of mornings.

The reading moved in one beat across five towns and the beat was clean.

The fields coupled.

People felt it as a pleasant relief at first, the way a room feels when everyone agrees to stand the same way for a photograph. Even the goats held their heads at the same height, ropes in the same slack. Then the relief went smooth. Then the smooth went thin. The hum grew perfect and white.

It was beautiful for a breath, and then it was gone.

Nema could not feel the bowl. Her hands were on it. The bowl had always answered hands. It did not answer now. It sat like a shape, as if someone had carved bowl out of silence and forgotten to put sound back inside. Bren's hoop did not hear a charge. He set it down and picked it up again as if he could learn the new rules between motions. The witnesses looked at one another without moving their heads. The Warden by the door shifted his weight and did not know why.

White weather took the belt.

In Riverplain the planned slumps took weight and held. Red ties flapped once and then lay still against posts. A bed settled into its trough with a low resigning sound; soil shouldered soil and did not go hungry. A rope lattice caught a jar that had fallen bravely and lay there as if jealous of how well the rope had understood its life. Water lifted in catch basins to the lip and did not spill. The honest crack on the market wall opened a shade and stayed clean, a line that told the truth and did not become a wound.

Nema's mouth shaped the second without naming it, and the market crews answered, not as defiance, as muscle. Hands at shoulder height as the script required; shoulders softened on the late blink the script did not name. The wave that moved through bodies did not announce itself. It kept feet from hurrying on braced spans and kept eyes soft enough to see a neighbor's hand before a misstep took it.

At Cliffmouth the wheel plaza sang a hurt note and a stair shed itself like a snake skin. Screws that had held too long let go cleanly because the mason with the tremor had left them a way out. The bowl on the hub lost its voice, but people crossed in pulsed waves that Savi would later describe without using the word teach. She raised her hands to shoulder height like a student, then let her wrists hinge on the late blink like a child. A boy on the third step mirrored her; the mirroring ran. The stair flexed, dropped a plank, held. The courier who favored tidy belts opened his mouth to recite a line from the script, then closed it because his body had chosen to remain upright.

In Saltspan the causeway shimmered like heat. The boulder garden took force and held the water's mind like a parent with a fevered child. Crew three opened the upstream cut by a thumb on Nema's signal relayed through four hands and a hoop, high for ridge, low for edge, middle for spine. The late beat smoothed a panic curl that tried to form at the jetty's end. The bowl near the water sat handsome and useless and looked as if it did not mind.

Elsewhere, plazas that had learned perfection forgot how to bend in time. In a city that had polished its floor until it held sky, the white hum made glass. Glass made cracks. Cracks made falls. People did not scream at first. Perfect rooms delay sound. When it came, it came in clean pieces, a jar, a bench, the name of a street used as if it were a person who might turn, a prayer that was really a list of tools. Bowls were covered to keep dust out and because there was nothing left for them to do.

Back in Riverplain, the Auditor stood with his tidy patience and watched the perfect moment fail. He did not look betrayed. He looked confused, the way a person looks when a map insists a door is a wall and the wall opens when a child pushes it. He reached for the tray of standard tokens as if weight and edge could account for a missing field. The tray felt like a tray.

The synchronized readings ended within the same count they had begun. The Wardens lowered their bark. The scripts curled at their corners where heat finally reached them. People's hands came down not together but close enough to call it together. The market did not cheer. There was nothing to cheer.

There was a sound like many small things choosing not to break at once and then remembering that some things had already broken.

The witnesses wrote nothing for a moment, because there was nothing to write that would not be a lie. Then one of them wrote a single word on bark, thin, and the other, after a time, wrote held. They did not show anyone. They put the bark under the ledger stone because a person must sometimes place a word where stone can decide what to do with it.

Bren lifted the hoop and touched it to the bowl one more time. He felt a ghost of charge where Lera had landed, a kindness from earlier, not the reading now. He set the hoop down like a cup for a person who would be thirsty later.

Nema tied the cloth over the bowl with the knot that comes free with a thumb. She looked at the plaque above the crack, leave daylight a line, and then at the square that had learned a different lesson: leave daylight many lines. She turned her head to find the Overseer; he was already looking at her, not for instruction, for witness. He nodded, once, as if to say: we saw the thing that cannot be kept.

On the ridge a goat shook and sneezed and decided not to sneeze again. Children exhaled the second out of their bodies and put it away, the way you put a tool back on a hook you will still need after the house is gone. The Auditor placed two fingers on the script to keep it from curling and found that his hand did not steady paper. He took his fingers away and let the page behave like a thing.

Night took the slope slowly, as if even darkness did not want to be synchronized. The five bowls were covered in five places that had been the same place for a breath. The breath ended. People went looking for each other, not for orders. The Great Keeping had kept a lesson and it did not belong to the Index.

***

Morning came with the decency mornings often have.

Light fell into the square by the same angles it always used. Smoke went up from cook yards. Stalls opened. People tried to stand the way they had always stood. Hands found their places. Eyes softened. A bell offered the first low tone.

Stilling failed at forty bodies and above. It failed without drama. The count would not catch. It was like trying to tie a knot in water. Eyes could soften but could not find each other. Breath slipped off the surface of the air as if the air had been oiled. Goats ignored the bell. They chewed and blinked in their own time and looked smarter than people again.

A Warden asked for a second try. He lifted the script and read the lines as if they could make a field by being tidy. The lines did not. A row of shoulders rose and fell out of time, close, then farther, then not at all. Someone laughed once, the small sour laugh of a person who has finally felt the shape of a mistake in their bones. No one scolded them. Scolding would have required a room to agree on what was happening.

Bren brought his hoop to the bowl and touched the rim where charges had always gathered after a reading. He found nothing. He carried the bowl across the square into a house where six people had slept in a pile because they were tired and frightened and did not want to name either thing.

He set the bowl on a low table. "One truth," he said. "Say it and set the token."

A woman spoke: "My hands shake when I carry water." She set a chip of fired clay. The bowl sang for a breath the way old bowls do, soft in the rim where two centuries of thumbs had learned its edge.

A man spoke: "The gate creaks because I did not oil it." He set a bent nail. The bowl hummed once more, a tone like a dry reed remembering river.

A child spoke: "I do not want to go to the square." He placed a button. Bren listened and heard nothing.

He tried again with another small circle in the yard: three bodies, then four, then five. The bowl sang at three, held at five, failed at six.

"Nets above hearth size will not render," he said, and hated himself for the beauty of how clean the sentence was.

Nema stood at the edge of the square and watched people pretend nothing had changed until they remembered the way pretending wastes work. The council gathered and dissolved and gathered. They were good people. They had kept a place. The keeping no longer kept. Their hands still knew how to stack wood and measure lentils and move a patient on a cloth without spilling pain. They did that, and the work looked like breathing.

The Auditor sat with his neat hands and watched. He did not gloat. He had wanted a thing that had worked elsewhere in small rooms and over short distances. He had believed a bigger version would work better. He joined a crew that moved planks the rest of the day. His strength was useful when it was asked rather than taken. He kept the scripts in his bag and did not look at them. Paper makes a sound when you do not open it. He heard that sound.

Index Wardens did what people do when a rule loses its field: they helped. One held a ladder while a cloth was taken down. Another carried water to a goat that could not be coaxed to the trough. A third fetched a midwife without being asked. Their white looked less like law and more like cloth. It suited them.

Savi ran the second along a lane and let it die when the lane opened into the square. In courtyards the hinge held. In courtyards people found one another. A woman made a circle of seven, then shrugged and sent two to boil millet on the other side of the doorway. The two did not feel exiled. They felt useful. When they came back with bowls, the circle had become five and was singing quietly without sound.

At Cliffmouth, the wheel plaza woke to the same failure and the same discovery. The flat wheel could not call more than a small ring now. Children made their own rings between spokes and kept their grandparents competent. The steward took the bowl off the hub and put it on a doorstep. "This is where it can live," he said to no one and everyone.

In Saltspan, the causeway crew tried to hold a mass stilling against the long water. It did not take. Five fishers, kneeling on their own planks, caught a rhythm that calmed a small stretch of wake. Boats moved out one by one with a child on each bow showing the hinge to the person who had forgotten it overnight. The boulder garden kept being a garden. It asked for no field to do that work.

Back in Riverplain, the council posted a notice that read like a person trying to talk a room into coherence: Great Keeping complete. Afterkeeps to be scheduled. The words curled at the corners within the hour. Nema did not take the notice down. She tied a red cloth to the post beneath it. Anyone who knew how to read work could see the sentence she had written with her hands.

Bren moved through the square drawing small circles. "Three to five," he told people. "If you are eight, be two tables. If you are ten, be three. If you are forty, be a market." He spoke with a voice that did not call itself a rule. People obeyed because their bodies told them he was not asking for anything they did not already know.

A trader stood by his wagon and watched the road as if it might decide to be clean again. It did not. Two teamsters unhitched and led their animals to shade. "We can go as three," one said, looking at the other two. "We have done that in flood years." The trader nodded and put away the extra harness.

The witnesses who had written thin and held on bark sat under the ledger stone and practiced writing what could be written now: names of households where small keeps were holding, lists of courtyards where someone had a pot big enough for ten small bowls to take turns. They did not try to keep the square all at once. They used bark the way bark prefers to be used, small, specific, tied to a door.

A woman from the ridge came down with a question in her mouth. "If we cannot have a festival," she said, "can we have ten suppers." Nema said yes without turning it into a plan. The woman smiled the way people smile when permission aligns with what they were going to do anyway.

A boy stood under the cracked plaque and read the words as if they were new: leave daylight a line. He traced the crack with a finger and then leaned his forehead to the stone. "More than one," he said, not to be clever. He was tired. He wanted the wall to tell him how many lines would be enough. The wall did not do that work. The wall was busy being a wall.

Near noon, a man attempted to rally a big stilling one more time, the way a person goes back into a house for a chair they loved. He called, "Eyes wide." He counted. People tried to catch it for him out of kindness. Their kindness did not make a field. Nema crossed to him and put her hand on his arm. "Keep it for your table," she said. He nodded and cried once, quick and unashamed, then went to find his table.

The Old Overseer spent the day in doorways. He did not stand on things. He did not gather crowds. He looked for places where three became six and split them with a story. "During the dust years," he said, "we learned to put two families under one cloth and leave the third to keep watch. The cloth is lighter than the square." People remembered dust. Dust has a way of teaching that white weather imitated without the mercy of grit.

By evening, wagons had stopped waiting for corridors that did not form. People began to leave in handfuls and tens. No one called it flight. They called it visiting. They would call it other things later. They carried tone hoops and pocket bowls and food that would keep. They left the big bell for someone who wanted a clean object. Two Wardens unhooked it with care and set it against a wall so it would not hurt itself if someone bumped it in the dark.

Savi packed a bundle with a frying stone and a hoop and three slivers of bark. She tied the bundle with the wrist bell's strap. "I can go with the first group to the ridge schools," she told Nema. "Adults will come if a child shows them how the hinge lives in feet."

"They will," Nema said. "Do not hold more than five at once."

"I cannot," Savi said, and laughed for the first time since the white hum, because the word had changed from cannot as rule to cannot as fact.

The Auditor returned the tray of standard tokens to the council table and left it there. He took a plank on his shoulder and walked it across the square to a house that needed a new step. He set the plank down and, without thinking, touched his forehead to it the way people do when something has earned being called real. No one noticed. Which is to say, everyone noticed and chose to let the noticing be private.

Night thickened. Fires scattered the slope like punctuation marks. Each small circle held its own count. Some circles failed and tried again with one person fewer and held. Some circles made room for a traveler and learned a song that did not need a bowl. The square did not vanish. It flickered and stayed visible like a drawing someone continues to love after it has stopped being useful.

Nema stood with Bren at the crack and breathed. "We will write it," she said, meaning the rule that would help people leave plazas behind without shame. Bren nodded. "Tomorrow," he said.

"Tomorrow," she agreed, and did not wait for the square to agree with her. Squares have their own pace. Tonight, pace belonged to courtyards and to roads that would carry handfuls of bodies who had decided what size a net could be.

***

They wrote on bark and on clay with hands that had done this before for other reasons. Birth lists. Flood routes. Which door to leave open during dust. This time the page felt smaller than the thing it had to hold. That was right. A rule that lasts should fit in a pocket and in a mouth.

They did not make a speech. They made sentences that could be carried by a tired person who had no space for ornament.

Nema spoke each line aloud before she wrote it. Bren repeated it back, shaving the edges until breath could hold it without catching. The Old Overseer sat with his staff across his knees and hummed once in his throat when a line landed right. Savi listened with both hands, as if she might need to throw the words down the road and have them arrive unbroken.

"Say it plain," the Overseer said. "Paper tires. Ribs remember."

Nema dipped her reed in soot-water, touched it to bark, and began.

Post-Consensus Rule

Keep stilling below forty bodies.

"If you are more than that," Bren said, "you are a market, not a circle. Let the market be a market."

Prefer corridors to plazas. Prefer paths to squares. "Because corridors move," Savi added, tapping the side of her hand on the table. "Squares ask to be important."

Keepings must be deed-linked. One truth, one token, one act. Bren set three small tokens on the table, bent nail, mended hinge, chip of glaze from a shared bowl, and listened to the faint hum they made together. "No Hollow," he said. "We tie breath to what hands already did."

Randomize dusk windows.

The Overseer smiled at the oddness. "Scatter your lights," he said. "Let the sky teach us back. No more one rope."

Teach the second child-to-adult, hand-to-hand.

Savi rolled the hinge across Nema's knuckles and then across Bren's. "No scripts," she said. "If you can write it down, someone will try to pin it to a post."

Invite, do not command.

"Command works until it doesn't," Nema said. "Invitation keeps working."

They made five copies on bark and five on clay. Bark for doorways, clay for travel. The clay tablets took the nail-mark cleanly. When they baked, they would carry that cleanness forward longer than any one mouth.

The Overseer held the bark while Nema nailed it beside the plaque. The crack took the nail as if it had been waiting to be useful for a human thing. The old words, leave daylight a line, sat above the new ones the way a roof sits over a doorway. Bren placed the old bowl under the bark, not as a shrine, as a reminder. The bowl had been honest. Honesty was not the same as usefulness.

Across the square, a Warden watched with his hands folded around nothing. He had tied his white back with a work cord. He approached without his posture. "May I carry one to the gate," he asked, and when Nema nodded, he tucked the clay copy under his arm like a loaf he did not want to drop.

Savi took a tablet and a hoop and walked to the roadside stone beyond the last terrace. A stranger leaned there, the look of a person who had decided to be brave after deciding for an hour to be tired. Savi showed the hinge with her hands. The stranger blinked in twos, missed once, laughed without shame, and caught it. By noon the stranger had taught someone else. They did not call it school. They called it what it was: passing something along.

Runners went out on three paths. One climbed toward Cliffmouth with bark tied to his back, ready to lay the new rule on the flat wheel where children traced spokes with their palms. One followed the river to Saltspan with a clay copy in a sling, the boulder garden ahead like a sentence that had learned to survive without the word "plaza." The third runner cut across the fields to the two small towns that had always borrowed names from bigger ones. "Keep yourselves small," he told the first doorway that opened. "Small is not less. Small is how we keep anything at all."

People tested the rule in the next hour because the next hour is when real rules are tested. At the well, eleven bodies tried to stand together out of habit. When the count slipped, they divided into two, then three. Buckets moved faster. No one called it obedience. They called it "how it worked today."

A ledge above the ovens cracked with a sound like a person changing their mind. The red ties on the slump beds fluttered once and lay still again. Two neighbors who had not spoken since a winter argument passed a pot between their courtyards and did not name the act large. They placed a chip from its rim in the bowl and wrote meal on bark. The hum at the rim was faint and right.

Bren walked the market edge with his hoop, not to police, to teach ears. "Listen here," he told a steward in training. "Feel how three set-downs leave a warmth that persists. At four, it thins. Do not be greedy. Take the bowl to the next door before you are proud of holding many at once."

The Auditor came near at midmorning, hat in hand. He had been carrying planks since dawn. He read the bark. He read it twice. "I asked a thing too large," he said, not to be forgiven, but to give the sentence a place to end. Nema did not absolve him. She nodded and pointed to the stack of clay. "Carry that to the ridge school," she said. "Do not announce it. Hand it to the first child who looks like they already know." He smiled at the clarity of being useful and did as told.

Random dusk windows began that day. Households chose by pebble, three in a palm: if two smooth, read now; if two rough, read later; if one of each, sleep and read by the first star. The square's bell was not rung. It leaned in shadow the way a handsome chair leans when a family changes what sitting is for. People looked at it the way you look at a beloved tool you will not use again because the work has changed.

By afternoon, corridors had replaced plazas in language. "Meet me on the oven path," someone said, and no one asked "Which?" because there was only one path past that oven that had learned to hold a hinge. Children marked the safe bends with chalk, not lines, but tiny eye shapes that meant soften here, seeing happens here. If rain took the marks, hands replaced them.

At a door where a mother had kept a name behind her teeth for a year, the witnesses stood and wrote without being seen. She said the name into a bowl that held five bodies. The charge sang. Down the lane, a man fixed a gate, not as show, as keeping. He set the bent nail in the bowl and wrote hinge on bark because he liked the word and because his hand had trembled less that day.

Cliffmouth laid the rule on the wheel and, before supper, a child walked the spokes saying the lines to each plank. The wheel did not answer. It did not need to. It had already given the town a floor. Saltspan pinned the clay to a post at the start of the causeway. A fisher touched the word corridors with two fingers and then took their boat out on the late beat, which the boulder garden liked.

Near dusk, a man who had loved giving orders gathered a dozen in a yard and called for shoulders even and eyes wide. Nema stepped into his yard without crossing his threshold and lifted her hands, palms open. Invitation has a shape you can see from a distance.

"May I offer you a smaller thing," she said. "Keep your dozen for lifting the oven. Keep five for breath. You will accomplish both and be less tired by night."

He looked at his dozen, who already looked relieved. He laughed once, let the laugh soften into his ribs, and nodded. "Five for breath," he said. "Seven for the oven. Then we eat."

The Old Overseer walked the lanes as day dimmed and found places to leave one more copy: the school bench, a traveler's stone, the crack itself. He paused at the plaque and read it out as if to teach the wall to hear its own words louder: leave daylight a line. Then, quiet, to the air: "And leave room for many lines."

They did not wait for anyone to name what had ended. Endings do not require applause. They require tools.

At night, fires took the slope like stars someone had dropped closer on purpose. Each small circle caught its own count. Each small circle could render enough. The road held conversation the way rivers hold reeds, lightly, with room to move. Above, the sky did what it always does when no one tells it what to be. It pleased goats and children and those who had run out of words for a while.

At the edge of the market, the old bowl slept under the new rule. A breeze lifted the bark at one corner and set it down again. Savi sat on the roadside stone and taught a stranger how to pass the second across a gap without making a performance of it. The stranger taught someone else by noon. By morning after that, the rule had reached a place that did not know Riverplain's name.

No new equilibrium came. There was a way to keep walking and to keep one another from falling where the ground changed underfoot. People would carry practice instead of places now. The hum had air in it again, and it would not be coaxed back into one field. They left daylight many lines, and they learned to live along them.

Cycle V
Aftercause

They moved.

The ridge broke into a shoulder of broken stone. The pieces were palm-sized, sharp where they had snapped from something larger. When Lusa stepped on them, they slid and whispered against one another. The sky had that thin blue that made edges look closer than they were.

Fara walked near Lusa's hip. The child's clacking stones hung from a thong at her neck. She had not looked back at the frog since they left the swale. Lusa had not either, but she felt its weight in her ribs. The feeling thinned with distance. That was the way of it.

At the base of the shoulder, a low shelf of pale rock ran along the hill. Water had polished it smooth. Someone had skinned a rabbit there long ago. The smell of iron had sunk into the stone and stayed. Lusa tasted it as a ghost under her tongue.

"Mute minute," the elder said.

They stood, four bodies in a loose line, and let silence take the first count. Ilen adjusted his breath. Fara watched Lusa's shoulders and matched their lift, then added a small delay on the release to avoid becoming a copy. Proof by weather came back in little signs. The air felt easier to sip. A fly that had been trapped against Lusa's cheek lost interest and lifted away.

The shelf bent around an outcrop and became a shallow bowl. In the center, patches of gray-green moss made a soft field about the size of a cooking cloth. The moss puckered and smoothed, as if wind were touching it, but the air was still.

Fara clapped twice, out of order. One-two then nothing for a count, then four.

The space in front of her yawned a little, and then the bowl made a path. Not a line. A corridor of no weather. Sounds went quiet inside it. The moss stopped moving. The stone's iron taste dropped away.

Fara laughed and stepped into the quiet. Her foot went down before it moved. She took another step. Her braid swung before her head turned. She turned anyway and made a face, delighted.

"Before-after," Ilen said softly. "Keep your count."

They followed Fara into the corridor. Inside, Lusa's breath felt too late. Events drifted into place a blink before her body answered. The effect could be useful. You could move without friction if you did not try to make sense of the order.

Fara clapped again, this time in time. The corridor narrowed and then held. She clapped out of order. The corridor widened.

They reached the far lip of the bowl. Lusa put her foot down on normal stone and the sound returned. A small scrape of grit. Wind nosed at her neck. The before-after corridor hung behind them like a pale tunnel, visible only as a slight lack in the air.

"It will be good for crossings," Fara said.

"Not for keeping," the elder said.

Fara nodded. She was learning to answer with movement. She turned to go and then said, because she was still a child, "We should make it stay."

The corridor died on the word. It did not collapse. It snapped to a line and went flat. The moss retook its pucker. The iron taste came back. Lusa felt relief and a small ache. It would have been useful to carry.

Rule card: Carry and drop. Nothing persists by wish.

They climbed a slope of pale dust that held their prints like a book page. The prints did not seem to age as they moved away. Lusa rubbed a line with her heel to blur them and the dust answered with a small sigh of release. Proof enough.

On the high ground, the day turned cold. Clouds had pulled thin curtains across the sun. A faint aurora hummed along the northern rim, faint colors plucking at the air as if someone were testing strings stretched from hill to hill.

The elder called a halt before the light thinned further. They found a hollow under a tangle of scrub and settled without fire. The hollow smelled like old leaves and animal sleep. Lusa's back felt the ground through her cloak. The ground approved them or at least tolerated them. No rim crept toward the hollow. The air kept its softness.

"Practice," Ilen said.

They formed a ring small enough that their knees touched. Lusa took out the pebble. It was not the same pebble as before. It did not matter. She set it on her palm and let the ring see that her hand was empty of want.

"One small change," she said. "One breath. Then drop it."

The pebble traveled.

Ilen preferred sound. For one count the pebble made a clear, thin tone, like water dripping into a glass from too high. He released and the tone went quiet. Fara preferred weight. For a beat the pebble grew heavy and sat into Lusa's palm as if it meant to leave a mark. Then it did not. The elder preferred a thinning of heat. The pebble grew cold, not unpleasant, like morning light before full day.

Lusa took it and simply preferred rest. Not sleep. Not anything that could keep a body from moving if needed. Rest as a loosening of the jaw, a softening in the shoulders. She dropped it and passed the stone.

"Shiver-right," the elder said.

They all broke the ring by one step, each in a different direction. They reformed it one breath later, slightly offset. It kept the practice from calcifying. It kept their bodies honest. You were not allowed to become an edge that someone else would lean on.

When they finished, they did not speak. The aurora thinned with the night's cold. Lusa slept with her knife as a tuning fork under her palm in case the count needed a quick adjustment. She dreamed of pears and did not reach for them.

Near dawn the air changed. It lost its sweetness. Lusa woke and tasted iron. Proof by weather.

A narrow rim was nosing toward the hollow from the south. Not racing. Curious, almost. It moved in a clean line as if drawn with a chalked string held taut between two hands.

The elder put a finger to her lips. No words now. They slipped from the hollow with the smallest change that would get them clear. Ilen altered his split-breath by a hair. Lusa lifted her foot a fraction earlier than felt good. Fara stepped on three, then counted two, then stepped again, making a little out-of-round wheel out of her own pace.

The rim hesitated and slid past their empty bed as if it had been looking for a committed line to bite. It found none and kept going, straight as a blade across the field beyond.

Rule card: Straight lines attract teeth. Break symmetry on purpose.

The morning brightened, thin and gray. They reached a slope of fallen basalt, dark hexagons stacked like a collapsed wall. Lusa felt in her pocket for the small length of cord she had carried since she was a younger walker. It was looped in a neat knot. When she had tied it years ago, the knot had felt like a good thought. A way to remember a rhythm in her fingers if her mouth could not say it.

The basalt chunks shifted underfoot. Fara slid on her heel and caught herself with a small hop. Ilen placed a hand against a block and steadied it for a breath, then took his hand away before the block could think the steadiness belonged to it.

Lusa looped her cord around a small outcrop to give herself a hold for one heartbeat as she crossed a slick patch. The cord tightened and answered perfectly. The hold felt good, and the feeling of good sang through her like a relief.

A seam opened from the knot outward. It was thin and white at first, like a hair caught in light. Then it deepened to black with a blue rim.

Ilen said nothing. He went shiver-right and re-entered the slope on a crooked count two paces lower. The elder made a small sound in her throat that was not language and moved three paces up. Fara froze, her weight balanced between two stones.

Lusa's fingers tightened on the cord. That was the wrong thing. She felt it even as she did it. She forced her hand to open. She unwrapped the cord and cut it in the middle with the knife she used as a tuning fork. The cord parted without drama. The seam did not vanish. It throbbed at the place where the knot had been and tested itself in both directions like a worm sniffing.

Lusa breathed in, preferred nothing at all, breathed out, released. She placed her foot on the next block with the care you give something you will not own. The seam slowed. It stopped spreading when she stopped wanting the cord to have been a good idea.

Fara exhaled, a sound that was almost a sob, and moved again. The elder nodded once at Lusa and then looked away to keep the nod from becoming weight.

They crossed the basalt field one careful step at a time and did not use the cord again. Lusa coiled the two cut pieces into a pocket and felt them there like useless teeth. She thought of throwing them away, then did not. Carry and drop. She could carry the lesson longer than the cord.

Rule card: Do not tie the world to you. It will come apart where you loop it.

By midday the land went soft. Low sedge, damp soil, hidden pools the color of old tea. The sky lowered with it, a ceiling of light-gray cloth. Wind moved in sheets that brushed the sedge and then lifted away like a hand leaving water.

Their path narrowed to a strip where boots had pressed the sedge smooth enough to show a direction. Lusa did not trust it. She stepped off the strip and found the ground was better on a slightly higher line to the left. Ilen mirrored her on the right, not as a counter, but to keep the set of possibilities wide.

They entered a place where sounds repeated. A plop of water to their left came twice, then once more, then came back later in the wrong place. Fara laughed and clapped in the offbeats, making a braid out of echoes. The sedge liked the game and flattened in twists like hair woven by a bored child.

The air turned iron without warning. Lusa lifted a hand. The line stopped.

Ahead, a wedge of stillness had formed, its pointed end aimed at a low hummock. On the hummock, a hare chewed. It did not look up. The wedge crept toward it at a polite speed, as if it had been told to walk in halls.

"Rescue?" Fara whispered.

"Rescue that does not anchor," the elder said.

They did not speak after that. They moved.

Ilen and the elder went left and right, breathing on the wrong count so the wedge would not smell a pattern to chase. Lusa took Fara's shoulder and set their steps in a broken cadence that would look like accident to any rule that watched for lines.

They reached the hummock before the wedge did. Lusa did not scoop the hare. She did not name safety for it. She bent a knee and presented her thigh as a step, then turned her body with a twist that would erase the shape of the offer the moment it was used. The hare stepped up without looking at her and off the far side onto lower ground that led away from the wedge. It moved as if it had always planned to, not as if it had been saved.

Fara grinned. The wedge continued to creep until it found nothing to punctuate and lost interest. It dulled its point and thinned away.

Rule card: Rescue without claim. Shoulder, turn, release.

The sedge gave way to gravel. The gravel to flat clay. The clay to a shallow river edged with reeds. The river looked ordinary except that a straight, clear lane ran down its center like a road beneath the water. Where the lane ran, the surface did not ripple.

They drank from the edge, not from the lane. The water near the reeds tasted of tannin and silt and living rot. The lane had no taste at all. Fara touched its surface with one finger, then pulled her hand back and shook it. "Like licking a polished stone," she said, making a face.

Ilen tapped the back of his knife against a reed. The knife did not sing. He tapped it against the bank. The knife hummed a low, true note.

"Count is good here," Lusa said.

They followed the bank upstream for a while until the lane swung toward them and cut the bank in a neat bite. The cut was so clean it looked false. The bite took a half-moon of bank and left a lip of clay undercut and ready to drop.

The elder did not try to fix the undercut with a named brace. She altered her breath. Lusa and Ilen did the same. The lip softened around them as if the river had remembered that it liked to be messy. The bite lost its edge and crumbled, and the river took the crumb as if it had meant to all along.

They left the river when the light moved from gray to a gold that did not warm. A thin rain began. It fell in lines that looked too straight. Each drop hit where a line said it should, not where wind would push it. The lines ignored the curve of the land. They ignored any reasonable thought about where rain belongs.

"Break the sky's count," Ilen said.

They did not try to touch the rain. They altered the soil below it. Lusa stepped off the easy line and lifted her heel at the last instant before it left the ground. Fara counted wrong on purpose, not sloppily but with intent to disrupt. The rain did not stop falling in lines, but the lines blurred at their feet as if the ground had turned to a different page. The rain accepted this without fuss. The world did not always fight back. Often it simply preferred lazy answers. You could encourage it to prefer laziness toward life.

By late day they reached a broad, open terrace. The clouds thinned. Sun came through in the color of old brass. On the far side of the terrace, a seam waited. It ran full length from rock to rock, black with a blue rim like the last skin of a bruise. It did not move. It had already finished whatever work it had been doing.

Beyond the seam, the land looked tired and perfect. A stand of young trees would never grow older. Grass would never seed. The air had a dry clarity that Lusa associated with rooms where nothing lived.

They did not go that way.

The elder stopped and looked to the left where the terrace sloped to a low saddle between two rocks. She pointed once. Lusa and Ilen nodded. Fara watched their faces and then looked at the saddle herself instead of at them again. She was learning.

They crossed the terrace. Their steps made a soft sound like hand on cloth. Lusa felt the energy go out of her shoulders as if a hand had patted it away. She let that go too. Walk. Breathe. Prefer nothing you cannot drop.

On the saddle, a small shrine had once stood. Not the kind with a name. Just a flat stone with a bowl cupped into it and a thin plaque leaning against a stack of smaller stones. Rain had done its work. Lichen had done its work. The bowl held water filmy with pollen. The plaque had flaked. If there were words, they had gone back into grain.

Fara looked at the bowl. "What was it for?"

"Someone else's breath," the elder said. "Not ours."

They did not touch the bowl. Lusa ran a finger along the plaque and felt only the softness of rot. She thought of scoring new lines. She did not. The wind made a small sound in the dry grasses. The sound was kind.

They continued to a bluff where the land fell away into folds of hill and shadow. Birds looped below them, finding little thermals under a sun that did not promise much. Their loops were not perfect. Good.

The elder nodded at Lusa. "Say it simply," she said. "So the child can carry it."

Lusa looked at Fara and then past Fara at the land. She spoke while watching the land so that the words had to keep up with the world and not the other way.

"The ground here answers words. If you name an outcome, it tries to give you all of it at once. That stops the world where it stands. If you prefer for one breath and release on the next, the world will help for a step and then forget. That forgetting is our friend."

Fara nodded. "And the rules?"

"Own one breath. Do not name for others. Carry and drop. Rescue without claim. Break straight lines on purpose. Consent every breath. Proof by weather."

Fara repeated them once and then again while rubbing her thumb against her forefinger as if counting a string of invisible beads. She smiled, not because the rules made her happy but because she could keep them all in her mouth at once without chewing.

"Now show me," the elder said.

Fara took the pebble and the knife and the clacking stones. She set the count with her chest. She stepped toward a patch of grass that had been flattened by the last wind. She preferred that it lift and then released. The grass lifted and forgot. She moved her step on the next count so as not to set a pattern the straight rim would enjoy. She looked at Lusa only to ask for nothing.

"Good," Ilen said.

They lingered at the bluff while the sun slid. The air cooled and turned clear. The tired perfection beyond the seam looked no closer or farther than before. It would wait forever for anyone who wanted to hold something until it stopped breathing.

Lusa took a piece of bark from a low branch and scored on it with the point of her knife. Not a sign to hold. Only a practice to carry.

Prefer lightly. Release on the second beat. Step crooked when the air turns iron. Help only if it can be dropped. No naming of others. One breath is yours.

She showed the bark to Fara, then rubbed the words with her thumb until they blurred into little rivers. She let the bark fall and watched the wind encourage it down the slope.

They ate in quiet as the light thinned. Bread and a small pot of dried berries that had not been asked to be more than they were. Ilen warmed the air above the pot for one breath and took his hand away before the berries grew tough. The elder cut the last of the cheese into four exact pieces without giving the knife a name.

Night arrived on small feet. The stars came in their own order. The aurora hummed again, faint and patient.

"Tomorrow?" Fara said.

"Tomorrow we cross the chalk fans," the elder said. "Then the oak flats. Then we see."

"Where are we going?"

"Away from here. Toward a place that will move when we ask politely."

Fara smiled at that. Lusa did too.

Rule card: Arguments end in movement.

They slept without marks. They woke to a sky the color of rinse water. Between two breaths the wind shifted and tasted of distant rain. Proof by weather.

They set their count. They stood. They moved.

On the far rim, a bird started a loop, lost it, found it again, and kept going.

To Hold One Thing

The earth slid from stone to water between her feet, and Jara didn't slow.

"You're leaking again," Marro said, two paces behind, barefoot, toes curling into what was now warm moss.

Jara crouched and picked up a small black pebble, turning it between her fingers. Its edges stayed sharp even as the moss beneath her knees slid into cracked clay.

"That one's solid," she murmured.

Marro frowned. "For now."

"No, " She closed her eyes and felt it: the precise weight, the cold bite in her skin. The clay around her wavered, tried to become reeds, then gravel, then stopped. "See?"

He spat into the moss, now sand, and squinted at her hand. "You keep holding on to things, the rest of the world comes loose, like it's been waiting for permission. And we need the ground under us to last longer than a breath."

"Maybe I want to keep *something*."

They moved on. A line of mountains bled into the air like wet ink. Behind them, two of the others were still anchored to yesterday's rain-smell, sitting cross-legged in the middle of a plain that changed shape every few breaths.

"You'll have to let it go eventually," Marro said.

Jara slipped the pebble into her pocket. "Not yet."

They found the valley by accident.

It announced itself in scent, sharp green after rain, threaded with warmth, like bread baking somewhere just out of sight. The moment they stepped into it, the ground was soft grass, the sky a pale sweep with swallows carving lazy arcs overhead. Nothing shifted.

Taran was the first to speak. "I could stay here."

"You always say that," Sorelle replied, but she was already pressing her palm to a birch trunk, testing its skin with her thumb like she might a ripe fruit.

"This one's holding," Jara said. She bent, pinched a handful of grass. It stayed grass.

Marro set down his pack with a thud. "We anchor it, we lose the river behind us. That was our water."

As if to punctuate his point, a faint splash echoed behind them, the river collapsing into mist.

"We can find another," Taran said, lying back in the grass with a sigh. "You can't drink from beauty, but sometimes you should try. We never get places like this."

Sorelle's gaze stayed on the far horizon, where the hills wavered in and out of form. "Marro's right. It's already fraying. The edges are crawling inward."

"We've held things before," Jara said.

"Small things," Sorelle countered. "A stone. A smell. A minute, maybe two. This is the size of a season. The cycle doesn't like being gripped this hard."

Taran opened his eyes slowly, as if listening to something underground. "Maybe that's worth it. One thing whole instead of a thousand things gone before you can even touch them. A season you can keep."

At his words, the air warmed and stilled, as though the valley approved.

A crack split the air. Everyone turned. The mountains to the west folded inward, collapsing into a hole so black the light bent around it. What it left behind was perfect and unmoving, a frozen wasteland, every detail caught mid-motion: a bird mid-wingbeat, a tumble of rocks in mid-fall, locked forever.

Sorelle stepped back from the birch. The bark began to run like water. "We don't get to keep this without paying for it."

Taran tilted his head toward the black. "It's just... stillness. Not the worst fate. Better than watching it all turn to soup."

Marro's voice went flat. "Tell that to Elen."

Jara's hand stilled on the grass. None of them spoke for a moment.

"She anchored the orchard outside Kael's Step," Marro went on. "Wouldn't let it go. The black reached her before she could move. You can still see her there, on her knees between the trees, hands on the soil. She's holding one of the early pears. Green skin, just turning gold. You can smell it if you get close enough."

The swallows above them kept circling the same loop, cutting the same angle of light.

"This isn't new," Marro said. "First there's something worth keeping. Then it starts to eat the rest of the world. Then you have to choose whether to save it and lose everything else, or let it go and trust the cycle to give you more."

"And sometimes the cycle takes," Sorelle murmured. Her eyes flicked to the horizon. "And keeps taking until there's nothing left but scraps."

"And sometimes it gives," Marro replied.

Taran looked around the valley as if already memorizing it. "Or sometimes it gives once, and never again. That's the gamble, isn't it?"

The wind shifted, carrying the bread-and-rain scent deeper into the valley.

Jara kept her hand on the grass. She could feel its slow pulse through her palm, as steady as her own heartbeat.

The air grew heavy, as though each breath had to be pulled through wet cloth. The black's edge was wider now, its rim flickering with blue.

"If we let it go," Sorelle said, "the valley will vanish."

"And we'll be back to running," Jara said.

Taran's chuckle was low. "Running to what? More flickers we can't keep? More near-moments?"

The swallows dipped lower at his words, almost brushing the grass.

"Running to possibility," Marro said. "Better to have a shifting world than a fixed one that's dying."

At that, a faint wind curled through the valley, breaking the swallows' perfect loop.

Sorelle shook her head. "Shifting isn't the same as living. Sometimes holding is the only way to survive."

Marro gestured toward the black. "Sometimes holding is how the world dies standing up."

Jara kept her gaze on the swallows. One swooped low, passing so close she could hear the whisper of its wings, and for a heartbeat, its body flickered into a silver fish, then back again.

Her fingers brushed the pebble in her pocket, last week's Flicker, still cold, still perfect. She could keep this valley too. Keep *something*.

The sky split with a thin white seam from zenith to horizon.

Sorelle's voice was tight. "Jara."

The scent of bread and rain wrapped around her. The warmth of the grass seeped into her legs. The swallows circled, wings catching the pale light. She could hold them. She could hold it all.

Her hand lifted from the ground.

The grass wavered, blurred. The scent thinned. The swallows dissolved like blown ash.

The valley sighed away.

They stood in a plain of shifting fog. Shapes began to form, a ridge, a path, a stream that might last an hour or a heartbeat.

Jara's hand stayed in her pocket, wrapped around the pebble.

Marro started walking first.

Hours later, they crossed a stretch of bare rock, warm from a sun that hadn't been there a moment before. Jara paused, crouched, and touched the stone. It was smooth, almost oily under her fingertips. She closed her eyes and felt its heat sink into her skin.

For a few breaths, nothing else existed, not the shifting ground beneath her knees, not the wind's restless turnings, not the fog on the horizon. Just the stone.

She let it go before anyone could speak. The warmth slipped from her fingers like water, leaving them strangely light, as if they'd been carrying more than she realized.

When she stood, her chest ached, not from loss exactly, but from the hollow it left behind. It was an ache with edges, sharp enough to remind her she was still moving. And in the quiet under that ache was something else: the faintest sense that the hollow might be meant for something new.

No one said a word, but when she started walking, they fell in step beside her. Somewhere behind them, the fog folded into the suggestion of a tree, and then let it go again.

The Last Practice

The rain fell in lines as if someone had ruled the sky and asked the drops to mind their places. Each line ignored the wind. Each line ignored the curve of the hill. Along the far rim a seam ran through a birch stand and cut it so cleanly that leaves hung from halved branches like coins sawn in two.

Tovin tasted iron. He held his breath for a count, not to hoard it but to feel how the air kept time. Too even. He lowered his hand on a count that never quite landed. The rain in front of him blurred for a heartbeat and remembered how to be messy. That was proof. Not enough to matter, but enough to show the direction of work.

People came in ones and twos because they felt what he felt. No calls. No marks. A tired woman with wet wool sleeves and a knife that had tuned a dozen small nights. A boy who counted with his tongue against his teeth and stopped when he saw the seam. Two old men who walked like they were listening for a low drum in the ground. Rae crossed the slope without hurry, rain tapping her hair and sliding off the line of her nose. She showed her hands empty and then taught the carries palm to palm. Split breath. Shiver right. Rescue without claim.

"In on one," she said, quiet enough to make listening easy. "Prefer only what you can drop. Out on two, let it fall. Shiver right means anyone can break the line if it stiffens. Rescue without claim means shoulder, turn, release. No names given. No debts made."

The boy copied her split breath. He missed the release and held it inside his chest for a sliver too long. The rain to his right crisped into neat little cords. Rae did not correct him with words. She stepped wrong on purpose and brushed his sleeve with her fingers. He felt her count and lost the extra half beat. The cords loosened.

Tovin listened. Numbers came to him as tones. He heard the land as a low choir that liked to fall into straight song when tired. He set his own chest to a crooked meter, almost four and then a soft catch before the next. The iron taste thinned. Proof enough to move.

Rule card: Proof by weather.

They walked to the river because the glass lane down its center had lengthened since morning. Shouted orders from the far bank pinned a section of reeds the way a thumb pins a bug. A man there yelled "break it" and the bank locked in a clean bite that the river would carry for a mile if it could.

"Quiet," Rae said, almost laughing. "Always back to quiet."

They turned their faces to the water and stepped off the easy line. Tovin set his breath so the release fell between his second and third toe instead of at his heel. Rae lifted her foot a fraction sooner than she wanted to. The old men made a small wheel of their counts, one late, one early, touching hands only at the rim of their turn. The glass lane did not crack all at once. It frayed at the edges, then forgot to be where nothing pushed it to remain. That was enough for now.

The seam near the birches did not care about the river. It ran like a taut string held by someone who did not have to breathe. A tangle of runners below the seam had tried to anchor. They had stacked flat stones and named the place refuge. The stones were neat. The neatness smelled like chalk.

Rae let her knife hang in her hand by the cord and tapped its spine against her palm. No song. She tapped it against a stone at the edge of an old fire pit. The blade answered with a low, dull hum that said the meter here was already crooked enough to carry a change. Good.

Tovin crouched and put his ear near a shallow hollow under the hill. He clucked his tongue and the hollow gave the sound back a heartbeat late and lower.

"Stone lungs," he said. "It will hold a bar longer than we can."

No one nodded. They did not make a ceremony of agreement. Rae stepped into a space with no corners and began the count with her chest. In on one. Prefer heat a hair. Out on two. Drop it. Three nearly landed and then caught like a laugh you swallow. Four was only almost four.

Hands touched without holding. The old men stood where the ground seemed too straight and took the count wrong together on purpose. The boy kept wanting to help more than his breath could release, but he learned each time the knife stopped singing. Rings formed because circles make it hard for rulers to find a corner. No one called the start. No one would call the end.

The hollow caught their crookedness like a drumskin that liked being spoken to. Tovin felt the answer as a pressure against the front of his teeth. He lifted his head. A far field of grass took the bar a breath later. The blades rippled from right to left, then forgot and fell back into their own small winds. The seam near the birches hesitated as if it had stepped into a shallow where it expected depth. Then it resumed.

"Not enough," Rae said. No disappointment in it. Only a description.

Rule card: Teach without binding.

They went to work like people mending a net without a pattern. Tovin tasted the air in three places and found it too clean each time. He walked until the knife sang dull and scratched a note into the dirt with his heel that would be gone the first time rain took the slope. Rae showed the carries again to the newest faces and kept her body loose so no one would learn her outline as a rule. They seeded rhythm in shallow caves, in a line of old willows, in the mouth of a culvert where water mumbled simple truths all day.

A cluster up on the hill began to build a better refuge. You could see the idea in the lines their bodies made. Straight. Kindness that wanted to last. Rae climbed to them and said nothing. She stepped through their neatness with a count that did not respect corners and put her shoulder under a woman's arm and turned her, then released her. The woman blinked and laughed, not at Rae but at the relief of not being a brace. Two men followed. The rest did not. The seam found their stack a few hours later and took it cleanly. No screams. Just a line that did not want to curve and would not be taught today.

The rain eased. The wind turned thoughtful. People drifted out, then back, following changes in taste and tone the way animals follow shade. Tovin noticed that when he let his breath fall on the offbeat the embedded specks in his blood listened. You could not see them. You could only feel the way boundaries answered. The specks were old as bones now. No one had put them in anyone for generations. They were inherited the way hairlines were inherited. They did not make bridges or food. They tuned the world at its edges. If you gripped with a word, they hardened straight lines. If you preferred lightly and released, they reminded the land how to forget.

He had no use for the word machine. He noticed cause and effect changed when he thought that way. Better to think of them as dust that liked kind timing and quiet hands. Better to say they listened to breath.

They kept seeding until late light. At the hollow, the beat they had laid into the ground stayed for a bar and a half without bodies holding it. Weak but willing.

"Ambient," Tovin said, not as a command but as a hope. "Carry it. We will forget it. You will not."

"Again," Rae said.

They began a second push, smaller and crooked in a new way so the valley would not learn one answer too well. The boy nearly matched Tovin. Tovin drifted a half count away. He would not let the boy's body learn him. The knife sang dull. The wind softened. Proof by weather returned and kept returning.

Night thickened. Someone had brought bread wrapped in a dry shirt. They ate with their hands in their laps so the land would not mistake hunger for a lever. The stars came on. No one named them.

Rule card: Break straight lines on purpose.

They slept without marks. In the second hour the air changed. Tovin tasted iron and woke. A wedge of stillness was nosing downhill from the north. Not racing. Curious. It moved in a clean line as if drawn with a chalked string held taut between two hands.

Rae put a finger to her lips. No words now. They slipped from the hollow with the smallest change that would get them clear. Tovin altered his split breath by a hair. Rae lifted her heel a fraction earlier than felt good. The old men stepped in a stagger that looked like accident. The wedge tested their empty bed for a grip and found none. It slid past and lost interest. It flattened and blurred and forgot that it had wanted to bite.

Rule card: Consent without consensus.

Morning came thin and gray. The seam at the birches had not advanced. The river did not show a lane. The sky tried lines again and failed to keep them. People came from farther slopes. They did not ask for names. They did not give them. They showed their hands and copied what they saw until the knife sang dull.

The boy found Tovin at the edge of a chalk fan that sloped to a dry wash.

"What are we trying to make?" he asked.

"Nothing to hold," Tovin said. "We are trying to teach the world to breathe on its own."

"Like us."

"Yes. So we can think without turning it to glass."

The boy nodded, not because he understood but because he trusted the work to teach him. That was better.

Rae traced a map in wet soil with a stick. Not places. Not names. Only tones and the routes between them. She dragged the stick where the knife had sung dull. She lifted it where the knife had been bright. She drew lines that were not straight. She scuffed them away with her heel so the map would not desire to be a thing.

"We seed these," she said. "We do not seed the bright. The bright belongs to another day."

Tovin went left with three people who carried quiet well. Rae went right with the boy and a dozen more. The old men drifted between, listening and stepping wrong on purpose whenever something began to like an answer too much.

At the first site a cave mouth opened like a yawn in limestone. Tovin clucked his tongue and the cave gave the sound back a breath later. He stepped in until the air turned cool on his skin and the floor stayed dry. He disliked caves he had to name safe to enter. He liked this one. It liked him back with indifference.

They laid a bar into it. No words. No rhythm anyone could not drop mid step. In on one. Prefer lightly. Out on two. Drop. Then a small catch before what would have been four. Tovin felt the dust in his blood take the pattern. He felt the cave air take it. He stepped back into sun and tasted nothing sharp. Good.

They moved to an old willow that should have fallen years ago. Its trunk had split and then knit itself into a hoop. Wind sounded like breath inside the hoop. Tovin stood in it and let his outline soften at the corners for a count to see if the tree would carry him without asking. It would. He tightened again. He did not need to be sap.

A fox watched from the grass nearby with yellow eyes that did not ask questions. Tovin nodded at it and saw the small lift of its chest as it breathed on two. It had learned a rhythm it could forget. That was the correct kind of learning.

On the right side of the valley Rae found a culvert where water spoke in one language all day. She laid a different crookedness there so the valley would not sync too much. The boy matched her. She stepped away so he could keep the count as his own. He did, and the culvert liked it and held it. The water did not turn to glass.

Midday came and went. The seam at the birches grew a ragged edge. The people who had tried to make a refuge did not return. The valley had changed its mind about them and made a clean decision. No one mourned aloud. Grief lived as another rhythm through the work.

Rae and Tovin met near a low hill that hummed without touch. The stone lungs again. The hollow took their bar and answered from beneath as if fields below had kept count for years and had only been waiting to be told that forgetting was allowed.

"We are close," Rae said. She spoke like a person who does not want her words to be levers.

"What remains," Tovin said, "is the last practice."

The boy heard that and stood very still. He was old enough to know that last does not mean final in the way a wall means final. It means the practice after which the work carries itself.

Rae set her knife on the ground so no one would mistake her for a brace. "One breath," she said. "Each of us keeps the crooked count and lets our edges go soft for that breath. Not all at once. Alone. No one commands. When you decide, you decide."

The dust in Tovin's blood answered her as a thrill of fear. It did not like the idea. It had been born to be useful and usefulness loved edges. He thought of Lusa and Ilen and a child with clacking stones who had learned that rescue does not anchor and that a frog cannot be named free without a cost. He thought of a bowl on a saddle where words had rotted back into grain. He thought of rain that had forgotten its rulers. He tasted the air. No iron.

"Not yet," he said to himself. "Soon."

Rule card: One breath is yours.

They set the valley for the Unholding. Rings formed by drift. No one matched anyone exactly. The knife sang dull where it should. Bright where it should not. People moved to dull the bright. They sent the beat into the stone lungs. They sent it through willow hoops. They sent it across water that wanted to be a road. The valley took it and did not complain.

The boy looked at Rae. Rae looked away so he would not borrow her courage.

Tovin began when the air near his wrist tasted of dust and rain at once. He breathed in and let his edges go soft for the space of one heartbeat. He did not dissolve. He did not become a line. He stayed himself, only lighter at the corners, like a shape under thin cloth. The dust in his blood loosed its grip and retuned. Not to answers. To offbeats. It remembered what it had been made to do and then what it could do better. He breathed out and kept the crooked count as if nothing had happened.

A woman near the stone lungs chose next. Then one of the old men. Then two people Tovin had not seen before who moved like mist over grass and made no fuss. The boy waited, fists tight at his sides, then let them unmake themselves and took his breath without an edge and found that his skin still held his shape after.

Not everyone chose. That was allowed. The valley did not need all of them. It needed enough to change what the dust favored. It got enough.

The seam at the birches did not split and vanish. It frayed. It remembered wind and took a joke badly and then forgave the joke. The rain forgot its rulers. Birds found loops and lost them and found them again and no one took notes. The glass lane down the river did not return. The river did not need it. The culvert kept speaking. The willow hooped the wind and did not fall.

Rae stood very still and watched the way the ground carried the beat without being watched. She had become a person who measured by looking away. That is a hard way to live. It was what the day required.

"What are we now," the boy said, "if the valley does it for us."

"We are bodies who can think without turning the world to glass," Rae said. "We are animals who can want and let go and still move. We do not leave the world. We do not freeze it. We teach it to breathe and then we keep walking."

Tovin pressed his ear to the hollow one last time. He listened for an edge and heard none. He tapped the knife. Dull hum. He tasted the air and it tasted like nothing at all, which is what air should taste like when you are not trying to make it behave.

Rule card: Arguments end in movement.

The day leaned into evening. People drifted away in ones and twos. They left no marks. The valley kept the beat without help. The embedded dust in their blood stayed tuned to offbeats. It would not take orders as easily if someone tried to make a bridge by naming it. It would prefer forgetting. That was the same as mercy now.

Tovin walked the slope with the boy and found places that had been bright last week and were dull today. He stepped wrong on purpose anyway. Habits should be kept honest too.

They came to a low terrace where a bowl had been carved into stone and a plaque leaned against a stack of smaller rocks. Rain had done its work. Lichen had done its work. If there had been words they had gone back into grain.

"What was it for," the boy said.

"Someone else's breath," Tovin said. "Not ours."

Rae rubbed the plaque with her thumb and left no mark. She looked at Tovin and then at the sky. It did not try to draw lines. It let clouds smear and lift and forget.

"Will we need to do this again," the boy asked.

"Yes," Rae said. "Because we are alive. Things drift. The world likes neatness when it is tired. We will always be a small crookedness it can rest against."

The boy smiled. The smile had nothing to prove.

They went back to the hollow and sat without speaking. The stars came up in their own order. No one named them. The knife lay on the ground and hummed in the bones of anyone who held it. Dull. True.

Night deepened. A fox stepped across the slope with no hurry at all. It paused and looked toward the birches. It breathed in. It breathed out. It moved on.

Tovin slept and dreamed of fields forgetting straight. In the dream he could feel the dust in his blood liking the offbeat on its own. He could feel it refuse to sharpen a line without a hand to push it. He woke with the taste of rain in his mouth and the sound of willow hoops carrying wind.

In the morning the valley was itself. No more. No less. The crooked beat was a weather now. If someone tried to make a refuge that held, the beat would turn their corners to curves. If someone asked the river to be a road by shouting it, the water would pretend not to hear. If a child clapped out of order, a corridor might open to carry a crossing and then die when the child forgot it. That was the correct shape of things.

Tovin stood with Rae on a rise and watched the world breathe. This was not ascent in the old sense. No one left. No one turned into light. They had taught the land to carry a low patience. They had retuned the dust that rides every breath to prefer gentleness and release. They had kept consent a thing that happens every moment rather than a badge.

"What do we call this," the boy said.

"Nothing," Rae said. "Names hold. We do not want to hold it. We want to live inside it."

They walked. That was the end. Or what passes for an end when endings are only changes in weather.

Rule card: Carry and drop.

They left no altar and no speech. They did not gather everyone who had chosen and recite gratitude on a hill. They shared bread on their feet. They gave the boy the knife for a day so he could learn how not to be a brace. He tapped stones and found dull where he expected bright. He smiled each time.

They crossed a swale where frogs jumped and did not hang. They saw a pear grove that did not ripen all at once and did not stop to name it. They stepped along a slope where old tracks had pressed permanent lines into clay. The lines remained, but they did not desire to be roads. Desire matters.

Near the far rim a bird began a loop and lost it and found it again. Its wings did not pause. Its head did not turn to check itself. It trusted the air to be a little wrong in kind ways.

The boy said, "I like it this way."

Tovin said, "Me too."

Rae did not say anything. She was listening for an edge. She did not hear one.

They moved on. The valley breathed without them. That was the work. That was the statement. That was the lesson the dust would carry forward into children who would never learn the names for any of this and would not need to.

And when straight lines came back someday because tiredness is real, there would be people to step wrong on purpose and lay the offbeat down again. That is not failure. That is life.

The knife hummed dull. The wind slid over willow and learned the rhythm with no one counting. The river forgot any road it might have been and liked the taste of its banks again. The seam at the birches frayed until it looked like a mistake and then a story and then nothing, and even the memory did not want to hold.

They kept walking.

Epilogue

From the Last Archive, it is written:

The world breathes. We do not command it, not anymore. We listen with our fingers to the hum that follows a spoken thing, a charge that gathers at the rim of a quiet bowl. We walk paths that have learned to be messy, stepping with a crooked count that keeps the air from turning to glass. This is the work. Not a grand rite in a plaza, but ten thousand small practices, carried in the body, that remind the world it is allowed to forget.

Our oldest stories, the ones that live in the grain of the wood and the taste of iron on the wind, are of the First Collapse. They speak of ancestors who built towers of logic and reached for a sky they believed to be empty of mind. They sought to look too precisely, to resolve a structure below the scale where referents hold. At a place called Axis Verge, they built a great machine, a Subscale Resonance Stack, to force reality to "admit more precision than it was willing to give."

They crossed a boundary they named the Resolution Horizon. The universe did not break. It answered.

The final log from that time says it best: "The array did not fail. It did not destroy us. It translated us." The experiment forced an evolutionary leap. The machine's attempt to render the unseeable became a permanent embedding, a "nanoscale interpretive lattice" woven into the very substrate of our consciousness. These are the "embedded specks" that ride our blood, the quiet tuners at the edge of the world. They are the architecture of our unmaking and our becoming.

What followed was a long, terrible childhood with a new sense. We tried to command the substrate, to bind it with law and rite. We fought the Wars of Name, believing the right word could pin the world in place. We tried to hold all valleys to a single breath, a Great Keeping that made the hum perfect and white, and then made it shatter. We learned that a net that cannot be unknotted becomes cruel.

From that failure came the last practice. We are no longer trying to hold one thing. We learned to rescue without claim, to break straight lines on purpose. We seed rhythms in the land so it can breathe on its own, and we do not need to name them to make them real. Our magic is not command. It is consent, renewed with every breath.

The technology of the ancestors is now the biology of their children. The direct interface with the quantum substrate is not a tool we wield; it is a sense we inhabit. It is the hinge in the mind, the second blink, the ability to prefer lightly and release on the second beat.

We do not build walls against the drift anymore. We leave daylight a line, and we have learned to live in the space it makes. We are bodies that can think without turning the world to glass. The architecture is not a fortress. It is a dance. And the unmaking is never finished.

9 781969 445033